CU00687062

MIXTAPE SERIES TRACK 4

FOUNDED ON REJECTION

KAT SINGLETON

Founded on Rejection
Copyright © 2022 by Kat Singleton
All rights reserved.

This book, or parts thereof, may not be reproduced in any form without the express written permission of the author, except for the use of brief quotations in a book review.

Printed in the United States of America.
This is a work of fiction. The names, characters, and incidents portrayed in this novel are either products of the author's imagination or used fictitiously.

ISBN: 978-1-958292-05-1

Cover Design and Formatting Images by Ashlee O'Brien with Ashes & Vellichor
Edited by Victoria Ellis of Cruel Ink Editing & Design
Formatted by Victoria Ellis of Cruel Ink Editing & Design

DEDICATION

To the misunderstood. The ones
overlooked when it comes to falling
in love, yet often, the ones most
deserving of love.

AUTHOR'S NOTE

Founded on Rejection is a slow burn, unrequited, age gap romance. It is the fourth book in a series of interconnected standalones (Mixtape Series). While it is unnecessary to read the first three books before reading Founded on Rejection, I do think reader's will get the best experience if you've read the other couple's love stories before reading this one.

Founded on Rejection contains mature content that may not be suitable for all audiences. Please go to
https://www.authorkatsingleton.com/content-warnings
for a list of content warnings for the book.

EPIGRAPH

"SHE IMAGINES HIM IMAGINING HER..."

-MARGARET ATWOOD

CHAPTER
1

SOMETIMES I WONDER what our "meet cute" would've been if we were in a romance novel.

He definitely would've noticed me. His eyes would've lingered on me a fraction of a second too long. I would've been able to see his extremely chiseled jaw flex. Our fingers would've slightly brushed, forcing my breath to hitch in my chest. And he'd notice. He'd think about it later that night, wondering why he couldn't stop replaying it in his head. He wouldn't have been able to stop thinking about me.

But none of that happened, not in reality.

He didn't even make eye contact with me. His eyes were trained on something over my shoulder.

Poe didn't notice me when we first met, but I noticed him.

It felt like I already knew him, and our gazes hadn't even collided.

They didn't have to. There was a hurt in his eyes that I instantly recognized. It was the same hurt I saw in mine when I stared at my reflection. His demons were calling to mine.

At that moment, I knew I wanted him. During that moment, I'm not sure he knew I existed.

Clutching my book to my chest, my current read where the

hero most definitely knows the heroine exists, I sit in a corner of the backstage area designated for meet and greets.

There's a door to my left, and behind it, ravenous Nash Pierce fans line up, waiting to meet their idol in the flesh. Some fans fawn over the members of Nash's band—Poe included—but for the most part, they're there for Nash.

It's still weird, knowing that my older sister is engaged to arguably one of the most famous people of our generation. His brother, Aiden, plops down next to me. I didn't want to sit too close to the meet and greet action, so I chose to sit on a trunk filled with different sound equipment. It isn't the most comfortable spot, but he doesn't seem to care.

"Got your head in the clouds again?" Aiden tries to snatch the book from my grip.

"Better than being bored here," I answer, gesturing to the small group of people in the room with us.

Aiden's eyes follow the same path as mine. Shrugging, he says, "You're probably right. Maybe I should get into reading."

I snort, trying to imagine Aiden reading any kind of book, especially a romance. Aiden is the same age as me. He just doesn't always act like it. Maybe it's because he's much more carefree than I could ever dream of being. Or maybe it's his constant pestering of Nash's manager, Monica Masters, that makes him seem younger. I don't think he'd be able to take any kind of fiction seriously. Sometimes I wonder if he takes life seriously. It doesn't seem like it.

"What's so funny?"

I shake my head at him, tucking my book into my lap, safe and away from him. "The thought of you reading. Do you even have time to read while trying to make Monica's life a living hell?"

This makes him shut up. Rolling his eyes, his back rests against the wall behind us. "I just don't trust her," he mumbles, flicking my thigh just to be annoying.

I blow a piece of hair out of my face, turning to look at him. "Oh, we know." I point to the door, where a horde of fans will soon pass through. "They'll all know soon enough. You're not good at hiding it."

Aiden sticks his tongue out at me, furthering my point of his childish tendencies. "Well, you're not good at hiding your crush for Nash's bassist, so I don't want to hear it," he jabs, trying to strike a nerve.

My eyes fall on the man in question—Poe. He sits in a director's chair next to his best friend, Landon. The two of them are always together. We're part-way into the North American leg of Nash's tour, and it didn't take long for me to notice how much time Landon and Poe spent together. I thought it was cool. I'd never had a friendship like theirs.

I guess Aiden and I spend a lot of time together now, but it's new. The two of us formed a relationship as the kid siblings to both Nash and Nora. He's fun and encourages me to come out of my shell some, but there are times, like right now, where he's the most annoying person on the planet.

"I'm not very good at hiding things," I answer softly. Now that he's brought up Poe, I watch the man again. He plucks at invisible strings against the plastic cup in his hand. I've watched him closely from the moment I met him. It didn't take long for me to learn that he's always keeping his fingers busy. Whether it's tapping against his thigh, his cup, or rubbing a stone that he keeps in his pocket. Whenever he pulls that stone out, he gets a sad look on his face. One day, I hope to find out why.

"Lennon," Aiden singsongs next to me. Instead of my thigh, he flicks me on the forehead. "Stop fantasizing about Poe." Of course because it's Aiden, he says it loudly—too loudly. It catches the attention of others in the room.

Heat washes over my body as everyone looks at me. I want to disappear underneath all their stares. If only life was like a fantasy novel where I could have some kind of power allowing me to vanish from here. Sneakily, I reach between us and pinch Aiden on the arm as hard as my fingers can manage.

"Ow!" Aiden yelps, dramatically rubbing his skin. He whines, pretending I did actual damage.

Landon smirks at me from Poe's side, making me blush harder because there's no way Poe didn't hear Aiden's words from right next to Landon. Except Poe doesn't look in our direction. As if to be polite, he stares down at his drink, pretending he heard nothing.

Or maybe he's embarrassed—it could go either way.

It's not like I've been able to hide my crush on Poe very well. Trust me, I've tried. It never really worked out for me. He's always just too interesting for me to look away. I know I stare at him a little too long. Cling to every word he says just a little too much. I've never really even tried to hide it. There's no part of me that thinks he would ever reciprocate any feelings for me. So it feels like a safe crush for me to have. I can harbor these feelings for him without thinking too much into it. But sometimes, when I'm alone with my thoughts, I wonder what it would be like if he—even for a second—looked at me as long as I looked at him.

"I actually hate you," I mutter under my breath, refusing to acknowledge anyone looking my way. Now would be a great time for any kind of superpower to kick in that would allow me to disappear out of thin air.

"You two always seem up to trouble," my sister, Nora, jokes, stopping to stand in front of us. Her hands find her hips, bunching up the Nash Pierce concert tee she proudly wears tonight. It's probably because it has lyrics scrawled across the front that are about her. Or it's because Nash begged her to wear it.

I frown, looking at the pain in my ass to my left. "You mean *he's* always up to trouble? I just get sucked into it, unfortunately."

Nora gently nudges my shoulder. "Scoot over." Her voice is sweet, like always. I don't think she ever has a bitter tone to her voice, especially now that she's head over heels, happily in love with Nash.

Following her direction, I scoot my butt over on the box that was only supposed to be a safe spot for me. Both Aiden and my sister have infringed on my reading time. It's rather annoying. There's a reason I chose a spot in the corner and away from everyone else.

"You know there's a ton of other seating options in here," I offer. My hand lifts to gesture around the decorated space in front of us. It fits the aesthetic of the current tour Nash is on. Black and red surrounds us. People with a "Nash Pass" get to come meet Nash in the room we're currently in. Behind two black curtains there's a separate room for the fans to hang out for an hour—or until security kicks them out. "It's really nice out there. I heard they spent a lot of money to make it that way. You should check it out."

"Aw, but why would we sit somewhere different when we can bother you, Len?" Aiden mocks from my side.

I groan, bumping his leg with mine. "You know I'd just gotten to the meet cute when you ruined my fun." I lift the pastel covered book between our bodies, shaking it at both of them angrily.

"What the fuck is a meet cute?" Aiden asks, leaning forward to ask Nora. Straight pieces of his shoulder-length hair fall around his face.

She shrugs before lightly elbowing my arm. "Beats me. I've never been into books the way Lennon is."

I feel sorry for both of them. Sighing, I play with the pages of my book. "I can't believe you don't know what the meet cute is. It's honestly embarrassing, and I'm ashamed to be seen with the two of you."

"Is it though?" Aiden pipes up. He pauses, listening to Matt,

Nash's head of tour security, as he alerts us they'll be opening the doors in five minutes.

That's five minutes I could be reading. If only my sister and best friend would leave me alone.

"The meet cute is one of the best moments in the book," I explain. Cheers erupt from outside the door. They've probably spotted Nash as he makes his way to the meet and greet area. Normally he's already back here by now, but his manager, Monica, pulled him away to discuss something, so he's a bit later than normal.

"I'm dying to know how," Aiden quips. I don't appreciate his sarcastic tone one bit.

Nora softly giggles next to me.

I glare at her, which makes her smile apologetically. My older sister tries to hide the smile by covering her mouth, but it's not worth the extra effort. She's betrayed me and gone to Aiden's side, AKA the dark side.

"The meet cute is the first moment they meet. When the two of them realize the other exists. It's like the moment in the book that sets up everything else. And you made me stop reading halfway into it."

Aiden lifts his hands in apology. "Holy fuck Lennon, I'm *so* sincerely sorry," he apologizes, his tone mockingly sweet. "I won't ever dream of doing it again." He flutters his eyelids, making the whole scenario far more dramatic than it needs to be.

Done with his shit, I hit him in the stomach with the book. A loud *smack* echoes in the room as my book meets his abs. "Don't make promises you'll never keep," I snap.

He laughs. "You're right. I'm definitely going to bother you and your *meet cute* again."

"And I'll hate you for it," I tease, knowing I could never hate him. As much as he annoys me, he's also a breath of fresh air. I need to take life a little less seriously sometimes, and he's the perfect friend to help me do it. Even when he's being a dick.

Nash walks through the doors. Before acknowledging anyone else, his gaze searches the room until it lands on my sister at my side. Beelining across the room, he lifts her into his arms immediately. "Missed you, Rose," he whispers against her lips, using the nickname he coined for her.

She wraps her arms around his middle. "It wasn't even twenty minutes."

He winks at Aiden and me. "Twenty minutes too long, babe."

Monica claps her hands together from across the room. "Okay, it's go time!"

People shuffle around us as everyone gets into their places. Nash goes to stand in front of a backdrop with his name and tour logo all over it. The band members stand off to the side, there to take pictures in front of the backdrop only when asked by fans.

Aiden gets up, leaving me alone with my book once again, happy to live through somebody else's meet cute since I won't be getting one of my own anytime soon.

I'VE BEEN DEEP IN MY BOOK FOR AN UNKNOWN amount of time, comforted by the sound of the meet and greet taking place around me, when I get the sensation that someone is watching me. I try to fight it at first, well aware that there are many people in this room. Eventually, I can't shake my curiosity. Looking up, I find the last pair of eyes I'd expected aimed right at me.

CHAPTER 2

I'VE ALWAYS BEEN someone who enjoys reading. There's something about being lost in somebody else's world that brings me joy. It's similar to the feeling that I get when I listen to music. There's something to be said about art that transcends people into a different world, a different place.

I've never seen someone who enjoys getting lost in different worlds in the way she does. It's crazy that there could be a million things going on around her, and she seems completely unaware of it all. It's as if the people around her fail in comparison to her fictional characters.

For some reason, it fascinates me.

I find myself watching Lennon, Nora's baby sister, wondering what world she's lost in right now.

When she first came on tour with us, I never watched her. But the more people gave her grief about watching *me*, the more I became fascinated with watching *her*. Not that I was interested in a romantic sense—that was the last thing on my mind when it came to Lennon. I just wanted to know why she chose to set her sights on me. I needed to know more about the person who could feel something for me, knowing virtually nothing about who I am.

I'm lost in wondering what she sees in a man in his mid-thirties like myself when she's so young, when the woman in question looks up. Immediately, she catches me staring.

We both avert our eyes, hers moving a millisecond before mine.

Fuck. That wasn't supposed to happen.

The last few fans to come through haven't been as interested in getting photos with us as they've been with Nash, giving me too much time in my head.

In my defense, I'd listened to Landon, my best friend and also a member of the band, as he talked about this woman he saw in the crowd during the show. He'd gone on and on about how she was his dream girl. I couldn't help but point out how he falls in love with a different person each show we have. Landon's always doing things like that. He falls in and out of love at the drop of a dime.

It must be nice. I don't want to fall in or out of love again if I can help it. There's too much at stake, too much to lose when you care that deeply about someone. Landon lives his life differently than I do. It might be what drew me to him in the first place. He seeps happiness like a damn golden retriever. I, on the other hand, feel like I'm constantly walking around with a cloud over me. My life has been one traumatic event after the other. I need people like Landon in my life to keep me from drowning in the events of my past.

"Damn, we aren't popular tonight," Landon whines from my side. I look over at him. He scratches at the blond hair at the top of his head with a sad look on his face.

"We're never as popular as Nash," I point out. We never have been, and I'd never want to be. Being his bassist is enough publicity for me to handle. I first met Nash when I was hired as a bassist for him and his little teen boy band. We became somewhat close during those years, but as soon as Nash went solo and asked me to follow him, he became like a little brother to me.

That's when I met Landon as well. Nash has always been a little like me, the two of us lost in our own hurt. Landon's the opposite. I've wondered if he's ever been hurt in his life. If he has, he's never told me about it.

Landon watches something closely from across the room. I follow the direction of his gaze and find he's either watching Nora or Lennon. He looks away quickly, plastering a grin on his face. "That's because they just don't have good taste," he jokes.

Shaking my head, I twist the lid off my water bottle. I take a drink as Nash finishes up taking photos with the last few fans left.

"Should we crash the other side?" Landon asks excitedly. From time to time, we'll go over to where all the fans gather and mingle. Landon eats it up because, with the absence of Nash, we *do* become the coolest people in the room.

I sigh, not entirely in the mood to socialize. Tonight's show seemed to take everything out of me. I was thankful to have something going on today. The date is not a day I prefer to be alone on. But even with the excitement from the show, the crowd being amped the entire time, I still can't help thinking about what day of the year it is.

"I think I'm going to pass," I reply. I grab his shoulder, my own way of apologizing for not being a wingman for him tonight.

He pulls in his eyebrows, grimacing. The only time he ever has a sorrowful look on his face is when he's pretending. "Don't make me go in there alone, Poe."

"You'll eat that shit up. Think of all the individual attention on you."

He smirks. "I get all the attention, anyway. No one cares about your ugly mug." He punches me in the arm, knowing that the both of us have women swarming us anywhere we go. Even though I'm a bit older than both Landon and Nash, I can still get any woman I want.

The thing is, typically I don't *want*. I'm good with the friend-ships—practically brotherhood—I have with the two of them. I don't need the baggage of a relationship with the life I live. A relationship doesn't need *me* with the type of burdens I bring to the table.

"I'm going to go see what trouble I can get into." Landon claps, rubbing his hands together in anticipation. Heading toward the other room, he throws one last look over his shoulder before walking through the curtains. "Your loss," he says, disappearing.

Now that the meet and greet is over, people file out of the room quickly. Nash and Nora leave arm in arm, Nash whispering something in her ear on their way out. Matt and Monroe, Nash's bodyguards, follow closely behind the couple. Monica leaves immediately after, Aiden hot on her heels ranting about something to her. Sometimes I wonder if Monica has some kind of superpower where she can tune out Aiden without hearing a thing he says. He's berating her constantly. Most of the time it seems like it goes in one of her ears and out the other.

All too soon, the only people left are the people in charge of cleaning the Nash Pass room and packing it up for the next stop of the show. No one in Nash's circle lingers long. We never really do.

Somehow, she doesn't seem to notice. I stand off to the side, wondering how long it'll take Lennon to figure out that everyone is gone. Typically, she's glued at the hip with Nash's little brother, but I guess tonight Aiden was too busy bothering Monica to remember to get his friend out of her fictional world. Nash and Nora were also too swept up in their own world to break Lennon from her fictional spell.

I look toward the exit. I'm more than ready to get out of here. I can't wait to be drawing the curtains to my bunk on the bus closed and getting some sleep. That way I'll get to wake up tomorrow and not have to deal with this day of the year for another 365 days.

But I don't want to leave her alone. Morally, I *can't* leave her alone. It's not that I don't trust the crew members, it's just that I've been told bits and pieces of her past. She may not feel comfortable walking back to the buses alone. My nostrils flare with my deep exhale as I realize I've already made up my mind. I make my way to her, refusing to leave until I've offered to walk back with her.

Lennon sits cross-legged on an equipment box. There's a large piece of duct tape across the front, letters and numbers that are code for the crew members to know what truck it goes on. Her brunette hair falls around her face, spiraling down her shoulders. It acts as a shield from the world for her. The book is tucked in her lap. She rests her head in the palm of her hand, the other hand free to turn the pages.

My boots come to a stop in front of her. It takes a few seconds for her to feel my presence.

As soon as she looks up, her already large eyes widen. They dart from my face to over my shoulder.

"Oh boy," she mumbles. The book snaps shut in her lap, her eyes racing around the room. "Did everyone leave?"

She refuses to look me in the eye as she pops up from the box. I have to take a step backward to make space for her. "Uh, yeah," I respond, waiting for her to look at me. Even though she's no longer physically reading the book, I wonder if her mind is still somewhere far away from here. Somewhere that doesn't even exist.

Her hands are busy shoving the book into an old backpack she has thrown over one shoulder. She quickly zips it up, so in a rush that she leaves a small opening, inviting anything to fall out if she moves a certain way. "Aiden normally tells me," she offers, and it almost sounds like an apology. The words are muttered to her feet since she still hasn't looked up at me.

I remember Aiden's words from earlier. He'd embarrassed her by accusing her of having a crush on me. I'd tried to ease the sting of her embarrassment by not acknowledging it. But now it feels weird standing in front of her. His words from earlier are a big fat elephant in the room.

Remembering she'd said something, I quickly pull my thoughts together. "Yeah, well, he seemed angry with Monica about something, so when she left, he followed."

She nods, finally training her eyes on me. Tucking her hair behind her ear, she rolls back and forth on the balls of her feet. "Thanks for letting me know. I'm going to get back to the buses, I guess. I've got to give Aiden shit for forgetting about me."

My lip twitches. The two of them seemed to bicker often, their unlikely friendship fascinating to me. I have no doubt she'll stay true to her word and give him shit for leaving her.

Tucking my hand in my pockets, I tilt my head toward the exit. "Let me walk you?"

CHAPTER
3

IT'S A SIMPLE FAVOR. All he's done is offer to walk me back to the buses—the same place he's probably heading to. Unless he has plans tonight. Which I guess he might. It seems like he and Landon are always off doing something, causing some sort of trouble.

Even though it isn't putting him out much to walk me back, his offer makes my heart flutter in my chest. My only answer is to nod. I adjust the strap of my backpack on my shoulder to give myself something to do.

He points to the exit. "After you," he says quietly.

Poe follows a pace behind me as we exit the backstage Nash Pass area. As we leave, Poe exchanges goodbyes with various crew members. He seems to be on a first name basis with most of them. It's sweet that he seems to care about the people on the tour. He's busy. He wouldn't have to get to know everybody if he didn't want to, no one would hold it against him.

Both of us are quiet as we walk through the stadium. Some areas are packed with people doing the after-show cleanup. It's crazy how much they can get done in a short amount of time. They set up and break down Nash's stage set up in a matter of hours. Other areas are desolate, not a crew member in sight.

When we're met with the views of the parking lot, it's eerily quiet. Usually, there are lines of golf carts at the exit, assistants waiting to cart different crew members and bandmates around. Now, there's none. They must be busy taking people where they need to be. Poe and I probably missing them only by a few minutes.

Poe tucks his hands in the pockets of his jeans. "We could wait for someone to come back. Eventually they will."

I nod, my eyes roaming the empty parking lot around us. My guess is most people are at the loading exit. It's where the trucks can back right up to the stadium, making it easy for crew members to load them up for the next stop. Other carts are probably at the same place we're trying to go.

My phone vibrates in the side pocket of my backpack. Keeping myself busy, I pull it out, finding a text message from my sister. I shoot off a quick response to her, letting her know that I'm fine and will be back at the buses soon.

Looking up, I find Poe watching me curiously. Feeling the need to explain, I say, "Nora was checking in on where I am."

He lifts his chin. "We could always walk?" It comes out as more of a question than a statement.

My teeth dig into my lip. I look in both directions, not seeing any carts to escort us back to the buses.

"We don't have to," he adds, his voice rushed.

I try not to smile, finding the way he sounded almost sheepish way too attractive for my own good. "I'd like that."

"Yeah?" His head tilts to the side, his gaze intent on me. When he looks at me, it feels like I'm under a microscope. He stares so deeply I wonder if he can read my every thought. My skin feels hot underneath his gaze. I hope the flush isn't obvious to him.

I answer by walking toward our buses. Aiden and I both have bunks on Nash and Nora's bus, the bunks slightly larger than typical because they're on Nash's. Poe is on the same bus as

Landon and other bandmates and crew members. Even though we're not on the same ones, they're always parked right next to one another. It'll be a slight hike to them, but I've always enjoyed walking. It doesn't bother me to do it, *especially* with Poe as my company.

This is the first time I've ever been alone with him. It feels important. He's just being polite, but I don't care. I'll eat up whatever scraps of attention he'll give me, even if it's just out of courtesy.

His hair falls over his eye as he falls in step next to me. Every now and then his arm brushes mine, and even though I wear a long sleeve sweater, ensuring my skin doesn't touch his, I still revel in the feeling every time it happens. He doesn't seem to realize it's happening, highlighting the strike difference in how we view each other.

I wonder if the hair in his face ever annoys him. It's always flopping down, a barrier in front of his deep brown eyes. My hair often does the same, but I use mine as a shield. His doesn't seem like that, it just seems like it's too much of an inconvenience for him to worry about moving it.

"Enjoy the show?" His words make me jump. We'd been walking for some time in silence, both of us lost in our thoughts. I wasn't expecting him to really say much. Because of this, his words catch me off guard.

I sneak a glance in his direction. He's already looking at me, waiting for me to answer. I almost forget to respond, lost in how perfect his features are. His nose is perfectly straight, his lips thin but full. Finally, I remember he's waiting for an answer. "The parts I saw were great," I respond.

He raises his eyebrows. It's not a smile, but with him, those seem to be hard earned. It's still *some* kind of reaction. One I'll gladly take. "The parts you saw? Was your book more interesting?" His words aren't accusing or said with malice. They aren't even really that playful. Often Nash jokes that he's offended that my books are more interesting than his performance. Poe doesn't make it seem that way. It's as if he really is genuinely interested in the contents of my book.

He kicks a rock across the pavement, and the rock skips ahead of us. Poe follows the path of the rock, continuing to kick it even if it veers off the path we're walking.

"Maybe?" I answer awkwardly, not wanting to hurt his feelings. "It was the end of the story," I explain, thinking of the book I'd finished during the show before immediately starting a new one. Hopefully that's enough of an explanation for him. Truthfully, even if it wasn't the end, I'd still choose to read during most of the shows. The first few shows I stood and watched from side stage, but they got pretty repetitive. Eventually, I've kind of lost a little interest. Sometimes I don't even go out to the side stage, choosing to hole up in a dressing room with a book, or take Aiden's dog, Pepper, for a walk instead.

"Tell me about it?" It takes me a few steps to realize that he's stopped. His kicking rock is at my side, but he doesn't seem to be worried about it. He watches me, his hands in his pockets as he waits for my answer.

I'm now a good chunk ahead of him, even though I've stopped and turned to face him. I crunch the toe of my boot against the rock, pushing it into the asphalt. "You don't have to do that," I tell the ground.

He takes a few steps forward. "Do what?"

"Ask about my book. Act like you care…" I don't want my words to seem harsh or rude. I just don't want him to think that just because I'm Nora's sister he has to act like he cares about silly things like what happened in my book. My teeth grind together, keeping my mouth shut from saying anything else.

His head cocks to the side, his eyes traveling over my face. Whatever he's looking for, I don't think he finds it. His dark eyebrows stay lowered in concentration. "Who says I don't care? Maybe I want to read it."

An unattractive snort breaks free before I have the chance to compose myself. *So much for keeping my mouth shut.* "You most definitely don't want to read it."

His eyebrows narrow. "Why's that?"

I shrug, unable to look at him any longer. Turning around, I walk forward, hoping he'll follow. Finding the curb between the sidewalk and the road, I put one foot in front of the other as if I'm walking a balance beam. My arms outstretch next to me to help keep my balance. It's more for drama though, I don't really need it. I spent countless hours perfecting my balance during my years of dance; I don't need the extra support. It seems necessary, though, with Poe's eyes on my back. "It's a romance novel," I explain. "This one was very fluffy, a romance about a single dad falling in love with the woman next door."

"Fluffy?"

I glance at him over my shoulder. "Yeah, fluffy. Sweet, whole-some—*fluffy.*"

"Don't women normally like the shit that makes them cry? The opposite of fluffy?" He's walking directly behind me, his long legs able to eat the previous distance between us easily.

"Some women do. I'll read it sometimes if I'm in the mood, but often I like to feel happy when reading. Real life is harsh enough, you know? I don't need to read about it, too."

He's quiet. The vacancy of words lasts so long that I look over to check that he's still next to me.

Finally, he responds. "Yeah. I get that." His words come out quietly, like his mind is somewhere else.

I'm dying to ask him where his head is at. I've always wondered why he always seems washed in sadness, in pain. He tries to hide it, and he does it pretty well. But pain recognizes pain, and whenever I look at Poe, I see immense hurt written all over him.

I've always hated when people pry about what I'm thinking, so I don't ask him, even though every part of me wants to. If he wanted to elaborate, he would. So I let the silence wash over us once again. I focus on lining up the heel of one foot with the toe of my other. It entertains me for a few minutes before I tire of it and walk normally again.

The start of the bus line is now in sight. It'll take some time to make it to ours, them being tucked all the way in the middle of the group. Still, it makes me sad. I don't know if I'll ever get alone time with Poe again. Our time together is fading all too soon.

"You never answered my question, by the way," his words come from right next to me.

"Oh, the ending was good. Their love overcame the vindictive ex-wife of his. They ended up happy together. She was pregnant at the end."

He nods. "Good. That wasn't the question I was talking about, though."

It's my turn to stop and turn to face him. My hands run through my hair, a nervous tick I've always had. "It wasn't?"

"Nope," he clips.

It's the first time I've been able to study him in close proximity. If I was brave enough to reach out, I'd be able to touch him. I'd be able to find out if his T-shirt is as soft as it looks. His shirts always look so worn that I can't imagine that the fabric isn't soft to the touch from the wear. I could reach up and play with the dark brown tendrils of his hair, if only I had the nerve.

But I don't.

I allow my eyes to rake over him, committing everything about him to memory. That way, late at night, when I romanticize this otherwise innocent interaction, I can remember it in perfect clarity.

It occurs to me that it's my turn to speak. I was too busy marveling at how sharp his jawline is, how if I ran my finger down the bridge of his nose I'd feel no curve at all. My fingers twitch at my side, desperately wanting to reach out and find out how his skin feels against mine.

"Remind me of your question again?" I whisper.

He holds my gaze. His eyebrows furrow, and it seems like he's doing everything to figure me out. Or maybe it's just my brain playing tricks on me, just wishful thinking on my part.

I wonder if his deep brown eyes are able to see the things I keep hidden. "Who said I wouldn't care?" he asks, his voice thoughtful.

I try not to react, not expecting that question at all. For most of the duration of our walk, I haven't felt as shy around him as I normally do. He's seemed more normal, not some enigma made up in my mind. But I feel nervous all over again, unsure of how to answer his question. My stomach twists as my mind races with what to say.

All I've got is the truth, no matter how ineloquent the answer is. "Well, no one said you wouldn't. I just thought…"

Even though I can't look at him as I get through my thoughts, I can feel his stare hot on my cheeks. "Thought?" he presses.

I look up at him through my eyelashes. "I just didn't think you'd care. Not in a bad way, or in a rude way. I'm just Nora's younger sister to most on the tour. I'm not that interesting or compelling."

He stares down at me. His cheeks puff out, air hissing through his lips. Whatever he was going to say never comes out of his mouth. He stares at me one more long, drawn-out moment—at least it seems that way to me—before continuing to our walk toward the buses.

I spend the rest of our walk to the buses wondering if I said something wrong, his silence making me self-conscious.

CHAPTER
4

THE HEELS of her boots are loud against the pavement. She's always moving around the world so quietly. It's odd to be able to hear every single step she takes. It isn't as if she even walks that heavy. The way she moves her body, the way she effortlessly balances walking along the curb, it's clear that she was a dancer. Nash and Nora have explained that she doesn't dance anymore, but even in her movements, I can tell she used to.

It doesn't shock me she was a ballerina. She moves so effortlessly that there's no way she could've been anything else. Everything about her is quiet—except for those damn boots.

Even as I look forward, the numbered buses her and I both sleep on each night in sight, I'm aware of every move she makes. Lennon tucks her chin into her chest, seemingly making herself small. I should probably say something or tell her she *is* interesting. I do find her compelling, but I can't explain why.

And I don't want to instill false hope in her.

I'm well aware of her little crush. I find it as a compliment. She's beautiful, and no man in his right mind wouldn't find her interesting in her own unique way. But even with all of those things, I don't think of her romantically. And I don't want her to mistake my compliments for that, so I stay silent, even though I know I could boost her spirit by being honest.

We spend the rest of the walk in silence. Finally, we reach the buses. I'm relieved at the familiar sight of them. If we'd had any more time together, I may have come clean and told her what I was thinking.

She stops between the two buses, turning her body so she faces me. "Thanks for doing this." She awkwardly shifts from one foot to the other.

"Don't thank me," I answer. "I wanted to."

Her back straightens slightly. "Okay…" she mutters. "Well still, thank you."

She's getting ready to open the door of her tour bus when I do something stupid.

"Hey, Lennon?" I say, louder than necessary out of urgency.

Her hand pauses against the door handle. Looking over her shoulder, she watches me expectantly.

My fingers anxiously twitch in the air. Suddenly, I realize I probably should've just let her get on the bus and left it at that. I just feel like I have to get this off my chest, to give her one small sliver of something. I'm not sure of what…but just *something.*

"Today is a hard day for me," I explain, fumbling with my words. "The date is hard for many reasons." I pause. "So I guess I'm just saying thank you for keeping me company?" I blow out air, unable to find the words to express my gratitude. "I thought I wanted to be alone. But this, the walk, I don't know—it helped."

I anxiously await her response. I didn't divulge much, yet it seems like I told her everything. No one on tour with us knows about today—the significance of it. Only people from back home know why today is harder than others. I don't know why I told her about it, even if it was just a small mention.

It just seemed right—felt right.

"I'm glad," she gets out breathlessly. Her focus stays on me, like she's wanting to say more but thinks better of it. Quickly, her head turns to face the door again, her body disappearing into the opening.

I stand there a few beats after, wondering why I feel the urge to befriend her, to compare our demons and see what happens.

The door swings open, but it isn't Lennon on the other side. It's Aiden.

He halts at the top of the stairs. Angling his head to study me. "Looking for Nash?"

I scratch at the hair on my chin. "I was, but I figured it out."

Aiden's eyebrows narrow, but he doesn't press further. He finishes exiting the bus, letting the door snap shut behind him.

Before he can change his mind and ask more questions, I spin on my heels, getting the hell out of there. Closing the distance to the bus I share with the rest of the band, I'm surprised to find it empty. Troy, Nash's drummer, may be in his bunk. The curtain is drawn, so it's hard to tell. My bunk is in between two others, Landon above me and Luke, Nash's guitarist, below mine. Next to our bunks are Nash's backup vocalists. There's also a line of bunks across from ours, which houses some of the male dancers for the tour.

It seems as if most of the bus is out celebrating the show. Normally I'd leave and seek company, but tonight I'm just tired. I want to get to bed and wake up to a new day tomorrow.

My phone rings from in my pocket. I don't have to pull it out to know who's calling me. She's been calling me all day. I've just chosen to ignore it. The problem is, Veronica doesn't do well at being ignored. Not taking her call is only prolonging the inevitable. She won't stop calling until she gets a hold of me. It's her way of making sure I'm okay.

I'm not.

I probably never will be.

Sighing, I slide the phone out of my pocket. My intuition is correct. Veronica's name pops up on my screen. I stare at her picture for a few seconds, wondering if I can at least ignore her until tomorrow. I'll feel better tomorrow, I always do. Except part of me wants to talk to her. To acknowledge what day it is, the importance.

"Hi," I answer, my tone defeated.

I hear her sigh of relief immediately. "I've been trying to reach you all day."

My body falls onto the leather couch in the living area. There's a slight hissing sound as the air escapes from between the cushions. "I know. I've been busy."

"I like to keep myself busy on days that remind me of Connor, too."

And there it is. The first acknowledgment of him. Sometimes I think of my life as before Connor and after Connor. He was my childhood best friend. Our parents were inseparable, he was basically my brother. I was an only child, only ever having Connor and Ty as friends growing up. Connor was first, though. Ty came along in middle school and made the awkward duo Connor and I had going on a trio.

The three of us were inseparable until Connor died. It may have even begun before Connor died, from when he met and fell in love with Veronica.

"It's good to talk about him, you know," Veronica says gently. "It's been so long, yet it feels like yesterday."

It feels like a lifetime to me. I was a teenager when it happened. Now in my thirties, it was half my lifespan ago. But Veronica is right, the *pain* still feels as if it happened yesterday.

"I keep waiting for his birthday to not be so hard, but it's always awful."

He was six months younger than me, and I loved to remind him of it. I was the oldest in our trio. It made me feel superior to them, even though it wasn't the case at all. We should've had a joint thirtieth for all of us in Vegas. We should've reminisced when none of us had any idea how to talk to a woman, to shoot the shit while we blew way too much gambling.

We didn't have that.

Connor should be married now. Probably with five kids because that's something Connor totally would've done. Instead, Veronica, his girlfriend when he passed, is married with two kids of her own. She still honors him, though. Even though time has moved on, she hasn't. Not fully. She does things all time to remember him.

Like this phone call.

The line gets fuzzy as she breathes into the speaker. "Probably because he freaking loved birthdays. I mean, really, who gets into birthdays that much?"

I laugh, remembering how big of a deal he made each birthday—well, the ones he had until he never had one again. One time he and I got into a huge fight because I told him turning eleven wasn't that cool. You were already in the double digits, so it didn't have the allure that turning ten did, but it was also still far away from being a teenager. It took him three days to forgive me. And I still wonder if the only reason he let it go so quickly was because the third day was my birthday. No matter how angry he was with me, he wouldn't let a birthday go to waste. It's funny how a memory can stay so vivid, even though it was from over twenty years ago.

"It annoyed the hell out of me," I confess, my voice low. "But fuck. What I would do to have him here to make a big deal out of it just one more time. He'd be the only person in the world still excited about birthdays after turning thirty." My fingers play with the necklace on my neck. It has my stepdad's old Navy dog tags on it and a guitar pick from my very first sold-out show. Anytime I'm nervous or anxious I fiddle with the chain on my neck or with the stone in my pocket. They're both messed with often.

It's her turn to laugh. "Maybe eventually he would've

stopped getting excited about aging. I'm over getting needles stuck in my face to fight the wrinkles."

Veronica and I were never close back then. She ran in a completely different circle than I did. She was part of the popular crowd. Our minds were blown when she fell for Connor —even Connor had a hard time believing she was into him. It was years after his death when she first reached out to me. I was touring with Nash's old boy band, shocked when I heard her voice on the other end of the line.

Now, we speak from time to time. She always calls on his birthday and the day after the anniversary of his death. Never on the day of. It's too hard for her. She was there when he died.

"How are Maverick and the kids?" I ask to be polite.

"Sucking the life out of me," she answers fondly.

"That good, huh?"

The sound of the bus door opening distracts me for a moment. Two of Nash's dancers appear. They whisper to one another once they realize I'm on the phone. I lift my hand in greeting. They don't linger, both of them basically diving into their bunks.

"Maverick keeps saying he wants one more," Veronica continues, her voice tired.

"What's one more when you already have two?"

She gasps on the other line. "Poe, it's clear you have little experience with children. I rather love that my youngest is now old enough to tie their own shoes and get themselves a snack without asking me a thousand times. I don't want a newborn again."

All I can do is chuckle. Veronica Cunningham has had two weaknesses her entire life. One was Connor, the second was Maverick. I wouldn't be shocked if I were to find out that they end up with a third kid. I don't tell her that. It's fun to let her pretend she doesn't have the softest spot for her husband.

"Whatever you say, Veronica."

Neither one of us says a word for a few moments. Finally, she speaks up. "Are you taking care of yourself, Poe?"

I try not to roll my eyes. I'm a grown man, of course I'm taking care of myself. "You bet," I tell her.

Her sigh says enough. "Why don't I believe you?"

"Because I'm a grown man on tour with a child popstar?"

"*Former* childhood popstar," she corrects.

"You're only saying that because it makes you feel young because you've seen him in concert."

"I still remember the shock of seeing you on stage with him."

"Didn't think I'd end up so cool?"

"You're still not cool, Poe."

I shake my head even though she can't see it. "It's been nice talking to you, Ronnie. It's good to talk to someone who knew him."

"You can call anytime," she reminds me.

My hands pause on the necklace, letting it drop to my chest. "I know."

"But you won't."

"Probably not."

"At least you're honest." She laughs.

"'I've got to go," I lie. I don't have to go. It's not like I have plans other than going to sleep. But I've had enough reminiscing for one day, and I really am exhausted.

"Okay," she responds. "I'm always here if you ever need anything, Poe."

Before she can say anything else, I hang up.

The truth is, it's hard to speak to her sometimes. She was his girlfriend, there when he died. For years, she blamed herself when no one else did. But the fact that she's been able to move on and I haven't is something I hate.

CHAPTER 5

A JOLT of the bus wakes me from a deep sleep. Turning in my bunk, I pull the thin blanket to my chin. It's supposed to be a full day of driving for us as we reach our next destination—wherever that may be. Monica gave me a nicely laminated tour schedule at the beginning of the tour, but I don't recall where I stuffed it. I'm along for the ride. It doesn't really matter to me where we end up next.

I'm almost asleep when my bunk curtain is ripped open. Rolling over, I'm met with my sister's smiling face. "Hungry?" She keeps a grip on the curtain, waiting for my answer.

I rub my eyes with the heels of my palms. "What's going on?"

She's never woken me up on the bus. On travel days, we usually eat at different times. Occasionally Aiden will scrounge something up in the tiny kitchenette for us, but even on those days, he doesn't wake us up to do it. Typically, we all just grab something from the cabinets, living off pre-packaged foods and meals until we reach our next stop.

Nora looks at something I can't see. "Nash had the idea that we'd stop and get lunch." She chews on her lips as she mulls something over. "Well, I guess it's more like dinner—supper?"

she finishes, using the word our grandma always called dinner when she'd insist we'd eat early in the evening.

I stretch my legs underneath my blanket, trying to wake up. I'd been up all night, rehashing the unexpected moment with Poe over and over in my head. I'd spent hours obsessing over every word he said, which is saying something because he isn't a man of many words. Caffeine had kept me up long enough this morning, but I nodded off before I even had lunch. The nap was exactly what I needed. I may have slept late into the night if it wasn't for my sister.

"What time is it?" Throwing off my blankets, I swing my legs over the ledge of the bunk.

Nora side-steps out of my way. "Almost four."

Jeez, I'd been asleep for almost four hours. As soon as my feet hit the floor, I reach to the ceiling of the bus to stretch. The bunk is tall enough for me to sit up inside without hitting my head, but there isn't enough space between my head and the top to stretch when in the bunk.

Nora stands there quietly as I finish stretching, the pull of my muscles helping me get rid of the fog from my nap.

"I don't know how I slept so long."

She picks at a thread on the end of her baby doll dress. "You didn't miss much. Nash and Aiden have been playing some video game for most of the day."

"What'd you do?" I ask, pulling my duffle bag out from underneath my bunk. I rifle through it, wanting to change into a pair of jean shorts instead of my lounge ones if we're going to be getting off the bus.

She shifts her weight from one foot to the other, shrugging awkwardly. "Oh, you know, just…stuff."

I feel bad as her words fall off. The reason I'm on the tour is to spend more time with her, and I need to be better at making time to do that. She's trying to mend our relationship, and I need to put in the same effort. It's not that I don't want to be close with my sister. All I want is for us to get to the point we were at before everything happened in high school. It's just hard because I didn't know how to handle what had happened to us, so I did the only thing I could—I ran. Because I ran, left my tiny town, my family included, and my relationship with my sister suffered.

Sometimes, I wonder if she still blames herself for what happened. At first, I wondered if I blamed her. But I know I don't, I never did. I just couldn't look at her without seeing *him*.

I grab my shorts from my bag and stuff the bag back where I found it. Nora reads something on her phone in the meantime.

"Maybe tonight we could watch a movie together or something?" I ask. "We could choose some cheesy chick flick the boys would hate. They'll definitely leave us alone." I laugh and her eyes light up.

She enthusiastically nods her head. "Yeah, I'd love that."

I smile, excited at getting some one-on-one time with her. It seems like we're always with somebody, not getting time for the two of us. It was like that before the tour, too. I make a mental note to be better at getting away from all the people we're always surrounded by so we can do things together.

"Everyone else already went in to get a table, but I can wait for you to get changed," she offers, ambling toward the living area.

"I'll be one minute," I tell her, rushing toward the bathroom. It doesn't take me long to change into the new pair of shorts and run a brush through my hair. My mascara is slightly smudged from my nap. I run my fingers underneath my eyes to wipe the black splotches away. Once it doesn't look like I have a black eye, I run some Chapstick over my lips and call it good.

Nora is tidying up our small dining table when I finish.

"I'm ready," I say, pulling my phone off its charger in my bunk.

The two of us walk across the parking lot toward some small

restaurant. It's got vines traveling up the side of the faded yellow building. Underneath the vines there's a mural of a man holding a platter of spaghetti and meatballs.

Nora seems to notice the same thing. "Nash saw a billboard for the restaurant like thirty minutes ago. He spent five minutes looking at the menu online before he decided we had to stop."

"*I'll die if I don't get this chicken alfredo,*" she says in a low voice, imitating Nash. "*It's world famous, babe. We* have *to go.*"

I laugh at her terrible impression of her fiancé. It's crazy that they'll be married next month. Her impression of her future husband sure needs some work. "That sounds exactly like Nash." He's hard to say no to when he knows what he wants. It's how she ended up with him.

She hooks her arm through mine as we near the entrance. "He then got Aiden roped into wanting the food, and before long, they'd told three other buses full of people we were stopping."

I look over my shoulder, just now noticing the two other parked buses next to ours. One of them being the band's. I haven't seen Poe since I left him standing at the door of our bus last night, a sad look on his face.

I wonder if he'll act any different after last night. Shaking my head, I get a grip on myself. Of course it won't be any different. He simply walked me to the bus. It doesn't change anything.

"Sounds exactly like the Pierce brothers," I joke.

A petite elderly woman smiles at us from a hostess stand. "You must be the wife," she says, her tone matter of fact.

Nora looks at me with one arched brow.

The woman doesn't give us time to respond, a breathy laugh falling from her. "He told me that your face would be great if I said that."

Nora rolls her eyes, freeing her arm from mine. "Apparently my future husband is full of jokes."

The woman ushers us to follow her. Talking over her shoulder, she says, "My granddaughter is obsessed with you. She's always jabbering about the woman who stole this Nash Pierce's heart. I told him that, calling you his girlfriend, and he was quick to correct me. He told me I should call you his wife when you arrive." We weave through empty tables with white tablecloths. I look down at my outfit, wondering if this restaurant is nicer than I was expecting and feeling self-conscious in my fraying cutoff jean shorts.

Nora nods in understanding. "Tell your granddaughter I'm really not that cool," she says shyly. Being in a relationship with Nash has made her famous in her own way, yet she still seems shocked when people are fans of *hers*. She made a name for herself as a dancer on his tour, having a large social media presence before she ever even met Nash. I don't know when it'll occur to her she's almost as famous as him now because she's marrying the guy.

The woman takes us into a separate room where the rest of our party waits, all of them already digging into baskets of bread laid out on the long table.

"Did she make a face?" Nash calls from across the room. He sits tucked away in a corner. Aiden sits at the head of the table, Nash seated in the chair to his left. There's one empty seat next to Nash and then one next to Aiden.

"Len, sit next to me," Aiden calls, pointing at the spot next to him.

Nora and I separate, each of us rounding the table to take our spots.

The lady chuckles. "She made a face."

Nash wraps an arm around Nora as she takes a seat. "I knew you would, Rose."

I can't hear whatever Nora whispers back to Nash. Taking my seat, I find myself stuck between Aiden and Poe.

"Have a nice nap *Sleeping Beauty?*" Aiden jokes, pushing a water cup my way.

"I did," I say, taking a sip of my water.

"Late night last night?" A deep voice questions from my other side. Eyes widening, I look over at Poe.

What do I say to him? *Oh yeah, spent all night replaying our brief time together like an obsessive schoolgirl.*

Aiden saves me from having to answer. "She probably spent most of the night reading. The real world isn't cool enough for our Len."

There's a mischievous glint in Poe's eyes when he looks at me. He doesn't respond to Aiden, the two of us knowing I'd spent a chunk of the night with him. I like that the two of us have a secret. It links me to him.

"Is that so?" Poe presses, a hint of humor to his voice.

My hands fumble in my lap awkwardly. "You know me, a total recluse," I fib. Typically, I *am* alone if I'm not with Aiden or Nora. It just so happens that things took a different turn last night.

I don't want to tell Aiden that I'd walked back with Poe. Aiden had seen us together at the door, but I think he thought Poe was just looking for Nash. Aiden would never assume Poe and I'd spent time together. I'll let him think that. It's not like anything happened anyway. It was as innocent as it could be, but still. I want to protect that small moment with him. It's exhilarating to know him and I share a secret, as innocent as it is.

Poe watches me carefully. He pulls the crust off his bread, crumbs falling onto the plate below him.

Looking down, I grab the menu in front of me. I'm thankful that everyone around me has busied themselves by falling into their own conversations. There are numerous options on the menu, all of them sounding delicious. There's a picture next to every item on the menu with a detailed description of what's in the dish.

My stomach growls—loudly. I realize I never ate lunch.

Something gently nudges my arm. Looking up from my menu, I see Poe holding a piece of bread. He doesn't look at me, instead he continues to watch Landon as he animatedly goes on about a show he's watching.

I stare at the piece of bread, wondering what he's doing. Sighing, he brings the piece closer to him. He quickly unwraps an individually packaged butter. He slathers the butter onto the bread evenly. Setting the knife down, he places the piece of bread down on the plate in front of me. Pointing down at it, he simply says, "Eat," under his breath, his attention returning to Landon.

CHAPTER
6

LENNON STARES AT ME, her mouth hanging open. I look away from Landon briefly, looking down at the piece of bread I just placed in front of her. I angle my head toward it, silently telling her to take a bite.

She picks it up tenderly, as if the crusty bread will fall apart in her hands. Holding it up to her mouth, she takes the world's smallest bite. Her eyes close momentarily. The bread is good, the outside nice and crunchy, the inside warm and fluffy. Shortly after, she takes another bite, this one much larger.

Satisfied that she's eating something, I look back to Landon. He doesn't seem to notice the brief distraction. I'd been caught up in his recap of his latest TV binge when the growl of her stomach almost shook the table.

Every now and then, I risk a glance at her. She polishes off two pieces of bread and almost an entire pasta, her stomach placated and quiet.

Lennon sits back in her chair, rubbing her hand over her stomach. "I'm so full," she groans.

Aiden plucks her plate from in front of her. "I'll finish this for you then."

"What if she wasn't finished?" Monica chimes in from a few seats down the table.

A wolfish grin takes over Aiden's face. "Why don't you mind your own business, Monica?" He slurps a noodle into his mouth, glancing at Lennon. "Tell her you were done, Len."

Lennon looks like the last place she wants to be is in the crossfire between Monica and Aiden. "Oh I'm done," she mutters. She leans deeper into her chair, slowly slouching down as if she wished the chair would swallow her whole.

Everyone else finishes up their meals and engages in conversation. Travel days are often filled with the same people, the same conversations. It's nice to get our small group together and feel somewhat normal. We aren't often able to go out to eat, with Nash being who he is and all. But we're in the middle of nowhere at an odd time to eat. It seems like, at least for the time being, no one knows we're here.

"We need to get back on the road soon," Monica declares, in her usual bossy tone. She looks down at her phone, furrowing her eyebrows slightly at whatever she reads.

Nash sighs from across the table. "You're right." He looks at me. "Would you want to hop on over to our bus until we stop again to get some writing in?"

I nod, itching to get lost in the songwriting process. My head still isn't in a good place after Connor's birthday yesterday. Getting lost in the creative process of making a song is exactly what I need.

"Oh perfect," Monica says eagerly. "The label will be thrilled to know you're working on another song for them."

Landon, Luke, Nash, and I roll our eyes in unison. From the moment the tour began, Monica has been breathing down our necks to get some new music out. We've already been to the studio once to record some stuff, but we don't have an album put together yet. With Nash getting married next month and he and Nora taking a honeymoon after, I'm sure Monica is feeling the pressure to get something to the label before we all have some time off.

I'm dreading the break. Going on tour is always a great escape for me mentally. Keeping busy is exactly what I need. Being left alone is never good for me. The loneliness takes its toll.

Our group spills out of the restaurant, the owner following us out. She thanks us, requesting a picture with Nash to send to her granddaughter before we make our way to the buses. Instead of getting on my bus, I follow Nash to his. Sometimes Luke and Landon write with us, but for the most part, Nash writes on his own or with me.

I'd first found my love for making music in song writing. It was more in the form of poetry, but after Connor died, I needed some sort of outlet to get my feelings out. My school guidance counselor suggested keeping a diary to journal all my feelings. I was a teenage boy. I wouldn't have been caught dead writing in a journal. But my best friend had just died, and I needed something to help me cope.

It started with jotting down simple thoughts here and there. Those thoughts turned into lines of poetry, and those lines turned into entire poems. Eventually, I realized the poetry was morphing into song lyrics. When I was a kid, my mom had put me in guitar lessons. I picked it back up easily, instead falling in love with the bass guitar. After Connor died, I went from being the kid who spent his free time holed up at home playing video games to the kid always playing music.

In a way, music saved me. It's saved me over and over again. It saved me when Connor died, and it saved me when both my parents passed. It still saves me to this day.

Boarding the bus, Nora pulls on Lennon's arm. "Let's leave the boys to write their music so we can watch our movie."

"What movie are we watching?" Aiden asks.

Nora narrows her eyes at him. "We're having a girls' night. You're not invited."

Aiden fake pouts, his bottom lip jutting out. "Oh c'mon, I can be one of the girls for the night. I love a good chick flick."

"It's sister time," Lennon adds apologetically, running her fingers through her hair.

Aiden huffs, falling onto the couch. He crosses his arms over his chest, resting his head on the back of the couch. "You guys suck."

Nash claps him on the shoulder. "Aw Aiden, you can write some music with Poe and me."

Aiden grumbles, pulling a throw pillow over his face dramatically. "I hate writing music, and I'm terrible at it."

"Can't say I didn't offer." Nash pushes his brother's feet to the side, taking a seat on the end of the couch. He pulls out both his phone and song journal, two things that are always included in our songwriting sessions.

I follow Lennon and Nora to the back of the bus.

Nora flops onto the bed, pulling her sister with her. "Sorry Poe," she says. "No boys allowed."

I reach to the side of the bed where Lennon lays, grabbing the guitar that's always on Nash's bedside. "Just grabbing this," I explain, my fingers wrapping tightly around the fretboard.

Backing out of the room, I look at Lennon and Nora one last time before shutting the door. I focus on Lennon for a moment. "You two have fun." I wink, shutting the door behind me.

Walking back to where Nash waits, I sit down, soon forgetting the way Lennon's cheeks turned pink with the wink.

CHAPTER 7

PEPPER SITS CURLED up at my feet as workers all around us prepare for the show. When Aiden first got the dog, she would've never sat so calmly as people rushed around her. Now that she's a certified tour dog, she doesn't even flinch as they roll a giant speaker right past us.

I've become accustomed to the hustle and bustle of tour life. I used to thrive in silence. That was before, in the after, I hate being stuck in silence. There's something about sitting off to the side of the stadium seats, tucked away in a corner while they set up for Nash's concert that brings me peace. Nash and Nora get married in a few weeks, leaving us with only a few shows before we're already halfway done with the tour.

Pepper's tail whacks me in the calf. At first I ignore it, but once it doubles in speed, I look up, wondering what's caught her attention.

Turns out, it isn't a *what,* it's a *who.*

My heart does a funny flip-flop in my chest when I find Poe heading in my direction. His focus is solely on me, but I still chance a look in either direction to my side, not confident he's not looking at somebody else. It confirms what I already knew.

I'm the only person in the vicinity. Well, me and now Poe—plus Pepper.

"There you are," Poe says smoothly. His voice must be what every author envisions when they describe the hero's tone. It's deep, rich, incredibly husky, almost always sounding like he just rolled out of bed.

"Here I am…" I reply, my words sounding more like a question instead of an answer.

He takes the stadium seat next to mine, stretching his legs out in front of him. There's a hole in the knee of his khaki pants, but it isn't one that looks like it's meant to be there. It's small, allowing a small peek at his tan knee.

Pepper jumps up, putting her paws in his lap to reach his face. Poe laughs, moving his head from side to side to evade the assault of Pepper's tongue. Unfortunately for him, Pepper has great aim. It's hard to really get away from her when she's dead set on licking your face.

Something falls to the ground in his attempts to get away from her. It's only then that I notice he was holding something. It's a small rectangle wrapped in newspaper. There's something written across the front of it, but it's too far away for me to read it. The handwriting is too small.

"Okay, Pepper, that's enough." Poe chuckles. Gently, he pushes on her chest, forcing her front paws down to the cement below him. He scratches her behind her ear for a moment. Satisfied with the attention she's receiving, Pepper sits down next to him. Her tongue hangs out of her mouth in pure joy.

His shoulders rise, and he breathes air in through his nose, out with his mouth, letting the breath out slowly. "Hi." He sighs. He doesn't smile, but the way his eyes crease at the corner kind of feels like one.

I bite back my smile. "Hi," I respond, my voice coming out breathless.

"You always sit out here?" He looks toward the stage. Stagehands roll out various instruments while other crew members work on setting up lighting and other things. One guy has a large cord wrapped around his elbow and hand. It reminds me of my dad, how he used to be so anal about how he'd wrap up the Christmas lights. I watch the man wind up the cord for a few more moments before I remember Poe asked me a question.

"Yeah," I say, averting my gaze. I've caught many of their sound checks, like the one they just wrapped up, from spots similar to the one I sit in now. He'd know that if he looked out into the crowd, but he doesn't. I feel like I'm always absent-mindedly searching for him, no matter where we are. It's clear he doesn't do the same, not that I expected him to.

He hums. "I didn't see you out here."

I know. You never see me.

But I see you.

I swat at the air dismissively, trying to play it cool. "I'm easy to miss."

Poe does this thing where he draws you in with eye contact. He maintains it so well, so even at times like these, where I feel incredibly awkward, I feel like I have no choice but to look at him, to stare into his brown eyes even though I'd much rather disappear into thin air.

His dark, straight eyebrows pull in. He frowns. "Not anymore."

My. Heart. Skips.

Sitting up straighter, he shakes his head, clearing his throat. "I'll keep a lookout for you next time." His words run together with the rapid pace of his words.

I can't do anything but nod. My tongue feels heavy, like if I tried to speak, my words would come out jumbled. All I've wanted for months is for Poe to notice me. The thought of him looking for me next time he gets on a stage for sound check makes my heart flutter, even if he only said it to make me feel not as lame.

We fall into a comfortable silence. Pepper keeps Poe busy by placing her head in his lap any time he attempts to stop petting her. Eventually, my eyes wander, focusing on the package that fell to the ground earlier.

I point. "What's that?"

Poe jumps out of his seat, making it seem like he forgot about it as well. "Oh, yeah." Grabbing the carefully wrapped package, he holds it up between us.

"So, I got you something," he begins. His fingers grip the package tightly as he inspects the wrapping closely. Now that I can see it closer, I notice creases in the paper where it appears he messed up and started over with the wrapping.

"You w-what?" I stutter.

Is this real life? I pinch my thigh with the hand farthest from him, making sure I'm not dreaming.

He smiles. An actual, real smile—and it's at me. I've seen him smile while talking to others, or when performing on stage. But never so up close, and never aimed directly at me.

I'll do whatever I can to have it happen again.

"I got you a present," he repeats.

Holding it out between us, he gives it a small shake. "Open it."

My hands tenderly take the gift as if he's handing me over a newborn baby. I want to cherish whatever is wrapped inside. Now that I hold it, I notice the countless pieces of tape covering the newspaper, the tape not doing a great job of hiding the small rips in the paper. I run my finger over one of them.

"Yeah." He scratches at his facial hair. "I'm not the best at wrapping," he says, his tone apologetic.

I'm too excited about the gift to tell him I love it more with the small rips. I imagine him trying to wrap whatever is underneath the newspaper. It's even more special to me that it seems it took him multiple attempts to get it right. The fact he took the time, trying repeatedly, to wrap this gift nicely for me makes my heart soar.

Get it together, Lennon.

I've held enough books in my life to be pretty confident that what hides underneath the paper, but I don't say anything. Carefully, I glide my finger underneath one of the folded edges. Pushing up, I try my best to not rip the paper—at least not in a place he hasn't already ripped it. I slide my finger through the tape, gently moving the paper to the sides to expose the gift.

Underneath, I find the embossed cover of a book.

Poe watches me unwrap the gift closely. As I pull the paperback out, he shifts in his seat. "I just finished it last night. I thought you might want to read it."

Taken aback by the gesture, I stare at the cover. It's a map of a made-up kingdom, with crumpled flower petals scattered across it. My finger runs over the title, the words sticking out of the book in a 3D effect.

Poe must take my silence as disappointment. Quickly he mutters, "It's a fantasy, so you may not like it." I don't answer right away, so he continues. "You probably won't. There's a bit of a love story, but nothing huge. At least not yet, it's only book one," he explains. He seems a little flustered, but I must be reading him wrong. I don't know why he would be. I could never hate a gift from him. I'll lap up any attention, any gift, *anything* if it's coming from him.

"There's also a plot twist at the end I didn't see coming." His voice has gotten tighter, like he's regretting the gift.

"I love it," I get out quickly. I grasp it to my chest, inhaling the scent of him mixed with the scent of a book—my new favorite smell. I'm careful not to crumble the paper as I set it on the empty seat on my other side.

His eyebrows raise. "You do?"

Nodding, I can't hide my smile. "I do. I can't wait to read it. I've been in the mood for a good fantasy recently."

It's not a lie. I had been in the mood to read fantasy. It's why I picked up this book a few months ago when it first released and people went nuts. It was all over my social media. The book was phenomenal. I've already preordered the second. But there's absolutely no way I'll tell him I've already read it. I don't want to disappoint him, and I'm excited to reread it. To read the same pages he read.

A lock of wavy brown hair falls in his face. He doesn't move it from his forehead as his lip twitches. "Cool. We'll have to talk about what you think of the plot twist."

I'd guessed the plot twist a few chapters into the book. It was pretty obvious that the rebel that was helping her save her kingdom from the evil, tyrannical king was actually the son of the king—the crowned prince. But it was probably only obvious because I've read so many books. I've figured out their formulas. It's fun guessing what the plot twist will be. I feel a certain kind of pride when I guess right.

I'll fib and tell him it took me by surprise, though. It'll give me the chance to have another conversation with him. To discuss who we think she'll end up with. Will it be the prince or her best friend who has always been in love with her?

My money is on the prince.

"I'm sure I'll have it finished in no time," I answer honestly. He doesn't have to know that the second I'm alone in my bunk, I'll scour the pages of this book. I hope the scent of his cologne with the familiar scent of book pages envelopes the tight space. I can't wait to run my finger over the same places his fingertips have touched. Sometimes, if I get distracted and hold my book too tight, I'll leave teeny tiny imprints on the pages. I wonder if he's left any of those on the thin paper.

"No rush," he says coolly. "Just whenever you have time."

I have to catch myself from saying I'll always have time for him.

"Luckily, I've got lots of it," I respond, still telling the truth.

CHAPTER
8

I NOTICED the book on a gas station bookshelf. It wouldn't have caught my attention, except two people ahead of me in line had plucked it off the shelf and purchased it. Standing in line, my mind had drifted to Lennon. I'd thought about how she was probably on Nash's tour bus reading a book of her own. I'd recently finished a murder mystery and needed something new to read. The book wasn't one I'd typically go for, but I'd absent-mindedly wondered if it was one she'd enjoy. Before I'd thought too much into it, I'd picked the last one off the shelf and bought it.

The entire time I read it, the book surprised me by being enjoyable. I'd wondered what she would think of certain scenes, thought deeply into what she'd think of the characters.

As she inspects the book next to me, fanning the pages, creating a slight breeze that moves the long tendrils of her hair, I realize the reason I'd bought the book was because I wanted to discuss it with her. It didn't seem like she was someone who was into psychological thrillers or murder mysteries, so I chose one that I thought she'd like.

I don't think too much about it, or at least I try not to.

She sets the book in the discarded wrapping paper, my

pathetic excuse for wrapping paper, that is. I could've just handed her the book and told her I think she'd like it. It didn't feel right to do that, so this morning I took the time to wrap it, albeit *horribly*, to hopefully make it more exciting for her.

The way she marvels at the book tells me I could've given it to her plain and she'd love it. She's tender about putting the book back in the paper, treating it delicately.

"Thank you," she whispers. Her body turns in the seat to face me. The sun hits her green eyes just right, showcasing small gold flecks. Pepper perks up, moving from my side to rest at Lennon's feet.

Her knee brushes against mine slightly. "It's nothing," I say, trying to play it off as if I hadn't bought it for her in the back of my mind.

"Sound check went well." Lucky for me, she changes the subject.

I nod, sitting back in my chair. She'd chosen a row in the front, allowing me to stretch my legs out in front of me without anything blocking my path. "This deep into the tour, it becomes almost second nature. I'm glad you thought so, though," I add.

It bothers me that I've never noticed her sitting through our sound checks. I feel guilty, and then I feel guilty for feeling guilty. This is Nora's little sister. The woman who has a crush on me even though I nowhere near deserve it—or want it. I shouldn't be noticing her. I shouldn't be paying her any attention at all. I don't want to be feeding into her crush; I don't want to give her any false hope. There's a reason I don't allow myself to form the attachment she deserves. The way she no doubt hopes for. Her romance novels are filled with the love I'm sure she wants, where the men are fixable and able to surpass their demons. And then there's her past, feeding into the notion she deserves way more than a man like me. Her crush will eventually go away. But that doesn't mean I'm not all too aware that I shouldn't be seeking her out like this. I shouldn't be reading books just to have an excuse to talk to her.

Yet, here I am.

The worst part of it all is that I'm already anxiously waiting for her to finish so we can discuss it. The excitement she has when discussing books is intoxicating. I'd thought it the night I walked her back to her bus after the show. She'd told me about a book I'd never read, but to see her light up talking about it was refreshing. She could've been reciting a cookbook, and I would've eagerly listened to every word if it meant she'd light up the way she had that night where it was just us and the stars.

And maybe that's the reason I found myself giving her a reason to talk about a book with me again. One we could both discuss.

"How'd you get into music?" Her words take me by surprise. She's typically shy and minds her own business. Her question isn't intrusive by any means. At least I know she doesn't mean it that way, but she's always been so quiet, and in her own world, so I wasn't expecting her to ask me anything personal.

My fingers run through my hair, messing with it as I try to come up with a suitable answer. One that doesn't divulge too much. "It's, uh, complicated," I finally get out.

She laughs. It's soft. Everything about her is soft. Her voice, the way she phrases her words, her laugh.

I wonder what else about her is soft.

The thought jars me. I shake my head, focusing back on the question she'd ask, and how I'd even begin to answer it without making this encounter depressing.

"You don't have to tell me." She pulls one of her legs into the chair with her. Her foot plants on the seat, her knee sticking up in the air. Her chin rests on her knee as she watches me. She blows a piece of hair out of her face, finally swatting it away when it doesn't cooperate the way she wants it to.

Air escapes my lips slowly as I let out a deep breath. "It kind of just happened," I answer sadly. "Something happened when I was a teenager that I wasn't quite equipped to deal with. My guidance counselor first suggested therapy," I say it jokingly, remembering that at fifteen there was no way I was going to therapy, even though I desperately needed it. At the time, the idea of a fifteen-year-old guy talking about his feelings was unheard of. "Then she suggested journaling"—I bump her with my shoulder—"which wasn't about to happen either. So, the next best thing was music."

"Tell me more." She barely blinks, hanging on to my every word. Her green, gold-flecked eyes are wide as saucers as she waits patiently for me to elaborate.

"There's not much to tell." There's a mountain of things I could say to explain why music is the one true love I've ever had, even though I found it later in life than most. It doesn't take away that it's the one constant I've had in my life. Those I've loved have left me, have died, but music has stayed. "I started writing poetry, it turned into song lyrics, and the lyrics turned into songs. I realized I needed music to go with the lyrics, and then I was obsessed with picking back up the guitar skills I'd learned as a child. One day, I picked up a bass guitar, and then I lost myself in music. It's twenty years later, and I'm still lost in it."

Lennon shifts, now resting her cheek on her knee. "I used to feel that way about dancing." Her words are so soft I wouldn't have heard them if I hadn't been listening intently.

Nash has never shared all the details with me about what happened to Lennon. The only reason I know something happened is because one night he'd felt the need to explain to me the reason Lennon was going on the tour was to get closer to her sister. I hadn't pressed for more, but he'd told me, anyway. All I know is that when she was in high school, Nora's boyfriend mistakenly sexually assaulted Lennon, thinking it was Nora in the bed. Apparently Lennon had been a talented dancer before it happened—ballet, especially. But Nash told me after that the assault, Lennon never danced again.

There's more to it, I just haven't pried. It isn't my business unless she decides to make it mine.

I'm quiet, busy gathering my thoughts when she speaks again.

"Now I lose myself in books." She taps the book resting on the seat next to her. I want to ask her if she thinks she'll ever dance again, but I keep my mouth shut.

"Hopefully that one does the trick," I say, trying not to stare at her too long.

Her hair falls in her face again. She tucks it away in a motion I've caught her doing frequently.

She smiles, placing her foot back on the ground. "Something tells me it will." There seems to be a hidden meaning in the way she says the words, but I don't know what it could be.

I run my hands down my thighs, clapping them down on my knees. "I should get going."

Lennon nods, picking the book up and placing it in her lap. "Thank you again, Poe," she says in that soft voice of hers. One I've taken too much of a liking too. "It means a lot."

"It shouldn't," I mutter under my breath, regretting it the moment her lips pull down in a light frown. I didn't mean for the words to come out harsh. I just don't want her thinking more of me than she already does. I don't deserve it, and eventually, whenever the crush she has on me expires, she'll realize I was never worth the time.

CHAPTER
9

"I FEEL like I'm going to be sick," Monica groans from her seat in the limo. Her head falls into the window, her forehead pressing against the cold glass.

"Maybe we should give her some water?" Nora offers. She hands me a water, leaning across the limo to take it, I hand it to Aiden on my left. He uncaps it, holding it out to Monica.

"If I put anything in my mouth, I might vomit," she whines.

Surprisingly, Aiden keeps the dirty joke I know he's wanting to make to himself. Monica tries to shift in her seat, but she gets tangled up in the birthday sash Nora and I'd created for her. Aiden quietly helps get her arms out of it, pulling it off and throwing it to our feet.

Birthdays have always been my favorite. Not necessarily my own. I don't enjoy being the center of attention. The only time I did like being the focus of everyone was when I danced. Now? I'm more of a stay on the sidelines kind of girl. But celebrating other people's birthdays is my jam.

Even if it is celebrating Monica Masters.

The first time I met her, I wanted to run for the hills, and I wasn't even on the receiving side of her wrath. I've slowly begun to admire her as the tour has gone by. She doesn't take shit from anyone, and she's fiercely protective of those she cares about. Both admirable qualities.

So when Nora and I found out it was her thirtieth birthday, we had to celebrate. Monica argued profusely, but the group didn't let up. We begged and pleaded until she'd finally agreed. The night had been fun. We hopped from one place to another, ending at a karaoke bar. Before I knew it, time had flown by, and it'd been time to go.

"I hate you," Monica mumbles under her breath. Her eyes are closed, so I'm not sure who she's talking to. It could be aimed at any of us.

"I've heard those words before." Aiden chuckles. He then immediately winces. I try not to smile, knowing Monica must've been the reason behind the wince.

Looking up, I find Poe staring at me from his spot next to Nash. He flicks his eyes to Monica and then looks back at me. *"We're in so much trouble tomorrow,"* he mouths.

This time I do smile, because there's not a doubt in my mind that tomorrow she will be out for vengeance. She's already always a tad moody, throw in the hangover she's guaranteed to have, and I'm already scheming how I can avoid her at all costs.

"I know," I mouth back.

The rest of the ride back to the buses is filled with the sound of Monica's moans and Landon drunkenly singing along to the radio, belting out the words as if we were still at the karaoke bar. Matt even turns the music down from the front of the limo, but it doesn't deter Landon in the slightest. Even drunk, his voice isn't bad.

Poe cheered his friend on from the side, goading him to sing louder and louder as the miles passed by.

Once we arrive at our destination, we all pile out of the limo.

"Hope you had a great birthday, Monica," Nora says. Nash offers his hand to her as she steps out of the limo. She gladly takes it, her steps a little wobbly from the few drinks she had.

Monica teeters on her heels, and Aiden steadies her by grabbing her elbow. "It isn't for another week," she grumbles. "I'm going to bask in the fact that I'm still in my twenties for a few moments longer." She lifts her hand, pointing at Nora and I. "Enjoy it ladies. Eventually, you'll be old and doing whatever you can to fight the aging process."

Aiden rolls his eyes, pulling on her elbow slightly. "Let's get you to bed."

She swats his hand. "I can get there myself. I don't need your help."

He ignores her, pulling her toward the bus she shares with the rest of Nash's personal relations team.

The remaining group watches them bicker as they walk toward her bus in silence. Landon breaks it by clapping his hands together loudly.

"I'm going to hit the hay," he declares proudly. He puts his arm around Poe. "This was fun, friends. I thought hell would have to freeze over for me to celebrate Monica, but shockingly, that was a damn good night."

He turns to the bus he shares with his bandmates.

Nora bumps me with her shoulder. "It might take a few days, but I think Monica will thank us for the celebration."

"Maybe." I giggle, knowing that'll probably never happen, but it's a funny thought. I watch as Matt and Monroe head to bed as well, only leaving Nash, Nora, Poe, and me.

Nash throws his arm around Nora's waist, pulling her in close to him. "Let's go to bed, Rose."

I scrunch my nose in disgust. "Gross," I whisper, knowing exactly what Nash meant by that.

If it wasn't so dark out, I know I'd be able to see the blush on Nora's cheeks. She playfully hits Nash on the stomach. "Stop it, Nash." Her voice has no trace of anger at all.

"I'm going to hang out in the fresh air a bit," I tell them, pulling my book from my backpack.

Nora gives me a disapproving frown. "It's late"—she looks around—"and dark out here," she adds, resignation in her tone.

Poe reaches behind his head to scratch his neck. "I can keep her company for a bit. Landon always snores for at least an hour after he first falls asleep. I won't be able to fall asleep, anyway."

I'm glad that no one is standing too close to me. I'm afraid they'd notice my small breath of excitement when he said he'd keep me company. My heart pounds in anticipation in my chest, thrilled to be alone with him again.

It looks like Nora wants to say something, but she ends up biting her tongue. Nash whispers something in her ear, and she responds with a nod.

Nora runs her hand down my arm. "Goodnight, Lenny. This was fun." She squeezes my hand before letting Nash pull her to our bus.

The night around us is silent. I'm all too eager to be left alone with Poe, the shadow of the night making it seem like we're the only two people in the world.

Turning around, I search for somewhere we can sit. There's a slab of concrete with a few bench seats not too far away from us. In the middle there's a statue of some athlete they named the stadium after; at least I *think* the stadium was named after them. I'm not fully confident in that fact. Either way, the guy must be important to be immortalized in stone.

Poe's footsteps ring out behind me. Picking the bench farthest from our parked buses, I sit down. He takes a seat on the same bench as mine, although he sits as far away from me as the bench allows.

I pull my legs into a cross-legged position, placing the book in my lap. "You didn't have to keep me company, you know."

He taps away at the medal on the bench. "It was more to avoid Landon's snoring," his tone is joking, but the words slice through me more than I'd care to admit.

"Yeah," I say, feigning disinterest, while my stomach is in knots. "That's what I meant."

"You weren't so bad at karaoke," he teases.

I bite my lip, remembering earlier in the evening when he'd pulled me up on stage to do karaoke with him. It's something only Poe could convince me to do. I was too enamored in wanting to hear his singing voice, in sharing his space, that I'd let him lead me to the stage. If anyone was shocked to see him and I singing a duet up there, they didn't show it.

"That was the *first* and *last* time I'll ever do it." Singing is not a talent I possess, and I'd prefer to keep the only thing that hears me belt out lyrics to be my showerhead.

"It was one of my favorite parts of the night." He bows his head, his fingers fluttering down his thigh with his nervous tick.

It was *my favorite part of the night.* At least, until now, in this moment.

There's an awkward silence between us. I'm running through things I could say to break it when he reaches toward me. His fingers brush against the inside of my knee as he grabs the book in my lap.

He doesn't even seem to realize he's touched me, but it's all I can think about in this moment.

"How'd you like the book?" he questions, opening my new book, one different from the one he lent me. He flips through it, his eyes scanning the pages. He pauses when he notices there's writing on some of them.

I liked it a lot better when you were reaching for it in my lap.

It was such a mundane touch, yet there's still warmth on my knee from where I felt his skin on mine.

"What's this?" he asks, reminding me he's found my annotations.

I want to pluck the book from his arms, but I know there's not much he can find in the one he holds. It wasn't really a spicy one, so there aren't any notes in there that I'd necessarily be embarrassed for him to read, but it still feels weird to let him in on the parts of the story that caught my attention. No one's ever asked me about the things I scribble in the margins of my books, so I've never had to explain them.

"Just little notes," I mutter under my breath. "I've recently been into annotating my books. That way I can look back and see what I thought while reading."

He looks up. "Did you annotate the one I gave you?"

I bite my lip, shaking my head. "No, it's yours. I didn't want to ruin it."

He once again focuses on my little notes in the margins. He runs a finger over one of them. "That's too bad," he says, his voice so slow I wonder if I'm supposed to hear it or not. "I would've loved that," he adds.

"You would?" My words come out breathy. Luckily, he seems too interested in what I jotted down to notice it.

Finally, he closes the book, handing it back to me. "Yeah. I would. I wouldn't have thought you making notes would've ruined it, by the way."

I grin, trying my hardest to play cool. Inside, I'm freaking out. "Noted."

He smiles—wide and perfectly. I take a mental picture, that way I can remember it forever.

"Noted," he mimics, shaking his head. "I see what you did there."

Flying on the high of having his smile aimed at me, I twirl a piece of hair around my finger. "I finished the book," I say, my fingers playing with a loose thread in the hole of my jeans. "I loved it."

His eyes light up. "You did?" His voice sounds like he's relieved.

"Yeah, I didn't see that ending coming," I lie. I just don't want to wipe the excitement from his face.

He throws his arms up in the air. "Right?"

"Thank you again for letting me borrow the book," I say before I break and admit that one, I'd already read the book, and two, I saw the rebel being the prince by the fourth chapter. "I'll make sure to get it back to you."

"Don't worry about it. I'm more just disappointed I wasn't special enough to get a book with your small little notes."

CHAPTER 10

"ANNOTATIONS." Her green eyes watch me carefully.

I raise my eyebrows, confused. "Annotations?"

"The little notes." She tucks a piece of her wild wavy hair behind her ear. "They're called annotations."

Sitting back in surprise, I shake my head. Lennon has this thing where she's constantly taking me by surprise. "Here I am confessing that I wasn't special to you, and you're correcting me on my terminology?"

Lennon's cheeks turn pink. It seems like they do that a lot. "It's not that," she says hurriedly. "I really just didn't want to ruin your book."

It's dangerous territory, acknowledging the fact I know she has a crush on me. I could make some comment that I thought I was special to her or something along those lines. I don't want to broach the subject. Saying it out loud, hearing it from her, isn't something I'm prepared for. While I've wondered what drew her to me, I'm not sure I actually want to know.

What if I don't like her answer?

What if I do?

"Let's make a deal," I begin, sliding slightly down on the bench to bring our bodies closer.

She lets out a sigh of relief. She probably didn't want to have to approach the elephant in the room—well, in our case, it's more like the elephant in the night.

"A deal?"

I allow myself to get closer to her by a few more inches. We're still a platonic distance away from one another. A respectable amount of difference between a man that is over ten years older than his female counterpart. "I want to read your books—or at least ones you've annotated."

"You aren't reading my books," she states matter-of-factly.

Stretching, I rest my arm across the back of the bench. "Why not? I let you read mine."

Her lips part slightly, her mind deep in thought. She plays with her hair, twisting it around her finger to avoid the conversation. I keep watching her, eyebrows raised, making sure she knows I'm not dropping the subject until she answers me.

After what seems like forever, she groans. "That's different. You wouldn't like most of the ones I read."

My teeth run across my bottom lip. "Shouldn't I be the judge of that, Lennon?"

Her eyes widen when my finger brushes a long piece of her hair that fans over the back of the bench. "I'll pass," she mutters, tilting her head back slightly so the tips of her hair brush over my fingers.

Damn. I wasn't expecting her to tell me no.

I feel this intense need to read more of her little notes. I can't explain why I feel this way, but the need to know what she writes isn't going away. She's so quiet, always reading in the corner or letting Aiden do the talking for her. I want to know more of her thoughts. I want to know more of *her*. I only got to glimpse at a few of her notes in the book she's currently reading, but I'm greedy and want more of them.

"What if I find the books?" I blurt. What's best for the both of us is for me to just drop the subject. If she doesn't want me to see these annotations, I should drop it. But I can't. The thought of reading a story through her lens is too enticing, something I can't let go.

Lennon watches me silently, waiting for me to elaborate. Any other person would grow uncomfortable with the lull in conversation, but not Lennon. She's standing her ground. Her green eyes shine in the moonlight as she trains them on me. Her fingers gloss over the cover of the book in her lap, something I'm not sure she even realizes she's doing.

My mind races with different ways I could make this work. Finally, I come up with some semblance of a plan. "I can find the book, make sure it looks interesting, and then I'll give it to you to read."

"Don't you want to read it?"

I tilt my head, thinking her question is silly. "Of course I do. I just want to read it *after* you. To see your annotations and all."

She fidgets, crossing her legs only to uncross them. "Why?"

If only I knew, Lennon.

"I want to see the fictional worlds you're always escaping to through your eyes."

She stares at me. I stare back. And in the silence of the night, this moment feels…momentous.

"I don't understand," she whispers, even though there's not another soul in sight.

"I don't either," I respond. Uncomfortable with her silence, I pull my arm to my side, sitting up straighter. "We don't have to. I just thought you'd maybe want to."

Lennon rolls her lips together. "Okay, but don't be disappointed when my notes aren't too interesting."

I laugh. "You don't give yourself enough credit."

"Why do you say that?"

"I think it's super cool that you do the whole"—my words break off, trying to remember what she called it—"annotation thing. I hadn't heard of people doing that before."

She wipes the palm of her hands against her legs. "It really just started with me wanting to have a way to remember my favorite parts. Then it just snowballed into more and more notes."

My hand slides into my pocket, finding the familiar stone I always carry with me. I rub the stone between my pointer finger and my thumb. "So…" I wonder why I suddenly feel nervous. "Is that a yes?"

She scrubs her hands down her cheeks. "I guess it's a yes, but don't say I didn't warn you about the disappointment."

I click my tongue. "Lennon, there's absolutely no way I'll be disappointed. Trust me."

She stares at me. I want to ask her what she's thinking, what she sees when she looks at me so intently. My teeth grind from clasping my jaw tight, ensuring I don't voice the questions spinning through my head.

When she doesn't answer, I keep talking, not wanting our conversation to be over. "So, what's your favorite book of all time?"

She lets out a dramatic breath. "You can't ask a book lover that question," she chides.

I smirk. "Sure I can. I love books, and I can definitely tell you my favorite."

"What is it?"

I adjust my body on the bench, angling it toward her. "I'm not telling you mine until you give me yours."

"We need to narrow down my options first."

My eyes narrow. "That defeats the purpose of picking a favorite."

"Okay, but it varies by genre, at least. Like I can't put fantasy in the same category as rom-com so it's hard to compare. And then I can't put rom-com books with angsty books because they elicit *totally* different feelings. I need more constraints here, Poe. Your question is unfair."

Time passes by quickly as I sit there listening to Lennon passionately speak about books. The topic makes her come out of her shell. Once she's explained the difference between a genre and a trope and her favorites of each, it's late. When we decide we both should call it a night, I don't want to.

I want to stay there on that bench, hearing her rave about things I really don't care about and only do because they're coming from her mouth.

When I climb into bed, I'm already thinking about what book I'll bring her next.

CHAPTER
11

SLIPPING MY SHOES OFF, I close the distance until I'm standing at the foot of a king-sized bed. Large, white, fluffy pillows pile in front of the headboard. A thick blanket is folded nicely at the end, a box of chocolates perched on top of it. Not waiting another second, I face plant into the covers, loving the way the thick comforter catches my fall. If I laid in this position for a few moments, I'd probably fall asleep and nap for hours upon end.

"This is heaven," I mumble into the soft comforter. After spending night after night sleeping on a bus bunk, this luxurious hotel bed is better than I could've ever imagined. I'm stoked that this is where I'll be sleeping for the next two nights as we celebrate Nash and Nora getting married this weekend.

I'm never leaving this bed.

A hand tickling my bare foot makes me jerk. Pushing off the bed with my palms, I turn around to find a grinning Aiden.

"I'm busy." My face falls back into the comforter, hoping he'll take the hint and leave me alone.

"Too busy for me?" he argues. I feel the dip of the bed as he unfortunately climbs in. "That's impossible."

I groan, turning to face him. My arms pull up to rest underneath my head. I'm too comfortable to fully sit up.

"I want to nap," I whine. It figures he wouldn't even allow me five minutes of peace alone in my room before he bombards in. If it was anyone but Aiden, I'd have already kicked them out.

"We need to go over our speeches," Aiden states, pulling out his phone. He thumbs around on it for a moment, probably finding what he's got for it so far.

"Don't remind me," I plead. It's not that I don't love my sister. She's my sister, of course I do. I want everyone else to know how amazing she is, but the thought of giving a speech in front of all of their guests tomorrow makes me nauseous. And of course she had to go and marry someone famous—meaning I'm going to be stumbling over my words in front of the world's most famous people.

Lucky me.

Aiden is Nash's best man, and I'm Nora's maid of honor. At first, they decided they didn't really want to do the conventional wedding party thing, but then they changed their minds, leaving me to give a speech. I'm dreading it.

My entire body feels itchy at the thought of so many eyes on me tomorrow night.

A hand smacks my side gently. "Hey, stop worrying about it."

Rolling to my back, I stare up at the ceiling of my room. Nash and Nora chose a venue tucked away in the California coastal hills. It's got a setup that makes it feel like you were in Spain—a country I lived in for a brief span of time and adored—without ever having to travel. The ceiling is high and arched, exposed mahogany beams covering it, reminding of Spanish architecture.

Aiden passes me a pillow. Grabbing it, I stuff it underneath my head to prop myself up. "I can't *not* worry about it, Aiden," I argue. "I'm not like you. The thought of public speaking gives me hives."

When I had to testify in court in high school, I spent the entire time before and after throwing up. It's just not my thing to speak in front of groups of people. Dancing in front of them was fine, speaking, not so much.

"Just imagine all of them in their underwear," he offers, giving me his usual smug smirk.

I kick his outstretched leg, laughing at the idea of imagining some of the A-list celebrities that'll be attending the wedding in their underwear. "Oh my god, that doesn't help at all."

He wags his eyebrows. "I know one person you'd love to imagine in their underwear."

I roll my eyes, wishing he'd just drop the Poe thing and let me have my crush in peace. "I could say the same thing to you."

This shuts him up. The perks of always being on the outskirts of things, of observing instead of being the one observed, is that you notice things. Things that other people may not notice. Like the way there's *clearly* tension between Aiden and Monica. He's always had it out for her, angry with her for some of her past decisions. But lately, it seems different, like they're both hiding something.

Aiden coughs, stretching his legs out in front of him. He links his fingers together, resting them on his stomach. "Point taken," he admits. "Let's discuss your speech so you aren't nervous, Len."

Sighing, I sit up and scoot across the bed until I can reach my backpack on the floor. Reaching into the pocket, I pull out my phone and fall backward into the sheets, already dreading the speech.

Aiden and I spend the next hour reviewing it. I've recited it enough times that I could definitely say it in my sleep. However, the thought of saying it in front of a hundred people tomorrow still doesn't seem any less daunting.

Pulling my legs underneath me, I look across the bed at Aiden. "Do you think Nora will like the speech?" I wonder, vulnerability to my voice. It doesn't really matter what anyone else thinks of it. I just want her to love it.

"Of course she'll love it, Len." He nudges my knee with his foot in encouragement. "Why wouldn't she?"

Shrugging, I pick a loose feather off the down comforter. "I don't know. She's marrying someone who's always good with words. I'm not…"

Sitting up, he scoots across the bed until our knees bump together. "Listen," he demands. "I've obviously never had a sister." He pauses for a moment, tilting his head. "Well until you—and I guess maybe Nora. We'll be considered siblings now, right?"

I furrow my eyebrows. Nash will be my brother-in-law. I don't know if Aiden also gets some special title after Nash and Nora's nuptials. It doesn't really matter. My head hurts trying to think of all the fancy titles that come with a new marriage. "Either way, you'll be considered a pain in my ass," I tease.

Aiden rolls his eyes. "If I had someone say that speech to me, a sister, I think it would be the best shit ever. Nora will fucking love it, Len. I'm glad I go first so I don't have to follow up your masterpiece."

My hand slides across the comforter until my fingers grasp the edge of the pillowcase. Trying to be sneaky, I pull on the pillow until I quickly pick it up and hit Aiden square in the face. "You better not be lying," I wheeze, trying to talk through a fit of laughter. The look of shock on his face is one I'll never forget.

He grabs his own pillow, aiming it right at my face. I try to get another good hit in, but he's too quick for me. I'm laughing through the repeated hits to the side of my head when a throat clears behind us.

Craning my neck to see over Aiden's shoulder, I find Poe standing in the doorway, his eyes wide. He clutches a book in his hand, his eyes burning into the spot where Aiden's knee rests between my legs.

Giving Aiden a shove so I can get around him, I smile. "Poe. Hi," my voice comes out more breathless than I'd intended. Not because it's Poe, but because I just spent all my energy trying to get a good hit in on Aiden.

Poe awkwardly holds the book up for the two of us to see. "I was bringing the book back." He looks down at the book, lowering it to absentmindedly tap it against his thigh. "Your door was ajar, so I thought it was safe to come in."

"Oh," I answer, trying to pull my foot out of a pile of twisted blankets.

Poe's hair falls in his eyes as he turns toward the door. "I'll go. You're busy."

I about face plant into the ground as I practically leap off the bed to stop him. "You don't have to go." I'm still trying to catch my breath, but he turns back to face me.

He looks over my head at Aiden. "I don't want to interrupt anything."

I shake my head, waving the hand dismissively. "You're not. Right Aiden?" I turn to face Aiden, trying to tell him with my eyes to get lost.

Aiden is quiet for a moment. He stares at Poe, a thoughtful look on his face. Eventually, his face breaks out in a smile. "No, man. I was just about to leave."

He tosses the pillow in his hand to the side and gets off the bed. Stopping by me, Aiden messes with the hair on the top of my head. "You're going to nail that speech, Len. I'll catch you later."

I'm busy trying to smooth out my hair as he and Poe exchange goodbyes. The click of the door lets me know that Poe and I are alone.

"What'd you think?" I ask, tugging at the hem of my T-shirt.

Poe stares at the door for a few moments before turning to look at me. "I really didn't mean to intrude," he explains as a hand runs over his facial hair. "Are you and Aiden uh…"

I scoff, not bothering to hide the disgusted look on my face. "Oh my god, *no*," I say, horrified. "He's like an annoying brother I can't get rid of."

He nods, his facial expression not giving anything away. The only thing that gives a hint to his emotions is the muscle ticking furiously away along his jaw.

The silence makes me uncomfortable, so I continue to run my mouth to fill it. "Plus, I'm fairly confident he's got something going on with Monica."

Finally, he breaks his composure. His eyebrows rise to his hairline. "So you picked up on it, too?"

"Yeah, it's kind of hard not to." I don't add that at the beginning of the tour, I swore I found them after they'd had some kind of moment. Aiden didn't divulge anything to me, and I didn't press him on it. But the tension behind them is getting pretty obvious to anyone around them.

"Well, I still mean what I said. I don't want to bother you if you're busy."

Before I can stop it, I mutter, "You could never bother me."

I regret the words as soon as they're out. The last thing I wanted to do was to bring attention to the irritating crush I have on him. He's so much older—and cooler—than me. I'm sure the women he's with never word-vomit to him like I do. But I've thrown the words out there, unable to take them back no matter how much I want to.

He sighs, looking uncomfortable while he scratches his gelled hair. "Lennon, look—"

"Did you like it?" I interrupt, reaching to grab the book from his hand.

Trying to forget how lovesick I made myself look, I turn away from him and plop down on the bed, book in hand. There's a line down the spine where he broke it. Normally, I'd hate a broken spine on a book, but when he does it, it intrigues me more.

I feel the dip of the bed as he takes a seat on the edge. Looking up, I find him a respectable distance away from me. Luckily, he no longer looks uncomfortable, and when he speaks up, I'm thankful that he's allowed me to change the subject. "Do you want me to be honest?" he asks hesitantly.

"Of course."

He looks down at the book in my lap. "It wasn't really for me. I found myself not rooting for the main character the way I should have."

I laugh. "I think that might've been the point. I don't know if the author wanted you to love him or not."

"Well, I most certainly did not."

"See and I did. I thought the way he protected his heart was endearing."

He whistles. "Is that what we're calling being a dick to people these days? Protecting our hearts?"

"Hey, remember, there's a whole trope of books where the hero is an asshole. Girls love it."

His mouth hangs open. "Girls aren't *actually* attracted to guys that are that much of an asshole."

I shake my head at him. "You'd be surprised. There's something romantic about an asshole having a soft spot for you and being able to be the one that saves a broken man."

He runs a finger over his lip. His mouth opens as if he wants to say something, but it snaps shut right after. It's an excruciating few seconds as I wait for whatever he's about to say. "In fiction it may be. In real life, it's just loving a man who could never love you back."

For some reason, I feel like we aren't just talking about the book anymore. His words seem to have a double meaning. And not for the first time in my life, I wish real life was more like fiction.

I wish the broken hero would fall for the heroine.

I wish Poe would look at me the way I look at him.

Too bad love doesn't play out the way it does in romance novels. What a beautiful story that could be.

CHAPTER
12

THE LAST WEDDING I ATTENDED, I had to break up with my girlfriend because she'd spent the entire night saying she couldn't wait for it to be our turn. We hadn't even been dating a year. I hadn't considered it serious, but her viewpoint on the relationship was obviously different. It probably wasn't my best move, but I'd told her we had to end things between the last dance and the sparkler exit.

She'd slapped me before hurrying out, which I probably deserved. She was a nice girl, it's just...I never had the intention of getting married. Apparently, I hadn't made that clear. Since then, I've been transparent with anyone I've been involved with that I had zero intentions of getting serious with them. Some took it well, some didn't. I hadn't cared. They weren't going to change my mind, no matter how much they wanted to.

I wonder if I've made that clear enough to Lennon or not. When I'd shown up at her door earlier, I hadn't expected to spend the rest of the afternoon alone in her room together, discussing more random things.

I'm enjoying her company, but in the back of my mind I know I shouldn't be. It must be sending mixed signals. I don't know how to tell her I'd love to be her friend but she needs to get rid of her crush on me without disappointing her. It stings to even imagine letting her down, even though I know it's bound to happen.

Right now, the last thing she looks is disappointed. Her chipped painted fingernails wrap loosely around the stem of a wine glass as she engages in a conversation with Landon. My best friend seems to hang on every word she says. He leans forward, his eyes purely focused on her even though the rehearsal dinner is in full force around us.

A hand slaps me on my back. "I expected you and Landon to be off causing trouble somewhere." Nash undoes the button of his suit jacket and takes a seat next to me. "It seems we've got a brooding Poe today."

I scowl. "You're calling me broody? You're known for being the broody popstar."

Nash looks in Nora's direction. She's in the midst of talking to her best friend, Riley, while holding Riley's little girl. "Not anymore. Not since her."

"I'm so happy for you, man. I've always wanted this for you. For you to be happy."

He focuses back on me. "I guess I no longer have my head up my ass, do I?"

I try not to laugh. On many occasions, I was left being the one to tell Nash to get his shit together. The two of us have been through a lot together during our years on the road. He's like my little brother, because of that I often had to lecture him. "No, you don't."

He unscrews the lid to his water bottle, taking a sip. "I never thought I'd be this unbelievably fucking happy, Poe. But here I am, one day away from marrying the girl of my dreams."

"That's if she doesn't know what's good for her and runs for the hills," I tease. We both know Nora would never. The two of them fought hard for their relationship, if there's any relationship I believe in lasting forever, it's theirs.

"I'll track her down," he responds. "That's what we do. She won't get far."

"Are you excited?" I ask, taking a gulp of my beer. There was a time where Nash and I would be pounding beers, or something harder, right now. Nash got sober, I tried to find better ways to cope. Things have changed.

"I'm psyched for all of this"—he twirls his finger in the air— "to be over. I love the girl, I don't love sharing her with everyone."

"That is the most Nash answer ever," I say, amused.

He shrugs. "I am who I am." His eyes track over the crowd. He'd told me earlier the rehearsal dinner would be small, but the amount of people seated around the courtyard doesn't feel small to me.

"Where's Landon?" he asks, his eyes searching the crowd.

Lifting my finger, I point to where Lennon and Landon stand off to the side. There's a table of appetizers a few feet away from them that people occasionally stop at to grab a bite to eat, but for the most part it's just been the two of them talking for a majority of the night.

"Interesting combination," Nash observes. I hold my tongue, not sure I have any right to comment on it. Interesting isn't the word I'd choose to describe it. Infuriating is more like it. And I have no right feeling that way.

Nash takes my silence as his cue to go. Standing up, he pushes his chair to the side. "I'd love to sit and talk all night, but I should probably keep mingling with my guests." He winks, his words coming out sarcastically. I know Nash well enough that he would prefer to be locked up somewhere alone with Nora, not having to make small talk with anyone.

The moment Nash walks away, I look back to Landon and Lennon, finding them not where they used to be. I sit there, watching people mingle while finishing my beer. Once it's empty, I stand up to stretch my legs and maybe actually talk to a few familiar faces.

I need to stop wallowing.

I'm weaving through the bodies when I spot Lennon. She's found an empty table, a book propped against the vase of the floral arrangement in the middle as she reads. I smirk, forgetting about everyone else to take a seat next to her.

"You know there's a real world going on around you, right?"

She keeps her eyes trained on the words as she shakes her head. "Fiction is so much better."

I'm recalling our earlier conversation in her room when she looks at me. "I socialized for the first hour or two," she explains, as if she really owes me an explanation.

"I can leave you alone then," I offer, not wanting to. I've become so used to her presence these past few weeks that I'd rather spend time with her than anything else. It slowly happened, but even earlier today when I brought her book. I didn't have to do it at that time, I'd just wanted to because I hadn't seen her since we'd checked in. And even then I hadn't spoken to her as the staff welcomed all of us to the venue.

When she doesn't answer, I stand, leaving her to it. Her hand juts out immediately, stopping against my chest. "You could stay."

I stare down at the place where her hands rest against me. Even through the fabric of my suit jacket, I can feel warmth radiating from her palm. Out of character for myself, I like the way it feels. "Would you actually maybe want to go take a walk around the venue?" I ask, missing the weight of her hand against my chest the moment she pulls it away. "I was going to take a breather for a few minutes, if you want to join."

The book snaps shut as she closes it. "I'd actually love that," she says, relieved. "I've done my part rehearsing, and the dinner is over. No one should even notice I'm gone."

I find it hard to believe that people won't notice her absence, but I keep my thoughts to myself. She's called me out before for not noticing her, so I'm not in a good place to talk. Her fingers fumble with the zipper of her backpack. I bite back a smile as she slings it over one shoulder. She's in a nice evening dress with a tattered backpack on her back. It's such a Lennon thing to do.

"I'm so excited to escape," she admits, pushing her chair back and standing up.

"Me too." Our footsteps fall in sync as we head in the direction of a stone path that circles the venue's grounds.

"Really?" she asks, surprised. "You always seem excited to be around others."

I duck underneath a tree limb that cuts into the path. "I'm getting old," I joke.

We're getting deeper into the land of the venue. If it were lighter outside, we might be able to get a peek of the coast through the rolling hills. In the dark, all I can see is the old cobblestone path and the plants that surround it.

"You're really not that old," Lennon suggests.

"I am compared to you. Too old to be doing this," I add half-heartedly.

She stops. I stop along with her.

Hooking her thumbs through the straps of her backpack, she trains her eyes on me. "What is this?" she questions.

"What is what?"

Blinking, she lets out an aggravated sigh. "You know what. *This,* Poe. I know you and every other single person on this tour know my feelings for you. So I guess the question is not what is this, but what is this to *you?*"

My mind struggles to come up with a response, her bluntness takes me by surprise. I wonder what's changed to make her more bold with her questions. Maybe she's had a drink or two, giving her some liquid courage. Or maybe she's just fed up with my mixed signals. I'd understand either way. "I don't know," I finally answer. My hand reaches into my suit pocket. Once my fingers find the familiar feel of the stone, I rub it.

"You don't know?" she repeats. "It just seems odd, you know, for you to seek out a friendship with someone you know already has a crush on you, with your aversion to relationships and all."

I wish I was able to voice my feelings for Lennon. They aren't romantic, but they aren't platonic. They're something else completely. I let out a controlled breath. "I know it's odd. I don't understand it either, and I wish I could tell you more—give you more—but I don't have anything else right now. Can I just call us…friends?" The word tastes weird rolling off my tongue, but I don't know how else to label this.

"Friends?" She tilts her head to the side, saying the word like it's a stupid question.

I nod, taking a small step closer to her. Both her thumbs still wrap around the straps of the backpack, her hands in little fists around the fabric. She clutches the strap tightly. If I took another step forward, I'd feel the brush of her knuckles against my chest. "You shouldn't even want to be my friend, Lennon," I warn.

She blinks, those big green eyes staring up at me expectantly. "Why not?"

I have to look away from her for a moment. She looks at me with so much hope, it hurts to know I nowhere near deserve it. I don't want to hurt her, or let her down, but that's exactly what I'm bound to do. I'm a man incapable of loving her, of really truly caring for her the way she so desperately wants. "Because I'll only disappoint you."

Her fingers unwrap from her backpack. Being bold, she reaches up to touch my cheek. My hand catches her wrist while my head rears backwards. Stopping her from touching doesn't deter her from saying, "I don't think you will."

Gently, I pull her hand away from my cheek, letting her arm

fall to her side. "I know I will. Especially if you think this will ever be anything more."

"I'll take whatever I can get," she whispers.

For some reason, her words feel like a brutal hit to the gut. I'm trying to be as honest with her as possible, yet it still feels like I'm leading her on, which isn't my intention. It would help if I knew what the fuck my intentions were. She deserves more than someone who won't give her anything. I should try to stifle her hope, but I don't want to hurt her. I haven't had someone look at me the way she's looking at me right now, and I don't want it to stop.

Feeling uneasy, I realize I'm walking a very thin line. I know she has feelings for me. I know I'll never have feelings for her. I should stop this friendship immediately, knowing that no matter what I say, she doesn't see me as just a friend, no matter how many warnings I give.

I can't do it. I know I'll hurt her eventually. There'll be a time that she'll regret the silly little crush she has on me, wondering why she spent so much time and effort on a man far older than her who didn't deserve it.

But for the time being, I can prolong the hurt. So that's what I'll do, even if in the back of my mind I know it's a terrible idea. Tonight, I don't have to hurt her.

Tonight, I selfishly get to keep the way she's looking at me.

Reaching out, I tuck a piece of her hair behind her ear. The silence of the secluded path allows me to hear her quick breath in when my finger trails over the shell of her ear. "It won't be enough," I answer sadly.

"That's not for you to decide," she responds immediately.

For her, I let Lennon have her way, well aware I should know better.

CHAPTER
13

A KNOCK SOUNDS at my door. My hand pauses next to my ear, the dangly earring hanging loosely in my grip. My eyes flick to my phone on the counter, wondering if somehow I'm late for wedding pictures. Checking the time, I confirm that there's still almost an hour before I'm supposed to be dressed and back to the bridal suite.

Nora is getting her bridal portraits done. The photographer had said they needed an hour alone with her before the bridal party pictures began. Instead of hanging out in the bridal suite with my mom, Riley and whoever else ended up in there, I opted for some time alone. I've gotten used to being around people so much again, always having to socialize. But it's nice to have a few moments to myself before spending the rest of the night chatting with people.

I reflect on the rehearsal dinner last night. It'd gone well. The rehearsal for the wedding was pretty simple. The planner last night eased some of my nerves for the wedding. We'd gone through the entire ceremony a few times, making sure we all knew what to do and when. There's not too much I have to remember. Luckily, Nash and Nora didn't really want anything out of the ordinary for their ceremony, so we were done practicing in no time. They'd tried to keep the dinner low-key, but there were still a lot of people there last night. By the time Poe caught me reading alone, I was over having to make simple conversation with people. There's nothing worse than small talk. It seems rather pointless when you can be reading instead.

When it comes to Poe, I can't say no to him. I don't *want* to say no to him. Being in Poe's presence is like a drug, and I can't deny a hit even if I know becoming addicted will only end in pain. When he'd asked to get away, I'd lapped up whatever attention he'd give me.

Another knock sounds against the wood door to my room, the sound demanding my attention.

My dress kisses the ground as I walk toward the door. I don't bother looking through the keyhole, figuring it's probably Monica telling me something I need to do—or maybe even Aiden coming in to go over our speeches one last time.

What I don't expect to see is Poe standing there, an unreadable look on his face.

My eyebrows pull in. "Poe?" I say, stating the obvious. It's him. He's standing at my door, and I don't know why. My heart thumps wildly against my chest at the sight of him in a suit again. The one last night was hot, but this one is even better. It's tighter around the arms than the one last night, showing off his toned biceps. I thought I was into his tour look, but the sight of him dressed like this makes butterflies take flight deep in my stomach, even though I know it shouldn't. Even though he'd been persistent in his warnings to me last night, it didn't help anything. He still gives me more butterflies than any other man ever has before.

His large hand points behind me. "Mind if I come in?"

I dumbly look over my shoulder at my room. Lucky for me, it's mostly picked up. I'm just trying to figure out why he's here. Yesterday it made sense why he showed up unannounced. He wanted to bring back the book. But his empty hands show me he has no book in hand. Today, his best friend is getting married...why is he here with me?

"Uh, sure," I mutter quickly. Stepping aside, I let him in the room.

As he walks by me, I'm met with the familiar smell of his cologne. It's stronger this time, like he's sprayed a bit more than normal. I hope it lingers in the room even after he leaves. I want to crawl into bed tonight, still able to smell his familiar scent floating around the room.

"What are you doing here?" I try not to sound too shocked as I close the door behind him.

Ignoring me, he rakes his eyes over the small space. When he was here yesterday, he didn't seem to look twice at my small space. Today, he's taking in every inch of the room, almost like he's looking for something. It isn't even my personal room, yet somehow it feels intimate to have him looking so closely at everything. Or maybe it's the fact that we're alone in a room once again.

Maybe it's both.

I need to get it together.

I could guarantee that he doesn't care if he's alone with me in a bedroom or not. His mind isn't having the same thoughts as mine. He'd made that crystal clear last night.

This little crush has me wondering what it'd be like to feel him next to me as we laid tangled in the sheets of the bed.

"Nash is busy with the videographer," Poe explains, his eyes finally done assessing my room—focusing on me.

I nod, wondering why he's pointing out the obvious to me. Nora's my sister. I know the schedule for the day.

Picking up a book I'd left at the end of my bed, he flips through the pages. "Did you get a new book for us to read?" he asks innocently.

It's something he's done before. It's an honest mistake for him to think this book is one he'd eventually read. The problem is, this isn't a book I ever wanted him to know about. He'd chosen some dystopian book for me to read and annotate before it was his turn. I wasn't in the mood to read dystopian, so I started reading this one at the same time. Typically, it wouldn't be a big deal, but the contents of this book are vastly different from the books we've been reading together.

Like totally different. Opposite ends of the spectrum different.

My heart drops when I realize how different this time is. I'm well aware of the annotations I have in this book—ones I never dreamed of him seeing.

Ones I never dreamed of *anyone* seeing. That's why I didn't think twice when making them more explicit than anything else I've ever done.

It happens in slow motion. He fans the pages of the book, his fingers stopping when something catches his eye. He flips through the pages until I know what he's noticed.

My legs don't move fast enough. Lunging for him, I try to grab the book from his grip.

Unfortunately, he's way too tall for me. Holding the book above his head, he looks down at me.

"What is this?" he asks tightly. His lips are set in a thin line. There's a muscle in his jaw that ticks away angrily.

My face is hot as I watch in horror as he looks at my annotations on the side of the page. Writing that was supposed to never be seen by anyone else by me.

I try to jump to grab the book from him, but my efforts are futile. His large hand softly pushes against my chest, deterring me from reaching for the book. The floor-length dress makes it even more difficult to jump. My heel keeps catching on the hem when I move a certain way. I have to be careful not to trip over it completely.

"It's none of your business," I answer, trying to mask my embarrassment. I give one last attempt at stealing the book from his hands, but it's no use. He keeps on flipping through the papers as if my attempts are nothing.

"None of my business?" He licks his finger, turning the page. His eyes scan over the words.

Giving up, I sigh in defeat—embarrassment—probably both. The man I have a massive crush on is reading my dirty annotations, and I can't do anything about it. He's used to the innocent ones I've written. I've kept them innocent, knowing he'll read them. What he hasn't seen are the ones I make in books that have a lot more romance.

"Hook up somewhere spontaneous, somewhere someone could catch us," he reads, his eyebrows narrowing in concentration.

In a motion I shouldn't find so sexy when I'm dying of embarrassment, he pulls at the bowtie around his neck. It loosens, hanging lower on his neck.

"Finish from a guy going down on me," his voice lowers an octave.

I jump when the book snaps shut.

I feel hot under his stare. As much as it mortifies me having him read these notes I'd taken, I think having him look me in the eye after is way worse. There's a burning in my chest from the way he looks at me.

"What is this?" he asks, his teeth clenched tight.

My arms cross over my chest. I don't know how to respond to him. I'd asked him that same exact question last night, but on a totally different topic, in a totally different context. Alone, I've definitely fantasized about doing some of these things with him, but that's with the knowledge that he would never have those thoughts about me. It's not like now he is having those thoughts about me, but something about him knowing what I've been writing in my books feels different.

It feels like I've made us cross a line without either of us really doing anything. Paired with our conversation last night, with me basically falling at his feet and telling him I'll take whatever scraps he'll give me in a moment of weakness, I definitely feel like the air is different around us now—more charged.

"What kind of notes are these?" he pesters, seemingly annoyed I didn't answer his first question.

I snatch the book from his hand, cradling it to my chest as if clutching it will erase everything he just read. "Private ones," I snap.

He scoffs, having the nerve to roll his eyes. As if it's him that should be annoyed by the invasion of privacy. "Who else has read those?" he demands.

My eyes narrow, shocked he would ask such a dumb question. It should be clear as day by the flush of my cheeks that not another soul has read these. And not another soul should have read them. "Oh, you know, just a few people," I say sarcastically. A piece of carefully styled hair falls in my face. I'm even more annoyed because I know how long it took the hairstylist to pin it back this morning, trying to make it appear effortless when it really wasn't. My attempts to get the book free from Poe's hands must've made it pop loose. I'll have to try to fix it before the wedding starts.

"Who?" he demands, his voice low. The words sound strained. I must be hallucinating, or my crush on him has reached an all-new low of false hope, because I swear he looks jealous. His jaw flexes. He works it back and forth as his eyebrows gather on his forehead.

Why do I think he's jealous?

Shaking my head, I rid it of the thought. There's *no* way he's jealous. Even with our newly developed friendship, he's made it more than clear that for him, he doesn't see me as anything more than his—much younger in his eyes—friend.

I've never hated a word more. *Friend.* It sucks hearing it straight from his mouth, even though I wasn't really expecting him to say anything different.

He reaches up, running his tattooed hand through the gelled locks of his hair. They were neatly styled into place, now a few of them rebel and fall on his forehead. "Lennon, who?" Poe takes a step toward me until he's crowding my space.

Any other man abruptly standing this close to me would trigger something dark in my mind. I feel none of that with him. My eyes flick to the space between us, marveling at how little space it is.

"No one else," I say softly, stating the obvious. My arms still clutch the book to me, as if hugging it will erase everything he just saw.

He stares down at me, something unrecognizable in his eyes. His lips are pressed together in a thing line. His shoulders lift as he takes a deep breath in. I'm waiting for whatever he's about to say, whatever words they may be, I'm not sure I'm ready for them. I'm already mortified enough.

Before he can say whatever was on the tip of his tongue, he abruptly turns on his heel. His dress shoes squeak against the stone floor as he beelines for the door. I don't even have time to ask him where he's going, or to even explain to him what he just read.

He's gone before I realize what he was doing. And all I'm left with is my embarrassment and the intense smell of his cologne surrounding me.

CHAPTER
14

NASH AND NORA embrace each other in the middle of the dance floor. They stare into each other's eyes as if they're the only two people in the world. For a slight moment, I wonder what it would be like to find love like that—to allow myself to be *that* happy.

There was a time where I never thought Nash would ever get married. Hell, there were times I wondered if Nash would even make it to twenty-five. If anyone knows what it's like to live with addiction, to live in your own misery—it's me. It's been a long time since addiction had pulled me under, but the memories from my lowest point last forever. For a time, Nash and I were in that addiction together, only fueling each other's demons.

Nash overcame it. I watched from the sidelines as he fought tooth and nail to overcome his addiction, to be with Nora, and I've never been happier to witness him get everything he's ever wanted through marrying Nora today.

It was a beautiful wedding. But the entire time Nash and Nora stood at the altar, I found my eyes wandering to Nora's little sister. Last night, she was upfront about her feelings for me, even though I persistently told her I'd only disappoint her in the end. At first, the crush was flattering. I couldn't figure out what she saw in me, but I'd figured it'd disappear as easily as it began. Yet here we are. She's made it abundantly clear it hasn't gone away. If anything, she makes it sound like it's grown stronger. Landon's always giving me shit about it now that Lennon and I have become friends. It's taken everything in me not to throw his words back at him, to point out that he's been awfully friendly with her recently.

No matter what, I know my focus shouldn't have been on her while my best friend stood at the altar. Ziggy, the officiant and someone who used to tour with us, rattled on about how beautiful Nash and Nora's love story was, and all I could do was sit there and replay everything that's transpired between Lennon and I since we'd arrived at the venue.

First, it started with her shocking me by asking what we were. I wasn't expecting her to call me out last night. She's always been so quiet, someone who listened instead of being the one who was listened to. Except, last night she'd demanded to know what I was doing, and I couldn't give her more than a *I don't know* and a *we're just friends* excuse.

I'd been obsessing over the way I'd handled things with her last night when I decided to stop by her room. Our conversation was cut short when Nora had called Lennon, letting her know they had some last-minute things to discuss before the wedding today.

When I'd shown up at her door, I'd wanted to reiterate that I valued the friendship we were developing, but that it had to stay that—a friendship. I'm thirteen years older than her. I wanted to explain to her that having feelings for a man her age would be a much better way to spend her time.

That's what I should've done when I got there. Instead, I ended up barreling out of her room, more confused on how I viewed her more than ever. After reading the words she'd carelessly scrawled in the margins of her book, nothing about this is simple anymore. The entire ceremony, I repeated what she'd written over and over again in my head.

I was fixated on it. I was desperate to know why she'd written what she had. Was it some kind of sexual bucket list of hers?

It dawns on me that that's exactly what it seemed like.

But why?

And more importantly—with *who*?

And why does the mental image of another man doing the things she'd listed make my blood heat?

"Are you listening to a damn thing I'm saying?" Landon says from my side.

I straighten, focusing my gaze on him. "Hm?" I question, having no clue what he's been talking about.

Landon looks at the people at the table with us before looking back at me. "How many of those have you had, man?" He gestures to the whiskey glass in front of me. The sweat from the glass drips down the sides, pooling onto the nice tablecloth.

All I do is smile tightly at him, not wanting to admit that this half-drank whiskey is only my first one. My best friend doesn't need to know that the alcohol wasn't the culprit of making my brain fuzzy—it's the little sister of the bride.

"You caught me," I answer half-heartedly, trying to stay focused on him instead of letting my gaze wander to her. The girl I've sworn is like a little sister to me, the girl last night I'd confirmed that we were just friends. The problem is, my brain is nowhere near thinking she's a younger sister of mine right now. It's too busy seeing red at the thought of any other man touching her—of another man ever being given the chance to take advantage of her again.

A hand smacks me on my back. "Don't mind him," Landon

explains, squeezing my neck. "He goes to these faraway lands from time to time."

His words catapult me to my past. To the words Connor used to say. The shit he'd give me about spacing off. I plaster on my fakest smile to my best friend. Landon came into my life when I had no direction. I was living day to day in my own misery. The only thing keeping me going was music.

Now I'm in a better place. I've left the pain of my teenage years and twenties behind. Now, in my thirties, I shouldn't be sitting here wondering what conversation Lennon is having with Aiden.

Whatever he says to her, makes her beam. I've learned it isn't easy to get her to smile that brightly. It has to be earned, and right now *he's* earned it.

Nash's brother and Nora's sister.

They'd be the perfect pair together.

They're the same age.

They make sense.

So why does the sight of them together make me toss back the rest of my whiskey like it's nothing? She made it clear she didn't have feelings for him when I interrupted them in her room. But looking at them right now, it doesn't look like that's true. She smiles at him so brightly it makes my stomach knot. She hasn't smiled at me like that.

"It's going to be one of those nights then?" Landon asks, humor in his voice.

Nothing about what's going through my mind is humorous.

"It sure is," I agree, wiping the wetness from the glass off my hand.

The DJ calls for other couples to join Nash and Nora on the dance floor.

"I'm taking my lady to dance," Sebastian, Nash's best friend and head of security for LA, says from across the table. He doesn't give Riley any time to object. His hand reaches out to take hers, pulling her up and out of her chair. She trips over her dress as he escorts her to where a crowd gathers.

Landon and I watch them retreat to the dance floor. It is now filled with couples embracing, all of them swaying to the beat of the song the live band plays. Once the others at our table have all vacated to the dance floor, Landon looks over at me. He smiles as he presses the bottleneck to his lips. "I've got to find myself a lady to dance with."

He chugs the rest of his beer, slamming the bottle down on the table with a *bang*. His wolfish grin is all he leaves me with before disappearing into the crowd, no doubt finding himself someone to flirt with for the rest of the night—or for the time being, at least.

My eyes track over all the couples on the dance floor. I tell myself that I'm just taking it in, focusing on my friend in the middle of it all.

That would be a lie. I know deep down I'm searching for her again. When I find her, something uncomfortable settles deep in my chest.

My eyes land on Lennon eventually. She's wrapped up in Aiden's arms. They stand a respectable distance apart as he jokingly shimmies in front of her. Even from afar, I can see the eye-roll she gives him. He pays her no mind, continuing to shimmy for a moment before he pulls her in closer. It isn't too close, at least for anyone else paying attention to them. But to me, it seems *far* too close.

I thought she didn't dance. Maybe like this, it's different. I don't know if I would've even thought about it too deeply if she wasn't dancing with Aiden.

I'm confused by the thoughts that bombard my mind. This morning I woke up and thought of Lennon as nothing more than a close friend—emphasis on the friend. Now I'm wondering if I wasted my breath last night when I emphasized how I saw her as nothing more than a friend.

It wasn't until I read her carefully scrawled words on the pages of her silly, smutty romance books that something changed. She wasn't just the quiet, nose in a book little sister of Nora. She's the woman who took the time to write the things she wanted a man to do to her. The things she wanted to do with other men.

Reaching for my drink, I'm reminded that I already emptied the whiskey I was sipping on earlier. I stare at the melted water at the bottom of my cup, wishing some liquid courage would magically reappear in my glass. After staring it down for a few more moments, disappointed that it's still empty, I take a deep breath, needing to fix the issue.

I don't look toward the two of them dancing as I stand up. My eyes stay averted as I make my way toward the open bar. This morning, I hadn't any plans of getting wasted at the wedding. I'd left waking up with a hangover in my twenties.

Tonight, I may have to go back to my old ways. I don't want a clear head—it's too full of replaying the words she'd written in the margins of her book. Tonight, I want a brain that's muddled by alcohol. At least maybe then I won't have to imagine what her motives were with her apparent sexual bucket list.

"What can I get you?" the bartender asks, her voice sultry. She works at wiping the inside of a glass as she waits for my answer.

"Something strong."

She nods knowingly, her eyes raking over whatever she has behind the bar. "I definitely have the good stuff. Tell me, what are you into?" Looking up at me, she gives me a flirtatious smile. Any other night, I'd humor her. I'd flirt back, see where the night took me. That isn't my sentiment tonight. All I want is for her to make me a drink so I can take part of this edge off.

"Whiskey," I clip. Not giving her the answer it seems she wants.

Her hand pauses for a moment before she nods. Turning around, she grabs a bottle of the good stuff. "I can do that."

I'm silent as I wait for her to pour it over a large ice cube in the shape of a sphere. Taking the glass from her, I reach into the pocket of my suit and grab my wallet. I shove some bills into the tip jar in front of her, retreating with my drink before she can say anything else.

I manage to stay away from Lennon for the time it takes me to get halfway through my drink. I'd call it a win. I'd shown restraint as she stood off to the side of the celebration, seeming to only be half listening to whatever her mom is saying from her side.

Aiden appears to have switched Lennon for Monica—an interesting choice at that. I recall what Lennon had said the other day, how she thought something may be happening between Nash's manager and little brother—quite an interesting duo.

Lennon repeatedly smooths out the fabric of her bridesmaid dress. It's a dark emerald, silky material. It hugs her petite frame, and by the way she keeps smoothing out the wrinkles, it may not be one she's the most comfortable in.

I watch her, and for the first time ever, she isn't just the kid sister to Nora. She's a woman, one I can't help but wonder what it looks like underneath the dress that hides the slopes and planes of her body.

When her eyes find mine from across the party, I wonder if something unexplainable connects us. It's as if she knew I was watching her, her gaze finding mine immediately. I expect her to avert her eyes. It's what she's always done. Until last night, I've been used to the way she tries to hide the fact she has a crush on me, even though it's been clear to all of us on the tour. She hasn't been that good at hiding it.

This time is different. She doesn't give me the courtesy of looking away. She isn't bashful or shy. She holds my gaze for as long as I'll hold hers. It's as if me reading what she'd written in the margins of her book hadn't just changed things for me, it changed things for her as well.

And without a shadow of a doubt, I know things between us just got way more complicated.

CHAPTER
15

I'M NOT sure where the courage comes from, but I don't look away from his burning gaze. I used to feel bashful around him—maybe I still am slightly. But having him read my most private thoughts has changed something. It's given me confidence—made me more brash. There's no way I'm looking away from him. He'll have to be the one who breaks contact.

This moment seems like it would be in a romance book. I feel cliché for making the comparison, but I can't help thinking it. We've locked eyes from across the room, neither one of us looking away. Time seems to have stopped. Those around us have faded to black in the background. It's exactly how the books describe it. Maybe even better.

My stomach drops to my feet when he stands up. His hair falls over his eyes as he makes his way across the crowd. His fingers work to button his suit jacket back up. For a moment, I feel a sting of pain, wondering if he's going to somebody else.

The look on his face, the way his gaze doesn't falter from me, makes my heart soar with hope that maybe it *is* me he's heading toward. It could be false hope. He never looks at me this way. It isn't often that he seeks me out in a crowd.

And yet…he comes to a halt directly in front of me.

My eyes find my mother through my peripherals. She smiles at Poe, quietly excusing herself, leaving Poe and I standing alone.

"Hi," I mutter. Out of habit, I go to tuck my hair behind my ear, but there's nothing there. The hair stylists fixed it earlier. Per my mother's request, they'd used more bobby pins and hairspray to get the hair to not have a mind of its own.

"Make sure it doesn't hide her beautiful face," she'd said sweetly. If only she knew the reason my hair came around my face *was* to hide. It was kind of the point.

I wish I could hide behind my hair at this moment. I'd have the chance to look at Poe in front of me without feeling like I'm checking him out. Poe doesn't smile, he rarely does around me. Not like he does with Nash or Landon. But the corner of his lip twitches, and that almost feels just as important. It feels significant.

"Enjoying yourself?" he asks, his eyes flicking down to where I rub the fabric of my dress between my thumb and index finger nervously.

Shrugging, I look to where my sister stands with Nash, a swarm of people surrounding them. "Not typically a crowd person, especially when the attention goes to me like it did being in the wedding and giving a speech, but I'm happy for her." No matter what transpired between Nora and I, the things we're still fixing about our relationship, I'll always want her to be happy. She deserved to find the right man—someone who was nice, and who treated her well. And it seems like she found exactly that in Nash.

"I'm not much for crowds either," Poe agrees. He looks at me as I'm a puzzle he's trying to solve. If only he knew how bad I wanted to figure him out.

My eyebrows narrow. "You're not much for crowds?" I mock. "Your job is to be in front of thousands of people." My head shakes as a quiet laugh passes through my lips. "For some reason, I don't believe you."

This time he actually does smile. It feels like such a victory. He smiled at me—at my words. As if I wasn't already infatuated with him enough. "You called me on my bullshit. I don't mind the crowds at all."

I nod, having to look away from him for a moment just to get a grip on my composure. "Yeah, your job is probably my worst nightmare."

He stares at me for a drawn-out moment. It seems like he wants to say something. Taking a deep breath, I'm waiting on pins and needles for whatever he's about to say. Except he pauses, shaking his head. Neither one of us say anything for a moment. I'm too busy wondering why it always feels like he's biting his tongue, not saying what he wants to say. He disarms me, I say things I don't necessarily want to say, but they still pour out of my mouth anyway.

Poe looks over his shoulder. He nods toward the dance floor, his shoulder lifting in the same direction. "Dance with me, Len?"

I blink, processing his words over and over in my head. Did he just say what I think he did?

Poe. Just. Asked. Me. To. Dance.

I'd already told Aiden earlier that the dance floor was the last place on earth I'd wanted to be. He'd managed to sweet talk me into going out there even though I hadn't wanted to.

But Poe's invitation is different. I *do* want to. I'm just still trying to figure out if I heard him correctly.

He offers his hand out to me. I look at it, taking in the calluses at the top of his fingers.

What would they feel like against my bare skin?

Even though I hadn't danced in years, somehow I'm finding myself on the dance floor twice in one night.

Once, with my best friend. The only person who doesn't walk on eggshells around me.

And now, with the man I've harbored an intense crush on since the moment I met him. The one I've found myself developing a friendship with. A friendship is the one thing I don't want when it comes to Poe, but it's the only thing he's willing to give.

Unable to speak from the nerves, I carefully place my hand in his. His fingers wrap around mine, his warmth seeping into my bones.

I'm too focused on putting one foot in front of the other to pay attention to what goes on around us. A meteor could land on the dance floor right next to us, and I'd have no idea. I'm concentrating on making sure I don't fall on my face at his feet.

When he turns toward me, pulling my body into his, I forget to breathe. His hand slowly drifts down my back, and I revel in the way it feels. I wish my back was exposed in the dress. If that were the case, I would have the honor of feeling his skin against mine. I'd know how the scratch of his calluses felt on places other than my hand.

I'm so caught up in wishing my sister had picked out a different dress that it doesn't even occur to me how much I'm enjoying his touch. How that hasn't happened to me ever, or at least for the past few years.

Hours ago, he'd left my room like he couldn't get out of there fast enough. Now he keeps me pressed against him, like letting me go is the last thing he wants to do.

I allow him to lead us around the dance floor, not risking correcting him on the steps as he sweeps me across the floor. He's sure in his movements, even if they're incorrect.

His fingers dig slightly deeper into my back as he clears his throat. "Hey, Lennon?"

Slowly, I arch my head up to look at him, marveling at our nearness. "Yes?"

His Adam's apple bobs as he swallows. He averts his eyes for a moment before looking back at me. "I want to talk about earlier."

"Well, I want to never speak of that again," I mutter, trying not to trip over his feet from the secondhand embarrassment of remembering the moment.

"Do you do that in all of your books?" he presses, not dropping the topic. "The ones you don't share with me?"

I hope he doesn't feel the way my hand has turned clammy from the nerves. I don't know if it's him bringing up finding my list or if it would've gotten clammy either way from just holding his hand. Either way, I pray he doesn't feel it against his skin—that it isn't too obvious.

"Poe, why are we having this conversation?"

When he looks down at me, my breath hitches. For the first time, I feel like he's looking at me and not just seeing Nora's baby sister. He's actually seeing me, and I don't know how to feel about it. I don't know how to feel at the hope blossoming deep in my chest.

"Because it's all I've thought about all afternoon," he admits.

"It is?" I manage to get out.

He looks at something over my shoulder. "Yes. I just—"

"You just?" I ask, wondering what is going on right now.

"I just can't stop thinking about it."

Nodding, I wonder what that even means. Why does he care? And why does he insist on bringing it up again? I was hoping he would pretend it never happened.

I'm about to ask him those exact questions when he speaks again. "Are you doing those things with someone?"

"Does it matter?"

"No," he answers immediately. Frustrated, he looks down at our feet for a moment. "Yes. I don't know," he adds, looking back up with a resigned look on his face.

"Look," I begin, trying to think of what I even want to say to him. "You weren't supposed to see that. Nobody was, *obviously.*"

"Are you going to answer my question?"

At this point, I don't even know how long we've been danc-ing, or how many songs have played. I take a deep breath, avoiding the question at hand. "I haven't…yet."

"Yet?" His voice is tight. He pulls me into him further. Before our bodies didn't touch, now our fronts press against each other slightly.

"Yes, yet, Poe. Now, can we drop this?"

His warm hand squeezes mine tightly. "I don't think I can," he says under his breath.

"Find a way," I demand. "Please," I add, my tone gentler.

"Do you want to do those things with someone?" He keeps pressing me, and at this point I don't know if he'll stop until I answer his questions. It's the last thing I want to do, even though I know it'll allow me more time on this dance floor, more time in his arms.

Taking a deep breath, I look him right in the eye. "Yes. I do. I've answered your questions. Can we stop talking about it now?"

"Why?" he asks, breezing right past my desperate plea to stop having this conversation.

Spinning me, I drift closer to the other bodies for a moment before he pulls me back up against him. His brown eyes bore into me as he holds me even closer to him than before. Some-thing about the way he's looking at me compels me to answer him.

CHAPTER
16

It seems like an eternity for her to answer. "Because I want to do those things," she finally admits.

I chew on my lip for a minute, wondering what question I want to fire at her next. There's a million running through my head. I've got plenty of options. "So it's like a bucket list?"

Lennon shakes her head. There's a layer of makeup brushed onto her skin, but even through it I can see the flush to her cheeks. "Not really," she starts. "I don't know what to call it." Her words drift off, and for the first time during this conversation, I stay silent, waiting to see if she'll say something else.

One song ends before another begins. It doesn't stop me from keeping her clutched against my body. I know everyone we know has probably noticed us by now. I'm sure I'll have to explain to some people why I was out on the dance floor for so long, but at the moment, that explanation is the last thing I care about.

Her eyelashes flutter against her cheek as she looks at the ground. She continues to stare at where our bodies touch with her next words. "I'm sure you've been told what happened to me. When I was younger…"

I've been told bits and pieces of it. Not the entire story, but enough to understand she's been through things that no person should ever have to go through. "I don't know much," I offer.

The hand planted on her lower back feels her shaky inhale. "After, like a year after, I was in denial about what happened. So, after some expensive therapy sessions and traveling the world, I decided to take back what was taken from me. I wanted to take hold of my…" she pauses, looking at me as she thinks how she wants to finish her thought. "I wanted to take hold of my sexuality. To not shy away from being intimate, but instead, to find what I like…what my preferences are."

"So you found it in books?"

"Sort of. I met this woman in Barcelona while working at a cafe. Within five minutes of knowing her, she was going on and on about the night she'd spent with a man the night before. I'd hung on her every word, wondering why it'd never been like that for me."

I catch Nash's eye over Lennon's shoulder. He looks confused as he watches Lennon and I closely. I ignore it, waiting idly to hear what else Lennon was going to say. "I hate that I'm having this conversation with you, you know." She sighs. Her hand loosens in mine slightly, but I don't let her pull it out completely.

"I don't need the details on what it's been like for you," I add, curious why the thought of her with any other man doesn't sit well with me.

"Good. Because I'm not going to share that with you," she emphasizes the last word. As if it was preposterous to discuss that with me. "Anyway, in listening to her story, I realized how confident she was. She knew what she wanted, she knew what she preferred. I wanted that. So I had the idea to highlight the things I think I may like in my books."

"To do them?"

Lennon lifts one shoulder in a shrug. "To try them."

The song in the background builds, all of the instruments

coming together in beautiful harmony. Leaning over her, I guide her body into a deep dip. She holds onto me tightly. One hand clutching the fabric of my suit, the other squeezing my palm. Her back arched, the long tendrils of her hair almost dusting the dance floor, words slip from my mouth before I can stop them.

"Try them with me," I whisper. If our faces weren't inches away from one another, there's no way she'd be able to hear me over the music and the crowd. I know she hears my words, no matter how quiet they were, because her eyes get wide, my words taking her off guard.

She's stunned. We're still locked in an embrace, neither one of us budging. My words don't only surprise her, they surprise me as well.

"With you?" she questions, her voice shaky.

I pull her up, hugging her frame to mine as I answer. "Yes."

"No."

I try to hide my shock. It wasn't the answer I'd expected from her. "No?"

She takes me off guard by pushing her tiny hands against my chest. I release my grip on her instantly. For a moment, the two of us stand in the middle of the dance floor, oblivious to the couples moving around us.

Something burns in her eyes, and I'm left trying to figure out if it's anger, surprise, or something else completely. "Absolutely not," she states, squeezing her body between two couples to leave.

Without even thinking, I follow after her. "Lennon," I call.

Her steps don't falter. She doesn't even look over her shoulder as she walks past every single person at the reception. Ziggy calls something out to her, but whatever she says back to him, makes him shrug and return back to the group of people he was originally speaking with.

Finally, she slows down, coming to a halt in a hallway of doors that lead to different guest rooms. I believe one of them is the room where she and the rest of the bridal party got ready earlier today.

Turning around, she stares at me, raising her eyebrows as if she's expecting me to say something. Not wasting my chance, I speak, my throat feeling tight at what I'm about to ask. "Do you trust me?"

"I think that's a loaded question," she answers, her fingers nervously turning the bracelet on her wrist round and round.

My eyebrows furrow. "It is?" I offered for her to use me to find what she likes without thinking twice about it. I didn't even give myself time to think about all the reasons it's a terrible idea. Her *no* shocked me, but her honesty about whether she trusts me hurts more than I thought it would.

Lennon ignores my question. "Poe, you barely knew I existed a few weeks ago. I spent all my time looking at you, *wanting* you, and you didn't even know I was there."

I swallow, regretting all the times I hadn't noticed her. "I know. But now I do. I *do* notice you. You're the first thing I notice when I walk into a room."

She runs her hands over her forehead, keeping them on the top of her head in shock. "What is happening?"

I open my mouth to answer, but she speaks first. "Am I dreaming? Poe it was last night where I basically threw myself at you, admitting how I felt, that I was willing to take scraps from you, and you did nothing. I remember you very clearly telling me that we're just friends."

"We are friends," I add.

My words seem to make her angrier. "You've mentioned that. Friends don't do what I want to do. What I want to learn."

She's right, I'd made it clear to her last night I don't reciprocate the same feelings. Except here I am, imagining myself between her thighs, helping her learn everything about herself and what she desires.

What the fuck is wrong with me?

"I just thought if you trust me...then I could be the one to help you."

"How chivalrous of you," she seethes. I've never heard her sound so angry. Typical soft-spoken Lennon has a bite to her words when she wants to.

Angry with myself about how much I've fucked things up, I shove my hands in my pockets. "I just don't want anyone to hurt you."

"But what about you? You yourself told me last night you'd only disappoint me."

I take a step closer to her because it feels wrong to be standing so far away from her. Not when she looks confused and angry all at once.

My hands stay in my pockets because if I don't keep them there I'm afraid I'll do something stupid like touch her and make things even worse than I already have. "I'm still scared I'll disappoint you."

"Then why are you making things more complicated?"

"Because I can't help myself."

A sad laugh slips through her lips. She looks up at me, the glitter on her eyelids sparkles underneath the soft lighting of the hallway. "I don't know if I can say yes to you." Her small hand reaches out. Slowly, she places it against the lapel of my suit. She applies the lightest pressure, probably waiting for me to stop her from touching me like I have before. "Part of the purpose of my list was to find someone that not only drove me crazy, but someone I drove crazy. I want someone to *want* me. And you've already told me that person won't be you."

I'm silent because there's not much I can say. To argue with her would just end up in me further contradicting myself. I have no doubt she'll find a man that will want her desperately. It wouldn't surprise me if she found a man that wanted her more than she wanted him. Lennon has a way she can effortlessly pull you in just by the way she interacts with the world.

She slides her hand down the lapel of my suit. I don't stop her. The sad look on her face stops me from being able to do anything, to say anything.

"Let's just pretend none of this ever happened, okay?" she asks, her voice pleading. "We'll exchange books. You'll tell me how cheesy the heroes are, and we'll both act like you never read what you read. I can keep my dumb crush, and you can keep telling me how damaged you are, and it'll be like what it used to be. We'll just forget, okay?"

I nod, my tongue feels heavy in my mouth. There are so many things to say, I just can't get my head clear enough to say them.

Taking a deep breath, she pulls her hand away. I miss the warmth of it the moment it's gone. She gathers her dress in her hands, glancing up at me before stepping around me. Her footsteps are soft as she walks away from me.

I wait until she's about to disappear around the corner to finally speak.

"Lennon?" My hand nervously runs through my hair as she turns around.

"What?" she asks, defeated.

"What if I can't?"

Her pink lips thin. "What if you can't what?"

I rub the stone in my pocket between my thumb and pointer finger anxiously. "What if I can't pretend?"

"That's the only option," she answers breathlessly. Before I can say anything else, she turns around, returning to the reception, leaving me standing alone once again.

All I can do is stand there, wondering what I've done, blaming myself for complicating things.

CHAPTER
17

I'VE NEVER SEEN Poe drunk.

It's not like I haven't seen him drinking. Often he has a drink in his hands, but to me, it always seemed to be more of a social thing, like he was only drinking because those around him were. I'd never seen him drink a ton. Maybe it was because Nash was now clean. Maybe he had other reasons. No matter what, tonight, I'm seeing a whole new side to Poe. It's the Poe I've heard Landon tell stories about.

Landon and Poe stand at the bar, a few other members of Nash's band surrounding them. Landon and Poe seem deep in a conversation with a gorgeous blonde manning the bar. She doesn't seem to notice that there are other people trying to get drinks from her. She eats up every word Poe says to her, a wide smile on her face the entire time.

It sucks because I can't blame her. I know it's the same look people have caught me throwing his way many times. He smiles freely at whatever she says to him, and I feel a sharp twinge in my stomach at the sight. It took me so long to earn a smile like that. He's giving it to her with barely knowing her. I can only hope that he gave it so freely thanks to the alcohol, and the one I'd earned earlier was more because it was well-deserved.

Looking at him, you'd never know that only two hours ago, he was lighting my world aflame by offering to help me gain experience. I felt like I'd been on a rollercoaster discussing his offer. My heart was getting jerked up and down, left to right, with each word that left his mouth.

I hit the peaks when he admitted he did notice me. For the briefest of moments, I'd wondered if maybe his warnings from the night were all but forgotten. But in the next moment, we were plummeting down to the ground when he'd reiterated that we were just friends.

I didn't know my heart could feel so much hope and so much rage in such a short time span. All I wanted was for him to notice me, for him to have even an ounce of a feeling for me that I have for him. But the last thing I wanted to happen was for him to notice me because of some silly wish I'd written in my book. He was only offering because he felt sorry for me. Mortification hits as I wonder if he thinks that no one else would ever want me like that.

"Lennon," Aiden singsongs, falling into the chair next to mine. He looks nice, all dressed up in his suit. The night has taken a toll on him, however. He's discarded the suit jacket and unbuttoned the first two buttons of his shirt.

"I was finally getting some peace and quiet." I stab at the wedding cake with my fork, wishing I was still alone to obsess over every single thing Poe had said to me tonight. After returning back from my conversation with him, I'd been swept away into the excitement of the reception. Many people wanted to have conversations with me, but I was only half invested in what they were saying. My world had been tilted on its axis with his request. Chatting about the weather wasn't something I could manage.

"You're at a wedding. It's like a sin to get peace and quiet at a party like this." He reaches to take the fork from my hand, but

I keep a death grip on it. If the asshole thinks he's getting a bite of my cake, he's sorely mistaken.

"Back off," I warn, holding my cake close to my chest. I hover over it, attempting to protect it from him.

He groans dramatically. "Aw c'mon, Len. I'm starving."

"Then get your own cake." I stuff a large bite of the cake in my mouth. My eyes roll back at how good it tastes. The chocolate frosting melts in my mouth perfectly.

"All the chocolate cake is gone. Now it's some kind of almond one that doesn't sound good." He scrunches his nose. I'm sure the almond cake tastes fine. Nash and Nora wouldn't serve anything that doesn't taste amazing. Chocolate is just better and he's deciding to be dramatic.

My eyes roll. "If you're hungry enough, you'll eat it. Plus, it's not my fault you weren't around when they served the cake."

Aiden falls back in his chair. He crosses his arms over his chest. He probably doesn't even realize he's doing it, but his eyes keep flicking to Monica. I only notice because I know my eyes are doing the same, except they focus on Poe.

"I've been busy," he answers vaguely. He fiddles with something in his pocket, not pulling it out.

I laugh. "I've noticed. You disappeared there for a bit."

His eyes grow wide, like he'd expected no one to notice. I'd gone searching for him before we were supposed to give our speeches, but he was nowhere to be found. The rest of the night, he's been jumping around, chatting with many people that may be famous, but I don't know who they are. I'm not sure what he's up to. His bottom lips juts out in a pout. "I want chocolate cake."

Sighing loudly, I push my plate to him. "You can have two bites. But I'm not sharing a fork with you. It's gross, and I do not know where your mouth has been."

He coughs, clutching his chest as if I took him off guard. My eyes narrow, wondering what sent him into the coughing fit. Finally, he gets a hold of himself.

"Deal, two bites," he agrees, snatching my cake from in front of me. I figured he'd get his own fork and take a bite. I should've known better when it comes to Aiden. He picks up my cake with both hands and takes a giant bite out of it. Chocolate frosting is stuck on his lip, but I keep the information to myself. It's his karma for scarfing down half my cake in one single bite.

"Have I ever told you that you're a butthead?"

This makes him smile through a mouthful of cake. "Hate to break it to you, Len. No one says butthead."

Thumping him on the back of the head, I allow him to eat the rest of my cake as I once again look back at Poe. The rest of the band has left. Even Landon has moved on to flirt with somebody different. Not Poe. He's saddled up to the bar, taking a shot of whatever the bartender just poured him.

No matter how many times I try to look away, to engage in a conversation with Aiden, I can't help it that my attention always seems to go back to Poe. The more the night goes on, most of the guests leaving until it's just Nash and Nora's closest friends and family, the more I get annoyed. I know Poe wasn't interested in me. But I don't know how he can go from asking to hook up with me, even if it seemed like he was just taking pity on me, to him spending the rest of his night flirting with an older, probably more experienced, woman.

Looking away from him, I search for my sister. A few hours ago, she ditched her wedding dress. Now she wears a short white dress paired with a black jean jacket with *Mrs. Pierce* embroidered on the back. Nash has also changed. He and Nora both wear matching sneakers, roses hand painted all over them. They're so cute it's almost sickening.

"Was tonight everything you hoped for?" I ask, taking a seat next to her.

Nora smiles in newlywed bliss. "No," she pauses. "It was even better."

My head falls to her shoulder. "That makes me so happy."

The two of us watch the remaining people mull around. The air has grown colder, and even though it's dark and you can't tell if there're clouds in the sky or not, it smells like it may rain again.

"Do you think people had fun?" Nora asks. Her voice is tired. I'm sure she's exhausted from all of the excitement today.

I nod, my cheek still pressing against her shoulder. "Definitely. Everything was so perfect. People looked like they were enjoying themselves all night." I'm not lying. All night, people were laughing and socializing, having the best time. Even the scattered rain didn't seem to spoil anyone's time. The highlight seemed to be when Nash shocked everyone by taking the stage and performing a song he'd written for Nora just for their wedding day. It was beautifully romantic.

She pulls my hand into her lap. Both her hands trap mine between hers. "I hope so, Lenny. But is it bad that part of me doesn't care if I know that Nash and I had the perfect day?"

"That's how you're supposed to feel. You're the bride. It's *your* day."

Nodding, she lets go of my hand. "Okay, good. Now I don't feel so bad."

"You shouldn't feel bad. All that matters is that you and Nash had the time of your lives."

She crosses one leg over the other, looking to her left where Nash speaks to Ziggy and Aiden. "It was everything I could've ever wanted and more. I, for one, had the time of my life. Did you have a good time?"

I suck in a breath. Her question shouldn't feel so loaded, but it is. In theory, I was offered everything I could've wanted tonight. I have the opportunity to do more with Poe. Things I could've only dreamed about. But the offer comes with limitations, and I'm not sure my heart could differentiate the physical aspect with the emotional aspect to be able to agree to him.

"It was the best night," I fib. My definition of a good time isn't watching Poe flirt with a woman for hours on end, but my sister got married today. She got her happily ever after. It overshadows anything that happened with Poe—or anyone else for that matter.

CHAPTER

18

THE WORLD AROUND ME SPINS.

"Bacon?" Landon asks, shoving a piece of limp bacon in front of my face.

The smell, and sight of it, almost makes me throw up in front of all the people seated at the breakfast table. They're all way too loud and chipper considering how late we stayed up celebrating Nash and Nora getting married.

Groaning, I shove his arm away from me. "Absolutely fucking not," I say in disgust, closing my eyes to stop from gagging. Even with my eyes closed, I feel sick to my stomach. My head falls to rest on my forearm as I do whatever I can to keep the small amount of liquid I've been able to drink in my body.

"Been there, done that," Nash notes from his seat. I don't need to look up to know it's him talking. "I don't miss those days," he adds, his tone sympathetic.

I grunt, wishing I hadn't taken shots last night. Or had that last long island.

I'd take the hangover if I hadn't also thrown myself at Lennon, somehow expecting her to agree to my stupid offer. I'd feel like this for weeks if I didn't have to look her in the eye and remember how I somehow thought it was a great idea for me to suggest us essentially being friends with benefits.

Instead, I'm stuck with the worst hangover I could imagine and having her sit a few chairs down from me, throwing subtle jabs my way. Suddenly, the smell of maple hits my nostrils, making me pop out of my chair.

Covering my nose with my hand, I look apologetically to Nash and Nora. "I've got to go," I explain, making sure to breathe through my mouth instead of my nose. The smell of maple is sending me over the edge.

"I hope the two of you have the best honeymoon," I say, rushed. I feel terrible that I can't linger with them longer, to send them off on their honeymoon with all the others, but it's all I can do to not puke at their feet right now. "I'm sorry to run."

Nash waves in the air unbothered. "I understand, Poe. Go take care of yourself. We'll catch up later."

I manage to get a quick goodbye out to everyone before making a break for my room. A hotel staff member tries to stop me, asking if I needed any help. All I can do is shake my head as my feet rush toward my room.

The second my knees hit the ground in front of the toilet, the limited amount of liquid I've had this morning empties into the toilet bowl. My body heaves over and over until I have nothing left, and even then it tries to expel stomach contents I don't have.

"I'm never drinking again," I groan, clutching my stomach. Drinking in your thirties is ten times worse than drinking in your twenties. The amount of alcohol I had last night used to be nothing. I used to drink triple the amount and get up with a smile and a minor headache the next day.

I manage to brush my teeth and splash cold water over my face without throwing anything else up. In the back of my head,

I'm wondering if I'll be able to get everything packed and ready to go without having to vomit again.

A soft knock raps against my door. I contemplate ignoring it, but I take a peek to make sure it isn't somebody important before leaving it be. Peeking through, I find Lennon standing on the other side. She's got a water bottle clasped in one hand, and something in the other that I can't make out.

My forehead falls against the wood door. I groan, wishing she wasn't standing on the other side of it. The last thing I want to do is explain my behavior from the night before. I'm older than her, by a good amount, yet last night I hadn't acted that way at all—in many ways.

I pull the door open. "Hey," I manage to get out, this time wanting to throw up from embarrassment.

"Thought you might need these," she quips, not bothering with any kind of greeting. She holds up the water bottle in one hand, a bottle of pain medicine in the other. Pills rattle in the bottle as she moves it in the air.

My eyes soften, appreciative of the gesture. "Thank you." I nod my head toward my room. "Want to come in?"

She looks shocked. Shaking her head, she hands over the water and the pill bottle. "No, I don't want to interrupt you if you have, you know"—she pauses, her fingers running through her hair—"company." Company comes out as a whisper, like it pained her to even say it.

I feel like I'm going to throw up all over again, but not because of the alcohol. It's the thought that my actions last night made her think I brought somebody back to my room.

If only she knew I drunkenly mulled over what I'd said to her for hours before sleep finally took mercy on me and pulled me under.

My fingers tighten on the door. "There's no company. There never was last night."

She peeks up at me from under her eyelashes. "There wasn't?"

My head shakes. "No, Lennon. I wouldn't have done that. Not after…" My words fall off. I'm unsure what else to say.

"Oh. I just thought." She twists her hands in front of her anxiously.

"You thought?"

"You just seemed friendly with the bartender last night."

I wince, faintly remembering the woman and how strong she was coming on to me. At one point, I think she would've been fine with either Landon *or* me with the way she flirted with the two of us at the same time. Some things are fuzzy, but I remember her sliding the long island across the bar top at the end of the night, a napkin with her number on it placed neatly next to it. "It wasn't like that," I explain.

She's silent, chewing on her lip as she mulls my words over. I step into the room for a moment. Unscrewing the lid from the pill bottle, I shake a few into my hand and chase them down with a sip of water.

Looking over my shoulder, I find Lennon still standing in the doorway. She stares down from where the wood changes from one pattern to another as it switches from the hallway to my room. Stopping in front of her once again, I rest my head against the doorframe.

"Are you going to come in?" I ask, the corner of my lip pulling up at the way her eyes widen.

"No." She looks up at me. "I just wanted to make sure you had water. In case, you know, they didn't have any in here."

Even though it feels like someone took a hammer to my skull, I somehow still manage to smile. I could've found water easily, the pain pills too, but I like that she still thought of me. Even after I made an ass of myself last night.

"About last night," I begin.

She throws her hands up between us. "We don't have to talk about it. Please don't talk about it," she adds.

"I just have to get this out, okay?"

All Lennon does is nod, giving me the floor. Except now that she's allowed me to explain, I don't even know where to begin. I spent a chunk of my night lying in bed, my head spinning, going over exactly what I wanted to say to her. I'd planned out apologies so perfectly in my mind. Now, in her presence, I can't remember any of it.

"Last night, I hadn't really thought things through when I said what I said. I know now that it came out all wrong."

"How so?"

"I didn't want it to come out like I felt sorry for you or that I thought you wouldn't find someone who you know would want to help you…"

"That's exactly how it came out, Poe."

I sigh, turning my forehead to rest against my hand on the doorframe. "I'm such an ass."

Her only answer at first is a timid smile. "Something like that," she whispers.

Clearing my throat, I continue on with my apology. "It wasn't that I thought no one would want to. It's that I was afraid too many people would want to, and they wouldn't treat you the way you deserve."

Lennon nervously twists her hair around her finger. "Is that for you to decide?"

"No." I answer immediately. "It doesn't change the fact that I want to be the person you experiment with. Until…"

Her big green eyes seek mine out. "Until?"

"Until you find the man that won't just treat your body with respect, but your heart, too."

She nods in understanding. "And that's not you."

"Not your heart, no," I answer honestly. At least now she seems to have expected it. Maybe last night she saw my true colors. Maybe it opened her eyes to the fact that I'm not as special as she's made me out to be in her head. I've got flaws, more than most, and there's absolutely no way I deserve the blind adoration she has for me.

"I just don't think it's a good idea," she gets out, a sadness in her voice. I want to ask her why, but I don't, afraid I already know the answer. I've warned her with my words, and last night my actions, that I'm not a person worth having feelings for.

Pulling my body off the door frame, I take a deep breath. The pain in my head has dulled, along with the nausea. Now all that's left is an uneasy feeling that somehow I messed up the friendship I'd created with Lennon shortly after it began. "You're probably right. You can find a guy younger than me, cooler than me." I wink. "Who definitely has his shit together.'"

"Do you want that?" she questions, her voice soft.

My eyes rake over her. At her hair, that somehow always looks messy no matter how much she smooths it out. Her high cheekbones, and the place below each cheek where dimples pop through when I'm awarded with a smile. Her long, thick eyelashes that frame her moss green eyes. She rarely wears makeup, and she's still always one of the most beautiful women in the world, even if she would never know it. There are so many nuances to her that draw me in, but I'm not capable of wanting someone the way she wants me to. I want her to be happy. Deep down, I know eventually she'll find a man that can do it all. That doesn't mess up and call her a friend and offer ridiculous ideas just because it pains him to think of somebody hurting her. And I want that for her, even if it makes my stomach turn at the thought.

I take a step back into the room, slightly distancing myself from her, from her smell and the magnetic field that somehow draws me to her.

"You should probably get going. I bet they're wondering where you are at breakfast."

"Uh," she says, confused. "Okay."

Reaching out, I do something I shouldn't. My finger trails down the soft skin of her cheek, coming to land underneath her chin. I feel the faint thump of her pulse underneath my fingertip. The beat wild and strong. "Thank you for the water and pain meds, Lennon. I already feel better."

Before she can say anything else, I shut the door softly. When my stomach empties again, I'm not sure if it's because of the lingering alcohol or the look of disappointment on her face as I closed the door on her.

CHAPTER
19

"PEPPER, SLOW DOWN," I plead, tugging on the leash. Her giant, furry body doesn't slow down in the slightest. My fingers wrap around the leash tightly as Pepper pulls me in the direction of her choosing.

With Nash and Nora on their honeymoon, taking Pepper on walks has become my new hobby. My days have been spent reading, exercising, and taking Pepper on walks. We've gone on numerous walks to kill time. As nice as the fresh air is, I've mostly spent my time in my room, pouring over book after book to keep myself busy.

Every time I tabbed a scene or made a note in the margin, I thought of Poe. I imagined trying it with him. The longer I've had to think about his offer, the more I ponder if it's a deal I want to take. It may be hard for me to separate the physical and emotional aspect of what he suggested, but I don't know if I can deny the opportunity to know him in an intimate way. Even if it's purely physical from his point.

Even with the door slamming in my face the day after the wedding, I believed what Poe had said. I didn't think it was him taking pity on me. It isn't my mind playing tricks on me. The look on his face told me that this is different for him. I won't give myself false hope that anything will happen. I have to protect my heart from him, the pieces that I haven't offered up blindly at least. But now that I've had time to think about it with a clear head, I want to know what it feels like to be with him.

I'd told him I'd take whatever scraps he'd give me. At the time, I hadn't realized the weight of my words. I hadn't expected for him to ever suggest something like a friends with benefits type agreement. Now selfishly, I want to snatch the opportunity to experience what it would be like to *really* be with him. Even if he hasn't allowed me the false pretense of thinking it's anything more than him allowing me to explore my sexual preferences with his aid.

I want to take it.

I want to have him in any way he'll give me.

My arm almost pops out of its socket as Pepper lunges forward. I'm barely able to stay on my feet as I trail behind her, refusing to let go of the leash. She whines, clearly having her sight set on something. When my feet finally find a rhythm that can keep up with her without the fear of falling on my face, I look up.

Right away I see what's caught her attention. *Who* caught her attention.

Poe stands at the end of Nash's long driveway. I wish Pepper wasn't so hellbent on reaching him so I could stop and take him in for a moment before he notices us. He leans up against his car. A giant, slate-gray SUV that seems so *him*. He props one foot against one of the front tires, a hand tucked lazily into his pocket. His other hand holds his phone as he appears to type something on there.

Pepper lets out a loud whine, catching his attention. I must be a sight for him to see. My feet barely keeping up with the pace Pepper sets as she races to him. If I'd known he would show up, I'd have cared more about my appearance.

My entire body is coated in a layer of sweat thanks to the California sun. When I left, it'd been cloudy. I'd worn a thin long sleeve T-shirt and a pair of biker shorts. Halfway into our walk, the clouds had disappeared. I'd only made it a few minutes with the sun hitting me until I had to strip out of the shirt. It's tied around my waist, leaving me in the matching bra and bike short set. I'd messily thrown my hair into a claw clip on my way out, not even checking to see what it looked like in the mirror.

I've never been one to fuss over what I looked like. I preferred not to make myself stand out, wanting nothing to do with unwanted attention. But as I stop in front of Poe, his eyes directed at me and only me, I wished more than anything I'd spent a small amount of time making myself more presentable.

"Poe," I wheeze, out of breath from chasing Pepper. I pull my headphones from my ears. "What are you doing here?"

Pepper excitedly throws her body into his legs, demanding his attention. Pulling his body from the car, he reaches down to pet her, his eyes still focused on me.

The stare sends tingles down my spine as he focuses a second too long at the sheen of sweat in between my small amount of cleavage.

He stops as quickly as he begins. Clearing his throat, he looks back at my face. "I'm here because you've been holding out on me."

"I have?"

Poe reaches out, grabbing Pepper's leash from me before she can yank me in the direction of the next thing that catches her attention. "You sure have, Lennon Mason." He takes off toward Nash's house, leaving me the only option to stand here and stare or to follow behind.

As I trail behind him up the driveway, I'm grateful that Aiden texted me he'd be gone all evening and to keep the doors locked. If he knew Poe showed up, I'd have to explain myself, and I don't care to do that. It's kind of like he didn't want to share after I'd caught him and Monica together a few days ago.

"I've been waiting for a book from you," he adds nonchalantly, acting like it's totally normal for him to show up at Nash's house, knowing full well his best friend isn't here.

"You were?"

He nods, slowing down until we walk shoulder to shoulder, Pepper trotting happily in front of us. "I was. Not very patiently I must admit."

He rattles on about how he tried to start a few books, but they weren't the same without my writing. I only half hear what he says, my mind racing with so many things I want to say but I'm afraid to.

"I just don't want things to be awkward since—" he pauses. "Hey, you listening?"

"What?" I ask, shaking my head to clear my mind.

"I don't want things to be awkward between us after everything that happened the wedding weekend. I want to go back to what we used to do with the books. To hanging out."

Asphalt crunches underneath my tennis shoes with my abrupt stop.

Poe doesn't notice. He's going on about a book he saw an ad for. Something about a football player that gets injured and has to return to the small town he grew up in as he rehabilitates his injury. He lets go of Pepper's leash as he nears a side door that leads to Nash's massive garage.

"Poe?" I say loudly.

He turns to face me. "Yeah?"

"I changed my mind."

He frowns, shifting on the balls of his feet. "Look, we don't have to do the book thing if you don't want to." His fingers run through his hair. "If I ruined it, I get it. Just don't tell me we can't be friends anymore. I don't know if I could handle that."

The last words are said softly, with a vulnerability I hadn't heard to his voice before.

I shake my head. "That's not what I'm talking about."

"Oh."

Despite my racing heart, the lump in my throat, and the nervous feeling in my stomach, I manage to gather my thoughts enough to speak. "I changed my mind about what you offered. I want to do those things with you. I want to find out what I like…with you."

His hand runs over his chin. "I thought you said—"

"I don't care what I said," I interject. "I've changed my mind. You were right. I trust you. Why would I choose someone else right now?" My words run together as I try to get every single thing running through my mind out. I'm afraid I'll lose the confidence to go after what I want, to seize this opportunity to have him in some sort of capacity.

"Lennon," he breathes.

"You can't take back your offer. You said I should do it with you because I trust you, and I've made up my mind, Poe. No take backs."

"No take backs."

Heart racing, I put one foot in front of the other until I stand directly in front of him. His eyes flick down, no doubt noticing how I've invaded his space. "Are you sure about this?"

Nodding, I say, "I've never been so sure." I reach out to touch him. My fingers trail over the ink across his arm until I stop at his hand. His body is tense, but he doesn't stop me as I lift his hand between us. My fingers wrap around his wrist, my clean skin contrasting with his dark inked flesh. Using the opposite hand, I link my pinky through his. "With one promise."

He uses his free hand to tilt my chin up, forcing me to look at him. "What is it?"

"Promise me you'll make me forget. I want no memory of every unwanted touch someone had the nerve to take without being given permission. I want every memory to be filled with you and only you."

I feel the sharp intake of his breath against my cheek. Quickly, he unlinks our fingers, clutching my hand to his chest. "Fuck, Lennon." He leans forward, resting his forehead against mine as he holds on tight to my hand. "I promise," he says, his voice steady and sure.

"Come inside?" I ask, aware there's no going back now. One day, far from now, I may regret this. But for today, I'm going to pretend that my heart will recover from only having his physical touch but never having his heart.

CHAPTER
20

MY HEART BEATS ERRATICALLY in anticipation as I follow closely on Lennon's heels. We walk past Nash's various cars until she's pushing open the door that leads to the large powder room. As soon as the door is open wide enough for her to fit through, Pepper runs off, disappearing somewhere inside.

Lennon leads me to the kitchen. "Want anything to drink?" she asks, her voice slightly shaky.

"I'm good."

She nods, turning around to open a cabinet. Her arm extends as she stands on her tiptoes to reach a glass. Her fingers narrowly miss it.

"Let me help," I offer. Coming around behind her, my front slightly presses against her back as I reach over her shoulder to grab it. Turning around, she looks at the glass in my hand.

"Thanks," she whispers, her fingers turning white from grasping the glass so tight. Her face flushes as she takes in how close our bodies are. The nearness gives me the opportunity to take in all the creamy skin she has on display. Her bare shoulders have freckles splattered all over them. The freckles trail all the way across her chest, disappearing underneath the fabric of her sports bra. They make her skin appear tanner than it actually is. The parts of her skin not covered in freckles have a pink tinge to it. I briefly wonder if it's from her walk with Pepper and will disappear soon or if it's a slight sunburn.

I take a small step backward, giving her enough room to slide past me. At first, her feet stay planted, eventually stepping around me to guide her toward the fridge. Soft clinks fill the silence as ice falls from the ice dispenser into her empty glass.

My hip leans against the counter as she quietly sips on her water.

"So," I murmur, breaking the silence. When I'd stopped by earlier, I hadn't expected her to change her mind on checking things off her list with me. I'd really just missed her. Even though most of our time is spent in silence, the two of us lost reading ink on paper, I've grown accustomed to her presence. I missed hearing a pen scratching against paper as she wrote her thoughts on whatever she's reading. Or the familiar sound of her pulling a tab off its dispenser. I'm all too used to the anticipation of knowing that soon I'd be able to read her thoughts, know the parts of the story she found interesting.

Nash and Nora going on their honeymoon was supposed to give me a nice break from being around people. I'd been looking forward to catching up on sleep and maybe even getting some song writing in. I'd done both things, but it hadn't been enough. I'd even gone out with Landon, Luke, and Troy a few times to get myself out of the house.

None of them were who I really wanted. Turns out, all I wanted was something I had no business desiring—spending time with Lennon.

Lennon cradles the water in between both hands. Her back pushes into the pantry door as she watches me carefully. "So," she repeats.

"If we're going to do this, maybe we should have some rules." My mind flashes to the promise we made only minutes ago. I would've found my pinky wrapped around hers childish if it wasn't for the serious look on her face. A crease had appeared across her forehead as she'd looked at me in desperation. Something dark had passed through her eyes as she made me swear to make her forget about the man who took something she wasn't willing to give.

At that moment, I wanted to ask her what happened. I wanted to know so I could understand her more. But I know how hard it is to talk about past trauma. I've sat through many therapy sessions trying to unpack the things that's happened to me. I know how it hurts to be asked about something you aren't ready—or interested—in talking about. So I kept my lips pressed together, even though I desperately wanted to know what happened to her so I could make sure I'd do exactly what she asked—help her forget.

"I didn't take you for a rule follower," she argues, humor in her voice.

My arms cross over my chest. "Lennon, are you making fun of me?"

She cocks a shoulder, a shy smile on her face. "All I'm saying is that you've got this quiet, broody vibe to you. I don't know if I'd necessarily call it *bad boy*, but it definitely doesn't scream *rule follower*."

My back slides across the edge of the counter as I get closer to her. "Oh, yeah?" I tease. "And what makes you an expert on this?"

"Easy," she breathes. "For one, remember my obsession with books? All men can be labeled just like the male main characters in a story. They can be nerdy, possessive, a jock, a bad boy, an alpha male—so many options. I've read about them so many times that I can see the same qualities in real people."

I laugh, seeming to find myself doing that more and more in her company. Her obsession with books is one of the qualities that drew me to her in the first place—that and her fascination with me. It intrigues me how much she'd rather be in a fictional world than the one she lives in. If she pulled her nose from the pages of the book, she'd realize the effect she had on people. How she's a magnet drawing people in without even realizing she's doing it. She's too busy living with fictional characters to notice how all of us in her real life want to steal her attention the way the characters in her books do. I've noticed it more and more over the tour. Aiden, for example, is always finding Lennon. He's the asshole little brother of Nash who never seems to care about making friendships with women—except for her. I've even noticed how my best friend has made excuses to find himself in her presence more and more.

"And for two?" I press.

She rolls her eyes, as if the answer is obvious. "For two, I know everything about you. Well, all the things you make obvious to the world. Maybe even some of the things you don't."

My stomach clenches at her admission. She'd said it so matter-of-factly, without a drop of shyness in her voice. She's becoming bolder with her feelings toward me, bringing more attention to the fact they've always been there. Her confidence is messing with my mind—making me feel things I won't ever acknowledge.

"That's exactly why we need rules." I take a deep breath. "I just don't want to hurt you, Lennon," I say sadly. "You're free to use me in any way you need. I just don't want this agreement to make you think that anything else will come out of it."

"Oh my god, Poe." She sighs in annoyance. "I know you look at me and see a child, but I'm not. I can make my own decisions. You've made it abundantly clear how you'll never feel about me the way that I feel about you. Cool. I get it. I reminded myself of it many times before agreeing to do this with you. It's because of my feelings for you, no matter if you reciprocate them or not, that makes me confident that I want this."

"You're sure?"

She steps forward and sets her glass down loudly against the marble countertop. "Yes. Now stop asking. Any other rules you have floating around in your mind?"

Yeah. A few.

My head shakes in disbelief. "Since when are you so sassy?"

"Since forever. You just hadn't bothered to notice."

"Speaking of, I do have another rule. I want you to stop making it seem like I don't notice you. You're so fucking hard not to notice that it makes me mad you think it could be any different."

Her mouth falls open, forming a little O.

"Agreed?"

Lennon manages to nod and pull her mouth shut. "Yeah," she mutters. "Understood."

"Good." I'm quick at bringing my body directly in front of hers. She takes a step back in surprise, her hips hitting the edge of the countertop. "I have one more," I say, looking down at her.

Both her hands clutch the lip of the marble. "And what is that?"

My head nods down to where my fingers hang midair in front of her stomach. "Can I?" I ask, gesturing to where she has her shirt tied around her waist.

"Yes," she breathes, staring intently at where my finger slides into the space between her skin and the fabric. My finger hooks into where the shirtsleeve is knotted. I pull until I get it undone. My other hand helps to pull on the other sleeve until the shirt falls to the ground.

I place my hands at either side of her hips, pressed up against her own hands that still grasp the lip of the counter like it's the only thing keeping her standing. Leaning in, I slide my nose across her neck. "If at any point you want me to stop, or if you feel nervous, uneasy, any kind of negative feeling—I want you to tell me immediately. Okay?"

She nods her head fervently. "That won't happen. Not with you," her voice comes out breathless.

"I need you to say yes," I beg. "I never want you to feel that way with me. Please, for me, just promise you'll tell me."

"I promise."

I swallow, trying to bring moisture to my dry throat. She's got me wrapped in some kind of spell where I can't think clearly. All I want to do is pick her up by the hips and make her mine in ways I nowhere near deserve. But we aren't doing this for me—we're doing this for her. So I keep a handle on my restraint, no matter how much it pains me.

"Now Lennon," I whisper against her cheek. Reaching up, I move some stray hairs that stick to her lips. I tuck the pieces behind her ear so I can take in every aspect of her face.

"Yes?"

I cup her cheek in my palm. "Tell me, what's first on this list of yours?"

CHAPTER
21

IT'S a miracle I'm able to form words. My heart thumps so loudly in my chest it feels like the only thing I can focus on is giving my lungs air and fixating on the way his fingertips press into my cheek. I have no idea what I want to do with him, where to even begin, but feeling his touch in this moment seems like a perfect start.

My thighs clench together as I clear my throat. "I don't know." I swallow. "I haven't thought that far."

He tsks, his brown eyes watching his finger closely as it traces my cheekbone. "I figured you'd know exactly what you wanted to do...where you wanted to start."

I may have. His touch has made my brain so foggy that I can't think straight. "Anywhere," comes out of my mouth before I can think of a more eloquent answer.

Poe stares at my lips. Mine part in anticipation. I've dreamed of kissing him so many times I've lost track. I'd never imagined it standing in my sister's kitchen on a random Thursday night. "Where are your books?"

"What?" I blurt, my brain unable to function at the possibility of him kissing me.

This makes him smirk. Standing this close to him, I can tell that one of his canines is chipped. You'd never know it unless you had the opportunity to be this close to him. "Your books," he repeats, his voice steady, a stark contrast from the way my words keep coming out shaky and jumbled with his hands on mine, his breath against me. "Where do you keep your books? The ones I haven't had the pleasure of seeing until now."

"They're in my room."

Stepping away from me, he cocks his head, that smirk still plastered on his face. "Lead the way, Len."

It takes a moment for me to gather my wits to peel myself away from the counter. With my skin still on fire from his touch, I head toward my room. He's probably been in this house more than I have. I'm sure he knows where the guest rooms are, but I like the thought of leading him to where I sleep, regardless.

Neither of us say a word as we walk through the large living area where the setting sun pours in through the wall of windows. Turning, I take us down a dim hallway. The only thing illuminating our path is the small amount of light escaping from the living room and the line of lights along the floor that leads the way.

Stopping at the end of the hallway, I grab the doorknob to my room. "This is me."

He rubs his lips together. "Are you going to let me in?"

I turn the knob, pushing the door open and stepping inside. I hastily search the room, wondering if I should've picked it up more. Aside from a few random things, my room is tidy. My suitcase sits in the corner, perched on a chaise lounge hanging open. Clothes spill out of it from where I haven't fully unpacked yet. I didn't find the need to unpack everything. Before we know it, Nash and Nora will return from their honeymoon, and we'll be preparing to travel abroad for the international leg of the tour.

"Lennon Mason, you're messier than I was expecting," Poe jokes, gently pushing past me in the doorway. To prove his point, he lifts a bra I'd hung on one knob of my dresser. Lunging for him, I pluck the simple white bra from his grasp.

"I obviously wasn't expecting company," I retort, unable to hide the blush that's crept over my body.

"Do you always keep it this messy? Neat freak Nash would hate it in here."

I smack him playfully in his abs, shocked when I discover how hard they are underneath my touch.

Groaning, I quickly pick up a few other pieces of discarded clothing. I throw them in a pile, putting my hands on my hips and taking inventory of the rest of the room. Technically, there's more I could pick up to make it neater in here. A few random empty energy drink cans are littered on various surfaces in the room. There are also books scattered around the room in no specific order. "If you're just going to give me grief about my room, then you can leave."

He throws his hands up in surrender. "I won't mention it again." Mockingly, he puts his fingers to his lips and salutes. "Scout's honor."

My eyes narrow. "I can't picture you in Boy Scouts."

He chuckles. "Oh Lennon, I was a lot different when I was younger. Would you believe me if I told you I was a nerd?"

I gasp. "Absolutely not."

He picks up one of my books, licking his finger before flipping through the pages. "I was a huge nerd. Think spending all my time playing video games in a dark basement with my friends. Boy Scouts may have been too cool for us."

I pick my jaw up off the floor. "You were into video games?"

He nods, glancing up at me to prove his point. "Big time. *Huge* nerd."

My hand runs over my comforter as I walk the length of my bed. "I would've never guessed that. At least you had friends."

"Something tells me it was the opposite for you. You were one of the popular ones, weren't you?"

Poe's question is innocent, but no matter his intentions behind it, it still brings a rush of sadness—of pain.

Shrugging, I take a seat on the edge of my bed. I pull my knees to my chest, wrapping my arms around them. "I guess. Only because I was on the dance team. At my school, the dancers were more popular than the cheerleaders."

Lost in my own memories, I don't realize he's come to my side of the room until I feel his touch against my shoulder. His hand is warm on my skin. "I didn't mean to pry or bring up anything bad."

I shake my head. "It's fine. I should be able to talk about these things, you know? I had so many amazing memories throughout my teenage years. One bad memory from one night shouldn't ruin the rest of it."

"But it does," Poe says in understanding. I want to ask him what bad memory stole all of his good ones, but I resist the urge.

"It fucking sucks that it does," I answer sadly.

His knuckle runs down my arm, making my skin break out in goosebumps. "If you ever want to talk about it, know that I'm here to listen. I'll never force you to. I just want you to know that if for some reason you do want to talk about it…I'm here."

Feeling brave, I catch his hand in mine. Squeezing it tight, I look up at him. "The offer goes both ways."

I'm lost in his brown eyes, wondering what happened to him to cause the sadness that lingers in them, but then he shuts them slowly. When they open back up, the sadness is gone, a blank stare left in its wake. "Before we start this, I have an idea," he says, completely changing the subject.

I rest my chin against my knees. "What's that?"

"For me to know how to make you feel good, first I think I should watch you make yourself feel good."

My stomach drops. "Make myself feel good, how?"

"Like this," he says, his voice deep and gravelly. His palm

presses softly against my chest, guiding me to lay back on the bed. I scoot my bottom back a few inches on the bed so there's room for my feet as well.

Slowly, he comes to stand between my legs. His hands are light as they come to rest on the sides of my thighs. My heart wants to jump out of my chest watching him pay close attention to my every reaction. I know without a doubt that if he saw me have any hesitation to his touch that he'd back away immediately. The small gesture means more than I could ever admit.

His long fingers snake around my thighs until his fingertips press into the muscle between my legs. He's slow about pulling my thighs open. He spreads them wide open. I don't wear underwear underneath the biker shorts. I'm nervous the thin, orange layer of fabric doesn't do much to hide the wetness soaking the spot between my legs.

His strong fingers wrap around my wrist. He guides my hand from the comforter, down my stomach, until my fingers rest right above the waistband of my shorts. He gently nudges my hand until they slip underneath the fabric. "I want you to show me. Show me what makes you feel good, Lennon."

He backs up, taking a seat on the chair in front of my desk. The desk is merely a decoration piece, something I never sit at in the room. He places his elbows on top of his thighs, watching me closely.

I almost feel like I'm having an out of body experience when I close my eyes and do exactly as he says. My fingertips trail deeper into my shorts until they're met with my wetness. I close my eyes, unable to look at him at the moment as I settle deeper into the blanket.

"Are you wet?" Poe asks, his voice raspy.

All I can do is nod. I slip one finger inside, shocked by how I'm doing this in front of him. This isn't something I'd typically do. Normally to touch myself, I have to know nobody's home, and it's still done in the darkness of my room behind a locked door. Never in front of someone. The primal way he looks at me, the desire in his eyes, has me acting out of character. I'd do anything to keep the fire in the way he looks at me right now. I feel powerful as my finger moves in and out of me, playing around with my wetness.

"Is it because of me?" he pushes. I wish his voice was closer, that it was him doing these things to me. Even with him across the room, only his voice coaxing me into the building tension in my abdomen, I'm more turned on than I've ever been in my life.

CHAPTER 22

I T T U R N S out I have way more self-restraint than I ever could've imagined. It takes everything in me to stay planted in this chair. To allow her and *only* her to explore herself. By the way her hips arch slightly off the bed, her hand buried in her shorts, it's clear she doesn't need my help to get herself off.

But boy, would it be fun to help.

I'm just here to watch. To study every single movement, the pace her hand keeps underneath her tight little shorts. To discover every single thing that makes her feel good.

"How's that feel?" I ask, marveling at the way her cheeks get more and more flushed the longer she touches herself.

"I think it'd be better if it were you."

My tongue clicks. Leaning back in the chair, I adjust my cock in my jeans. "Then I wouldn't have the luxury of watching you play with yourself."

"Yeah, you could be doing it yourself."

Her response makes me smile. "Oh, but now when I finally do, I promise to make it worth the wait."

She moans, her small little hips squirming against her mattress.

I bite down on my thumb, aching to reach down and stroke

my cock but resisting the urge to. I hadn't expected to have such a primal reaction to her, but watching the way she plays with herself has me hard as a rock. "You're doing so good," I tell her.

"I'm close," she pants.

I focus on what she's doing between her legs. Part of me wishes there was nothing obstructing my view of how wet she is. I'd love to see the way she pushes a finger in and out of her greedy pussy.

"Tell me what you're doing, Lennon," I growl. "Are you playing with your clit? Pushing in and out with a finger? With two? Walk me through it so I can make you feel good."

"Oh my god." Her moans have become louder. It seems like she's said to hell with any shyness she had left in her. The hand not in her shorts untangles from the blankets. She strokes the side of her ribcage before playing with one of her nipples through the bra. Both of them are hard, trying their best to break free of the restricting fabric.

My hands dig into the leather armrest. I grip them as tight as possible, needing to keep myself grounded before I ditch my idea and finish her off for her. "Lennon?"

"Yes?"

"You better start telling me what the fuck you're doing inside those shorts before I say to hell with it and find out on my own."

"My clit," she moans. "I'm playing with my clit."

"Fast or slow?"

"Slow."

"And your fingers on your perky little nipples," I say, locked in on every movement of her body, every breath she takes. "Are they pinching hard or soft?"

Her toes curl as she palms her breast. I haven't seen any extra skin other than what she wore on that walk of hers yet watching her bring herself to the edge of a release completely dressed is just as sexy as seeing every naked inch of her body.

"You going to come for me, Lennon?" I ask, desperate to watch her lose herself to an orgasm. "Show me what it looks like when you fall apart. Show me how you scream so I can make you scream louder when it's me."

"Poe," she moans loudly, without reservation.

Her hips buck up and down on the mattress as she rides each and every wave of her orgasm.

"Good girl," I rasp. "Let me hear how good it feels."

To the world, Lennon is quiet, reserved. But right here, in the shelter of her own room, away from any prying eyes or ears, she's wild and untamed. Her moans echo through the room, showing me an entirely new side of her.

My cock protests in my jeans. The head presses against my zipper, begging to be released.

Her breaths are loud as her chest heaves up and down rapidly. She stays lying on the bed, stretching out her legs with a sigh. With one hand, she pushes herself up on the bed, pulling her other hand out of the shorts. I see the wetness coating her fingers from across the room.

I'm up and out of my chair immediately. My feet don't stop until I'm standing between her spread thighs once again.

"How was it?" I question, anxious to hear her answer. By the way her moans filled the space, she pleasured herself well.

I can't fucking *wait* to show her how I can do it better.

She chews on her bottom lip, bashfully looking me in the eye. "It was..."

I cock my head, wondering what she'll say next.

"Better than I could've imagined."

"Just wait until I get my chance," I state. I don't miss the way her thighs tighten against my hips at my words.

Pieces of hair fall from the hair clip she's fastened at the nape of her neck. Reaching around her, I press the two sides together until her hair is spilling over her shoulders and down her back. Tossing the clip onto the bed, I take in the unruly waves of her hair. It falls all the way down her spine, and the ends play with the bare skin in between the edge of her bra and shorts.

I run my fingers through it. Her hair feels softer than I was expecting. Lennon is silent, letting me do whatever I want. Eventually, I stop, moving the blanket of hair so her bare shoulders are on display once again.

She shifts, reaching up to grab me by the hand moments before I'm about to step away. The movement brings attention to her coated fingers again. Lennon looks down to where I stare at the wetness coating two of her fingers. Her grip on me slacks. I use the opportunity to grab ahold of her wrist. Holding her fingers up in between us, I nod my head toward her glistening fingers.

"Look at how good you made yourself feel. So wet and messy."

Her eyes widen, her already hard nipples getting even harder underneath her bra.

Leaning forward, I refuse to look at anything but her as I bring one of the wet fingers into my mouth. My mouth closes around it, moving down until her entire finger is in my mouth. Pressing my tongue against her index finger, the taste of her immediately hits my taste buds. It's sweet—just like her— tasting exactly what I'd imagine Lennon to taste like.

Lennon grabs on to my biceps with her free hand, her nails digging into me as she watches me closely. Her large, pink lips part slightly, her tongue coming out to lick her lips as I taste her on herself.

My cheeks cave in as I suck hard, making sure I taste all evidence of her arousal. Her finger comes out of my mouth with a *pop*. She acts like she's going to lower her arm, but I keep a tight grip on it.

"I'm not done tasting you," I scold, shaking my head at her. I press her middle finger to my mouth, running it across my lip in a small taste. "You taste like heaven, Lennon. And this is the closest I'll ever get, so I have to savor every last bit." I don't give her time to respond. I'm closing my mouth around the digit, twirling my tongue around to make sure I don't miss anything.

Slowly, she pulls her finger out. I let my teeth graze down this one, almost coming in my pants at the way she watches me so intently. Like it isn't me trying to figure out what she likes, but the other way around.

"Do you feel like you got what you needed?" she asks, her voice timid.

I nod, giving her a wolfish grin. I run my thumb over her lip, over her chin, until my hand falls to my side. "Yes. I most definitely did. But we're not ready for it. Not yet."

The edges of her lips turn down. "Not yet?"

I shake my head, taking a few steps back. More for myself than for her. Standing that close to her, smelling the scent of her mixed with the lingering taste of her in my mouth, has me almost throwing her books out the window and doing whatever the fuck I want with her. "Nope. We've got to find something from your books, remember?"

"How could I forget?" she answers.

My eyes scan the room, to the piles of books that litter the space. I think there's more books in random places than there are books actually on the bookshelf in the corner of the room. "Next time I see you, I want you to have picked what you want to do."

"Next time?" She stands up, her voice sounding shocked.

I nod. "Yes, next time."

Looking down, her eyes widen. Quickly, she loops one leg in front of the other to cross her legs. "Why not now?" she asks, looking back up at me.

My eyes flick down to the obvious bulge in my jeans. "Because right now, I'm two fucking seconds from saying to hell with your books and taking you in every single way I want to."

Her mouth falls open.

Taking a step closer to her, I grab her by the neck and tilt her face to look at me. "And this isn't about what I want to do to you and that sweet little pussy of yours. It's about what *you* want. So before I lose the last shred of self-control I have, I'm going to leave."

"You don't have to." She takes a step forward, letting her hand brush over my cock. She shrugs as if it was an accident, but it's clear she knows exactly what the fuck she's doing.

I press into her, letting my hardness push against her hip. "Yes, Lennon, I do. But I'm anxious to see what you have in store for us next."

Ripping myself away from her before I do something stupid, like throwing her over my shoulder and tossing her onto the bed to have my way with her, I head toward her bedroom door. I pull it open, stopping to turn around and face her once again.

"And Lennon?"

"Hmm?" Her hair is messy, and every inch of her skin on display is flushed. It's the sexiest thing I've ever seen and I hate myself for thinking it.

I focus on the seam between her legs. "Don't ever hide the evidence of you being turned on again. Seeing that wet spot, knowing I watched you soak yourself through, is the sexiest thing I've ever seen."

I'm rushing through the hallway before she's able to even process what I said. Pepper whines as soon as she catches me leaving in the kitchen. I feel bad that I don't give her an ounce of my attention. I'm too desperate to get away from this house—away from her—before I lose all sense of control. My legs quickly take me down the long driveway until I find the safety of my car.

As soon as I'm in there alone, my palm comes down against the steering wheel. "Fuck!" I yell. Hitting it again and again. "Fuck, fuck, fuck."

There's absolutely no fucking way I'll make it out of this agreement with my sanity or any respect for myself.

I have no business being this hard for her. Yet here I am, cock pressed against my zipper, aching for the next time I'll see her.

CHAPTER
23

I SIT CROSS-LEGGED at the breakfast nook, a bowl of cereal in front of me and a book in my lap, when I hear the house alarm chime. Confused, I rack my brain about who it could be. About twenty minutes ago Aiden had come into the kitchen for water before disappearing to go back to sleep. It could be someone with security, but typically I'll hear from Sebastian if he's coming over.

It could be Monica, but even then I feel like Aiden would've told me if she was coming over. We hadn't talked about it again, so maybe he didn't want to have to explain himself more.

I'm watching the entrance to the kitchen carefully when Poe steps through it. He quirks an eyebrow when his eyes land on me.

"Good morning." He halfway smiles, coming to a stop at the edge of the table. "I should've known you'd be in another world by nine in the morning."

Tiny little droplets of water drip from his wet hair. His already dark locks appear even darker with the wetness. He smells like fresh winter air, the scent of his body wash, or maybe it's his cologne, surrounding me.

My spoon tings as I let it drop into my cereal bowl. Smiling, I sit back against the bench. "I wasn't expecting any visitors."

His fingers strum against the fabric of his shorts. They're a gym material, the hem of it coming to rest a couple of inches above his knee. A tattoo peeks out from underneath the fabric. I fight the urge to slide the shorts up so I can find out what he'd permanently marked on his skin. "Yeah," he breathes, scratching his head. "I was wondering if you'd maybe want to do something today?"

My stomach drops, excitement washing over me. "You and me?"

"Obviously." I'm surprised by his invitation. We haven't seen each other since he'd watched me give myself an orgasm. He'd texted me later in the night. All it said was goodnight, but I'd obsessed over it for hours. Wondering what it could mean, hopeful that he was thinking about me in some sort of capacity.

Stepping closer, he pulls the book from my lap. His knuckles brush my inner thigh, sending goosebumps over my skin. My sleep shorts do little to cover me, not that it really matters. Only a few days ago, he was watching me lie on my bed, my fingers down the front of my shorts as I let his words coax me to a climax. "Anything naughty in here?" he teases.

"It's a young adult dystopian novel," I point out, standing up and grabbing my bowl. "It's a great book. I think you'll like it. But there's nothing naughty in it."

I brush past him, stopping at the sink to rinse out my bowl. He waits quietly behind me. Once it's rinsed and loaded in the dishwasher, I turn around to face him. A muscle in his jaw ticks as he works hard at maintaining eye contact with me.

It just so happens I wore one of my skimpiest night sets last night. It wasn't on purpose. In fact, it was because a lot of my laundry is dirty. Nash had given his housecleaner the week off with both him and Nora being gone. He'd offered to keep her on since Aiden and I would still be here, but we'd both insisted that she got some time off. Typically, she's great about doing my laundry even though I tell her I can do it myself. It turns out when I tried to do it on my own, I had zero idea how to work Nash's fancy washing machine. I'd even gone online to see if I could figure out how to turn the washer on, but it was no use. Now I've been left to work through the small amount of clean clothes I have left before she returns tomorrow, the same day Nash and Nora are getting back.

I fold my hands over my chest, waiting to see if he'll look past my eyes then. He's probably trying to do the respectful thing, but the thing is, I don't want him to be respectful. I want him to look me up and down because he can't help it. Now that he's seen me come, his name on my lips as the fireworks erupted over my body, I've lost my sense of bashfulness around him. I want to push his buttons, push his restraint, to see what else I can get from him.

It's selfish of me to think this will ever be anything more than what it is. But it won't keep me from trying, from stealing whatever I can from him, even if it's in the form of his self-restraint.

He swallows, eyes unwavering from looking at my face. "Have you picked what you want to do next?"

I'd spent every minute I'd had alone yesterday poring over my books, wondering what I wanted to do with him next. There were so many options. Now that we've got this thing started, I'm not sure it even matters to me what we do as long as we're doing something. Even though he barely touched me the other night, the power I felt in myself was unmatched. I'd hopped around the world trying to find men who would make me feel like that—powerful and sexy, yet still vulnerable. This man had only brushed his fingertips across my skin, and I'd felt all of those and more.

"I don't know," I say, looking at his shoulder instead of his eyes. Different scenarios I'd read in my books fly through my head, and I can't help but envision doing all of them with him. It's hard to look him in the eye as various possibilities roll through my head.

"Well, I have an idea. If you're okay with it." His voice sounds strained with the last part, like he thinks I'm going to turn him down. It's odd to me he hasn't realized I'd do anything if it meant I got to do it with him.

I place my hands on the counter next to me, the movement causing my sleep tank to ride up slightly. Air kisses a sliver of skin on my stomach. For a slight second, his resolve slips. His eyes flick down to the exposed skin before looking away just as quickly. If I hadn't been looking for it, I would've missed it. "What is it?" I ask, making it seem like I'll have to think about it. Whatever he's got in his mind, I've already decided to say yes.

I'm preparing myself for things like him touching me, me touching him, or even skipping all the bases and going all the way. "I want to take you to a bookstore." Well, I wasn't expecting that.

"A bookstore?" The confusion is apparent in my voice. When we'd agreed to tick items off my sexual bucket list, I hadn't thought it would entail outings that seem a *lot* like dates.

He nods his head, as if it isn't an outlandish idea considering what we'd agreed to. "Yep," he says, popping the P. "The other night when I was looking through your books, I'd noticed that you had a line highlighted where he takes her to a bookstore and lets her pick out a book." He shrugs, anxiously wiping something off the counter. "You know, only if you want to."

I'd highlighted that spot in the book, thinking it was one of the most romantic things a man could do for a woman. Books are my love language. All I need is to be fed and have a book in my lap. I hadn't even realized he'd picked that book up. I was too focused on having him in my room, on the ghost of his touch I'd still felt on my body even though he'd been across the room. Going to a bookstore with Poe is the best way I could spend my day. Taking a deep breath, I try to reel in my feelings, trying not to get too excited. It may be my dream date, but it's just a normal day for him—not even a date.

"That sounds cool," I say, trying to keep my voice steady. Inside, butterflies flutter around in my stomach, as if they've been caged for years and are finally being set free. On the outside, I try to act nonchalant.

"If it isn't something you want to do, we don't have to. I was just thinking with your love for books and you having it noted in your—"

"Poe?" My voice is loud, having to break through his ramblings.

He wipes his hands up and down his thighs, pulling the hem of his shorts up slightly, giving me another slight taste of the tattoo on his thigh. "Yeah?" His voice is hesitant.

"Of course I want to."

His eyes light up with relief. "Good, because I already have coffee waiting in the car and a place in mind."

How the hell am I not supposed to fall in love with this man?

For someone who's adamant about not falling in love, he makes falling for him too easy.

Pulling myself off the counter, I look down at my PJs. "I just need to change first."

He finally takes a moment to look at me from head to toe. I feel it all the way down my body. "Good idea," he says, clearing his throat. "I'll just wait out here."

Our eyes linger on one another for a few moments before I spin on my heel, beelining for my room.

I'm never the girl who worries about what I'm wearing. I don't dress my body to impress men. Yet as I hurry toward my closet, I can't help but wonder what I want to wear. What outfit will make him notice me?

I rifle through the small amount of clothes I have, finally

settling on something. Throwing it on quickly, I put a small amount of mascara and Chapstick on my lips. It's all the makeup I ever wear comfortably. My hair is a bit of a mess, so I grab a ribbon from my bathroom drawer and tie it around my hair, creating a ponytail that travels down the nape of my neck. I finish tying the ends in a bow before grabbing my bag.

Allowing myself one last glance in the mirror, I see the excitement written all over my face. I'm about to go on a date with Poe, even if he doesn't know it, it's the most excited I've been in a long time—maybe the most excited I've ever been.

CHAPTER
24

MY FINGERS GRIP my steering wheel tightly as I guide us toward the bookstore. Lennon sits next to me, the tiny little dress she put on showing a dangerous amount of thigh. The fabric keeps sliding up little by little as she absentmindedly dances along to the song playing through the speakers. It's taken all of me to not reach over and get a feel for the creamy white skin she's put on display.

Her lips move with the lyrics of the song. She's totally unaware of how I'm crumbling in my seat next to her, my mind unable to think of anything but the way she looked the other night with her small little hand pushed between her thighs.

"Thanks again for the coffee," Lennon says, breaking the silence. She picks hers up from the cupholder between us. The lid presses against her lips as she takes a sip of the cold liquid. I'd taken a guess at what she wanted, apparently not too far off by the way she's enjoying it.

Peeling my eyes from the road for a moment, I look over at her. "I'm glad you like it."

"It's from you. Of course I like it." She smiles, immediately turning pink in the cheeks. She might regret her words by the way she focuses her stare out the window, angling her body away from me.

I keep my mouth shut. Her words are just a reminder that I shouldn't be doing this. I have no business stealing this one-on-one time with her, yet here I am, not about to change it. I'm not the man who deserves to share these small moments with her. A better man should be taking her to a bookstore, getting her a coffee, not because it's the polite thing to do but because he's memorized her order and knows how she gets without caffeine. I should walk away and give her space. I should leave her alone so she'll fall for a better man and not for a man like me who will never fully want her the way she imagines.

The car doesn't stop. I don't turn it around even though every part of me says I should. The thing is, she seemed so happy when she came barreling out of her bedroom. I'd been standing awkwardly in the foyer, the thought just occurring to me that Aiden could appear at any moment, and I'd somehow have to explain to him why I was there. It'd only been a few minutes since she'd gone back to her room to change when she reappeared. I was thankful to not have to look at her in the tiny little sleep set for another second longer. I'd been holding on by a narrow thread to not reach out and feel how soft the silk was for myself. The shiny fabric had done nothing to disguise her body. It clung to every small curve of hers, driving my mind wild.

The entire time we spent talking in the kitchen, I'd focused on staring only at her face and getting lost in a deep hole of how she walks around in front of Aiden in tiny little outfits like that. She didn't have on a bra. Her peaked nipples were visible through the thin fabric.

Anything she chose to change into would've been better than the pajamas she'd had on. At least, that's what I thought, but when she'd stepped out in a dress with barely there straps and a hemline that's dangerously high on her thighs, I'd wondered if the pajamas were better.

She pretty much skipped all the way to my car. I'd walked behind her, wondering what the hell I'd gotten myself into. She looked way too fucking innocent with her hair pulled back in a nice little bow. Looked way too innocent for me to be thinking about how easy it would be to slip my hand underneath that short little dress of hers. Or how the way she's tied her hair back with the ribbon would make damn sure her thick hair wouldn't get in the way of her blowing me.

The rest of the car ride is quiet. I know I should probably say something to get her mind off what she'd said, her body language proving to me she was embarrassed about it. My mouth stays closed, my mind too busy wondering if this is possibly the worst idea I've ever had.

Finally, I pull the SUV into a small parking lot, joining only two other cars in the closed off space.

"Have you been here before?" Lennon asks, her voice unsure. I don't blame her. From the outside, the bookstore doesn't look like much. I'd spent the early morning hours when I couldn't sleep looking up the best bookstores in the area. There were a few that seemed more touristy than I was hoping for. This one had a stream of loyal customers, all giving it really excellent reviews.

Partly because it's known as a romance bookstore, which I guess isn't typical. I'd learned that most bookstores only have small sections dedicated to romance, but this was not the case. Apparently, this one has shelves and shelves of romance books. The name of the store, *Catching Fictional Feelings*, is an homage to the books it carries.

"No," I tell her, trying to hide my smile when I see her eyes widen at the name.

"I didn't know a place like this existed," she says, voice full of wonder. She lets out a small little squeal of excitement. Easily one of the cutest sounds I've ever heard.

Eagerly, she pushes on the door handle. Her fingers fumble with the lock, working hard at getting the door unlocked. Once it's free, she excitedly falls out of the car. Turning to me, she gives me the widest smile. "Are you coming?"

Bending over the passenger seat, she grabs her coffee from the cupholder. She takes one last pull of the liquid before placing it back where it came from. Her hand wipes the excess liquid off her lips. "Poe," she whines. "Let's go."

"I'm going," I drag out. I take my wallet and phone from where I placed them in the console between us and slide them into their respective pockets of my shorts. Grabbing the keys as well, I step out of the car.

Her door slams slightly as she bounds around the car, jumping up and down in excitement. "I can't wait to see all the books."

Lennon takes off for the door, trusting that I'll follow. She manages to wait for me at the front door, but by the way she shifts from one foot to the other, I can tell it took a lot for her to even take that time before going inside.

I grab the handle to the door, holding it open until she steps inside. Without even realizing it, my hand finds the small of her back, escorting her into the shop.

A girl with purple hair sits at a desk not too far from us. She pulls a headphone from her ear, a friendly smile on her face. "Welcome in, guys. Anything I can help you with?"

"Uh, just looking," Lennon says shyly.

"Cool," the employee responds, already putting one side of the headphones back in her ear. "Just let me know if something changes."

Lennon looks at me. Her teeth dig into her bottom lip as she bites back a smile.

Rolling my eyes, I gesture to the rows of shelves. "Go look."

She claps her hands together, running off to disappear in between the countless shelves.

For a while, I wander aimlessly, giving her time to explore. Eventually, I find her tucked in a small alcove, a book cradled in her hands. She leans on an elbow against the shelf, delicately turning one of the pages.

I'm in awe of her for a moment, wondering how anyone has ever been able to hurt her. The way she smiles down at the ink on pages, totally lost to the world, captivates me. She seems so pure, so innocent, standing there, lost in her enjoyment of whatever her eyes are scanning over. Lennon seems to enjoy the simple things, like finding a new book to read. I hate that terrible things have happened to her. That there were moments in her life that broke that beautiful smile of hers.

She doesn't look up from whatever book she's devouring, allowing me a few moments to freely stare at her without her noticing. Watching her like this, seeing her so happy and content from something so simple as a bookstore, makes me wish things were different. That I could ever be a man deserving of the smiles she freely hands out. Someone who deserves the heart she keeps trying to hand over to me, no matter how many times I tell her I won't take it.

For just a second, I forget about everything in my past, and I wonder what a future could look like. I rid myself of the thought quickly, knowing myself enough to know that I'll never be the guy for her.

Years ago, I tried to love after loss. It crashed and burned and hurt for ages. I won't do that to myself. I can't do it again. So, I'll continue to keep her at arm's length, even though it's painful for me to do so.

CHAPTER
25

MY FINGER TRACES over the spines of the books on the shelf. Some of the titles written across the spines I recognize, some are new to me. All I know is that my pile of books I want to take home is growing and growing. I've created a small pile at my feet of the books that I'm interested in. Eventually I'll have to whittle down the pile to a more realistic number, but for right now I'm going to enjoy the growing stack.

Reaching the end of the shelf, I bump into a warm, firm body. Before I can freak out, a stranger touching me unexpectedly is my worst nightmare, I'm met with his familiar scent.

His hands are warm as he holds me by the elbows. "Having fun?" Poe asks, humor in his voice. My neck cranes to look up at him, finding a smirk.

"Definitely," I whisper, too focused on the way his thumb brushes up and down on my arm to form any other thought.

We linger in the position for a moment, his hands are sure against my skin. "Good," he says. "That was the goal."

"Already better than the book," I whisper. Commenting on the whole reason we're together, to check things off my list from things I read in stories.

His eyes darken. He pushes me against the bookshelf, his

hips against mine pinning me in place. "Yeah?" he all but growls. "You haven't even purchased a book yet."

I bite my lip, reveling in feeling his hard body against mine. "I don't have to," I assure him. "I just know it's already better."

His hands find my hips, gripping them tightly. The movement has the fabric of my dress bunching up, a breeze hitting my upper thigh. "Let me make sure of that." Goosebumps take over my skin when he brushes his nose along my jawline. I feel his breath hot against my neck. I want to turn my head, to catch his lips with mine and finally discover what Poe Hanson tastes like.

Before I can ask him what his words mean, his lips delicately press into the sensitive skin beneath my jawline. It's incredibly tender. While his tongue rakes over the soft skin, one of his hands slides underneath the skirt of my dress.

Even though we're tucked away in the bookshelves, someone could still walk by and catch us in this compromised position. The idea doesn't bother me. I'm too caught up in feeling his lips against me while his fingers slide into my panties.

Having him watch me touch myself was hot. Actually feeling him touch me is unreal. It's the last thing I'd expected when we stepped into the store, but right now, it's the *only* thing I can think about.

I'm wet, something I know he discovers by the way he moans into the crook of my neck.

"You're wet. What have you been reading to make you like this?"

My head hits the shelf behind me in pleasure. "It's not the books. It's you."

He grinds against me at the same time one finger enters me. "Good answer."

All I want is for him to move his lips from my neck. I want him to capture my mouth with his. He doesn't give me that. What he *does* give me, is one finger inside me while the other pushes against my clit. His lips and tongue continue to work at the sensitive skin of my neck while his fingers expertly work to bring me to the brink of an orgasm.

"Poe," I moan, knowing I'm moments away from losing control.

"God, my name sounds so good falling from your lips," he groans.

"I'm..."

"I know, Len. Go ahead. Let go. There's no one here but me and the books."

I'm so far gone that I don't think it'd matter if there were people here or not, the orgasm overtakes my body. He allows me to ride it out, my hips bucking between him and the shelf. The movement causes a few books to tumble off the shelf, hitting the ground with a *thump*.

Poe lays a gentle kiss against my collarbone before his head pulls away. There's heat to his stare when he pulls away, a cocky smirk forming on his lips. "You look good all flushed, your body pinned against the bookshelf."

My knees are wobbly as I recover from the orgasm. I look over his shoulder, seeing nothing but books in sight.

"I can't believe..."

His knuckles brush against the sensitive skin of my core as he pulls his hands from my panties. "I had to make damn sure it was better than your book. I couldn't just get you a book, I had to get you an orgasm, too."

He takes a step back, but his fingers trail down my arm until he drops his hand. Poe looks over my shoulder, his eyes raking over the books. "Find any good ones?" He totally changes the subject, and I let him. I'm too stunned at what just happened to really say anything else.

I laugh, my whole body feeling heated from him and the orgasm. I tuck a hair that's escaped from my ribbon behind my ear. "I've got a few contenders." I point to the growing stack of books on the floor a few feet away from us. "I'll have to narrow it down before we leave."

He gently picks up all the books that fell. After he slides them back into their places, he walks over to the stack of books I'd created. He easily picks up all the books, balancing them in one arm. With his free hand, he grabs mine, his large fingers wrapping around mine effortlessly.

"Let's go," he says nonchalantly, as if he doesn't realize the weight of him holding my hand in his. The feelings are heightened, knowing what he'd just done to me. The words he'd said, the way he made me feel mixing together to make my head spin. He gently pulls on my arm, leading me deeper into the store. "We've got more books to find."

He keeps walking through the endless shelves of books until we reach the back. To our left, there are bookcases with old marquee letters placed above them. The letters spell out "spicy." Letting go of my hand, Poe looks at me with a mischievous gleam in his eye. "I figured you could find some keepers in here."

"You *think* so?" I tease, feeling bold.

He nods. "Why don't you go take a look at them? We're going to need ideas on what else you want to do." His tongue peeks out to wet his lips, and I fight the urge to clench my thighs together. I'm for certain there's nothing hotter than a man with hungry eyes standing in the middle of a bookstore.

I don't need to be told twice. Leaving him standing there with my stack, I take off to look at more books. My body feels hot. I know he's watching me go. I feel his stare right between my bare shoulder blades.

I pull book after book from the case, reading the blurbs and flipping through the pages to see if I'm interested. Turning a corner, I look through another line of books, cradling a few that have piqued my interest in my arm. Suddenly, a book is pulled from the slot in front of me. Looking through the hole, I find Poe's brown eyes staring back at me.

His lips turn up. "Had to make sure you weren't lost in your smut," he jokes. I almost die when he winks. He probably didn't mean anything by doing it, but it makes me feel flushed all over.

"I'm close," I answer honestly, sticking a book in the spot where his face pops through. I need a moment to let my cheeks return to a normal color.

He doesn't give me the chance. Once again, the book is sliding to the side and he's looking at me with a grin. "Looks like you've found some more," he notes, his eyes flicking to the books in the crook of my elbow.

The book from the top slips. I quickly grab it, straightening it back out. We both stare at the cover, a man with tattoos and abs front and center. Poe looks from the cover back at me. Quickly, he's out from the other side of the bookcase and is standing in front of me. Picking up the book, he examines the cover.

He looks up at me. With a lazy shrug, he says, "Meh. I think my tattoos are better." He takes the group of books from my arms, placing the model cover back on the top. "Same with the abs."

Poe leaves me standing there with empty arms. I watch him walk away until he places the few books I'd just picked up in a pile with the ones I'd already picked out. He takes a seat on a long leather couch tucked away in the corner. My pile of books sits on a coffee table in front of him. He's got them all neatly stacked in two columns, the rest of the table a mess with strewn magazines and books. A potted plant sits in the middle, its vibrant green leaves spilling across the surface and onto the ground.

He grabs one from the stack, the one with the abs, before crossing one leg over the other until his ankle rests over his knees. Leaning back on the couch, he looks at me once again.

"Take your time." He waves the book in the air, the lights catching the glossy cover. "I'll be right here. Taking notes."

The only reason I disappear back into the books is to get a moment away from him. For some reason, he's acting differently this trip. I don't know if it's because we're away from everyone who knows us, or if it's something else. I try not to think too much into it, knowing that even if he seems more relaxed around me, it changes nothing—at least for him.

I finally make my way back to him, falling onto the couch cushion next to his. I sigh, my eyes wandering the store.

"Want a book?" he asks, barely looking up from the one in his lap. Without me even answering, he reaches to the pile and blindly hands one over.

I take it but leave it unopened. Placing it on my chest, I lean back on the couch, assuming the same position as Poe. "Right now, I just want to soak it all in."

"Soak what in?"

My head turns to look at him. "This place. The books. Being with you. Everything." I let my eyes focus on his lips for one small moment before I look back ahead of us. "I just want to remember it all."

"Me too." His words are clipped. He returns to reading immediately, seeming to be done with that part of the conversation.

Meanwhile, I'm replaying every single word that just came out of my mouth to figure out what part he was agreeing with.

"I think one day I want to own a bookstore," I state, interrupting the silence between us.

This gets him to close the book and turn his head to face me. "Tell me more."

"Or maybe just work at one," I backpedal, realizing how far-fetched it sounds for me to own a bookstore. I haven't even graduated college, and I barely graduated high school, opting to get my GED instead of a diploma. I'm not sure anyone would take me seriously enough to be a proper owner. "I don't know," I say, defeated. "There's just so many things I envision. I don't know if it'll be enough to just work there, you know?"

He blinks, nodding in understanding. "You can do anything you want, Lennon. If you want to own a bookstore one day, then I can't wait to be its first customer."

My cheeks hurt from smiling. "You would?"

He scoffs, as if my question offends him. "Of course I would." He picks up the book in his lap. "As long as you have countless shelves of covers with abs," he teases.

I can't help but laugh, shaking my head at him. "I don't think it'll ever happen." I look at the surrounding space sadly. "It's a nice dream, though."

His hand comes to rest on my thigh. He applies only the slightest of pressure, but it's enough to get me to look back at him. I look down at his hand, somehow already yearning for him to slide it underneath my dress again and feel him touch the part of me that's still wet. "Tell me all about it." He sounds like he's actually interested, so even though I'm already embarrassed I said anything to begin with, I start to list exactly what I picture in my mind.

"So for starters, I'd want to have a garden in the front. To make it seem homey before you even step through the door."

"Like vegetables?" he asks.

I shake my head. "No, I'd want it to be one that attracted butterflies. A space with flowers that attract them. I'm sure it'd be so pretty."

"You like butterflies?"

"Love them," I answer immediately. "I love the symbolism behind them. How they transform into something so beautiful."

"What's it like when you go inside?" he presses.

"As soon as you step inside, you're going to be hit with the smell of books and freshly brewed coffee. I'd love to have a little coffee counter where we make fresh lattes and espresso for readers to enjoy while they're there."

He angles his body toward mine, resting his head against his knuckles. Poe watches me so intently that I'd come up with ways to describe this bookstore for hours, if it meant he'd keep looking at me the way he is right now.

"I want it to be a place where people don't just stop in and buy a book and leave. I want it to be more than that. From the moment they walk in, I want them to feel like it's an experience."

"Coffee is a good start, then."

"Right? I feel like the scent of coffee could lure anyone in and make them want to stay for more."

He stares at me so intently I'm confident that for some reason, he really is interested in what I have to say. "Tell me more," he prods.

"There will be comfortable chairs and couches everywhere. Like almost an absurd amount of seating space. That way people will be invited to sit down with their book of choice. I want them to feel like they can test it out before purchasing."

I adjust my position on the couch, pulling my legs underneath myself and facing toward him a bit more. "I also want to have a blind date with a book table. Employees and I, and maybe even customers, can bring in a book that's wrapped in special packaging. On the outside, we'll write what tropes the books are or what genre, a bit about the characters or something to hint at what the books are about. People can pick them up without knowing exactly what they're getting, but that's the fun of it."

He rubs a hand over his mouth. His facial hair is longer than it is normally. Even though he showered this morning before coming over, he must not have had time to shave. Or he didn't care to. Either way, I like the slightly longer peppering of hairs covering his jaw.

"Basically, I just want it to be the most inviting place ever. I want people to come in and feel right at home. It'd be the place where they come to leave their reality for a completely new one." My words run together by the end out of excitement. "I can picture everything so clearly in my head," I chatter on. "The fun jewel tones I'd have throughout the place, how the couches will be overflowing with throw pillows. There would be tons of plants and maybe even a bookstore cat that would act like it owns the place. It'd be fat from all of the customers feeding it scraps of food."

This makes him laugh. It's a deep, quiet rumble through his chest. I feel it everywhere.

CHAPTER
26

"AM I TALKING TOO MUCH?" Lennon questions, stopping her well-thought-out descriptions of the store she wants to open.

Shaking my head, I smile. "No, I'm loving learning about this fat store cat. Tell me, what'll his favorite scrap be?"

Groaning, she throws herself deeper into the cushions of the couch. Her hands come up to cover her rosy cheeks. "Oh my god, I'm definitely talking too much." Her words come out muffled as she speaks into the palms of her hands.

I scoot across the couch, my leg now pressing against hers. "You aren't talking too much."

Her head rocks from side to side behind her fingers. "I absolutely am. You don't care about this idea. Why should you? I shouldn't have gone into so much detail."

Reaching up, I pry her fingers from her face so I can see those big, beautiful green eyes of hers. Unfortunately, she has them closed in embarrassment. Her long eyelashes kiss her cheeks.

My fingers tangle with hers, my knuckles brushing her cheekbone. "Who said I didn't care?"

I feel her breath hot against my fingers. "You did." She leans her cheek deeper into my palm. "At least you implied it."

My eyes soften. "Don't listen to me." Her lips shine with Chapstick. I wonder what the flavor is. If I were to lean in to find out, I know she'd let me. I almost kissed her earlier, in the privacy of the shelves. It took everything in me to keep my mouth on anywhere but her lips. Fighting the feeling, I stroke her cheek one last time before I pull both our hands from her face.

Lennon doesn't look away. She lets her eyes glide all over my face like she's trying to solve some sort of puzzle. I guess maybe to her I *am* a puzzle. She purses her lips. "I don't understand you," she mutters.

I scoot across the cushion until my side presses into the arm of the couch. I need space from her. Her words bring me back to reality. She's not wrong. I'm not giving her very clear signals right now. One moment I push her away, the next I'm pulling her in.

I can't help it. Being around her makes me want to challenge my feelings on love—on my ability to be loved. "I don't either," I joke, hoping to break the tension between us.

The tension still lingers in the air, but we both ignore it. She picks up the book I'd handed her earlier. I pretend to read the one that had caught my attention before. It's no use. My thoughts run rampant, wondering why I care about her bookstore dream. The entire time she talked about what she envisioned for her very own bookstore, I was sitting next to her, wondering where I'd fit in the scenario.

I stay seated for a few more moments, wondering what the hell I'm doing, before I get up. Sighing, I run my hands down my thighs. "I'm going to go set these books to the counter," I say, not bothering to look at her.

She hums an okay, clearly enamored in her own book.

I barely manage to get all the books in my arms in one trip.

My chin rests on the top of the stack, making sure the books don't topple over. The cashier's eyes are huge as she looks at all the books spilling over the counter.

"I'd like to check out, please."

Her eyes bounce from me to the books, back to me again. "Uhhh…you want all of them?"

I try to hide that I'm annoyed. Taking a calm breath, I give her a remnant of a smile. "Yes. I do."

Bending down behind the counter, she holds up a few canvas bags. "These are the biggest bags I have. It'll take a few."

Reaching into my back pocket, I pull out my wallet. Setting it on the counter, I slide my credit card out of its slot. "Those will be perfect."

Quickly, she rings up book after book. It takes a while, even with the two of us working together. She scans the book. I carefully put it in the bag with the bookshop's logo on the front. We work in the repetitive motion until we have three overflowing bags of books.

The girl with purple hair, Harley, if her name tag is correct, whistles. "It's not every day that we have men so into reading romance."

We both inspect the bags of books. I shrug. "They're not for me."

Her nails hurriedly glide over the keyboard of her computer. I wait patiently, telling her I don't need to see the total before handing over my card.

"Wait," I say, moments after handing it over. "Can I possibly add one more book? My friend is still in the back reading it." I'd forgotten that Lennon is still in the back of the room reading one of the books. I don't want her to have to pay for any of the books, especially since this was my idea in the first place.

She nods, holding my card between her fingers. She types something in again on her computer before swiping the card.

"Would you like your receipt?"

I shake my head, grabbing my card back from her. "Nope." Shoving my wallet back into my pocket, I take two of the bags in one hand and the last in my opposite hand. I look around the shop, deciding to take a seat in an armchair near the entrance. If Lennon is at peace reading her book, I don't want to bother her. When I'd decided I wanted to take her out today, before Nash and Nora return and we get swept up in tour life, I wanted the day to be about her. A day that she'd enjoy. I'd sit in this fifty-year-old highly uncomfortable arm chair all day if it meant she was content.

Turns out, she doesn't make me sit in it long. I've only been scrolling through my phone for about twenty minutes when her figure emerges through the shelves. Our eyes connect instantly, like we have this weird new thing where we can sense where the other person is without even having to think twice about it.

"You disappeared," she comments.

I nod, sitting up in the chair. "I didn't want to go back and interrupt your reading. In case you were reading a good part." I say the last few words with a double meaning, knowing she'll pick up on what I mean. Hopefully her mind goes to the same place as mine. To the both of us nestled in between the book-shelves, me working hard on making sure I not only check things off her list, but I make it *better* than her fiction.

She blanches. "No. Nothing like that," she says hurriedly.

"If you say so," I tease, standing up. I pull on the ribbon in her hair slightly, evening out the bow. "Ready to go?"

A line appears on her forehead. "I still need to sort through the books. I'm going to pick a few to buy and take home. I know I want this one for sure." She holds up the book that she'd been reading on the couch.

Holding up the bags, I smile. "Too late."

Her mouth falls open. "What do you mean, *too late?*"

I walk toward the door. My back presses against it as I push it ajar. "I mean the books are already paid for."

Lennon looks to the counter for clarification. Harley smiles wide at her. "Yeah, it's been paid for. The man must love you. My boyfriend would never."

Both Lennon and I speak at the same time.

"We're just friends," I argue, remembering how I'd told the cashier that.

"Oh, it's not like that," Lennon says.

Harley narrows her eyes, chuckling low under her breath. "Okay, whatever you say."

Harley's mistake has made Lennon turn bright pink. Even her chest is red with embarrassment, small splotches of red pop up all over it. Without saying anything else, Lennon bolts in my direction. Her elbow brushes against my stomach as she rushes through the door.

"Wait up," I yell, the bags swinging in my arms as I chase after her.

Lennon stops in the middle of the parking lot. Swiveling on her feet, she walks right up to me. "You didn't have to do that."

The sharp tone in her voice shocks me. I thought she'd appreciate the new books, not seem angry about them. "Lennon, I know I didn't have to. I wanted to."

She crosses her arms against her chest, still holding on to the book from earlier. "You wanted to?"

I take a step toward her, well aware that our bodies are way too close, even with the arrangement we have going on. "Yes, Lennon. I wanted to. I'm not one to do something because I feel like I have to. I'm too old to feel that way."

She rolls her eyes. "Your thirties aren't old."

"Well, it sure as hell isn't young. And damn well old enough to be past the people pleasing phase."

Her lips roll against one another as she takes a second to think through my words. "You know *just friends* don't buy each other hundreds of dollars' worth of books right after giving them the best orgasm of their life, right?"

My lip twitches. "The best orgasm of your life?"

"Poe," she warns, her tone annoyed. "You get the point. It's not *just friends'* territory."

I scoff, walking past her toward the car. "You're right. Just friends also don't watch each other come, but I guess we already blew right past that as well haven't we?"

I don't turn around until the bags are placed in my trunk. Once they're neatly tucked in the back, the trunk closed, I spin on my heels, finding her watching me closely.

She hasn't moved from her earlier position, even though it's in the middle of the street. She clutches the book from earlier to her chest, an unreadable look on her face as she watches me closely. Walking to the driver's side, I open the door, thinking that would make her move.

It doesn't.

I rub the bridge of my nose with my pointer finger and thumb, letting out a long sigh. "Get out of the middle of the road, Lennon."

She lets out a sigh of her own, dramatically walking to the SUV and yanking her door open. The two of us are silent as we both buckle our seatbelts. My arm finds her headrest as I turn around to back up.

We're a few miles into it when I finally lose the battle of wills. "Am I getting the silent treatment for buying you books?"

She scoffs, looking at me with a wild burn to her eyes. "It's not *just* the books."

"Then what is it?" I keep my voice even. I didn't intend to upset her by purchasing the books. I did it to make her happy.

"It's just that I can't keep up with you. One moment you're acting like you're not interested in the slightest, the next you're buying me all these books and making comments about how we aren't *just friends.* It's confusing as hell, Poe."

I swallow. "I'm not trying to make it that way."

"Well, you are. And the worst part about it is I really don't think you mean to, so it's hard to even blame you and stay mad."

"I'm sorry."

Her only response to my apology is to look out the window. She angles her entire body toward it, making it clear she doesn't want to talk.

The least I can do is respect her wishes. I stay silent, aimlessly driving down random streets instead of heading back toward Nash's house. If I drop her off while the two of us are still fighting—or doing whatever this is—I'll feel like shit. I'm going to keep driving until she's ready to talk again, until I can attempt to fix whatever I've already messed up.

Finally, her eyes stop looking out her window and instead focus on my profile. "If we aren't friends, then what are we, Poe?" Her voice is brave, every word controlled as if she's thought how to phrase that sentence repeatedly before actually saying it.

My cheeks puff out as I let out a breath. "We're just us, Lennon. We're Lennon and Poe. Why does it need to be more?"

She sighs, her eyes looking sad. "It doesn't. Forget I said anything."

I glance over at her. "You sure?"

Her smile is sad when she looks at me. "Yes. I'm sure." Reaching across the dash, she grabs my hand and squeezes it once. "Thank you for the books, Poe. I can't wait to read them."

I'd do anything to ease the tension, to have her smile at me without a hint of sadness. "No thank you for the orgasm? I really thought it'd be good, with the books surrounding us and all."

She bashfully covers her smile behind her hand, shaking her head at me with a soft giggle. "I already told you it was the best orgasm of my life. What else do you want from me, Poe?"

It all, Lennon. I want it all.

CHAPTER
27

WE'VE BEEN in the car way longer than needed. I'm not familiar with the streets of LA. There's no way I could get us even remotely close to Nash's place from the bookstore. Despite all that, I know that we've been in the car almost double the amount of time it took us to get to the store. Nothing looks familiar, and I don't even know if we're going in the right direction of the house.

From what I've gathered after listening in on different conversations, Poe has been in LA for a long time, even longer than Nash. He should be familiar with the streets, on how to get us back, yet it seems like he drives with no sense of direction. I don't say anything, not wanting to end our time together just yet.

Even though his words hurt inside the bookstore, they weren't something he hadn't said before. I've known from the very beginning we were just friends, it's just hard to remember things like that when he plans elaborate bookstore outings and buys every single book I'm interested in. I got mad when he'd told me he bought all the books because it felt like another thing he did out of pity for me. My mind can't figure out any reason he'd do something like that unless he feels bad for me or if he actually *does* have feelings for me and is too stubborn to admit it.

My heart holds onto hope for the latter, but my brain says it's something closer to the former.

It'd taken me forever to muster up the courage to ask him what we were. I don't know why it took so much out of me. I knew before I'd even asked that he wouldn't give me a straight answer. That's Poe, giving vague enough answers to not give me any clarity at all but still keeping me holding on, regardless.

I allowed his answer because the sad part of the entire situation is…I'd do just about anything to keep my name attached to his. He hadn't given me a definitive answer about what we were. There's no label to define us by. But he had said we were Lennon and Poe, and it's pathetic of me, but even being associated with him at all is enough for me.

Poe directs the car onto some small street with cars parked down both sides of it. He pulls into a parking spot and puts the car in park. Turning to face me, he looks at me apologetically.

"Look Lennon," he begins.

"You don't have to say anything else." Now that some time has passed, I wonder if I'd overreacted. Being in his presence is enough to make my head spin. Once you add in the orgasm I'm still recovering from, my body finally familiar with his touch, and the incredible gesture of him buying *all* the books I'd shown interest in, I can't think rationally. It's not something I'm used to. Typically I'm the most level-headed in the room. Not when it comes to him. "I really am grateful for the books. I hope it didn't come off that I wasn't."

"The only reason I bought the books was because I wanted you to have them. I wanted to get them for you. There's no hidden meaning other than it was something I wanted to do because I care about you."

My heart rate speeds up. I wouldn't be surprised if he can hear it with the quietness of the car. "You do?" I whisper.

His eyes soften. Reaching out, he swipes his thumb over my cheekbone. "Yeah, Len, I do."

Before anything else can be said, he leans back, taking the warmth of his hand away as quick as he put it there. "Hungry?" he asks, opening the door to his SUV.

I look out the window, wondering where we are. All I can see are the sides of brick buildings and cars. They give no indication of where he's taken me, not that it really matters. "I'm actually starving," I say, laughing softly. We'd spent way longer at the bookstore than I'd realized. The morning faded to afternoon as we spent our time lost between bookshelves.

Now, the clock on his dash tells us it's getting late in the afternoon. My breakfast had been a tad late, but now my rumbling stomach is proof it's been a while since I've had food. The caffeine from my coffee could only provide sustenance for so long.

Poe hops out of the car, pressing his forearm against the open door. The position makes it hard not to stare at his bicep. Tattoo ink covers every inch of the muscle, and I don't know if I stare more to admire the creativity of the ink or at the size of the muscle. Maybe it's a mix of both.

"If you're so starving, why don't you get out of the car?" Poe breaks me from my ogling. Before I get caught checking him out again, I hurriedly unbuckle my seatbelt. I'm about to open my door when it swings open, Poe smiling on the other side of it.

One corner of his lip lifting, he waves his hand through the air. "After you."

I step out of the car, following him down a sidewalk. His pace makes it seem like he knows exactly where he's going, like he's traveled this path before. I don't ask questions, instead enjoying the spontaneity in seeing where he'll take me next. If I close my eyes and forget every warning he's uttered, I could pretend this was a date between boyfriend and girlfriend.

We loop around a corner of one of the buildings, bringing us to a bright pink door. Poe stops in front of it, turning around to face me with a smug look on his face. "Just remember, we can't stay here forever, okay?"

I narrow my eyes. "What does that mean?"

Excitement shines all over his face. In his eyes, in his smile, the way he rocks up and down on his feet. "It means eventually we have to go home, return to real life and everything."

Pulling the door open, he watches me expectantly. I give him a confused look before stepping inside. There's a giant neon sign in the back, lighting up with the words *Purrfect Brew*. The scent of freshly brewed coffee hits me in the face. Looking around, I don't know what aspect of the cafe to focus on first.

There's a room at the back that's framed in glass. Behind it waits a cat's dream. There are cat jungle gyms, things hanging from the walls, and most importantly—loads and loads of cats.

"Figured since you talked about having a bookstore cat with your books and coffee shop, you may like this place," Poe says from behind me.

I'm too shocked to say anything. My eyes roam over the entire cafe. Some people sit with cats in their laps, sipping on a coffee. Others sit at swanky looking booths with artificial flowers falling down the backs, eating food out of large black bowls and plates.

After taking in every inch of the cat cafe, I look to Poe. "How did you know about this place?"

This makes him laugh. At first, I wonder if he isn't going to answer by the way he grabs my elbow and guides me to an empty booth. As soon as we sit down, he sighs. "One of my good friends, Veronica, knows that I'm not the biggest fan of cats. She came to visit before the tour started and insisted we come here. I hadn't thought much into the name when she'd told me she'd heard amazing things about it. When I realized it was a place with fucking cats everywhere, it was too late. We were already here, and I didn't want to be a dick and make us leave. She knew I was too nice to say anything. Apparently she'd seen some blogger post about it and she just *had* to come here." The way he talks about this *Veronica* sends a twinge of jealousy through me. I wonder what the history is between them. I know just by his tone that there's more to the story.

"You don't like cats?"

His nose scrunches. "Let's just say cats and I have a complicated past. They don't necessarily like me."

A large snort falls from my lips the same moment a server walks up to our table. "Welcome to Purrfect Brew. Will you guys be needing menus today?"

Poe stares at the giant picture of a cat dressed as Albert Einstein on the guy's shirt before looking the server in the eyes. "Yes, please." He coughs. I can tell he's trying to hide his amusement, which makes me work hard on biting back a smile. I know if I laugh, I won't be able to stop. I've always found myself cracking up at the wrong time.

My mind flashes to the time I couldn't stop laughing in court because I was so uncomfortable. What people said about me—about Nora—because of it.

Shaking my head quickly, I catch Poe's eyes. "Lennon?" he asks, concerned. His lips are flat as he watches me carefully.

"What?" The two of them stare at me like I've been asked something I've yet to answer.

"Are you going to want a cat?" The server says, his nasally tone annoyed.

"Like adopt?" I question, confused and a little shook up from the flash of memory.

Poe's foot finds mine underneath the table. "No. One to snuggle while here."

"Oh," I say in understanding. I look at the room in the back, full of cats I'd love to pet and snuggle. "Yes, I do."

"Great," the server says. He looks to Poe. "What about you?"

"I'm good. I'll just watch her."

"Sir, you can't go into the cat cafe if you haven't paid the fee."

"Then yes, you can put me down for it, too," Poe concedes.

The server disappears for a moment before returning with two menus. He places them in front of us without saying a word.

As soon as he's gone for good, Poe lets out a loud laugh. "Oh my god, I think he caught me staring at his shirt."

I laugh along with him. "I was barely holding on. It took all of me not to crack when I saw you notice the shirt."

Poe wipes the bottom of his eyes, moisture gathering at the bottom from laughing so hard. Taking a deep breath he says, "Fuck. I wasn't expecting that. The size of the cat's face on the shirt was enough to catch my attention, but the fact it's dressed up as Albert Einstein fucking sends me."

My abs hurt from laughing so hard. "I'm totally going to buy you that shirt."

He shakes his head back and forth. "I won't wear it."

I gasp, pretending to be hurt. "You wouldn't wear the gift I bought you?"

"I don't think I've ever worn something with such a blown-up image before. Plus, it's a cat, and it's probably the last thing in the world I'd ever choose to wear. But I guess for you, I would."

For you I would.

"Good," I answer smugly, sitting back in the booth. Picking up the menu, I hold it up in front of my face, making sure he doesn't catch my giddy smile. He probably doesn't realize he even said it, but it's all I can think about. I'm not sure what I've even read on the menu. My mind is too focused on repeating his words over and over again.

CHAPTER
28

LENNON'S LEGS kick up and down in front of the dash as she doubles over in laughter. "Oh my god," she wheezes, "I can't breathe."

"I'm glad you still think it's funny," I growl.

She sucks in a breath, trying to calm herself. "I just thought that cat was so sweet."

"Sweet?" I ask in disbelief. I point to the Band-Aids on my neck. "The cat attacked me."

She bursts out laughing again. "Your face. You were horrified." I'm barely able to understand what she's saying through her fit of laughter.

"Of course I was horrified," I argue, reaching up to stroke the group of bandages running down the side of my throat. "I was getting attacked by a tiny monster."

She straightens in the passenger seat, clutching her stomach. "My abs hurt from laughing so hard," she groans.

"Karma," I mutter under my breath.

Her voice is finally somewhat even when she talks. "It was a teeny-tiny kitten. I didn't think it could do so much damage."

"Yeah, well, I'm proof it can," I say gruffly, pointing to the evidence of its damage.

Things had been going well. Lennon and I had an easy conversation over a late lunch. We'd enjoyed our meals, neither of us in a rush to finish. We'd even both ordered coffees, despite having one earlier in the morning. Finally, it was time for us to go into the stupid cat room.

I'd hoped that she'd be able to go in there and play with the cats, and I could just watch in the corner. I was wrong. She'd insisted I hold the kitten she'd fallen in love with. The thing had been sweet as can be when she'd held him. His purring had rattled his entire body. He was perfectly content in her arms. She kept touching her nose to his little pink one and he loved it. Eventually, she'd asked if I wanted to hold him. Since he'd been so nice with her, I figured the little fucker was actually sweet. It's always one extreme or another with cats, it seems.

Turns out, he was only sweet with *her*. Or maybe he was only evil with *me*. Either way, I hadn't been holding him for more than a minute when the little creature went wild. He'd hissed loudly, clawing at my face immediately. I dropped him because he took me off guard. He caught his fall by sticking his sharp-as-fuck claws into my neck and holding on for dear life. A staff member had run in immediately, unhooking the claws from my neck and apologizing profusely.

"Buttons isn't normally like this," she'd said, cuddling the now calm kitten to her chest.

We left shortly after the incident. I'd told Lennon I would just wait for her in the non-cat area, but she'd insisted on leaving with me. She hadn't laughed at first. For a lot of the car ride to our next destination, she was quiet, but eventually she couldn't hold it in any longer.

We're parked at a gas station. There's a dull hum as gas fills up my tank.

Lennon takes a steadying breath, arching across the center console to touch my face. Her fingers run over the bandages on my neck.

"The kitten Band-Aids are fitting," she says sweetly, the humor gone from her voice.

My pulse thumps against her fingertips. If she feels it, she says nothing. Tenderly, she strokes up and down the path of Band-Aids. "They're probably unnecessary now."

"Keep them," she says, looking up from the Band-Aids and looking at me. Her face is right in front of mine, the air from the words she speaks caressing my cheeks. "They make you look manly."

"I'm happy you think so." Reaching up, I pull each Band-Aid off. I roll them up in a ball together, planning to throw them away when I put the pump away. "I can confidently say you will *never* find me at a cat cafe again."

This makes her giggle. She falls back in her seat. "What if Veronica wants to go again?"

I scoff. "Then Veronica can have Maverick take her. I don't think she really likes cats anyway, she did it only to fuck with me."

I leave the conversation at that. Stepping out of the car, I put the pump back and close the gas compartment of my car. Looking at Lennon through the open window, I say, "I'll be right back."

Running into the gas station, I load up on different snacks. I haven't paid much attention to what she enjoys on tour, so I have to take guesses on what food items I'd think she'd like. I grab a couple of water bottles while in there, knowing both of us have had our fair share of caffeine today.

It doesn't take me long to check out at the register. I pile all the items in my hand and walk out, thanking the clerk at the counter over my shoulder.

Lennon is busy looking at her phone when I open one of the backseat doors. I throw the snacks on the seat, keeping two of the waters to put up front with us.

"What's all this?" she asks.

I get into the driver's seat, buckling my seatbelt and putting the car in drive. "Snacks."

She rolls her eyes. "Clearly. What are the snacks for?"

"Our next stop. The last idea I had for our day."

"Are you going to tell me what that idea is?"

"Nope. It's a surprise."

"What if I don't like surprises?" she responds immediately.

My fingers stop tapping against the steering wheel when I glance over at her. "Do you not like surprises?"

She lifts a shoulder. "I don't mind them. I just wanted to know what you'd say."

"If you really hated surprises, I would tell you. But I'm hoping that maybe you don't mind them and you'll let me keep this a secret," I answer honestly. I never want to do something that makes her uncomfortable. If she wasn't a fan of being surprised, I'd tell her what we're doing next, even if it made me a little disappointed because I love to surprise people.

"You can keep it a secret if you promise to tell me one thing."

"Deal."

"Who is Veronica?" Her voice is unsure, and if I'm not mistaken, a little jealous. Veronica would get a kick out of it if she heard it.

"She's an old friend."

"Like *girlfriend*?"

It's my turn to laugh. I shake my head. "Not at all." Veronica has become an unlikely friend over the years, but her personality is not one I'd ever mesh romantically with. She needs someone sweet, who thinks she hung the moon. That was Connor. That's Maverick. "She dated my best friend in high school."

"Landon?" she asks innocently.

I shake my head sadly. Emotion creeps up my throat as I remember Connor. He probably would've cured cancer or done something amazing with his life by my age. "No. I didn't meet Landon until Nash went solo."

She's silent next to me. Her eyes stay focused out the windshield as we navigate the evening LA traffic. I can basically see the gears in her brain turning as she tries to figure out the connections. "Was your best friend the Maverick you mentioned?"

She's got a good memory. I'll give her that. I shake my head at this answer as well. "No, Maverick is her husband, but they didn't meet until college."

"So, who's the best friend? Does he live in LA?"

Her words slice through my heart. Connor would've never lived in LA. He would've found it completely cliché. The Poe he knew, the Poe I was when he was still alive, never would've ended up here either. But through his death, I found music. I found myself here, living a life he'd probably give me shit for. He'd probably be pissed at the way my life has turned out.

"No, he doesn't." My words are clipped. I don't do it on purpose. It just feels odd to discuss Connor with her. My life can be easily sliced down the middle in two parts. On one side, it was the side where Connor was alive. The one where I didn't need music to cope. Then there's the other side. The one that found music through Connor's death. The one that kept me alive when I lost two other people I loved more than life—my parents. It was also the reason the one and only woman I've ever loved left me—she told me I'd never love her more than it. She wasn't completely wrong. How could I love her more than something that has saved my life time and time again?

"Okay," Lennon says, her voice going up an octave at the end. "We don't have to talk about it then."

I'm quiet as we pull up to a man standing in a kiosk. "Here for the single or double feature?" he asks, hanging out the window.

"Double," I answer, pulling out some dollar bills and

handing them to him. Looking at the amount, he opens his cash register and pulls out some money. He licks his finger, counting through the bills in his hand. He tries to hand the change back to me, but I wave at the air. "Keep the change, man."

His eyebrows raise to his hairline, but he doesn't ask any further questions. Putting the change in the tip jar on the ledge outside his window, he smiles. "Thanks, bro. Appreciate it."

He writes something on a piece of paper and hands it over to me. "Just keep this on your dash and you'll be good for both. You'll be at the screen on your far left. The one with the most cars."

"Right, thanks again." I pull the car away, heading in the direction he instructed.

"Are we seeing a movie?"

"Technically, we're seeing *two*."

She bounces up and down in her seat. "I've never been to a drive-in!"

"I haven't either. But it seemed like some shit they'd do in a book, so I figured you'd like it."

Her eyes are bright with excitement when she looks over at me. "Is that your criteria for if I'll like something or not? If it seems like a hero would do it in the book, then I'd be into it?"

I smirk, backing into a parking spot in a far corner at the back of the parking lot. "Basically. Am I wrong?"

She huffs, crossing her arms over her boobs, bringing my gaze right to them for a moment. "No. Hate to break it to you, you'll never be able to compete with a book boyfriend. Fictional men are just built better."

I look at her wide-eyed. "Lennon Mason, challenge fucking accepted." The center console digs into my abdomen as I lean across it to get closer to her. My fingers brush against the soft skin of her neck. Moving her hair to the side, I trace her thumping pulse with the tip of my finger.

"I'd like to remind you of earlier…" I begin. She sucks in a breath, tilting her head to give me better access.

"Okay well maybe that *one* time," she comments. Her eyes shut. Maybe she's replaying the way it felt when I touched her. That's exactly what I'm doing, my mind never will ever be able to forget how soaked she was for me, her little noises as she tried to keep herself quiet in the public space.

"Do your book boyfriends make you feel like this?" I question, marveling at the way her pulse beats against my fingertip.

"Yes," she says under her breath. The position of her head gives me free rein of her beautiful, smooth skin.

"You sure about that?" My lips hover over the spot where her neck meets her shoulder. Licking my lips, I give her skin the smallest taste. My lips come down on the small wet spot left by my tongue. I nibble ever so softly, reveling in the way she moans at even the smallest of gestures.

"Mhm." Her eyelids flutter open and closed.

My mouth comes to a stop next to her ear. I run my nose over the shell. "What a shame," I say, my voice low. "I guess I'll have to stop then."

I peel myself away from her before I can do something stupid like keep going. She hasn't asked me to check anything else off her bucket list. Our entire day is already toeing dangerous territory, considering it was something unplanned, without any knowledge of an item on her list. I had got the idea from one of her books, so I used that excuse to drop by her house unannounced and begin our day together. I'd gone out on a limb at the bookstore, wanting to one-up the stupid fictional man she adored for buying his girl a book. I wanted to do better. When she ground her little hips against me the moment I placed my hands at her waist, I couldn't help myself. Selfishly, I wanted to give her something memorable. I hope every time she walks into a bookstore, she thinks of what I did to her nestled in between the shelves.

The cat cafe and the drive-in were purely excuses for me to spend more time with her. To bask in what it's like to be just us two, before the chaos of the tour potentially disrupts whatever we'd barely started. The great thing about being Nash's bassist is that I'm not recognized out in public often. I can go out in public without being noticed, but once the tour picks back up, once we're with Nash, everything changes.

I'd be more than happy to do something else with her. To be able to taste her, feel her, but I won't touch her again until she's told me it's what she wants. Until she's very clear about what item she wants off her list now.

I leave her to fix her hair in the front seat. I'm quick at grabbing the snacks from the backseat and transferring them to the back. Placing the bags of books in the backseat, I make room for us in the trunk. By the time Lennon leaves the passenger seat, I've got a makeshift seating area for us. The back windshield pops open, allowing me to keep half of the trunk closed while still giving us a good view of the screen. The sound is pretty clear as well, but even if it wasn't, I could tune in to the sound from the radio.

"I can't believe you did all this," Lennon says in awe. It's enchanting to watch her experience life. It's the fact her face can light up with so much joy from something as simple as a makeshift bed in a trunk at a drive-in movie

We spend the next hour tearing open different snacks, only half paying attention to the movie.

In her presence, away from our day-to-day lives, I almost forget all the reasons I'm keeping her at an arm's length.

CHAPTER
29

I DON'T KNOW what it says about me, but this is my first real date. At least what I'd consider to be one, and it isn't even a date. Not for Poe at least.

When I'd hopped from one city to another, roaming from one country to the next, I'd met boys. I'd met men that I'd spend time with. I'd even be intimate with them. But it never felt real. I never felt butterflies with them. There was no excitement, it was something to do to pass the time. It wasn't that I didn't enjoy myself, it was just that in the back of my mind, I knew nothing was going to come out of me spending time with them.

With Poe it feels different even though I know we'll never truly have a real date.

A fake half-date with Poe still seems better than a real date with anyone else.

Poe and I sit in his trunk, doing this weird not snuggling, but it's awfully close thing. The space isn't very large. Our legs press up against one another. I'm able to lean back and stretch my legs all the way out. My toes touch the end of his SUV, but I'm still able to do it. Poe has to have his legs bent at the knee to properly fit. His bent knee rests slightly on top of mine. It's all I can focus on, feeling the way his weight slightly comes down on top of my knee.

I'm biting the head off a gummy bear when he speaks up. His voice is quiet, laced with emotion.

"Connor, my best friend, he died."

My stomach drops. A funny feeling takes over my entire body as sadness washes over me. "What?" I ask. There are so many better things I could say, but that's the first thing that falls from my mouth. I don't know if it's the sad funeral scene that plays that has him telling me this, or if he's continuing our conversation from earlier about his best friend. Either way, it takes me off guard.

He adjusts his position. His arm comes to rest across the backseat. If I leaned back a bit, I'd be leaning into his arm. I'm almost tempted to do so, to find out if he would keep his arm there or move it.

Poe's eyes are sad when he looks at me. "He died when we were still in high school. It was an accidental drowning. Veronica was dating him at the time. She was also there when it happened."

Shock rolls through me. I feel terrible for pestering him with questions about his best friend. "I can't even imagine."

"Yeah." He takes a deep breath. "The two of us had got into a huge argument the morning before it happened. We were supposed to hang out that day, but he wanted to see Veronica instead."

The only thing I think to say is, "I'm sorry." I hate that at the moment I can't think of anything else. I know firsthand how terrible it is to hear people say "I'm sorry" when something traumatic happens to you. Of course you're sorry. Everyone's sorry, but sorry doesn't help the fact that it happened.

"I said awful things to him. About how he wasn't even my friend anymore because he was always choosing her. He'd told me one day I'd understand. I laughed at the comment. I couldn't possibly imagine choosing anyone over him—especially a girl. I'd told him that."

Tentatively, I put my hand on his chest, trying to find a way to comfort him. He doesn't push it away. His large hand falls on top of mine, squeezing my fingers tightly. "We both were angry, unreasonably so, but it doesn't change the fact we were. He told me we didn't have to be friends anymore if I couldn't deal with him having a girlfriend. Riled up, I told him I didn't want to be his friend. We both said some terrible things before I stormed out of his house."

"There's no way you could've known what'd happen."

Emotion wells in his eyes. "That's the thing. When you're a fucking teenager you don't think about the shitty things that can happen in life. You only think about yourself. At the time, I never would have dreamed that something would happen to Connor that night. That I'd have to live the rest of my life knowing the last conversation with my best friend before he died was that I no longer wanted to be his friend because I was stupid and jealous of him having a girlfriend."

His body trembles underneath my hand. It seems to take all of him to not break down at this very moment. Unable to stop myself, I throw one leg over him until I'm essentially straddling him. My knees rest on either side of his hips. Grabbing his face, I force him to look at me. "You can't let that be what you remember of him, Poe."

He leans into my arm. It's maybe the most vulnerable thing I've ever seen him do. "How can I remember anything else? He died before I could tell him I was a stupid fucking kid and didn't mean a thing I'd said."

Shaking my head, I tighten my grip on his cheeks. "I didn't know Connor, but I'm confident when I say he wouldn't want that for you. He would've wanted you to remember all the good times you shared."

He sighs, his breath hot against my face. It's inappropriate for me to think about how bad I want to lean in and kiss him. I wonder which one of the candies he's eaten he'd taste like. "I'm fucked up, Lennon," he says. "It happened so long ago, and I still can't let it go. I can't stop thinking about all the things I'd do differently—all the things I'd say—if I knew my time with my best friend was limited."

"You can't live thinking about the past, dwelling in the what-ifs." I don't miss the irony of my words. It's been years and I still get stuck in the past.

"Easier said than done," he responds sadly.

I can see it happening, see him retreating. He was happy, carefree today. He joked with me more than I'd ever seen. I was used to seeing him act that way around Nash and the band, but he hadn't really been that way around me before. I was used to the more serious Poe. This Poe is completely different. It's closed off, sad. I've always wondered where his pain came from, what had happened in his life to make him the person that he is. Now that I know part of his story, I want to do whatever I can to rinse the pain away.

"Poe?" I ask hesitantly. My hips dip a little lower, allowing my core to rest against him.

He grabs me by the waist instantly. Lifting me up so we no longer touch at the point I want him most. "Lennon, what are you doing?"

I try to press down, but he doesn't let me. His fingertips dig into the small narrow of my hips. He clings on to me so tightly I don't know if he's about to shove me off or pull me roughly against him.

"I know what I want to do next," I whisper, even though there's no need. The people in the parked cars next to us can't hear a word we're saying, or even see us in the privacy of his trunk, but it feels weird to tell him what I want with a raised voice. The only confidence I can muster up is to say it softly, hoping he'll hear me.

He rocks my hips across him once. We barely touch, and my body tingles all over. The anticipation of what could happen next has me aching between the legs. "Anything you want," Poe says, his voice strained. Looking down, I see the muscles in his forearms twitching. It's like he's doing his best to keep a hold on his control.

Even though it makes me nervous to look him in the eye and tell him what I want to happen next, I do it. I want to commit to memory what his face looks like when I say the next words. Maybe it'll give me a clue what he thinks about me, since he won't use his words to say it.

I can see the want in his eyes. The look of want written all over his face coaxes me to keep talking. "I want you to taste me."

Poe throws his head back, resting his head against the back-seat of the car. Groaning, he closes his eyes. "Fuck, Lennon, I don't know if I should." He digs his fingers into my skin. It feels like he'll leave marks. I love how unhinged he's getting, and nothing has even happened yet. "You're too sweet for me."

Getting brave, I let my fingers twist into his hair. It's the first time I've felt his dark, wavy locks between my fingers. I commit the feeling to memory forever. I've always wondered what his hair would feel like.

I yank at it to get him to look at me. "You won't know until you've tried."

It's crazy, being able to physically see the moment a person's resolve begins to bubble over. I've always wondered what it'd be like to drive somebody so crazy that they turn wild around me. Right now, I'm getting to see it firsthand.

"You sure?" Poe asks, leaning closer to me. We're so close that the tips of our noses brush against one another.

I nod. "I've never been so sure."

My comment snaps whatever thin thread of resolve he was still holding on to. He leans in quickly, and I'm soaring high, realizing I'm about to know what his lips feel like against mine. I've dreamt about it so many times, I can't believe it's about to happen. Our lips are a breath away from touching when he lifts me up, bringing my chest right to his mouth.

"These have been taunting me all day." His tongue runs directly over the spot where my dress covers my peaked nipple. I hadn't worn a bra underneath the dress, not feeling the need to. My breasts are small enough that I don't need the support. I knew the dress was modest enough to keep me covered, not revealing myself to anyone in public that I'd skipped the bra.

I'm so thankful I did. I couldn't imagine having another layer between us. I'm upset enough that I have to feel his hot breath through the thin fabric of my dress. I want to feel his tongue up against the sensitive flesh of my nipple.

"I can't wait to see what they taste like." His hands run down my side, sliding down the sides of my thighs until he holds the hem of my dress in his hands. He moves his face from my chest, no longer burying his mouth between my breasts, as he looks at me with confirmation.

I'd be upset about him denying the kiss if I wasn't so turned on. My thin panties are wet, and he's barely even started. "Taste me," I pant, arching my back and rocking my hips against his.

Not needing to be told twice, he hikes the dress up my body. The moment my bare breasts are exposed, he's diving in to taste them. I pull my fingers from his hair long enough to help him get the dress off. The dress discarded somewhere next to us, I'm left in only my small thong. If someone were to walk by, they'd see my naked back. The thought turns me on even more. The thrill of being caught sends shivers down my body.

His lips are soft and sweet against my breasts. He moves back and forth between the two, making sure to balance the attention he gives. Whichever nipple isn't in his mouth is getting individualized attention from his touch.

As good as it feels, I want him to get rough. I want him to

grab it between his teeth and pull. I've read about it countless times. I want to feel it for myself. He's caressing the pink skin with his tongue when I move my hips against his length hard and slow. "You don't have to be gentle," I moan the words out, loving how hard he is underneath me.

Immediately, he's lifting me off him, flipping me over to lie me down across the small space. I have to bend my knees to fit. Poe settles himself between my legs, eyes hot as they travel the length of my body.

"Do you like this, Lennon?" he all but growls. "Do you like being laid out all wet and ready for me when anybody could walk by?"

I try to clench my thighs, but he's in the way. I can't close them, can't hide the evidence of my arousal.

"Yes." My back arches, desperately seeking some sort of contact with him. Poe doesn't make me wait long. His knuckles run up the backs of my thighs as he slowly makes his way up to the sides of my thong.

His index fingers hook into the fabric, pulling it down in one swoop. "If someone were to walk by, they'd see how soaking wet you are."

Before I can try to squeeze my legs together, he splays each one of his palms out over my inner thigh, making sure I'm spread wide open. I could try to fight him, to push my legs together more, but I don't. The way he's looking at my core makes it only wetter.

He trails one finger down the wetness, applying slight pressure to my clit. "Is it me making you this wet? Or is it the possibility of being caught?"

I can barely form words with his finger moving up and down my center. He applies only the slightest pressure, enough to drive me wild and leaving me desperate for more.

His fingertip pushes inside me. "I can't make you feel good if you don't answer me, Lennon."

I try to stifle a moan. "It's both," I force out.

He nods in understanding, his eyes focused on the part between my legs that's soaking wet. "Good girl, telling me what you like. Now tell me, what part of you do you want me to taste?"

CHAPTER
30

HER SWEET LITTLE pussy is dripping wet.

There's a mess between her thighs, and I've barely touched her.

This is going to be fun. Licking my lips, I wait for her to answer.

Her toned thighs fall open, no longer needing my help to stay spread wide open for me. "Here," she pants. My cock threatens to spring free at the sight of her stroking herself up and down, showing me right where she wants me.

My feet hit the side of my SUV as I get into position. I place my hands underneath her ass, lifting her up to bring her square with my mouth. "Is that what you wanted?" I ask, licking along her center once.

Her chin raises to the ceiling as she tilts her head back. Her perky pink tits reach to the sky.

"Lennon," I warn. "If we're going to be ticking things off your bucket list, I need to know exactly what you want."

"I want you to use your tongue to make me come," she pants. Her fingers tangle in my hair as she tries to guide my face between her thighs.

Smiling, I look at her, not letting her press my mouth to her core just yet. "And if someone were to walk by?"

Her hips rock up and down. She's soaked, completely wet, and ready for me to ravish her. I, however, want to drag this moment out. To show her she doesn't need a fucking fictional man, she's got me. She can get her ideas from whoever or whatever the fuck she wants, as long as it's me bringing them to fruition.

"Then they can see. I don't care."

I click my tongue, shaking my head at her. "Sweet, shy, little Lennon. Who would've thought you got off on the idea of others seeing you like this? So puffy, wet and ready to coat my tongue."

She moans. It's so loud it echoes through the entire car. "Now," she breathes.

"Who would've thought you're so bossy?" Not giving her time to respond, I press my tongue to her clit. I lick up and down. She tastes exactly how I'd expect—sweet. Too sweet. I lick it all up, stealing some of the sweetness for myself.

Even if I wanted to, I don't know if I could pull my face from between her thighs. Her fingers fist so tightly through my hair, her grip strong as she holds me to her center.

"God, Poe, I can't." Her words come out breathy, almost strained. She seems to ground herself by holding on to my scalp for dear life. "I feel you everywhere," she pants.

I could come without her even fucking touching me. At the words that fall from her lips. I don't know what it is about her. The contrast of innocence and sultriness to her words. The way she's the sexiest woman I've ever seen, and she doesn't even try to be.

The fingertips of one hand dig into one of her thighs as I hold it open, allowing me access to all of her. My other hand snakes between her legs, helping my mouth to bring her to the brink of a release.

"How's that, pretty girl?" My thumb and finger pinch her clit while my tongue works her up and down.

"I'm close," she moans. The sound is the most beautiful thing I've ever heard.

"That's right," I say against her clit. "Come for me, Lennon. Let everyone hear how good it feels when you lose control."

This sends her over the edge. Her moans ricochet over the small space as she rides out her orgasm against my tongue.

Her body goes lax, her hips staying up only because I still hold her up with one hand. I don't know what beautiful part of her to look at first. I love the fact how you can tell she just came, no matter what part of her you look at. She looks thoroughly fucked, and I haven't even been inside her. Her cheeks are nice and pink. Tendrils of her hair spill all around her face, the thin bow she had earlier no match for her wild hair. Her pink nipples are still hard and peaked, as if they're starving for the attention her pussy just got.

Speaking of...looking between her thighs, I find wetness everywhere. "You've made a mess, pretty girl."

Eyes going wide, she brings her hands over her face to shield her eyes from me. "I'm sorry," she says, her voice full of embarrassment.

The words anger me. In a flash, I'm hovering over her, pulling her fingers from her cheeks once again. "Don't apologize," I demand, furious she even felt the need to do so. "This right here"—I run a finger through a spot of sticky wetness on her inner thigh—"is the sexiest thing I've ever seen. Never, ever apologize for coming so hard, pretty girl. Not with me. Not ever. You hear me?"

Something sparks in her eyes. She nods up and down, biting her lip. "Okay. I hear you." Her voice comes out hushed.

I tenderly move her hair from her forehead. "You should never feel ashamed of that, Lennon." My voice is sadness and anger all wrapped in one.

She averts her eyes. "I know." Her words trail off like she's going to say something else, but nothing ends up coming out.

"So how was it?" I ask, nervous for her answer.

"Better than expected."

My eyes narrow. "I don't know if I should be offended by that answer or if I should be flattered."

"Definitely flattered," she says. Lennon sits up. She grabs her dress from behind her, slipping it on quickly.

I shift, bringing my legs out in front of me in a more comfortable position. My cock protests in my jeans. It strains against my shorts, begging to be let free. Running my palm down it, I try to ease the pain. It's no use. I'm just going to deal with the pain until it calms down, or at least until I'm alone and can get myself off.

My tongue runs over my teeth. I'm trying hard not to smile, to show her how badly I needed to hear that she enjoyed it. It's all I want from this little agreement between us. For her to feel good, for her to be comfortable in her own skin and demand what she wants.

Lennon's eyes are wide when she notices the bulge in my shorts. "Your turn?" she asks softly. I hand over her discarded thong. She finagles it up her thighs quickly, fully dressed once again.

My cock jerks at her question. I shake my head. "This is supposed to be about you, remember?"

She nods immediately, not looking away from the outline of my hard-on. "I remember it's supposed to be about what I want. What I want to learn…"

Without warning, she reaches across the small space and grabs me through the fabric separating us. "And this is what I want."

Her small hand moves up and down my shaft a few times. I almost listen to her. It's hard to think with reason when she's touching me, something I've hated myself for wanting. But right now isn't the time. I'm afraid once we go there, once she touches me, that I won't be able to stop myself. I'll need to figure out what it feels like to bury myself inside her. To get lost in her.

She isn't ready for that. She hasn't asked for it.

Hell, I don't know if I'm ready for it.

It seems like our bodies joining could propel us into something I'm not ready to face.

Even though it kills me to do so, I push her hand away from me. "Not tonight," I say through clenched teeth.

Hurt washes over her face. Her plump bottom lip juts out slightly in a pout. "I just thought since you were, you know"—her eyes flick to my cock—"hard, that you maybe wanted me to touch you—taste you—too.

Groaning, my head falls backward, colliding with the car window with a subtle thud. My thumb and pointer finger pinch the bridge of my nose. "Lennon," I start, trying to figure out a way to say this without coming on too strong. "My cock is throbbing inside my pants right now. Trust me, I want you so fucking bad I'm in physical pain. But there's no rush. We need to ease into it. Check other things off your list first."

"Why?"

She's making it incredibly hard to keep a grip on my lust, the need I feel to pull her on top of me and show her what sex is really supposed to feel like. "Because I want to do right by you. By this. And tonight, I'm afraid I won't be able to stop with just feeling that small hand of yours gripping my cock."

Her mouth forms a little O. My words must stun her because she takes a while to come up with a response. And when she does, all she's able to say is, "Okay."

Not thinking too much into it, I grab her leg and pull her to me. Once she's pressed up against my side, I wrap my arm around her, pulling her in close.

It feels right to have her pressed up against me like this. *Too right.*

CHAPTER
31

"ANYTHING GOOD IN THERE?" A voice I'll never be able to forget says next to my ear. Poe takes the seat next to me.

"You should probably put your seatbelt on," I respond, ignoring his comment.

The change of subject makes his eyes light up. "Lennon, are you worried about my safety?"

Rolling my eyes, I try to find someone else to help me drive my point, but it seems all the other jet occupants are busy doing their own thing. Nora is cuddled into Nash's chest on a nice plush couch I'd never expect to find on a plane. It looks like the two of them may be asleep. Monica sits in a seat all to herself, a pair of headphones covering her ears, clueing us all in that she has no interest in speaking.

Well, most of us have gotten the clue. Aiden has tried to speak to her a few times, but he's been shut down quickly each time.

Landon has a silk eye mask over his eyes. He's the epitome of comfort in his jet seat, his legs propped up and a blanket thrown over his body. He'd flirted tremendously with one of the flight attendants before she brought him out a warm, thick blanket. The fabric appears to be much softer than the thin ones already laid out.

A few other members of Nash's entourage mill about, doing their own thing as we fly from LA to Vancouver. We're kicking off the international leg of the tour in Canada, something I'm pretty excited about.

Traveling has always been something I enjoy, and now I get to spend the next few months going from country to country. I'd be even more excited about it if Poe didn't pretend I barely exist.

At least he had been ignoring me. That was until he surprised me by taking the vacant seat next to mine. Private jet seats are much larger than the ones you find when flying coach. There's enough room to fit two bodies in one seat. Even so, he sits too close to me for someone who's been ignoring me for days.

His elbow is on my armrest, not his. Something that's hard to do because the jet armrests are plush and cozy, totally negating the need to take somebody else's arm space.

It's weird that only a few days ago his mouth was making me feel things I hadn't felt before. Now, it's almost like we're relatively strangers again. We've been busy, but not busy enough to justify why we've barely said two words to each other since that perfect day together.

At least I thought it was perfect. I'm guessing he had other opinions on it.

Poe encroaches on my space even more, leaning across the seat to lightly tap my forehead. "Hello, is Lennon there? Or is she still stuck in that fictional world of hers?

Shoving his hand away, I pin my eyes on him. "No, I'm very much here," I respond. I'd chosen a spot away from everyone else to have some peace and quiet, but even so, I keep my voice hushed just in case someone hears what I'm about to say. "I'm just a little confused about how you haven't said a word to me in days and now you want to talk?"

He runs his hand over his mouth. "I didn't know if you'd want to talk to me."

"What are you talking about? Why wouldn't I?"

"Fuck, I don't know Lennon," he groans out. "I haven't ever been in this type of...situation before."

"Few probably have," I toss back at him. "I can't imagine many people take their sexual fantasies from books and make them reality in an agreement to stay strictly platonic except for the moments we're, you know..." I try to think of a word to describe what we are, but none come to mind.

He laughs. "Yeah, you're right. I have no fucking idea how to proceed with this. I guess once we were around everyone again, I didn't know if you even still wanted to, you know..."

"Have sex with you? Or have you still talk to me after we hooked up?" I say dryly, not in the mood to beat around the bush. Him ignoring me got on my nerves. I don't really feel the need to hold back on how it made me feel.

"Yeah," he says, blowing air out of his mouth. "I guess both."

"The answer is still yes to both, for the record. But don't make this weird." I settle deeper into my seat, pulling my blanket snugly against me. "I thought we were past that."

I thought me pulling the blanket up to my chin and opening my book back up would give him the hint that I'm done with the conversation. I've said what I needed to say. We've seemed to come to an understanding, no more ignoring. But he doesn't move a muscle. Poe stays firmly planted in his seat, looking at me with an unreadable look.

"You're really not going to give me any more shit for it?" he questions. His fingers tap nervously against the armrest—my armrest. He seems anxious for whatever reason.

I place my finger between the pages of my book, shutting it slightly. I look at Poe. "No. You've made it clear where we stand.

I didn't expect much from you. It was just a little whiplash is all."

"I'm sorry."

"No need to apologize. Plus, everyone has been busy with all this label drama," I add.

"That was the most epic show of my life," he says, his voice excited.

It turns out Monica is even more of a badass than I'd originally believed her to be. The entire time we were on the US portion of the tour, she was secretly working on taking out the terrible label owner or Nash's label—Coleman Records. I don't really understand how all of it works, but Nash had signed the rights away to his music out of ignorance. He was young at the time, so was Monica. They had signed the typical contract that most artists were used to. It gave all the power to Coleman Records and not a lot of power to Nash. Monica had set out to change that.

And change that she did.

Things are still getting negotiated and figured out, but Roy Goodman, the previous owner of Coleman Records, has officially stepped down as the head of the label. He can't really run a label from jail. He was arrested the first night of two shows in LA. Turns out, he was a despicable human being taking advantage of young artists at the label. Monica and Aiden shockingly worked together to unearth a ton of dirt on him, bringing to light his blackmailing of artists and some other shady things he was doing with the label's money.

Everything blew up while Nash was on stage performing. Nash told the crowd of what Roy had been doing before performing. He even brought two victims of Roy's on stage to perform with him. It was epic. Nash Pierce knows how to stick it to the man. Everyone watched them in a frenzy, trying to process what they were saying. It was a whirlwind few days afterwards, everyone trying to figure out what the future will look like for Nash's music.

Nora and I had spent a lot of time together, letting everyone else deal with the aftermath as we minded our own business. Yesterday she and I spent the entire day on the couch, watching old reruns of a reality TV show as everyone else had meetings for a majority of the day. It was nice spending time with her. We spent half the time barely paying attention to what was going on as she gave me all the details of her honeymoon.

Well, not *all* the details. There are some things about my sister I didn't need to know.

"The energy was unmatched," Poe continues, finishing his thought from earlier.

"My ears were ringing from how loud the crowd was," I add.

He sits up, excited. "They went fucking insane for Sasha and Chelsea. I've never seen anything like it."

I nod in agreement. "I hadn't either. They're so talented." Both Sasha and Chelsea were women that Roy took advantage of. They'd stood up to him, so he ruined their careers before they even had the chance of taking off. Or he attempted to. Now that the world saw them perform with Nash for two shows, I have a feeling their careers have only just begun.

"So talented. Selfishly, I hope they perform more with Nash in the future. I loved sharing a stage with them." Poe gets this way when he talks about music, at performing. I love it. He always gets this dark, brooding vibe about him. Even when he's smiling and joking with Landon, there's always a slight dark edge to him. Not when he talks about music. Talking about music makes him light up with joy.

I wish the joy would stay on his face forever. Happiness suits him, even if it was the darkness that drew me to him in the first place.

I'm silent so long that Poe switches the subject. He leans in real close, trying to peek down at the book in my lap. "Are you going to show me what you're reading?" He looks at the pen in my hand. "Or what you're writing?"

The way he bites his lip makes me tingle all over. It's such a simple move, yet it's so hot. He's hot enough. Something as plain as biting a lip shouldn't be that freaking sexy.

"Poe," I scold, my eyes darting around the private jet to see if anyone is looking our way. Everyone else is lost in their own world, paying us no mind. If they did look our way, they'd find him hovering over me, his face so close to mine I can feel his breath on my cheek. "We can't talk about that here."

"Why not?"

"Someone may see. They might wonder what we're doing."

Poe glances over his shoulder, a mischievous look in his eyes. "Are we doing something wrong?"

I throw the pen in my lap, using the free hand to tuck my hair behind my ear. "You tell me," I begin. "You're the one who wanted to hide things in the first place."

He sighs. "That doesn't mean we're doing something wrong. But fuck, maybe it does. I shouldn't still be fantasizing about the taste of someone your age, Lennon."

Why does everything he say have to disarm me?

My heart flip-flops in excitement. "Have you been thinking about me?"

His head hits the back of his seat. He closes his eyes for a short moment before opening them back and looking at me with a heated stare. "It seems like that's all I've been doing."

And just like that, everything is forgiven—forgotten. I forget that he spent days ignoring me at the simple mention that he was still thinking about me. It may make me pathetic, but I don't care.

"Really?"

He runs his knuckle over my cheek. The hunger in his eyes has my thighs clenching together underneath the blanket. His gaze flicks to my lips. *"Really,"* he confirms. "I've tried not to, but it was no use. You're in my head, Lennon. I can't get you out of there no matter how hard I try."

His stare doesn't waver from my lips. The brush of his knuckle against my bottom lip makes me shiver. My core tightens when his tongue peeks out to wet his lips, his hungry stare making me desperate for him to claim my mouth with his, no matter if there's people around us or not.

"Don't try," I plead, riding a high knowing he's also been thinking about me.

When he doesn't answer, I press on, not wanting to stop the moment between us. "What were you thinking?"

One corner of his lip pulls up. "Things I shouldn't be thinking about..."

"Like what?"

He trails his knuckle down my neck, over my collarbone, before he lets it brush over my peaked nipple. I'm regretting the thick fabric of my sweater, wishing I could feel more. Even with the thick barrier between us, my nipples harden underneath the small touch. "Like how fucking good you taste," he says, his voice lowered.

"Poe," I moan, the moment his hand snakes underneath the blanket. Looking over his shoulder, I try to see if anyone's noticed us in the corner. I'm hot and bothered, my panties soaked from a few words from his mouth and the soft brush of his touch.

"I've thought about how wet you always are for me." His voice comes out strained, he yanks on the armrest, pushing it up so it no longer separates us. Scooting closer to me, his hand continues its path down my body.

He's inches away from finding out just how true his words are. The backs of my thighs stick to the leather plane seat. The tennis-skirt I threw on this morning gives him easy access to the part of me that wants him most.

His touch is light as a feather as he runs his knuckle along my inner thigh. I look down at us, wondering what it'd look like if someone were to walk by. Luckily, the blanket covers what he's doing, even though I know the flush of my skin would be an instant giveaway if anyone were to catch us.

When he reaches the fabric of my panties, he clicks his tongue. "These have got to go," he comments, hooking his thumb through the fabric on one of my hips. I expect him to slide the fabric over and inch a finger in. He doesn't do that. Instead, he pulls the fabric down my legs, leaving my completely bare underneath my skirt.

"What are you doing?" My voice comes out breathy, my body already missing his touch.

He smirks, looking down at the lilac panties in his grasp. "I'm going to keep these," he growls. We both look at the dark spot on the fabric, knowing what it's from—both aware it's him that made it that way.

"What?" I blurt, shifting underneath the blanket. My entire body feels tight. I feel like a rubber band that's been pulled taut, and I need some kind of relief before I snap.

He maintains eye contact as he stuffs the fabric into his hoodie pocket. "I'll need those when I take care of myself later," he says, his voice husky.

That's freaking hot. I try to stifle a moan, but it's difficult. The picture of him stroking his cock, thinking of me while he holds my panties is enough to bring me to the edge of a release. I love the idea of him having a piece of me, of knowing that for the time being, I drive him crazy enough that he *needs* that piece of me.

"I need you," I all but pant, rolling my hips along the leather seat.

Poe looks over his shoulder with a sly smile. "You sure about that? Anyone could catch us…"

I shake my head back and forth. "They won't," I start, arching my hips. "I really don't care."

He turns to face me once again, his lust-filled eyes pinning me to my seat. "Well, I feel like we *definitely* checked hooking up somewhere we could get caught off your list with the bookstore and the drive-in, but I'm happy to do it again."

I rub my lips together, trying to fight a smile. "We're just being thorough."

Shaking his head, he slides his hand up my leg once again, except this time he's not slow about it. He doesn't taunt me. His fingers are brushing against my swollen, wet core before I can think twice about it. The speed of which he enters one finger into me makes me wonder if he needs this as much as I do.

When another finger joins in, stretching me, I'm unable to hide the moan. It erupts from deep in my throat, the pleasure too much.

"I know it's hard, but you've got to be quiet, Len." The gentle but firm tone of his voice does the opposite of what he's asking me to do. It urges me to moan deeper, longer, while his fingers work in and out of me.

"Fuck," he curses, cupping his free hand over my cheek. "All I can think about is forcing you to be quiet by trapping your mouth with mine."

"Then do it," I moan.

His head shakes. "No, Lennon. When I kiss you, it'll be my undoing. I'm not doing it in some corner of a jet with one of our friends able to catch us. If—*when*—I kiss you, my fucking resolve will be gone, and I don't want to have to restrain myself. I'm afraid I'll never be able to stop. So, pretty girl, I can't kiss you, not now. We're going to have to find another way to keep you quiet."

The thought of kissing him, of knowing he wants it, has an orgasm building. The pressure builds in my core. I'm so close to coming when I feel a weight on my chest. My eyes flutter open, finding my book from earlier being slid up my chest.

Poe flips the hardback over, facing the spine toward me. "Bite down on this to keep quiet." He coaxes it into my mouth. I follow his direction, knowing any moment the orgasm is going to overtake my body.

My teeth press into the cover as his fingers throw me over the edge. My jaw clamps down hard on it, my hips bucking underneath the blanket as I ride the waves of an orgasm.

His fingers don't relent until my entire body relaxes. My eyes pop open. Poe stares at me intently, his teeth raking over his bottom lip punishingly. His fingers slide out of me, but he doesn't move his hand all the way. It stays placed on my thigh in a tender gesture. "Hope you didn't want to keep that book," he comments, using his other hand to pull the book from my mouth.

My chest heaves up and down as I attempt to regain my composure. "Why?" I look at the book in his hands, noticing the indentions from my teeth.

"Because that was the hottest fucking thing I've seen, and I'm keeping this book to remember it forever."

My jaw hangs open. He smiles at me, amused. His fingers squeeze my thigh before he pulls his hand from underneath the blanket, now grasping the book with both hands. "Now, Lennon, there's a reason I came over here in the first place. And no matter how fucking turned on I am right now, it wasn't actually to have you come all over my fingers. Even though that was a god damn *excellent* surprise."

I sit up in the seat, already wondering how I'm going to make it the rest of this flight without any panties in the short skirt. My wetness rubs up against the leather with the movement, not letting me forget what Poe and I just did even if I wanted to.

"Then what'd you come over for?"

He smirks, running a finger over my bite-marks on the cover of the book. "So, there's somewhere I want to take you…"

CHAPTER
32

STEPPING OUT OF THE CAR, I look at the building in awe. The entire roof is made of glass windows. It slopes and arches in different places. I can't wait to see what it looks like inside. After days of traveling, I'm excited to finally get to explore a new city abroad.

Poe drapes his arm over my shoulders, pulling me into his side. "You ready?"

My head nods excitedly. I was more than ready to go inside to see all the beautiful butterflies and flowers. The day we went to the bookstore together is one of my favorite days ever. But something about today—in this place —feels different. We haven't even stepped foot into the conservatory, and I already know this will not only be my favorite day with him; it might end up being my favorite day ever.

It's even more special because he planned it. He searched for places he thought I'd like along our tour path. The sentiment isn't lost on me.

There's a line to buy tickets at a counter. We join it, standing behind a mom and dad with their two kids. A little girl who can't be older than three looks back at us.

"Are you going to see the butterflies?" she asks. There's a large butterfly barrette in her hair. It's almost as big as her face.

I nod, smiling softly at her. "We are."

She smiles wide, her chubby cheeks lighting up with excitement. "I've been wanting to see them for years." The little girl emphasizes years dramatically.

Her mom smiles at us, an apologetic look on her face. "It's really only been a few months. She saw the conservatory on a show she was watching. She's been begging to visit ever since."

Poe looks at me, a smile on his face. "Lennon here has been wanting to see the butterflies, too," he tells the little girl. The sweet tone he takes while talking to her makes my heart melt. "We couldn't visit and not come see them."

Crouching down to get on her level. "I love your barrette."

She reaches up to touch it. "Thank you," she says proudly. "My Grammie got it for me. She loves butterflies like me."

My eyebrows rise. "Does she?"

The mom grabs the little girl by her hand, ushering her gently forward as the line gets closer to the window. Once we're all stopped again, the little girl returns to facing us. "She does. Did you know there's over twenty butterflies here?" She says it so confidently, it's the cutest thing ever.

"Really?" I gasp, feigning surprise. From what I read online on the way over, there's more than two-thousand butterflies at this specific conservatory.

"I had no idea," Poe says, feigning shock just like me.

We share a knowing look. I'd spent the entire ride here firing off different facts about the butterfly garden to him. He probably knows more about the place than the average person just because I had to tell him everything about it.

The little girl's head nods up and down. "Oh yes," she confirms, her tone very serious. "So many butterflies. And we're going to see them all!" Her chubby little hands clap together.

"We're next," the dad says, looking lovingly down at his

daughter. He's got a baby strapped to his chest in some kind of contraption that holds the infant snug against his chest. The chubby-cheeked baby naps softly on her father's chest, completely oblivious to her sibling's joy at visiting the garden.

We exchange our goodbyes with the family before it's their turn to pay. I promise to say hi to the little girl if we see her inside. My guess is the moment she gets in there, the butterflies and overall scenery will make her completely forget about the strangers she met in line.

Her joy was what I needed before stepping into the conservatory. Her excitement was infectious. I was already excited —*thrilled*—to be here today, and after meeting her, she has me eager to get to the good stuff.

I'm tempted to pull Poe by the hand inside. I fight the urge, keeping a respectable restraint on myself.

To get into the butterfly portion of the conservatory you have to step through a door that leads to a small room. There's a sign on the door, requesting people refrain from opening the door to the butterfly garden if the door leading to the conservatory is open. I bet it's in place to make sure that the butterflies stay in the closed off area.

There's also more protection in place when you step through the butterfly garden door. Thin, net-like material covers the doorway, adding another layer of safety to keep the butterflies in.

I'm able to reign in my excitement until we take a few steps inside. Then, I mimic the joy of the little girl from earlier as I jump up and down. No matter where I look, the view is stunning.

Light pours in from the windows at the top. It's warmer here than it was outside, but I love it. The hot, sticky air makes my dress cling to my skin. Everywhere we look, there's lush, green foliage and flowers. Even the sound of the garden is beautiful. It sounds like running water and pure joy. People walk around, but they're quiet, furthering the calm ambiance the garden has going.

And then there's the butterflies.

From where we stand at the entrance, I can only see a few in the distance, but I'm already in love.

Poe takes charge, reaching down to grab my hand. Pulling on it, he smiles. "Let's go."

I follow his lead, not knowing where to look first. He pulls me down a narrow pathway, deeper into luscious green leaves. A family walks past us in the opposite direction, pushing a stroller that seems to be as big as a car. We smile at each other and keep on going.

"I can't believe this," I say to Poe, looking at our surroundings in awe. Once we're tucked deep into the space, nobody in sight, we stop.

There's a small little pond to our left, surrounded in beautiful bright colors. Stepping closer, I find one of the most beautiful butterflies I've ever seen. Its wings are giant. I've never seen a hue like its bright, blue wings. It opens and closes its wings as it rests on a pink flower.

Smiling, I look at Poe. "I can't believe how big it is," I mutter, crouching down to get a better look at it. I don't get too close. I stay far enough away from it to take in its beauty without startling it.

A few moments pass by as I stare at it in wonder before I look back at Poe. He doesn't look at the butterfly, he's looking at me.

My stomach drops. The look on his face is one that could bring me to my knees if I wasn't already on them. The look could trick my mind enough to make me think that he may actually feel something for me.

Just maybe…

"What're you looking at?" I ask, gaining enough confidence to ask the question out loud.

The corners of his lips lift slightly. "You." He isn't shy about his answer.

There goes my stomach again.

"What about me?" I ask, standing to face him. If it were up to me, I'd take the few steps and mold our bodies against one another. I've felt his mouth on the most intimate parts of me, but that's not where I want him most.

I want to taste him against my lips.

I want to know what he tastes like.

I want to know how he kisses.

Mostly, I just want to kiss him and never stop.

My mind flashes with his words from the plane. *When I kiss you, it'll be my undoing.* I'm ready for it. I want him to be as unwound and undone as I am.

"Just you," he answers simply. He takes a step toward me, so I take another step toward him.

"I need more details than that."

"I was just thinking…"

Just then, a butterfly lands on me. It's the same butterfly from before, it's bright blue wings right in front of my face. It finds a perfect home on my nose. I don't know what to do. I don't want to move, to do anything to get the butterfly to fly away.

Poe and I both stare at it. The biggest smile overtakes my face. I'm getting a butterfly kiss. I've read about them. They're supposed to mean good luck. They're supposed to represent a new beginning.

Looking across to Poe, I wonder if maybe this is some kind of sign. Maybe whatever we're doing, even when it does end with him inevitably breaking my heart one day, is a new beginning for me.

"Hey Lennon?" he says. His tone is serious. "Can I tell you what I'm thinking?"

The butterfly leaves my nose, fluttering away to land on a

nearby flower. "Yes?" I ask. My voice is breathy because of the way he's looking at me.

"I'm thinking that I've lost all sense of control when it comes to you. My resolve is gone, and I don't care about getting it back. Not now, not here." He pauses, swallowing hard. "What if I wanted to do something that wasn't on your list?" His voice breaks at the end.

Please kiss me. I want his words from the jet to ring true. I want him to kiss me and never stop.

"Like what?" My heart thumps so erratically against my chest I'm worried it might beat right out of me. I've looked at him so many times, but never have I seen him looking at me. Not in this way, not with such want—*need* in his eyes.

"This," he says, barely a whisper. He catapults his body through the distance between us.

His lips plaster against mine in a way that'll be burned on my soul forever.

I'm actually kissing Poe. I've dreamed about kissing him more times than I'd ever care to admit. None of them could even begin to compare.

This is way better. *So* much better.

His lips delicately trace my bottom one. He doesn't even have to ask. My mouth opens for his, letting his tongue tangle with mine. Unlike the way the kiss began, the kiss is now tender, slow. My hands fist in his hair, pulling him against me like I need him to breathe.

His fingers dig into my sides, fisting into the soft cotton of my dress. There's air on my thighs there wasn't before from where he's hiked up my dress. I'm thinking about climbing up his body just to give myself more leverage, to feel him everywhere.

We could never do another thing on the list again and I'd be happy. As long as it meant he'd kiss me like this, I'd do whatever. Feeling his lips against mine, tasting him; it's not something I ever thought I'd get to experience.

Especially with the primal need he shows right now. It's been no secret how bad I want him, that it almost feels like I need him, but never once have I been sure that he feels the same way about me.

Until now.

Throughout the weirdness of our relationship, I've wondered if he's felt more about me than he was willing to let on. But sometimes I wondered if that was my hope getting in the way. My naïve brain playing tricks on me. It was almost like I could want him enough for the both of us. There were moments, like in the bookstore and on the plane, that I'd had hope. His small comments making my heart soar. Other times, I felt like I really was still the girl that had a crush on him, but the girl he didn't care about at all.

Right now, it doesn't feel like that at all.

He kisses me like his life depends on it. I kiss him back with the same ferocity.

Ripping his mouth from mine, he peppers kisses down my jaw, over my cheek. "I've thought way too much about what it would be like to kiss you, Lennon," he confesses.

His hands go down the fabric of my dress, over the hemline and then underneath it. We'd totally get kicked out if someone walked up to us right now. His hands are underneath my dress, palming the tender flesh of my bottom. I kiss down his neck, tempted to bite and suck so I can leave my mark on him.

I've never thought I'd want to give a hickey. It seems childish and unnecessary, but right now I want to do just that. I want to leave some kind of mark on him so when we meet up with everyone else, going back to our normal tour life, there'll be some sort of proof this happened.

"It's all I've ever thought about," I admit, not feeling the least bit embarrassed by it. The great thing about everyone knowing you have a crush on someone is that the constant reminders make you less and less embarrassed by it. My feelings for him have been pointed out so many different times that I'm no longer ashamed of it.

And now that I've seen this desperate want in his eyes, I'm not afraid to admit it to him either.

One of Poe's hands stays underneath my dress, digging into the curve of my ass. The other snakes up my side and finds my jaw. His hands are so tender cupping my cheek. If he wasn't holding me, I swear I'd melt from it.

"This wasn't on your list," he notes, coming in to kiss me again.

I bask in the taste of him, my tongue swiping across his lip. "You don't know that," I say, our lips barely apart.

His eyebrows raise. He rests his forehead against mine. His lips shine from my lip gloss. "Is it bad I don't want it to be?"

I look up at him, confused. Pulling my hands from his hair, I rest them behind his neck. "What do you mean?"

He looks down at the ground for a moment before looking at me once again. There's a bashful look in his eye. If I didn't know any better, he might actually be shy. "I don't want that kiss to be something you just tick off a list. It seemed too…" he tilts his head, trying to think of a word. "It seemed too *altering* to just be something completed off a list."

My heart is his. If I really think about it, I think my heart has been his for longer than I'd realized.

CHAPTER
33

THERE ARE times in your life when it's impossible to think with your head. You have to think with your heart.

This is one of those times.

I knew it wasn't a good idea to kiss Lennon, but I didn't care. Desperation took over me. I had to know what she tasted like. I didn't want to do it as some experiment to help her learn what she likes. I wanted to kiss her because the thought of not kissing her was driving me fucking insane.

She tasted like candy. I don't know if I'll ever get enough of it.

When we'd decided to go to the observatory, I hadn't expected things to take this kind of turn. I'd just wanted her to have a good day. She'd talked about how much she loved butter-flies when talking about her dream bookstore. When I heard this is one of the best butterfly gardens in the world, we couldn't not go. She needed to see it, experience it. There was no way in hell I was going to miss her reaction to it.

Her reaction was worth everything and more.

The thought of making today the day I finally kissed her had crossed my mind before we'd ever made it into the place. It may have been her excitement that seeped out of her the entire car ride. It may have been the way she talked to that little girl in line, her voice tender and affectionate. To be honest, it's been in the back of my mind from the moment she told me about her dream to own a bookstore. Maybe even sooner if I'm honest with myself.

Her tiny fingers grip the back of my neck, sealing my mouth against hers. She holds me against her mouth like she's trying to keep me forever. If only she knew I never want to leave this spot. I never want to stop tasting her.

I'd meant it when I'd told her I was afraid to kiss her because I don't think I'd ever be able to stop.

Lennon pulls away slightly, looking up at me with the most stunning smile that it takes my breath away. There's a pink tinge to her cheeks that wasn't there before. Her lips are red and puffy, looking like they need to be kissed again.

"I love it when you go rogue," she comments. Her teeth dig into her swollen bottom lip as she tries to fight a smile.

She'd never believe me if I told her it, but she's the most compelling woman I've ever met. She's beautiful inside and out, completely unaware of the effect she has on me—on everyone.

Tucking her hair behind her ear, I can't help but smile back. "Me too," I agree.

"Maybe you should do it more often." Her eyes look at me with so much hope. The way she's looking at me right now almost has me believing I could be better for her.

"Don't tempt me." I groan, molding her body into mine. I want her as near as possible. Maybe her optimism will rub off on me. If I keep her close long enough, maybe I'll break every rule I've set for myself for her.

"I want to do that again," she says, her voice full of wonder.

"I'll give you anything you want," I respond, diving in for another kiss. It's a lie, there's one thing I can't give her. It's the thing she probably wants most—me. Not in the capacity she wants at least. For right now, I pretend that's not the case. I trick my mind into thinking I won't ruin things.

Kissing her is like stepping into the sun after a week of rainy days. Her warmth radiates around me, seeping into your soul. Her mouth pressed against mine, it's hard to remember there's ever been a time in my life I was ever unhappy.

Time passes slowly with our mouths pressed against one another. We take our time tasting the other, biting and sucking, relishing the feel of something we both have been desperate for. In the back of my mind, I hope the kiss is better than any man that's ever kissed her before.

I know it'll be a kiss that's etched on my mind, heart, body, and soul forever.

We finally break apart, but not by far. I still cup her face, not wanting to let go and miss the thumping pulse against my fingertips. It's addicting, feeling the effect I have on her against the tips of my fingers. She's been upfront about her feelings from the start, but I've always wondered if the real me could compete with the version of me in her head.

I must come close, at least in the moment, because her pulse is strong and wild. It's quite possible I'm addicted to the feel of it.

"Feel free to forget about the list whenever you want," she teases, standing on her tiptoes to kiss my cheek.

She's the first to break contact, stepping away, she pulls at the hem of her dress. Forgetting where we were, I'd stuck my hands underneath it, unable to control myself. I'm losing my mind more and more around her. If only she knew how crazy she drove me, how much I lose the restraint I've kept on myself for years the moment she steps into the room.

"What have we talked about?" I ask her, shoving my hands in my pocket before I pull her into me again.

Her head cocks to the side, her face confused.

I smirk. "This isn't about me, it's about *you*."

She shakes her head. "Trust me, that was exactly what I wanted. I think the butterfly knew it." Lennon looks past me, to the long pathway surrounded in greenery and bright plants. Following her eyeline, I see the blue butterfly that'd landed on her nose earlier, or at least one that looks just like it.

"The butterfly?"

She's running her finger over the giant leaf of a plant when she answers. Her long, curly hair runs all the way down her back, the ends landing at her hips. "Yeah, the butterfly. When one lands on you, it means good luck. A fresh start."

"What did that have to do with me kissing you?"

Looking over her shoulder, she makes a face, as if the answer was obvious. "Because I've wanted to kiss you since the moment I first saw you chew your lip. It was only a few minutes after I first saw you. You can say I was a goner early."

Her honesty stuns me. I didn't realize she'd thought about me like that so early. It hurts to know that at the same time she was having all these thoughts, I probably hadn't even realized she was there.

She trails her hand down a rock wall, walking deeper down the path. I follow her lead, falling in line next to her. "I'm still not following what the butterfly has to do with it?" I confess.

"Oh easy."

"How so?"

"You kissed me."

"I see," I say, finally catching on. My hand runs over my mouth as I try to hide my smile at her words. In front of us, there's a huge bush. It reaches way over my head. All over it, there's small yellow and white flowers. Whatever the flowers are, it must be popular with butterflies because they're everywhere.

Lennon doesn't seem to hear me. She's too stunned looking at the various colors of butterflies swarming around us. They go from flower to flower, sometimes landing together to form a rainbow of butterfly wings. "It's breathtaking," she muses, eyes wide as she takes them all in.

"You're breathtaking," I say under my breath. If she hears me, I can't tell. Her eyes stay trained on the bush.

I've never given a shit about butterflies. I had nothing against them; they were just something I never noticed. Now I stare at her, wondering how I can keep this look of awe on her face. I will track down every damn butterfly garden if it means I can see her joy over and over again.

Plus, she isn't wrong. The butterflies are a sight to see. I had no idea they came in so many shapes and sizes. But the most beautiful thing about the moment is Lennon. My chest feels heavy as I watch her. It feels like I can't breathe. It's true, she's absolutely breathtaking.

It's weird, knowing all these things I didn't really think twice about until I met Lennon. Books. Annotations. Butterflies.

Her.

The thought douses me in hurt. I don't know how she could care about me so deeply when I barely knew her. The thought makes my stomach twist and turn in pain. I hate that I didn't notice her the moment she noticed me. She doesn't deserve that at all.

It's like she's forgotten I'm even here. She pays close attention to every butterfly that flies near her. She looks at them so intently it's like she's committing each color and pattern to memory. Maybe she is. I hope in the moments where things are hard for her, she can think back to right now. The thousands of dollars I've spent in intensive therapy have taught me that everyone needs a bank of happy memories to get through the hard days.

When my therapist had first suggested it, I felt pathetic. It was early in my bass career, right before I'd met Nash and a group of teeny bopper boy band members. I'd tragically just lost both my mom and stepdad when I hadn't even healed from the pain of losing my childhood best friend. The therapist had suggested I should think of a happy memory on the days I didn't want to get out of bed. I needed to give myself a reason to keep going. He hadn't known I didn't really have anything.

I'd lost my best friend. He'd died knowing the last thing I ever said to him was how I didn't want to be his friend. I'd fallen out of touch with the other. Then I lost my parents, the only other people on this planet I loved. It felt like any person I loved was bound to die. Remembering them was too hard, so he'd said think of a happy memory that didn't involve them to begin with.

It was a shame there weren't really any. The only thing I could think of were times I was up on stage, playing music. I ran with it, using the high of a crowd cheering for you to get me through my early twenties. Eventually, I became close with Landon and Nash and felt like I had people I cared about again. But I've never felt as intensely happy as I do right now, at this moment, watching Lennon feel the joy of butterflies.

I wish I could bottle this moment forever. The way her green eyes are bright with joy, the corners of her eyes crinkle with her wide smile. Her lips are still red and puffy from our kiss earlier. The moment they're no longer like that, I tell myself I'll have to kiss her again, my mission to keep her lips swollen red like that for the rest of eternity. She pushes her hair back, making sure the untamed tendrils don't block her view. In this place, no one from our real life with us, butterflies swarming around us, I can almost see a future together.

Almost.

Finally, she turns to me, happiness all over her face.

"Are you seeing this?" she asks, holding her finger out in front of the bush. It doesn't take long for a butterfly to land on her finger. She squeals in excitement when another one lands right next to it.

Fuck, it's the best thing I've ever heard.

"I'm seeing this," I tell her, knowing we aren't talking about the same thing.

She's marveling at the butterflies. I'm marveling at her.

Her entire body freezes the entire time the butterflies rest on her. Eventually, they fly away. For a short moment, she looks sad to lose them. A slight frown comes over her face. It disappears almost immediately as she looks at them once again.

"Lennon?" I say, keeping my voice steady.

When she turns around, she's still smiling. Two perfect dimples hollow out her cheeks. I make the mental note to kiss them, wanting to memorize the feel of them against my lips.

"What's up?"

"You're my butterfly."

CHAPTER
34

"WHAT DOES THAT MEAN?" I ask, replaying his words over and over to make sense of them.

"It means you're my butterfly, my good luck. Butterflies make you happy. They bring you so much joy. The way you look at butterflies is the way I look at you."

My mind races with his words. I don't even know how to process it. What to process first.

To me, this almost feels like him telling me he has feelings for me. Maybe it's his way of saying it. Or maybe it isn't. Maybe it's just a simple confession that I'm not supposed to read into. But I can't help it. It's all I can think about now.

You're my butterfly.

How am I supposed to breathe when he says things like this?

My pulse is so high I can hear it thrumming in my ears, the quiet of the observatory making it easy to focus on the racing heartbeat.

"Poe, you can't say things like that." My voice quakes.

"I already did." If he regrets it, you'd never know. His voice is steady, confident.

"Kiss me again," I demand. "Kiss me again and again and

don't ever stop it." Grabbing his shirt, I pull him into me, stealing whatever he was about to say.

He's ready for it. His tongue is eager against mine.

There might be a million moments in my life that define me, that brought me happiness. He told me I bring him the same joy that the butterflies do, but what he doesn't know is that the elation I feel is because of him. Because I'm here with him, I can be so happy with the butterflies.

If I was with anyone else, it wouldn't be the same. I'd love it and find it beautiful, but it's knowing that he found this place and took me here because he knew I loved them that brought happiness to my heart.

This man has no idea what he's doing to me, what he's making me feel. He warned me not to fall for him. He told me he'd never feel the same. But would it really be that bad? With our lips pressed together, I wonder if it wouldn't be so bad to know I feel more for him if I just knew he felt *something*.

It's not the first time he's made me think this way. He makes me unreasonable for his attention. I know that Poe will never voice how he feels for me, but at this point, he doesn't have to. At this point, he says it with his actions, not his words.

It's in the way he claims my mouth with his, erasing the memory of any other person I've ever kissed.

It's in how without even knowing it, he does things that make my heart melt. Planning a date to a bookstore, buying the books without me knowing. How he latched onto the fact I wanted to have a butterfly garden and took me here, the most beautiful place I've ever been. I'd forgotten I'd even mentioned butterflies, it was only a small detail in my plans to have a bookstore.

I don't think he even realizes what he's doing. If he did, I'm scared he'd stop. There's no way he realizes that all the little things he's done for me have piled up. I've fallen for him, and there's no going back. He could try and talk me out of it and it wouldn't work.

It's too late.

Poe quietly scratched his name on my heart from the moment I met him. Now, he's gone back and carved over the letters, making sure they last forever. Eventually, I know they'll just be a scar when he stops whatever we have going on, but I'll bear the scars proudly.

It'll be proof it happened. That for a short period of time, he cared enough about me to do it.

I miss his lips the moment he pulls away. He nips at my neck gently. Groaning he says, "Lennon, we shouldn't be doing this."

My fingers dig into his forearms, keeping his hands pinned on my hips. "That's your rule, not mine."

His whole body shakes with another groan. I clasp my hand to his mouth before he can say anything else. "Don't," I beg, applying pressure. "Don't say it. Don't ruin this moment for me. For *us*."

His face softens. He looks at me sadly and I hate it. I wish he'd allow himself this—allow himself to feel happy. His body, his heart, says what his words never will. He wants this, same as I, but his stupid head won't allow him.

"Today, we're happy." My hand doesn't move from his mouth as I get out what I want. People may pass by us, I wouldn't know. I refuse to look away from him, refuse to break the moment. I need to get these words out as bad as I need to kiss him. "Today, you're going to tell your mind to shut up. I'm done hearing all the reasons this can't work. Today, it's just Lennon and Poe."

"And tomorrow?" he protests, his words muffled against my hand. He playfully bites at my fingers, making me giggle.

"We'll figure it out when we get there."

I keep my hand over his mouth for a bit longer, making sure he doesn't say anything else to ruin the moment. I give him a cautionary look as I pull my hand away. As soon as it's removed, he's leaning down and kissing me tenderly.

I don't know what's better. The wild and crazed kiss from earlier when he almost came unhinged from tasting my lips or this calm and collected kiss. He's deliberate, thinking through each swipe of his tongue against mine.

"I'll give you today, butterfly," Poe says, his lips moving against mine.

My nose scrunches. "Butterfly?"

He kisses the tip, pulling away from me. Our bodies never break contact. He moves effortlessly from holding me to holding my hand. "Yes, *butterfly*." He squeezes my hand. I happily allow him to guide me a few steps closer to the honeysuckle plant. "I told you, you're my butterfly. The name fits."

This man.

I feel like one of those balloons they hand kids at the fair. The only thing grounding me is Poe holding my hand, much like the thin string they tie at the end of the balloons. If he wasn't keeping me here, I may just float away from the elation I feel in my bones. I feel weightless, soaring high on the rush of having him at this moment.

I don't dare try to think of the disappointment I'll feel tomorrow or the next day. He's bound to come back to his senses. His walls will come back, maybe even stronger, when he realizes he's allowed himself to be happy. He'll make sure he lectures me on all the reasons I shouldn't want him, even though I've told him I won't listen. No amount of lectures in the world could make me stop loving him. It'd make it easier if that wasn't the case, but that doesn't make it less real.

The aroma of honeysuckle is overwhelming as we stop in front of the bush. I'd read before that butterfly's love honey-suckle, and it must be true because there must be a hundred butterflies on this plant alone. We both stand and stare at it. I rest my head on his shoulder, taking in the moment, knowing it'll be one I never forget.

Sighing, I hold his hand even tighter. "I like the name."

"Good"—he squeezes my hand right back—"because that's what I'm going to call you."

I pull on his hand, wanting to keep exploring the beauty of the butterfly garden. I feel like we've barely explored, and I've already been amazed at the beauty.

"That was on my list, you know," I say to him as we walk down a stone path. The path gets wider with each step we take, taking us into the more populated area.

"What was?"

"Getting a pet name that's meant for me and me alone from a boy I like."

This makes him laugh. He runs the hand not holding mine through his hair, tousling the strands even more. "I'm not a boy, butterfly."

I remember the skill he had between my legs not too long ago. The way his tongue worked against me was enough to prove he's right. He's not a boy, he's a man who knows what he's doing. I hope I get another chance to feel him against me again. Before this ends I want to know what he feels like inside me.

Stopping us, he pushes my body until we're tucked behind the leaves of a large tree. "The look on your face makes me wonder if you're thinking of the times I've shown you that I'm no boy. I'm a man, someone who knows exactly what to do with that little body of yours to make you feel good."

I have to clench my thighs together. I've never had someone speak so dirty to me. No one's ever had the power to make me so wet just by words. If he tried hard enough, I bet I could come without him ever having to touch me—or me having to touch myself.

"I know," I whisper. Our hands are still intertwined. Guiding our linked hands, I let them run over the length of him, marveling at how hard he is.

"God damn, butterfly," he grunts. "You can't do that here. Not with people around."

"I wish they weren't here," I tell him, letting my knuckles rub over him one more time.

He jerks his hips away, no longer allowing them close enough to our hands for me to repeat the movement. "Fuck, I wish they weren't here, too. I'd love to take you right here, with your fucking butterflies all around us."

My breasts feel heavy. If he were to look down, he'd find my nipples trying to break through my cotton dress.

"Poe," I moan, needing to feel him.

He takes the hint. I try to keep pace with his large steps as he pulls on my hand. We weave in and out of the pathways. It seems like he's pulling me to one of the corners of the observatory. The deeper we get into the lush greenery, the darker it gets. The large leaves let less and less light in.

Finally, we end up in a small corner that is desolate. There's a small hut. He yanks at the door handle, letting out a relieved breath when he finds it unlocked.

The door shakes on its hinges as he rips it open. Before I can step through it, wondering where he's taken us, he's lifting me by my hips. It's crazy how much our bodies can talk without our mouths ever having to say a word. He says nothing to me, but I know to wrap my legs around his middle, sealing my mouth to his again.

He kicks the door closed, his hands kneading my ass. At first, I'm too lost in kissing him to look at where we are. He places me on a wood surface, pulling away long enough to hike my dress up. With our mouths not being fused for the first time, I take a moment to look around to see where we are.

It seems like we're in some sort of garden shed. There's an entire wall of small shovels, gloves, and other gardening tools.

There's also a corner with a wheelbarrow filled to the brim with soil. This must be where they keep some supplies to take care of the plants in the butterfly garden.

Lucky for us, there's no one here. The door is dinky and doesn't appear to have any kind of lock, but at the moment, I don't care at all. Hopefully, no one happens upon us. It's the weekend, my guess is maybe the upkeep takes place over the weekdays.

Or we just lucked out, finding it at a time it wasn't in use.

The wood is rough against the backs of my thighs. The workbench is tall, my head taller than Poe for once. He tries to lift the dress over my head, but I shake my head. I allow myself to make out with him for one moment longer before I push him away slightly.

"No," I demand, my chest heaving. I reach between us, grabbing him through the coarse fabric of his jeans.

"It's my turn."

CHAPTER
35

WE SHOULDN'T BE DOING this.

Lennon's small fingers work at my zipper, attempting to free me. If she didn't look so bound and determined to free my cock, I might be a better person and stop this before it begins. Except, I don't want to hurt her. I don't want her to think that I don't want this—*need* this. I'm desperate for it. Probably more desperate than her. After every time we've been together recently, I've gone home and jacked myself to the thought of her. My mind would race with all the little sounds she makes, how her whole body comes undone when she comes.

There are so many subtle things about her that make her incredibly sexy. It hasn't been hard to get myself off, remembering everything she did when I've watched her come.

She finally gets the fly of my jeans undone. It doesn't take her long to shove them down my hips, pulling at the waistband of my boxer briefs with the movement. "I want to feel you," she says, staring at my cock in awe.

Fuck. If she keeps looking at it like that I may just let her have her way.

Her fingers run the length of it timidly.

She looks to me for confirmation. The look is my undoing. I

can't tell her no. I need to give her this. I need her to know how wild she makes me.

"This was also on my list." Her voice is low, but confident.

"Oh was it, butterfly?" My jaw clenches, wondering how long I'll be able to last, when she wraps her small hand around my length. Her fingers barely touch wrapped around my shaft.

Her teeth dig into her bottom lip, discoloring the skin around her teeth. She nods enthusiastically up and down. "I've never…" her words trail.

My head snaps to her, lifting her by the chin to force her to look at me. "You've never what?"

Even though her jaw is gripped tightly in my fingers, her eyes look down at the place our bodies are connected. They focus on her hand as she's brave enough to move up and down my length once. "I've never touched a man," she answers, not looking me in the eye. "Not really. Not for long. Never long enough to…"

"To come?" I finish, already envisioning what my cum would look like sticking to her fingers.

Her body shakes as she exhales. Her hand picks up speed, finding a rhythm that drives me wild. "Yes," she finally answers. Her voice is tight.

"Fuck, Lennon," I groan, so close to coming. It's never been this easy, but I've never been this turned on. It seems like I've become a puddle at this woman's feet, and this part is no different.

"Am I doing okay?" she asks, her voice timid.

I run my palm up her spine, over her shoulders, ending at cupping her cheek. "I need you to listen to me right now," I demand, trying to keep my voice level as I get closer and closer to releasing. "You could never not do okay. Not with me, butterfly. A simple look from you has me as hard as a rock."

Her hand stills on me for a moment, my words stunning her.

"You got that?" I ask through clenched teeth. Her hand's

picked up pace again, and now she's begun to spin her hand a little, too. It'll be no time before I'm coming. I can't hold back for much longer.

She looks up at me before nodding her head.

"Good," I say, my gaze flashing to her lips. "Now kiss me as I cum all over you, butterfly."

Her head tilts back immediately, her mouth ready and open for me the moment our lips connect. She bites at my lip, trapping the tender skin between her teeth. Her body arches into me as she throws everything she has into the kiss.

"I'm going to come, baby," I tell her. I reach to grab my cock, not trying to make a mess of her, at least today.

She slaps my hand away. "Then come," she directs, her voice full of confidence. Her hand works hard up and down my length.

Her words send me over the edge. In no time, my spine tingles and my cum is leaking out everywhere. I try to free my cock from her hands, to let the liquid run all over my hand instead of hers. She doesn't let me, my hand stays on top of hers, letting her set the rhythm. Her hand keeps working, getting slower and slower until my body relaxes from the orgasm. We stare between us, both of us gazing at our hands.

Lennon's shoulders rise and fall in rapid succession. Her entire face is flushed. I know if I were to reach underneath her dress, I'd find her panties damp.

"How was it?"

I fight the urge to laugh at her question, knowing it'd only upset her. It's just comical that she would even dare to think that it was anything short of the best handy I've ever had. She looks around for a few seconds before she wipes her hand off on the bottom of her dress. I don't know why I find the gesture so sexy, but anything is with her.

Hell, I've seen her make reading a book sexy. Anything's possible when it comes to Lennon.

I use the hand not covered in cum to lift the skirt of her

dress. My hands push it up her thighs until I see the outline of her thong. Even though she's told me I don't have to, I look at her for confirmation before I continue. I never want her to feel like she doesn't have the power to stop what we're doing.

She arches her back at the same moment her thighs spread open, opening herself up to me.

I play with the fabric at her hip. "Do you need to even ask that, butterfly?" I joke, looking at where my hand is still covered in the proof of how she made me feel.

"Yes." Her body shivers. "I just want to make sure I'm doing it right."

Her words break my heart and infuriate me all at once. "Trust me, Lennon. You're doing it right. It's impossible for you to do it wrong."

Her shoulders relax a bit. It might be from my words. It might be from my fingers that inch underneath the fabric of her thong. I make a mental note to make sure I'm telling her how good she's doing in the future. I never want her to be second guessing how she makes me feel in the bedroom. Ironic, because I feel like all I do is make her second guess how I feel outside of the bedroom.

My hand raises. I hold my coated fingers in front of her mouth. Her lips fall open instantly as I swipe the proof of my arousal against her bottom lip. "Taste how good you make me feel, butterfly," I growl. My cock grows all over again at the sight of her tongue peeking out to do just that.

Slowly, I put two fingers in her mouth, groaning when her mouth closes over them instantly. Her tongue presses against them, greedily licking the cum right off my fingers.

"The next time you think for a second that you don't drive me fucking wild, I want you to remember this moment right here. Remember how I taste on your lips."

Pulling my finger from my mouth, I use both hands to rip the thong down her legs. She was adamant I had my turn first, but now it's her turn. I want to feel her come against my mouth again. It's been days since I've been able to ravish her. I've been craving it, desperately waiting for the next taste.

"Look how ready you are," I rasp, licking my lips. Her pussy glistens, aching for me to devour it.

Lennon's head falls backwards. "So ready," she pants, bucking her hips.

I circle her clit with the tip of my finger. I'll never tire of how reactive she is to every touch. One simple press of my finger to her sensitive flesh and she's almost jumping off this table in pleasure.

"You're so fucking sexy," I admonish, pressing her clit with my thumb as one finger enters her.

Her moan is loud, her thighs pressing open even further. She's got everything on display for me, and I fucking love it. She's shy for everyone else, but I'm a fucking goner for how bold she becomes when I'm touching her. Lennon's becoming more familiar with what she wants, and I'll be damned if I don't give her exactly that and more.

"More," she moans, moving her hips to get more friction. "I need more."

I pull out of her long enough to have a second join the first. She's tight around both of them. I can't wait for the day she's ready for my cock to be the one stretching her.

"Like this?"

She nods up and down. My fingers hook inside her, applying pressure to the spot that drives her wild. The way she writhes against me, I know she's close. It wouldn't take long to have her coming all over my fingers, but that's not what I want right now.

It's been too fucking long since her arousal has coated my lips. I need it.

My fingers pull out of her. "I need to taste you, butterfly. I need to taste how good I make you feel."

"Yes, please," she pants.

"I love that my girl has manners." I'm about to lean down to taste her when I get an idea.

Looking at her, I bring my fingers to her lips again. She looks at me, confused. There might even be a hint of fire in her eyes at the fact I'm prolonging her orgasm.

"Don't worry, I'm going to make sure you come all over my face. First, I want you to taste how good we taste together. My cum mixed with yours."

Just like she did the first time, her mouth opens wide. I don't waste another second. She eagerly sucks my fingers in, hollowing her cheeks out with the force.

"Good girl," I praise, pressing my fingers deeper into her mouth, careful not to go too far. "We taste so fucking good together, don't we?"

She nods, her teeth slightly biting into my fingers. I could go again at the sight of my fingers shoved down her throat, my mind envisioning her looking exactly the same except where my fingers are, it's my cock.

Shoving her thighs open as wide as they'll go, marveling at her flexibility, I pull her across the wood. She shrieks, her hands falling to the wood to brace herself.

"It's my turn to taste," I growl, looking at her puffy, soaking wet pussy. I love how she's always so wet and ready for me. She isn't greedy. She'll take my fingers or mouth, ready for whatever I'll give her.

CHAPTER 36

POE HOLDS my hand the entire way back to our hotel.

It was unexpected, something I never saw happening. In fact, the rest of the butterfly garden experience was like it was out of my greatest fantasy. It was the most romantic day of my life, even if I'd had to walk around with moisture still coating between my thighs. My underwear wasn't dry either. Every step I took, I was reminded of what Poe and I had done in that shed.

I'd do it over and over again if I could. Before Poe, I couldn't imagine hooking up with someone else in public. After him, I'm addicted to the thrill. I almost want to be caught. That way someone out there in the universe would know that even if for a fleeting moment, it was me that was driving him wild.

To a stranger, Poe and I may have looked like a couple as we wandered around the butterfly garden and the other exhibits at the conservatory. It'd been an easy conversation between the two of us. When he'd taken my hand in front of a garden of vibrant flowers, he'd made it seem so simple. It was like he hadn't even noticed he'd done it. Our conversation had continued, even though my heart was threatening to beat right out of my chest.

He'd done the same thing the moment we'd gotten in the

back of the car. Poe had rattled off the name of our hotel to the driver before reaching across the bench seat and grabbing my hand. It'd stayed in his lap the entire way back.

He still holds onto it, his hand warm compared to mine, as we pull up to the hotel. Nash's show isn't until two days from now, giving us time to rest as we travel from place to place.

I'm waiting for him to let go, for reality to sink in, and for us to pretend that we aren't hooking up in front of our friends and family. If it were up to me, we wouldn't be walking the narrow friends with benefits line. We'd be more than friends, and everyone would know it. I don't see myself as one of those people who'd be super affectionate in front of others, but Poe could change that. It's sad because I'll never actually know.

I won't allow myself to hope that we'll ever be anything more than this.

It hurts too much to wish for anything more than private dates, hushed conversations, and wanting looks across the room.

Poe stares at the door to the lobby. His eyes look sad. I want to ask him what's on his mind, but I'm scared he won't tell me. The deeper we get into the agreement we have, the less I want to ask of him. My heart is falling deeper for him with each thing checked off the list. I can't control it. The more I fall, the more I'm afraid he'll stop this. Maybe if I don't ask questions, he won't stop whatever we have going on.

The only problem is all I want to do is ask questions. I need to know why at moments it feels like this is more for him. Sometimes I could swear I'm not the only one who has feelings involved here. I long to ask him if things have changed for him. If just maybe he'd reconsider his stance on what we are—on what we *could* be. My mouth stays shut however, because deep down, I'm confident it wouldn't go my way. Even if he felt the same, he wouldn't allow it to be more. It's some sort of punishment for himself I'll never understand.

"I don't want this to end," Poe drawls, interrupting my thoughts. His hand clutches mine tightly. "I don't want to go back inside and pretend I want to do anything but get lost in you."

A horn honks from behind us. I'm pretty sure it's at our car. The driver lingers in the circle drive, politely waiting for us to exit the vehicle. So many things happen around us. The driver may even say something, but I tune out all of it.

I'm focused on Poe, on the vulnerable look on his face. "You what?" I manage to get out.

He pulls our clasped hands to his mouth, brushing featherlight kisses to my knuckles. "Stay with me tonight?" His voice is timid, quiet, his eyes solely trained on me.

I pull a shaky breath in, wondering if I'm hearing him correctly. "You want to…"

"Stay with you. Spend time with you. Fuck, just be with you, butterfly." Reaching up, he runs his hand through his hair nervously. The way he's looking at me has me wondering if he thinks there's any possibility that I'd ever say no to him, to this. "We don't have to do anything off your list or anything like that. I'm not trying to convince you to do anything you don't want to. I just really hate the thought of going in there and saying goodbye to you. Or worse, going in there and having to be in the same room with you, pretending I wasn't *just* having the luxury of kissing you hours ago."

"I don't want to pretend either," I admit. It's the last thing I want to do. Aiden is already onto us. He suspects more has happened between us than I'm willing to admit, but he's so lost in his own drama with Monica that he hasn't pressed me about it.

Nash and Nora don't seem to have a clue, but I don't think they'd care if they learned of it. Nora would just want me to be happy. I'm sure Nash would feel the same.

I almost tell him we could go in there and tell everyone that we were together today. That I didn't spend all day in my hotel room sleeping off the jetlag, the excuse I gave them when they'd asked if I wanted to do something today. Poe had just told everyone he was going to explore the city alone. They were used to him doing his own thing every now and then. They didn't question it much.

The two of us could walk in hand in hand, ready to tell anyone that questioned it we were getting to know each other. It would be perfect. I'm ready to suggest it, but he beats me to it. His words slicing through my heart.

"Would you want to hole up in your room tonight—just us? I could give Landon some excuse that I found somewhere else to stay for the night. He wouldn't ask any questions." I fight to hide the sting of his words, what the unsaid parts of it mean. Landon wouldn't question it because he's used to Poe finding women to spend his nights with. It's close enough to the norm that he wouldn't think twice about it.

The realization hurts. There's a dull ache in my stomach the more I think about it, but I know it'll hurt even worse if I don't get this chance with him. I'd rather spend time with him, not having to hide it in front of those we love most, but I'd rather have him in any capacity than not have him at all.

It's a sad thought, knowing you want to proudly show off someone and they just want to hide you. It's even sadder, coming to terms with the fact you'll allow it to happen just so you can keep them a little longer.

"That sounds great," I say, only half telling the truth. It sounds like the perfect ending to an already perfect day, if it didn't mean we were only doing it to stay hidden.

The way his eyes light up lessens the sting slightly. "It does?" His voice is hesitant. A side to him I fall harder and harder for. I find it crazy how this man can break me and put me back together again in a matter of moments.

My thumb swipes over the top of his hand. "I'll go up to my

room. Just text me whenever you're on your way and I'll let you in."

He nods, letting go of my hand. Reaching between his legs, he lifts the large bag from the conservatory gift shop. Poe holds it between us, waiting for me to take it. I do the same, shoving my arm through the handles to rest it on my shoulder. I reach for the floorboard, pulling the bag from my feet as well.

On our way out, we'd both picked out some items from the gift shop for the other person. The rule was to only pick out one thing for the other, but judging by how heavy the bag he handed me is, I'm worried he didn't follow the rules.

The item he picked out for me needed a far larger bag than the one I got him. That being said, I'm excited about what I purchased for him. Part of me wants to watch him open it, the other part is too anxious to. I'm nervous he won't like it or won't realize how much thought I put into it.

"How about we open these together?" he offers. "Wait to open yours until I'm there?"

Nodding my head, I grab the door handle. I push the car door open, looking over my shoulder at him. "See you soon," I breathe, swinging my legs around.

Suddenly, his fingers grab me by the wrist. They've got a tight hold on me. He yanks me toward him, fusing our lips together in a way that ruins me for anyone else.

His kiss is like a brand to my soul. It's simple. There's no tongue or teeth. He takes his time with it, like he's savoring the way our lips fit perfectly against each other. It's a goodbye kiss, full of promises.

It's everything I'd ever want. It just hurts a little because I know it's something he wouldn't do if he thought anyone was watching.

Pulling away, he smiles softly. "I miss you already."

The driver mutters something under his breath. We're probably pushing our luck before he turns around and gives us a piece of his mind. Hopefully Poe tips him well, or at least apologizes on our behalf. I don't wait to find out. I pull my arm from his and exit the car. I'm excited to see him again, but I also need a few moments away from him to get my head on straight.

Shouldering past people, I hold the large bag to my chest until I'm in the elevator. Once I'm inside, I press the button for my floor before letting out a deep breath. When I'd stepped inside it, I'd been too busy rehashing every single minute of our day today. I hadn't thought to see if I was alone or not.

"It's funny," a deep voice says from behind me. "I was *just* with your sister. She said you were sleeping away the jet lag."

My stomach drops. Turning around, I find Landon grinning at me from the corner of the elevator. His arms cross over his chest, his eyes watching me expectantly.

I look down at the bag in my hands, the bold, black writing on the white bag doing nothing to help my case here. His eyes travel there, too, making him grin even wider.

"I can explain," I hurriedly say. My mind races with different excuses, but none of them seem to be remotely convincing.

Landon's eyebrows raise to his buzzed hairline. He tips his chin down, inviting me to explain. "Go on then."

My teeth dig into my lip. All efforts to come up with an excuse are futile. I can't come up with a single one he'd believe.

"I lied," I finally admit, rocking back and forth on my heels. He doesn't act the least bit shocked by my admission. How could he be? The bag in my hand and the purse on my shoulder make it pretty obvious I haven't been in bed sleeping the day away.

He laughs. It's deep and rumbly, coming from his chest. "I'd gathered." He quirks one blond eyebrow. "Why'd you lie?" He holds a finger out to stop me from answering his question. "*Wait*. Does it have to do with the reason my best friend has been missing all day as well?"

I scratch my arm, wondering how to navigate this. It's one

thing being caught lying about not being in bed. It's another to admit to Landon that Poe and I'd been together.

The elevator dings, the doors opening to a floor that isn't mine. I watch him, wondering if he's going to get off. There's no one waiting on the other side, and there's no one else in here with us, so logic tells me we're on his floor. He continues to stare at me, not budging.

If it's his floor, he misses it. The doors close slowly and we're back to moving.

"Lennon," Landon says, a warning tone to his voice. "Were you with Poe?"

I shake my head, hoping I come off more convincing than I feel. "Nope," I answer, my voice getting pitchy. "I was all by myself."

His eyebrows narrow. "You were by yourself? In a different country?" There's doubt in his voice. It isn't totally misplaced, technically this time I wasn't alone. But I was alone when I traveled the world by myself before college and it turned out fine.

"Yes," I clip. The elevator beeps again, the doors opening on my floor. I step off quickly, hoping he'll get the hint and leave.

He doesn't.

His long legs follow after me.

"Your sister would want to know if you were out gallivanting alone."

"My sister isn't my keeper," I say over my shoulder. Stopping at my door, I grab the keycard from the front pock of my purse. I hold it up to the card reader, twisting the door handle when the light turns green.

Landon stops in my doorway, watching me with an unreadable look on his face. "No she isn't," he mutters, looking at something over my shoulder.

Sighing, I drop the bag from Poe at my feet. "Any way we could keep the fact that you saw me a secret?"

"On one condition."

"And that is?"

He takes a long breath. "Be careful," he finally gets out.

My head tilts as I look at him confused. "With what?"

"With whatever you're doing with Poe. He's one of the best guys I know. He's my best friend. But he still carries a lot from his past with him. It's heavy, and he doesn't carry it well sometimes."

I'm opening my mouth to ask him what he means, but he's already backing out of the doorway. He plasters the familiar smile on his face, winking at me. "Your secret's safe with me, Lennon. Just remember what I said."

Landon disappears, leaving me with even more questions after my day with Poe.

CHAPTER
37

N ERVES COURSE through my body as I hit my knuckles against her hotel room door. The door swings open almost instantly, Lennon waiting for me on the other side.

Her dimples pop out as she smiles, hooking a thumb over her shoulder. "Come in."

I look in each direction of the hallway, making sure it's empty, before stepping inside. Luckily, I didn't run into anyone on the way up to her room. This night can be between just her and I, not having the pressure of anyone else's opinions of us spending time together.

She closes the door softly after me. Her shoulders rest against it as she watches me in the small entryway to her room. Her palms are flat against the door. "Hi," she breathes.

I switch the bag I'm holding from one hand to the other. Closing the distance between us, I press my body to hers. Using my now free dominant hand, I grab her chin, coaxing her to look at me.

"Fuck, I missed you," I confess. It's nothing but true. It'd only been an hour since I saw her, Landon keeping me longer in our room than I was expecting. But it felt too long. For once, I hadn't cared to talk music with my friend. He'd been throwing out ideas for a song we were writing with Nash, but my heart hadn't been in it.

It was still with Lennon, in that damn butterfly garden, remembering the day we'd had together.

She rubs her lips together, trying to play it cool by hiding her smile. It doesn't do much use, Lennon doesn't just smile with her mouth, her whole face lights up. Even her eyes give her away. "You just saw me."

Leaning in, I plant a quick peck against her lips. I don't linger, knowing if I start something I won't be able to stop, and I've been anxiously waiting for her to open her gift—well *gifts*. I'd cheated and had to get her two things. I couldn't help it. "Yeah, well, it seemed like way too long."

Turning around, I step into her tidy hotel room. We'd gotten in last night, so aside from sleeping last night and getting ready this morning, she hadn't been here long enough to get it too messy. There's a stack of three paperbacks on the nightstand. The top book is crooked at the top of the pile, like she'd quickly put it there last night before falling asleep.

I take a seat on the edge of her bed, looking at her with a giddy feeling in my stomach. "Ready to do gifts?"

Picking up the bag I got her from the gift shop, she brings it over and takes a seat at my side. "I'm nervous you won't like mine," she whines.

I scoff, rolling my eyes at her. "There's not much you could get me I wouldn't like, butterfly. If it's from you, I'll love it."

She lets out a tiny audible gasp. "Really?"

Reaching out, I touch the upturned tip of her nose with my fingertip. "Of course."

"You first," she says, her head nodding to the small bag in my hand. The bag weighs next to nothing. I don't know what she could've found that was this light, but I'm looking forward to finding out.

I shake my head at her. "Ladies first." I smile.

A flush creeps up her cheeks. She looks at the bag like she already loves the contents of it, even though she doesn't know what's in it. Her fingers work slowly at opening the bag. It reminds me of when she'd delicately unwrapped the book I first got her, something that seems like ages ago.

Reaching into the bag, she pulls out a neatly folded blanket. It's wrapped in ribbon, a big bow at the very top of it. "Poe," she manages to say, her voice astonished. Her small hand rubs over the top of it. "It's so soft."

"You're always talking about how cold you are. I saw it and thought you might like it." I suddenly feel nervous, feeling the need to explain why I chose it. Her silence fuels my nerves. I scratch awkwardly at my neck. "If you don't like it, you don't have to keep it. I know it's a lot extra to lug around…"

Lennon looks up at me. Her large eyes shine with happiness. Her heart-shaped lips turning up in a smile. "Poe," she interrupts.

"Mm?"

"I don't like it, I *love* it." She runs her hands over the fabric once again, feeling the softness. Her finger traces over the pattern of the blanket. It has various butterflies all across it, their colors vibrant against the black background of the blanket. I'd stood in front of it in the gift shop for so long, wondering if it was something she'd like or not.

"You do?" I ask, unsure. The real reason I loved it was because it was the only item I'd seen in the store that had the blue butterfly on it. The one with the giant wings of different shades of blue. I'd wanted something with that butterfly now that I'm incredibly fond of it. Her face when it landed on her nose was something I could never forget.

She thought the butterfly brought her a kiss. I let her hold on to the idea. The truth is, I wouldn't have been able to resist kissing her for much longer—butterfly or no butterfly.

It doesn't take her long to tear the ribbon from the blanket.

She rolls the blanket out to its full length. Pieces of cardboard that helped keep the shape fall to the ground, leaving just the blanket in her hand. Standing up, she wraps the blanket around her. The fabric easily covers her body entirely, leaving a floating head and neck above the butterfly pattern.

Lennon beams, twirling around in a circle. The fabric lifts at her feet, giving the illusion that she's twirling in some sort of ball gown or robe. "I love it so much." She laughs, stopping. If I'd spun that much, I'd be dizzy, but my guess is with her past ballet experience, she's used to it.

It's easy to imagine myself falling for her in this moment. Her smile is so wide, her laugh so infectious, that I can't fathom a day that I don't get to experience them daily. It hurts to think that one day she won't freely give them to me. One day, I'm bound to hurt her. I won't be enough for her or be what she deserves. I dread the day where she doesn't look at me with the same wonder as she is in this moment.

"Which butterfly is your favorite?" I ask, standing up. She only stands a few feet away from me, but it's too far. I need to touch her, to feel her racing heart against mine.

My feet eat the distance between us. Our minds are on the same page. She opens her arms, the blanket still in her hands. It looks like one of those weird flying squirrel suits Landon once told me he wanted to buy. Her hands wrap around my neck as I pull her against me. It's warm in the blanket. Comfort washes over me, feeling her near again. Effortlessly, her legs wrap around my middle as I lift her from the ground.

For a moment, we stay in the embrace. Her legs around me, my hands cupping her ass to keep her in position. We're in a cocoon of our own making.

Lennon leans into me, rubbing the bridge of her nose against mine. "Shouldn't the answer be obvious," she whispers.

It's weird how the smallest of actions seem to be the most intimate. The peace I feel as our noses rub against each other is a peace I haven't known for years and years. I tighten my grip on her. "Tell me anyway."

"The blue one," she answers immediately. "*Always* the blue one."

She feathers kisses along my jaw. Something else that makes me feel things I have no business feeling.

I smile, my mouth inches from hers. "Why the blue one?"

"Because it brought me this." She closes the small distance between our mouths. Her tongue runs over the seam of my mouth, asking to be let in. I open, loving how she tastes of sour candy.

I back up until my calves hit the edge of the bed. Slowly, I bring us down, making sure I keep our bodies pressed against one another. We get lost in the taste of one another for god knows how long. I love that there's no rush to it. There's no risk of anyone stumbling upon us. It's just us, able to take our time and get to know one another.

Eventually, she pulls away, keeping her forehead against mine. "Which butterfly is your favorite?" she asks sweetly. Her arm comes between us, bringing the fabric of the blanket with her.

I pretend to look over it, inspecting each and every butterfly like I don't already know my answer. My finger runs over all of them as I pretend to have to think about it. Finally, I look up at her and smile. "Easy. *You.*"

This makes her laugh. She shifts her weight on top of me. "I'm not a butterfly, Poe," she argues.

I rock her hips against me, loving the way our bodies fit against one another perfectly. "Says who? Don't you remember? You're my butterfly."

Even her chest turns red with the blush. I marvel at the way her body speaks to me, even when her mouth doesn't. I love the effect I have on her. I'm curious to know what else I can find out about her. I could spend forever finding out the little nuances of Lennon.

"I'll let you get away with it this time," she whispers. The smile falls from her face. It falls from mine as well. The air around us changes. It becomes charged as our eyes roam the other's face.

"Poe?" My name is even softer coming from her lips.

"Yes?"

She reaches for the ground to my left. My hands steady her by the hips as she stretches her body as far as it'll go. Finally, her fingertips brush over the handles of the bag she got me. Lennon brings it to us, fitting it into the empty space between our bodies.

"It's your turn to open your gift."

"You haven't even opened your second one," I argue.

Her eyebrow arches. "The rule was that we only got each other one gift."

I shrug unapologetically. "I broke the rules."

Her eyes roll. "For someone who makes a lot of rules, you sure have no problem breaking them."

I chuckle. "I seem to be breaking them more and more when it comes to you, butterfly."

"The second gift, the one you *broke the rules* by getting, will have to wait." Lennon pushes the bag into my chest. "Open." Her voice is stern. The look on her face is so damn adorable. She's so concentrated on looking threatening, that I can't help but let go of her hips to grab the bag.

Now that I no longer hold onto her, she digs her knees deeper into the bed on either side of my hips. It brings her core even harder against my growing erection. I try to hide it, knowing this isn't the moment to be so turned on by her. I just can't help it, not when I'm around her.

"I'm nervous," she admits.

"Don't be," I say. "I'll love it no matter what."

Opening the bag, I look inside to find a small rectangular box. It's black, the logo for the conservatory etched in silver on the top.

I look at her in question, reaching in to pull the box.

She watches me with bated breath. Her face leaning in close as she waits eagerly.

My thumb hooks under the lid of the box, pushing it off slowly.

When I see what's inside, emotion clogs my throat.

I haven't even pulled it out yet, and it's my favorite gift I've ever received.

CHAPTER
38

I FEEL like I could throw up. I'm so anxious.

He stares down at the small box between us, his face void of emotion.

Suddenly, I'm regretting the choice of gift. It's silly. Clearly I haven't paid as close attention to him as I'd thought I had. The thought makes me sad, because the moment I saw it, I knew it was what I wanted to give him.

When he looks up at me, his eyes almost seem glossy. It could be my imagination. I don't know anymore.

"How did you know?" he asks. He has to clear his throat.

Maybe it isn't as awful as I thought it was. His reaction makes it seem like he may actually like it.

Feeling bashful, I try to play it cool with a shrug. "I just kind of noticed you always had one. You seemed to pull it out when you're nervous, so just in case you needed a new one…"

We both look at the box between us, at what sits in it.

It's a small, oval-shaped stone. I hadn't really known the meaning behind the object until I'd checked out in the small gift shop store. The lady at the register had explained that it was called a worry stone. The thumbprint mold in the center of it was there on purpose, a place for your thumb to rest as you rub the stone between your thumb and pointer finger.

"Lennon," he rasps. "I don't even know what to say." His thumb swipes over the top of it, the place where a bright blue butterfly is painted on. The stone was at the bottom of a bucket of other colorfully decorated ones. I was about to settle on one that had a music note painted on it when I saw the gray stone with the butterfly painted on it.

I'd had to stick my hand deep into the jar, moving other stones around to reach the one I wanted. Eventually, my fingers wrapped around it and pulled it out. I'd held it in my hand, inspecting the small, smooth stone, knowing immediately it was what I wanted to get Poe.

"You don't have to say anything," I tell him. "I just hope you like it."

He looks to me, reaching up to run the thumb of his hand not holding the box over my cheek. "This is the most thoughtful gift I've ever been given."

"It really wasn't that thoughtful," I say awkwardly, not wanting to make things weird. "I just didn't know if you'd need a new one eventually."

"I'm going to use it right away."

His words make my heart soar. I'm relieved it's something he likes. There for a moment, I was really worried.

He carefully pulls the stone from the box, flipping it between his fingers. He digs his thumb into the point of the thumbprint.

"The lady at the register told me that many people say that by the time the butterfly, or whatever is painted on, rubs off, that your worry should be gone."

"I like that thought," he mutters. His voice is deep and gravelly, like he's working hard on keeping it level.

I search his face, wondering if his words are true. "You do?"

His answer is kissing my forehead. He presses his lips so hard into my forehead it's like he's trying to tattoo the imprint on my skin. His words are spoken against the same spot. "You have no idea, Lennon."

His lips stay pressed there for a little longer. Time is coming to a standstill around us. Eventually, he pulls away.

Poe looks over the worry stone one last time before he sticks it in his pocket. Except, he doesn't come out empty-handed. In his hand, he holds the old stone. It's a bright jade green. It's not lime green or emerald, but a color in between.

Pulling on my arm, he places my hand between us. He flips my hand around, facing my palm to the ceiling. The stone is cold in my hand as he presses it into my skin. He folds my fingers over it, his fingers firm over mine.

"You keep this one."

I squeeze my palm so hard the stone digs into my skin. "I can't," I say, staring down at our intertwined hands. "It's yours."

"I have a new one. This one is yours, for whatever worries you have. I want you to pull it out and think of me. That's what I'll do with yours."

I look up at him. "You will?"

He sighs, one corner of his lip turning up. "How could I not? I wasn't lying when I told you it was the most thoughtful gift I've ever been given. I can't believe you noticed…"

My body shifts, bringing us closer. "It's hard not to notice when it's *you*," I tell him truthfully.

Letting go of my hand, he holds both sides of my face. I love the feeling of his fingertips against my cheeks too much. They mold perfectly against my skin. I relish in the feeling of his calloused fingertips against the sensitive skin.

I bring the stone he gave me to my lips. My lips press against the smooth surface, my heart doubling in speed at the gift he's given me. It's small, but the meaning behind it is gigantic.

"Tell me your worry?" I question. He may not tell me, but it's worth a try. I want to figure out what's going on in that head of his. It's so hard to get anything out of him, but I won't stop trying. I'll dig and dig until he has no option but to open up to me.

"You really want to know?" he asks.

My head nods eagerly. "I'll always want to know what weighs on you, Poe." I slide the stone into the pocket of my pajama shorts, hoping it's nice and safe in there. If it falls out, I will rip apart this hotel room until it's found.

"I'm worried that I'll somehow end up hurting you," he whispers. There's so much sadness and worry in his eyes that it breaks my heart.

"You won't hurt me," I respond, conviction in my voice. "I know you, Poe. You're better than you think, deserving of so much more than what you believe You won't hurt me. I know it."

He shakes his head, hair falling over his eyes. "You don't know that, Lennon. I loved Connor, and I hurt him. He died, thinking I wanted nothing to do with him. My parents had been begging for me to come home and visit them when they'd gotten in the accident that took their life. I'd been so swept up in this world that I hadn't made the time. I inadvertently hurt them, too. I hurt the people I love."

His voice breaks, my heart breaking right along with it. This man has been through so much, he's lost so many people he's loved. I don't blame him for how he's shielded himself from love.

I flatten my hand to his chest. He grabs it, gripping my wrist. "I can't hurt you, too." The words are said so softly, I almost miss them over the sound of my own heartbeat.

"Don't think about it," I beg, leaning in so our foreheads touch again. "I can make my own decisions. I know what you've told me, and I don't care, Poe. I don't. I'd rather be hurt by you than always wonder what it was like to be loved by you."

His fingers tangle in my hair. "I can't say no much longer,

butterfly. There's so many reasons this'll never work, no matter how much you convince me it possibly could."

"Don't think about them," I plead. Grabbing at his face, I make him look at me. "Don't think at all, Poe." I tap the spot on his chest my hand just left. "Think with this," I whisper. "And not this." I tap his forehead.

"I'm worried that I won't be able to help myself from asking for more from you, even though I know there's only so much I'm able to give."

"Let me worry about that, okay?"

Nodding, he pulls me into him. For a while, we just hug. He clings to me as tightly as I cling to him, maybe even tighter. We hold each other, the moment we're feeling significant.

"Hey Poe?" I speak into his chest. Sucking in a breath, I memorize the smell of him.

He runs his hand over my hair. "Yeah?"

"I just wanted you to know that it isn't just about the list for me. Not anymore."

I feel the breath from his laugh against my hair. "Deep down, I don't know if it's ever been about the list for me," he confesses, his voice just above a whisper.

His words are my undoing. I latch my lips to his, desperate to wrap our breaths together.

Desperate for him—all of him.

CHAPTER 39

I DON'T THINK there will be a day that I ever tire of kissing Lennon.

It'd be easier if I knew she was someone I could easily put in my past someday, but that's not the case. Every time we kiss, it feels like she's carving out more space for herself in my heart.

Her tiny hands clutch my face like I could disappear any moment. "I want all of you, Poe. Right here. Right now."

My head jerks away from her, something settling in my chest. "Lennon. We don't have to."

Her small hand finds my mouth. She covers it, giggling when I nip at her fingers. "I know. I don't have to do anything. This is something I *want*. Desperately."

My heart pounds faster now than it ever does during a show. She's making me feel things not even music can pull from me. "Are you sure?" I mumble against her fingers.

Smiling, she pulls her hand from my mouth. "I've never been more sure of anything in my life, Poe."

Her warm hands travel down my back, gathering the hem of my T-shirt in her hands. She lifts it, pulling her body away from mine enough to pull the shirt up. Everything goes dark for a moment as the fabric covers my eyes. She doesn't waste time pulling it all the way off and tossing it to the floor.

Looking down, she runs her fingers over the ink on my skin. "There's so many," she breathes. Chills run over my body when her fingertip traces over both of my parents' names tattooed on my chest. Her fingers brush against the necklace I always wear. The one my stepdad gave me when he married my mom when I was five, becoming a father to me even though we didn't share the same blood.

Smirking, I grab her by the neck and mold our lips together again. "There's still a lot of skin left," I say against her mouth.

Her hips rock against me, searching for friction. Falling backward, I keep a hold of her as my back hits the mattress. She straddles me, her long hair falling around us and caging us in.

She rocks back and forth so much it drives me wild. If making out was all she wanted to do, I'd be fine with it. But the way she grinds against me, it's clear what her little hips are trying to do. Her hands press against my chest as she pulls away from me, pushing herself up.

A ribbon holds on for dear life at the end of her hair. I reach up, pulling at it so her hair is completely free. Her dark, long, wavy locks cascade down her shoulders. Even when she's tried to tame it, her hair has a mind of its own.

Her green gaze glues me to my spot. She looks down at me so intently as she grabs the hem of her shirt, teasing me by pulling it up her body ever so slowly. It seems like years until I'm awarded the view of the freckles that span all of her body, bringing color to her pale skin. Surprising me, she wears nothing underneath the baggy T-shirt.

The moment it's pulled off, discarded somewhere with mine, I'm met with the view of her perfect breasts. They're heavy with want, her nipples hard and ready for me to worship them.

My hands snake up her bare, toned stomach, feeling the weight of each of her breasts. I know I've heard that she no longer dances, but her body still bares all the muscles from her years of training.

"These are so perfect," I say huskily, my breath catching when she scoots down slightly lower, aligning herself perfectly with my straining cock.

She rocks against it hard in a perfect rhythm. A tiny moan falls from her lips when I pinch one of the pink buds.

"I need more," she pants.

Leaning up, I give her exactly what she wants—more. I pull her nipple into my mouth, sucking the sensitive flesh. Her back arches at the same time another moan rocks through her body. Her head falls backward when I move to the other one, making sure each gets attention. The long tendrils of her hair fall all the way down her back and past her hips in the position.

"You're so reactive to me, butterfly," I notice as I remain against her peaked flesh. "Tell me what else you want."

Her eyes pop open. Lifting her hips off me, she fumbles with the button of my jeans. "I want these off," she demands.

I help her by lifting my own hips. Finally getting the button and fly undone, she pulls both my jeans and briefs down, freeing my cock.

I might come just by the way she's looking at it. Her eyes are wide as she looks it up and down, her tongue peeking out to wet her lips.

"Can I?" She gets quiet, a shy look on her face when she looks at me.

"Can you what, butterfly?"

Her teeth dig into her lip. She stares down at it in wonder, making it even harder. "Can I you know…"

"Suck it?" I finish for her.

She nods enthusiastically. "I've never…"

My cock jerks. I grab it, running my hand down the base to get some sort of relief. "Fuck, Lennon." I groan.

"Teach me?" She looks so innocent, but so damn determined it drives me fucking insane. "I want to make you feel good."

Her words unravel me. I remember a time I said the same thing to her, everything coming full circle. Part of me wonders if it'll be selfish to tell her yes. I'm going mad imagining what it feels like to have her tongue run up and down my shaft. I just want to make this night good for her, memorable. It isn't about me, it's about *her*.

But fuck, the way she's looking at my cock, I can't tell her no. I'll give her whatever the hell she wants. And right now, it's obvious what she wants.

She wants to learn how to suck my cock. I won't say no. I'll be the best fucking teacher for her. I'll teach her exactly how to make me feel good, even though I know if it's her doing it, anything would be perfect.

"I don't think it's possible for it not to be good with you, butterfly," I answer honestly.

I suck in a breath when her warm hand joins mine, wrapping around my length. Her hand is so small that her fingertips don't even touch. She pumps it up and down once, looking to me for approval.

Pulling away, I place my palm over hers. I guide our hands up and down, showing her the pace that drives me wild. A quick learner, she finds her own rhythm. It's one that could have me coming, and her mouth hasn't even joined in yet.

"That's it. You're doing so good, butterfly."

She settles her body between my legs, leaning forward until her hair tickles the tops of my thighs. Even as she adjusts her position, her hand doesn't falter around me.

Suddenly, her hot breath blows against the head of my cock.

"Can I?"

I nod.

Her tongue slowly comes out to taste the tip. I let her explore for the moment, content with any attention she'll give it. She shocks me by closing her lips around me, sliding her tongue all the way down my length.

Air whistles through my teeth. "Just like that," I moan out.

My hands gently tangle in her hair. They rest there, just needing something to hold on to.

Lennon is timid at first, letting her tongue explore every inch of me. Eventually, she grows more confident in herself. She pushes down, taking all of me down her throat.

"Mmmm." I relish the feeling of her lips around me. "Fuck, it feels so good," I praise.

Her mouth picks up pace. She bobs up and down, the pace driving me wild. It feels so good, *too* good. I'm dangerously close to coming, her eagerness to learn close to sending me over the edge.

In one quick movement, I grab her, turning both of our bodies so she's now the one pressed into the mattress.

Her hair falls around her face, all the pieces going in different directions.

"I wasn't done," she pouts. It's the cutest look I've ever seen, and I watch as her bottom lip juts out in displeasure.

I kiss down along her collarbone. "Butterfly, if you want more from me, if you want to feel me inside you, then I can't have your mouth wrapped around me for another second."

I continue to trace the curves of her body with my lips. Moving from her collarbone, I kiss around each peaked nipple and then feather kisses down the muscles of her abdomen.

"Why?" she asks, squirming when I kiss around her hip bone.

Air whooshes from my lips in a laugh. "Because you were too damn good at it, Lennon. I was going to come before we even had the chance to do what you're asking."

"Oh," she whispers. Her hands grab my head when I trace the spot above her sleep shorts with my lips.

I hook my fingers into the shorts, pulling them down her thighs, down her legs, until they're off completely.

It seems like Lennon forewent *any* undergarments. She didn't wear a bra earlier, and she wears no panties now. Once the shorts are gone, I'm left with nothing covering her from me.

My lips continue their trail south, my tongue joining in to tease her sensitive skin. She writhes underneath me and my mouth hasn't even hit where she's aching for me most.

I stare at the wetness between her legs. "So wet," I notice. "Did sucking my cock make you wet, butterfly?"

Her moan is loud and powerful. Her hands fall to her sides, fisting the comforter to give herself something to hold on to.

"Yes," she moans out, bucking her hips when I lick her up and down.

"So fucking sexy." I get to work driving her wild with my tongue. Every sound that falls from her lips, every arch of her back, eggs me on.

Before long, she's writhing and coming against my mouth.

I continue to lick until her body goes lax. Even after, I kiss up her body once again, being met with a soft smile when I make it to her lips.

She kisses me with no hesitation, not caring that my lips are coated in her arousal. By the way her tongue hungrily dives into my mouth, it might even drive her even madder, to taste herself on my tongue.

The new position we're in lines me up perfectly with her. It's not the first time our bodies have lined up completely, but it's the first time it's been done as we're both naked.

The head of my cock rests against her inner thigh. Only a slight change in my position and I'd be inside her.

Her smile is wide and radiant when our kiss finally breaks. "I want to feel you, Poe," she says. Her hands dig into my back, trying to push me into her. "Please," she adds, and it comes out as a half-moan, half-plead. "I'm on the pill and want to feel you

—all of you—with no barrier. So please, Poe, don't make me wait any longer."

"You're positive?" I ask, hissing when she finally lines us up perfectly. My cock presses into her wetness. I can already tell she's ready for me, her pussy coated with her first orgasm.

"Yes. I want this with you. I need it." The primal tone to her voice solidifies my decision.

I've never wanted something so bad as to join our bodies. To feel her wrap around me, to feel like we're one. If this is what she wants, I'm going to give it to her, because it's all I fucking want, too.

Not needing anything else, I push inside her, knowing from the moment I'm all the way in that I'm lost for this woman.

CHAPTER
40

It almost feels like too much.

He fits inside me impeccably, stretching me until it toes the edge of pain and pleasure.

I love it.

"You feel unreal," Poe says next to my ear. He pushes in and out of me softly, like he's afraid he'll break me if he picks up pace.

He may break me either way, just not in the way he's thinking. Feeling him inside me, finally joining our bodies, is too much to handle. It's like I no longer know where I end and he begins. We're a tangle of limbs, the two of us desperate to make ourselves one.

My nails are short, but they're still long enough to dig into his skin, trying to bring him even deeper inside of me. I want it to sting, to leave a lasting impression. I want to feel him everywhere, to take all of him.

He hits a spot inside me that has my toes curling, and a loud moan falls from my lips. He steals the sound from my mouth, swallowing it and making it his own. A loud rumble comes from deep inside his chest. He picks up the pace slightly, still ensuring his hips aren't too punishing.

"Is this okay?" he rasps. His hands cup either side of my face. It's something he's done before, but now with him inside me, looking down at me with a look in his eyes that feels a lot like love, it feels different.

His thumb brushes my lip. "Yes," I whisper against it.

My answer has him pushing even deeper inside me. It's got to be as deep as he can go. I don't think I can handle much more. The feeling of him buried inside me overwhelms my senses. It's like he's making sure I'll feel him forever.

"I'm trying so hard to go slow for you, butterfly," he says through clenched teeth. "I want to make this perfect, to erase everything that's ever happened before me. But fuck, I'm sorry if it's too much—too fast." He kisses the spot below my ear. "You just have to let me know if I need to slow down, okay?"

"Don't," I beg, wiggling my hips to get him to move faster.

Slow is great, but I need more. I want to lose control. I want us to lose control together. "Don't slow down. I need faster," I plead, gripping his back.

"Whatever you want," he says, giving me exactly what I've been craving.

I've never known sex to feel like this. There have been men before Poe, although I wish that wasn't the case. In my mind, this is my first time because this is the first time it's ever felt so good. The first time I've ever felt like if we didn't connect our bodies, I might die.

Poe isn't good at using his words. His actions and words rarely match up. He'll say one thing but his actions tell me something completely opposite. It's something I've gotten used to with him. You have to read in between the lines with him. Right now, his body speaks in a way that I don't know his words ever will. With every thrust inside me, he makes me his. It's written all over his face. It's likely his words would never say it, but right now, he makes love to me.

At least, it's what I've always envisioned love to feel like.

His lips travel all over my neck, like he wants to taste every inch of my skin. We're both fighting to touch the other everywhere at once, like we'll never be able to get our fill of one another.

Maybe that is our reality. I know it's mine. It seems unlikely that I'll ever feel like I've had enough of him. That I've had enough of *this*.

From the moment I first laid eyes on him, I've wanted to be his. Right here, him pushing in and out of me in a pattern that has pressure building in my core; I don't think I'll ever get enough.

I'm addicted. Now I just have to find a way to make sure it's not just me with this addiction. I need him to need me as much as I need him, to never want to stop what we've begun.

"I'm getting close, butterfly." He groans. "Tell me you're close, too. I need to feel you tighten around me."

His words bring me right to the edge of another orgasm. I never knew it was possible to come multiple times—not until Poe. I hadn't even had a good orgasm with anyone else. Not like this. Not the way it feels with him.

Without warning, he pulls my nipple into his mouth and sucks so hard it sends tingles all the way down my body. My chest rises to give him even better access to it. His teeth and tongue work together to punish and pleasure. He bites and sucks so hard I wonder if he's trying to leave his mark.

He squeezes my opposite breast, flooding my senses with him and only him. An orgasm rips through me, my legs trembling with the feeling.

"Good girl," he praises, biting my nipple. "I love the feel of you coming all over me." He pushes all the way one last time before he pulls himself out of me, cum coating my entire stomach.

Seeing him like this makes me feral for the man. He's so unhinged, sweat coating his brow from the exertion.

I expect him to get up, but he does the opposite. Throwing one of his knees over my leg, his body falls onto the bed. With his next movement, he pulls me into him. I need to clean myself off. His cum still covers my stomach, but I don't move.

We're cuddling. I'd stay here forever if he allowed it. Being held by him, the two of us coming off our orgasm high, is one of the best feelings in the world.

"Tell me that was everything to you like it was for me, butterfly," he says into my hair. For the first time, I feel the strumming of his fingers against my body instead of watching him do it against his thigh, steering wheel, or something else entirely random.

It feels right, like my body was made to feel his touch all over, even in the most mundane of ways.

I snuggled deeper into the cocoon of his body. If I could, I'd enter his body completely, molding us into one. Maybe then I'd be able to pick apart his brain, to get a read on what he's thinking. I'd be able to dissect his heart and see if my name is etched on his, the same way his is etched on mine.

"It was everything and more," I assure him, kissing the hand next to my cheek. "Anything with you has been everything to me. It always has been."

His body stiffens slightly. I'm wondering if I've said too much when he kisses the back of my neck. His lips stay pressed there, even when he speaks. "What are you doing to me?" he says so quietly I wonder if he intends for me to hear it or not.

Either way, I do. And either way, it feels like a win. Like maybe he's admitting to himself that this is more than he'd ever imagined it to be. And that's okay. It's *more* than okay—it's perfect.

I refuse to believe something that feels this good—feels so right—is anything less.

"Nothing that you aren't already doing to me," I answer him.

Poe buries his face in my neck. I can feel his breath hot

against my neck. He inhales deeply. I know I'll never forget the familiar scent of him. Hopefully, he won't forget mine.

"Fuck. I don't know what we've gotten ourselves into," he groans against my back.

I laugh, secretly loving that I'm getting to him the way he's gotten to me from the moment I first saw him.

He wraps his arms further around me, his fingers accidentally hitting the wet spot on my stomach.

"Let's get you all cleaned up." He lays a tender kiss to my temple before he rolls off the bed. I'm in the middle of pushing myself off the mattress to follow him when he scoops me in his arms.

His forearm rests underneath my knees, his other arm pressed against my back. It's the way the groom holds his bride when walking over the threshold to their new life. My arms wrap around his neck. He carries me toward the en suite bathroom like I weigh nothing.

I expect him to put me down before he turns on the shower, but he doesn't. His hold on me is tight as he reaches into the large shower, turning the water to hot.

"How hot do you like it?" he asks, his voice tender.

Why do the simple things seem so special?

"Hot. Like burn my skin hot," I joke.

Shaking his head, he cranks the knob even further. Water droplets splash everywhere as he brings us into the stream of water.

His hands are firm on my hips as he places my feet on the ground. I stand facing him, the water on my back. He towers over me, some of the water managing to hit him.

"How's the temperature?" he asks, pushing wet hair out of my face.

"It's perfect." If it was anyone but Poe, I'd feel bashful standing here naked. With him, it's always different. The things that make me uncomfortable with others is that of the past with him.

The pressure of the water is immaculate. I'm used to the soft, barely there pressure of the tour bus. This pressure is way harder, digging into the knots at my shoulders. I tilt my head to the ground, savoring the feel of the hot water against my skin.

"Can I?" Poe's voice is gentle. Looking up, I find him holding a bottle of the hotel provided body wash. The bottle looks so tiny compared to his large hand.

I nod my head, watching him carefully as he squeezes the white liquid into his hand. He rubs his large palms together, creating tiny suds between his fingers.

"Turn around," he directs, twirling his finger in the air to further his point.

Following his direction, I turn to face the showerhead. Water falls from it, the head twice the size of my head. When I traveled the world on my own, I wasn't staying in plush hotels like I am now. I was renting out rooms in stranger's houses most of the time, lucky to even have five minutes alone in the shared bathroom.

This tour is allowing me to experience the world in a totally different capacity—fancy hotel rooms included. The lush hotels don't really matter to me though, I'm just happy to experience some of these things with the man behind me.

I want to sink into him at the feel of his fingers on my skin. He soaps every inch of my body, massaging the skin while he's at it. He even pauses at my shoulders, digging his thumbs into the spots where I hold a lot of tension. I don't know if he noticed how I let the water run over those spots to relieve the tension, or if it's just a coincidence, either way his fingers bring so much relief to the muscles.

"That feels so nice," I mewl, my head rocking to the side.

"I can feel the knots," he notes, his thumbs digging into them.

"I always have them there." His hands move away from my shoulders, working their way down my back to make sure every inch of me is clean. "They were way worse when I was dancing."

"Why'd you stop?"

I focus on the way his fingers dig into my skin. The way he washes me right now isn't sexual. It feels like he's taking care of me, a way of him sharing affection, and I relish in the feeling.

My body stiffens, even though I try to hide the reaction from him. "That's a long story," I answer honestly.

"I have nothing but time," he responds.

He's opened to me about things that are obviously hard for him. About his childhood best friend, and about his parents. It's probably time I do the same. I'm just worried that he'll look at me differently when I tell him everything that's happened.

Turning around, I look up. He watches me carefully.

I take a deep breath. "I have to tell you something. Something I've never told anyone else."

He cradles my naked body to his chest.

CHAPTER
41

"You can tell me anything," I assure her. My hands are still covered in soap, but I'm too focused on whatever she's about to say to keep working at getting her clean. For the moment, it can wait. I want to give her my full attention.

Her eyes dart all over my face. She opens her mouth only to shut it again, as if it's hard to get the words out.

Finally, she looks down, her shoulders slightly caving in. "I know you've heard some things about what happened to me in high school. But there's more to the story. More than I've ever told anyone else."

My stomach drops at her words. By the way she won't look at me, and the way her body has caved in on itself, I'm terrified of what she's about to say.

I'm scared to find out the whole story. The parts I already know have me seeing red, but I have a feeling it's worse. It has to be, by the way she's acting right now.

"You don't have to tell me," I offer, even though I want her to tell me more than anything. I want to take her pain and her trauma and shoulder it as my own. I can pack it with the ones of my past, carrying the burdens of our lives for the both of us if it means she never looks at me again with the same sadness in her eyes that's there right now.

Shaking her head, she steps closer to me. Her arms wrap around my middle, holding me close to her.

She doesn't look at me, but she does speak up, her words said into my chest. "I want to tell you. I need someone else besides…him…to know."

I clutch her head to my body. Maybe I should've never asked her about dancing. I hadn't imagined it would lead to this.

"I don't know what all you know," she whispers. The water almost drowns out the sound of her voice. My ears strain to hear every word. "But one night Nora had a party at our house. Our parents were gone, and I was supposed to go to a friend's house."

Her fingers dig into my skin as she buries her face in my chest. "At the time, dance was my whole world. My life revolved around it. I wasn't one to party, knowing how I'd feel the next day if I risked drinking or even staying up late. My coaches were always pretty hard on us, making sure we didn't do anything to get in the way of dancing. I didn't mind it. I was in love with dancing, with the way it made me feel."

I'm quiet, letting her tell the story at her own pace. I won't pressure her to divulge anything she doesn't want to. There's already a sinking feeling in my chest, knowing where this is going.

"Nora was disappointed I wouldn't be there for the party. I hadn't realized she'd been wanting to spend time together so much, but she'd convinced me to stay home that night, to party with her and her friends. She and her boyfriend at the same time had just broken up. She'd wanted to celebrate, so I canceled my plans, opting to stay home."

Her body shakes in my arms. I hate it. I'd take her pain and make it mine in an instant if it were possible.

"I'd hung around for an hour or two, but it wasn't my scene.

Nora had friends of her own, and it wasn't her fault but she got caught up in spending the evening with them. It didn't matter to me, I was tired anyway. I told her I was going to bed, and she understood. She was kind enough to tell me I could sleep in her bed. It was the room in the house that was farthest from where the party was taking place. Unlike my room, which was the first room at the top of the stairs. The sounds of the party would've been loud in my room, so I took her up on her offer."

She takes a shaky breath in. All I do is hold her tight to me, words failing me. There's a pit in my stomach already, and she hasn't even gotten to the part that did the damage.

"I'd been asleep for I don't know how long when I heard the door creak open. I didn't think much about it at first. Since I'd been in such a deep sleep, I didn't know what time it was. I'd figured it was Nora. Except, it *wasn't* Nora."

"Take a breath." I give her body a squeeze, silently reassuring her that I'm here. Her hands tremble against my back. I almost tell her to stop. Except at this point, I can tell she needs this. She needs to get it off her chest, to no longer carry the burden of whatever part of the story is unknown to everyone else, so I keep my mouth shut. I'm ready to be here however she needs me once she relieves herself of this secret.

I'm confident that whatever she's about to tell me will no doubt break my heart.

"It's weird how even in a deep sleep, out of consciousness, you just know something's wrong. By the way the bed dipped around me, I knew it wasn't Nora. It's like my mind was screaming for me to wake up, to move, but my body wasn't catching up. I was still waking up when I felt a weight on top of me. Before I came all the way to it, my hands were above my head, getting pressed into the pillow."

Bile rises in my throat. I swallow, trying to stifle the urge to throw up.

"When I opened my eyes, I could barely see. It was so dark

in her room, but I could see enough. I recognized the voice, the smell, the shape of the body above me. It was her ex-boyfriend. Nora's ex-boyfriend. It was him but wasn't him. There was something vacant in his eyes. He was looking down at me, but he wasn't. His breath reeked of vodka. It made my stomach churn. Well, maybe it was the smell, or maybe it was the way he held my hands so tightly I couldn't move them. I couldn't get him off me."

"Fuck, butterfly," I say, my voice hoarse speaking through the emotion. I want to cry, hating that she's been through this.

"I'd told him to stop. That it wasn't Nora, that it was *me*, Lennon. He didn't hear me, or he didn't care. I hadn't expected anyone but Nora to come into her room that night. I'd thrown on a big T-shirt as pajamas. The only thing underneath was underwear. They weren't great at keeping me covered. They made things too easy. If only I'd had on something different. If I'd worn leggings or pants to bed."

Dread settles all over my body when I picture the scenario she describes. As my mind fills in the holes on what happened next. "They were too easy for him to rip away. He was just so *heavy*. His grip was too tight. I couldn't stop him, Poe." She sobs. I cry with her, salt coating my lips from my own tears.

I clutch her so tightly I'm afraid I might break her. In my mind, if I hold her tight enough, I can ease her of the pain. I can shield her from her trauma with my own body.

If only that were true.

"He pushed my shirt up too easily, ripped the side of my underwear too quickly. I'd barely woken up, and I was almost naked in front of him. For someone so drunk, he was quick at getting his own pants undone."

My teeth stay clenched. I'm afraid if I don't keep my jaw set that I actually will throw up, and she doesn't deserve that. I didn't go through this, she did. I need to stay strong for her. Later today or tonight, the next time I'm alone, I know this'll catch up with me. I'll allow myself to process what's happened to her. But right now, she needs me. I stay strong for her, even though every word she says rips a hole right through me.

"He kept saying her name, and I kept saying it wasn't her. It was me. I'd repeated my name so many times, pleaded with him so many times, that my voice went hoarse. I didn't know when I started crying, but I was. My body went into shock when he pushed inside me. If I would've yelled, if someone were to have heard, maybe I could've stopped it before he took everything from me. But at the moment, I couldn't yell. I even stopped fighting. I just went completely still. I did nothing. I couldn't do anything."

I cradle her to my chest as she falls apart. Her sobs are so loud. I feel them as my own, her pain causing damage to me.

"He thought it meant I wanted it. He still kept saying her name. It didn't stop, not for what felt like forever. It hurt so bad, but I couldn't do anything about it. It felt as if I was watching it all unfold from outside of my body. I'd always imagined what my first time would feel like, never thinking it would be like that."

My chest shakes. I'm trying so hard to stay strong for her, but it's becoming way too much. My mind can't stop imagining this pathetic excuse of a man. I imagine all the things I'd do to this piece of shit if I ever see him in person.

When she looks up at me, her eyes are swollen and red. I've never seen her cry, and I never want to see it again. Seeing her like this destroys me. I've felt my pain for years, but seeing her pain—feeling it—is so much worse than my own. My vision goes blurry from the mix of rage and hurt, knowing what she's been through.

"Eventually, Nora found us. She came in and hit him over and over with her mirror until he stopped, but it was too late. The damage was done." Her voice breaks at the end. She sounds defeated as her body collapses.

I pull her into my arms, lifting her from the ground and bringing us chest to chest. Backing up, I take a seat at the large shower seat. Now that we're seated, I pull her all the way into me. Leaning over her, I wrap my arms around her and shield her from everything else.

"I don't know why, but Nora just assumed it hadn't gone all the way. My shirt was long enough that she couldn't see the ripped underwear, or see the blood between my legs. It was dark, so I don't think she saw the blood on him either."

My arms cling to her. At this point, I don't know if it's for her benefit or for mine. I hold on to her tightly, just to know that right here, in this moment, she's safe with me.

"She was so messed up over what happened. Felt so guilty because the first thing he'd said to her when she got him off me was that he thought it was her. I was already afraid she wouldn't be able to live with the guilt of knowing he assaulted me. If she knew how far it actually went, what he stole from me...I was terrified she wouldn't be able to handle it."

My lips press the wet hair of her head, needing to feel her, connect with her somehow. I've never been the best with words, but right now, I feel absolutely terrible at them. I don't know what to say. I hate myself for having words fail me. "You've had to keep this to yourself for years?" I rasp, choking over my words.

She nods, reaching up to wipe at her eyes. I stop her, cradling her face and wiping the tears away with my thumbs.

"She's my sister. It wasn't her fault. I didn't want it to hurt her more."

"He raped you, Lennon," I say, the words vile on my tongue.

Her entire body shakes as she takes a deep breath. "I know, Poe. Trust me, *I know*. I've relived it over and over, thinking about everything I could've done differently."

I lower my face to hers, keeping her head clutched in my hands. "This wasn't your fault, butterfly. It wasn't your responsibility to do anything differently. That was all on that piece of shit."

Sniffling, she looks at me sadly. "I know. I've had countless people tell me it wasn't my fault. And I know it wasn't. It wasn't Nora's either. I never blamed her for it. It was *his*, but it's easier to say that to actually come to terms with it."

"I wish I could erase that from your past," I say, not hiding the tears from her that roll down my cheeks. If I wanted to, I could probably pass them off as the water from the shower, but I don't care if she sees them. I don't care about anything other than her.

Her hands leave my chest. She places them in my hair, threading her fingertips through the wet locks. "You already have."

CHAPTER 42

I NEVER EXPECTED Poe to react the way he has to the rest of my story. Maybe it's because I hadn't ever told anyone about it. I didn't know what to really expect once I finally told someone my truth. Maybe it's because he's always seemed so closed off. I haven't seen a ton of emotions from him yet—until tonight.

His arms never faltered as he held me to his chest, even when I could feel his body shaking against my trembling one.

He looks good with wet hair. I saw it damp the day we went to the bookstore, but not this wet. It's soaking, the curls weighed down by the water. Droplets slide down his cheeks. Some of them are from the showerhead, but some pool from his misty eyes.

"What do you mean I already have?" His voice sounds broken. Mine does, too. We're just two very broken people trying to figure out how to heal the other without quite healing ourselves.

I snuggle deeper into his body, loving how we both smell of the same scent. "Tonight, it felt like what a first time should've felt like. It was everything I could've ever wanted. I've forgotten anything that happened before."

He reaches over me, grabbing the bottle of shampoo. Just

like with the body wash, he squirts it into his hands and rubs his palms together. His fingers feel like magic when he lathers the shampoo into my scalp. They massage the skin expertly, working it into my hair.

I'd accepted he wasn't going to say anything else when he speaks up. "You shouldn't have to forget anything, though. I hate how that fucker took something so special from you." He takes his time working into my hair, even caring enough to work it into my ends.

"Yeah, but you gave it back to me." I pull my knees into my chest, wrapping my arms around my legs. It feels like a weight has been lifted from my shoulders, telling him about what really happened.

It's no longer a secret between me and…him. The boy—undeserving of being called a man—that took something precious to me. It's made me sick all these years that the two of us were the only two people who really knew what happened. Even in court, he tried to play it off that nothing happened. That it was a mistake that stopped before anything could happen.

He was such a liar.

My family had wanted to do the whole court thing, to punish him for what he did. I was so numb I went along with it, when deep down it didn't matter to me. The damage was done. There was nothing that could give me back what he took from me. Jail time wouldn't bring it back. I wasn't going to put my hope in him getting a real punishment, because from the beginning, I knew it would never be enough. It would never feel like he got what he deserved. If I put too much thought into what I wanted to happen to him, I'd only be disappointed.

Eventually, he moved away. Charges were pressed, he was found guilty, it's supposed to stay on his record forever, but that wasn't enough. Nothing will ever be enough because nothing will ever bring back what he stole.

Tonight with Poe was as close as I'll ever get. I finally got to experience what it was like to be with someone I care about. I envision what it felt like with him is what the first time feels like for others that don't have it stripped away from them in an instant.

The shampoo has been sitting in my hair, needing to be rinsed out as Poe lets me feel everything I need to feel. He stands up, pulling me up with him. He doesn't let my body get too far from his. Just enough to stick my head under the cascading water, gently washing the suds from my hair.

"If I ever see him in person, I think I'll kill him," Poe says. It comes out so easy, so nonchalant, even though his words are vicious and angry.

I keep quiet. I've imagined the scenario many times, wondering what I'd do if I ever saw him again. Once my part in the legal stuff was over, I'd fled. High school wasn't for me. I couldn't walk the same halls, have people look at me like it was my fault their all-star athlete had to leave. Many people thought I'd been lying, that Nora and I had plotted it together to get back at him for the breakup. None of them even thought about the fact it was her that had ended things.

Sometimes I wonder if I'd want to kill him, too, if I ever saw him. Other times, I'm terrified at the thought of ever being in the same vicinity as him. I hope it's never a scenario I have to find out.

Poe works conditioner into my hair, somehow knowing to focus the product more on my ends than at my roots. The only times I've ever had someone else wash my hair was when I'd had my hair done, and even that hasn't been often. I've never had the time to get it done. Or wanted to spend the extra time I had sitting in a salon chair. The deep chestnut color of my natural hair has always been fine.

But I remember the few times I had it done, how good it felt to have someone else wash my hair for me. None of it compares to Poe, however. It's slightly unfair. He could do anything and I'd think it better than anything before.

I'm so deeply in love with this man. I just can't tell him. I don't want to scare him. I can't lose whatever we've started. Label or no label, I'm scared to backpedal on how far we've come.

He runs his fingers down my hair, making sure to remove all the product. The two of us are lost in our own thoughts. I like that about Poe. He doesn't feel the need to fill the silence. He understands that sometimes that words aren't needed. He doesn't apologize for what happened to me. He doesn't say things just to be nice. Instead, he uses his actions to comfort me.

The tenderness he's taken with me means more than words ever could.

Once my hair is clean, he spins me around, pulling me into him once again. If he keeps cradling me in his chest like this, I might get too used to it. We have a serious height difference, but the difference feels perfect. My head fits right up against his heart. I love that if I were to turn my head and place my ear against him, I'd be able to hear each one of his heartbeats.

"Thank you for sharing that with me." His words still seem a bit shaky, like he's trying to get a grip on his emotions.

"Thank you for listening."

This makes him sigh, his hands fisting in the hair he just spent so much time cleaning. "Don't you ever thank me for something like that, Lennon. I listen because I care."

I listen because I care.

He doesn't know the weight his words hold. It's just another way for him to admit to feelings he's swore he'd never have without flat out saying it.

I cling on to them for dear life, repeating them over in my head until I could repeat back exactly how he said it.

Reaching around me, he turns the shower off. I only miss the warmth the water brought for a few moments. It doesn't take long for him to wrap the large white plush towel over my shoulders. He takes another towel, wrapping it around his trim waistline.

Him taking care of me doesn't stop once he leaves the shower. He continues it by telling me to take a seat on the bed. I listen, watching him carefully as he walks around my space. He looks good, mixed with all my belongings. I could get used to him being in my space like this. Showers would be much better if they always involved him.

"Do you have more pajamas in your bag?" he asks.

I'm too busy staring at his abs to answer. They glisten from the leftover water of the shower. He takes great care of his body. Mixed with the tattoos that cover so much of his skin, he's the hottest man I've ever seen.

"Lennon?"

I jump, looking up to him apologetically. "Uh yeah, I do."

He nods, unzipping my bag and shuffling. His hands disappear inside it. He pulls one article of clothing out after the other. They're all day clothes, not suited for bed. His lips turn down in a small frown when he reaches the bottom, no pajamas in sight.

I'm about to tell him that my pajamas are in the suitcase in the closet, but before I can do it, he's walking across the room. He reaches into the small duffle bag I'd only just realized he brought with him.

Pulling out a large T-shirt of his, he smiles at me. "Wear mine?"

My eyes take it in, already knowing it's a few sizes too big for me. I don't care. I'd proudly wear it as a dress if it means I get something of his.

He crosses the room, stopping directly in front of me. Smirking, he holds it up. "Put your arms up."

I do as he says, the towel falling to the floor. He doesn't make it sexual. His eyes don't even travel over my naked body before the fabric is covering me. I wouldn't mind if he looked, but I appreciate knowing the moment isn't about that right now.

I fight the urge to pull the shirt to my nose and sniff. It smells just like him. If it's up to me, he'll never get this shirt back. It's perfectly worn, the fabric soft against my skin.

"It looks better on you," he notes, taking a step back. The towel around his hips slips slightly lower. The movement gives me a better look at his toned obliques, the muscles leading down to the point of him I've now had a taste of.

"Great," I smile, grabbing the towel at my feet and drying my hair with it. "Then we both agree I get to keep it."

He gasps dramatically, turning around and walking to his bag once again. Even with his back to me, I'm able to take in the view of him. I didn't know what I'd expected from him, but I wasn't prepared for all the muscles he has. The muscles ripple down his back with each movement.

I could stare at it forever. Sadly, I wish he wouldn't put on the clothes he grabs from his bag. I'd way rather stare at him like this.

"I've had that shirt for years. It's one of my favorites." In one fluid movement, he rips the towel from his hips, tossing it on the chair by our bags.

Averting my gaze, I look down at the shirt. *Anticipation Rising* is scrawled against the front in bold letters. The shirt must be pretty old since it's merch for Nash's old boy band. One he hasn't been a part of for years. It makes it even more special. He'll have to rip it from my hands if he wants it back.

I love picturing what Poe must've looked like at the time he first got the shirt. Even though he likes to point out how much older he is than me, I don't care about it. I like his age right now. I'm into the fact that he's older, wiser, and has more life experience. But it is fun to picture him when he was still in his twenties. Thank god for the internet. I've been able to look up what he looked like at various stages of his life. Through the years, more and more tattoos popped up on his body. His hair becomes longer, shaggier, the locks less styled and messier.

I hug the fabric to my chin as he steps into a pair of boxer briefs. "Well, it won't be one of my favorites. It'll be my favorite."

He shakes his head. "If you want it, it's yours, butterfly. Just remember me when you slip it on each time."

I take the spot next to him, rifling through my bag until I find a pair of underwear. I slide them up my legs, fully content with my pajamas for the night. Any chance I get, I'll be wearing this shirt. Searching my bag, I pull out my hairbrush.

All I want to do is climb into bed and have Poe hold me in his arms. My body is spent from earlier, my emotions as well, after finally telling someone else about my past. But I know that if I don't brush my hair, it'll be one giant knot tomorrow, and I don't want that either.

Walking to the bed, I take a seat on the edge. I run the brush through my hair, working out knot after knot.

The brush is running smoothly through my hair when Poe steps next to me. Without saying anything, he grabs the brush from my hand. He takes a seat next to me, making the bed dip. I scoot closer to the middle a bit, his weight heavier than mine, almost making me slide off the edge.

He follows suit, the two of us seated in the middle of the mattress. I didn't think he could be any sweeter, but he proves me wrong when he runs the brush through my hair.

"I used to beg Nora to brush my hair."

He chuckles. "Yeah? Did she do it?"

I pull my legs underneath me. "Only if I paid her or did something for her." If I wanted her to brush my hair, it usually ended up in me taking on one of her chores or giving her a dollar. I didn't mind. I liked her brushing my hair, and I liked spending time with her even more.

Our two-year age gap doesn't seem like much now, but back then, it was just close enough where I felt like I could do what she was doing, but just far enough to where we were at slightly different places in life.

The brush stops. He places it by my knee, running his fingers through my hair once. Taking me by surprise, he leans close to my ear. His breath on my neck gives me goosebumps. "You tell me when you want your hair brushed, and I'll do it, butterfly. I need nothing in return."

It's hard to imagine a time that my heart will never be his. The things he does and says, not realizing how much they mean to me, will stick with me forever. I'm convinced no other man will even compare.

I'd never tell him this, but he puts my book boyfriends to shame.

I tuck my chin to my chest, trying my best to hide my beaming smile from him.

His fingers find my hair once again. At first, I think he's just going to play with it, something I wouldn't complain about in the slightest. But he seems to work with more purpose. He softly runs his fingers through the hair, sectioning it off in three sections down my back.

"What are you doing?" I ask, my voice just above a whisper.

"Attempting to braid your hair." He laughs. "Although I may be shit at it."

As he does his best to braid my hair back, his knuckles keep brushing over the back of my neck. It sends shivers down my spine. The room around us is silent. Now and then, he mutters a cuss word or two under his breath when I can feel hair fall out of the braid he works so hard on.

It takes him a few attempts, but eventually he finishes the braid. He unwraps a ponytail holder from the handle of my brush, securing it to the end of the braid. When he flips it over my shoulder, I have to swallow to keep a laugh in.

He's right, it's horrible. Wet pieces of hair from different spots of the braid. There are chunks I'm wondering if he even used three strands. Halfway down the middle, it looks more like a twist than a braid.

"It's perfect," I fib, running my fingers over the hair.

He lets out a load groan. Wrapping his arms around my middle, he pulls me into him. Our bodies mold together perfectly. "It's awful but thank you for lying to me."

For the next few hours, we don't move from the bed. Our bodies never stop touching. It's the perfect night after an already perfect day. I try to enjoy it, having this one-on-one time with him, but in the back of my mind, I can't help but wonder how things will change tomorrow. We'll have to face everyone, and no matter how bad I want to tell them about us, I don't think Poe will. And I'm worried how long having him in secret will suffice for me.

CHAPTER
43

THE SUN PEEKS through the gap in the hotel room curtains. If Lennon wasn't sleeping soundly against my chest, I'd reach over to the nightstand and grab my phone to check the time. I don't budge, too comfortable with her nestled against me to dare move.

She looks so peaceful in her sleep. Her hands are tucked underneath her cheek, her nose pressed up against my shoulder. My arm tingles from falling asleep, but I ignore it. I don't want to do anything to wake her up.

There have been times since I first met Lennon that I caught her watching me. I know there's even more times that she watched me, and I didn't notice because she's told me so. So for now, I use the opportunity to watch her without her knowing.

We spent most of the night talking. Most of it wasn't important or life changing, but it was still a night I'll never forget. She discussed her favorite books for an hour, at one point making me get out my phone to make a list of books she'd read that she thought I'd enjoy.

I wrote them down, thinking one day I may read them. Even though I much preferred her telling me about the stories. It was intoxicating to watch her get all excited about them. Even laying down, she'd start talking with her hands, waving them around everywhere, heated when I told her I'd just watch the movie adaptation of one of her favorite books.

We'd talked about how I got the gig with *Anticipation Rising* and how Nash and I quickly became friends, more than friends, he became like a brother to me.

Lennon stirs, her eyes slowly blinking open. Squeezing, I lean in and place a kiss to her forehead.

"Good morning," I say. My voice is still raspy from not using it in my sleep, the little of it I got. She'd fallen asleep hours before me. I'd known I should sleep too, but I couldn't. My mind raced with the story she'd told me. I couldn't help wondering how she found her way to my arms, but I knew I needed to keep her safe. I never want another man to be in the position to hurt her again. The problem is, if I really swear to that, that means I'll have to keep myself from hurting her. And I don't know how to do that.

Her feet stretch underneath the covers, her toes running across my shin. "Good morning," she responds, her voice sleepy.

It's adorable. I'm fucking obsessed with it.

If I believed in love, if I allowed myself to love, I'd think I was in love with her.

My pathetic excuse for a braid falls down her back when she buries her face into the crook of my neck. I don't know if she can get any air in the position, but I say nothing because I love the feel of it.

It's been years since I've snuggled with someone. Intimacy like this was not something I craved. In fact, it was something I avoided at all costs. Things have changed. Now I'm trying to figure out how I can wake up to her in my arms every morning. The thought is dangerous.

I feel like we're playing with fire, except it's worse because her heart is on the line.

I'll do whatever I can to make sure I don't hurt her. I just don't know what that is. I don't know how to not hurt the people I care about, but it's something I want to change for her.

None of this I tell her. She doesn't deserve for me to give her false hope. I need to figure my shit out. I lied to her when I told her I'd never have feelings for her. What I hadn't lied about was that I couldn't keep her heart safe, no matter how hard I wanted to.

"What time is it?"

I keep one arm around her, keeping her snug against my chest, but reach behind me with the other. My fingers fumble around the various things on the nightstand before they connect with my phone. I hold it up in the air so we can both see the time.

She sighs, stretching her body out once again. "How many missed texts do you think I have?"

This makes me laugh. I look down at the two missed calls and seven texts I have. Most of them from Landon. "Considering no one has knocked on the door looking for you, hopefully not too many."

"Do you have anything going on today?" she asks, pushing off me to sit up.

Our bodies now barely touch. I already miss holding her.

I follow suit, the two of us now sitting up in bed, our backs pressed to the fancy headboard. The heels of my hands rub my eyes, trying to wipe the tired fog away.

"Only a few things. I'll have to check with Nash."

"Will I see you again today?" I hate the hesitation in her voice, ashamed of myself for my words and actions making her feel that way.

Following suit, I sit up, scooting over until we're pressed against one another again. I move some stray hairs from her face, looking her deep in the eye. "I don't know if I can go an entire day without doing this." I lean in, catching her mouth with mine.

"The feeling's mutual." She laughs. And not for the first time this morning, I wish I could make these moments last forever.

CHAPTER
44

I WAKE up to the feeling of hair being brushed from my forehead. My eyes pop open, finding Poe smiling above me. He wears a fitted T-shirt, a gray jacket halfway zipped over it. His normal necklace with a guitar pick hanging off it dangles against my chest.

Every morning since our butterfly garden date, I've woken up to either him pressing a kiss to my forehead, or to a long text saying good morning. It feels good. He makes me feel wanted, needed. I'm growing too used to it as we travel from city to city, country to country.

"I have to go," he whispers, even though we're the only two people in the room. "I've got a meeting."

Groaning, I grab a fistful of his T-shirt. I bring him closer to me. "Don't go," I whine.

He smiles, peppering kisses along my jawline. "I wish I could stay, butterfly, trust me. I'd love to repeat last night with you."

Blood rushes to my cheeks. We'd been lying in bed last night, both reading our own books, me carefully scrawling words in the margin of my book. The other thing he'd gotten me from the gift shop was a kit of annotation supplies. I'd gone crazy using the new tabs and markers, loving the way he'd been so thoughtful with the gifts he got me. The new pens slid across the paper of my books like a dream. I'd annotated way more with the new kit than I ever had before, loving using the supplies. I'd looked up from the scene I was in the middle of annotating, a blush to my cheeks when I'd told him I had a new list item.

We weren't still doing the bucket list thing, not really. But it was still fun to say it, especially when I wanted to try something new with him in the bedroom.

I'd told him I wanted to be the one on top. I wanted to be in control. He loved the idea. We'd spent the next hour tangled in the sheets, my thighs sore this morning from the fun we'd had.

He kisses the spot on my cheek that feels hot. "Never stop blushing for me. I'm obsessed with it."

This only makes me blush harder. I grab underneath his chin, bringing his lips to mine instead of responding. With his dirty mouth and him just being *him*, I don't see me blushing any less soon.

"Will you come back after?" I ask once he pulls away.

We've been lucky that for this portion of the international tour, we've been staying at hotels instead of on a tour bus. It's allowed for us to spend almost every night together, something we wouldn't be able to do if we'd been on the buses.

"If I'm able to sneak away with an excuse." He pulls me from the mattress, fully embracing me. I gladly wrap my arms around him, already dreading the moment he pulls away.

I wish I could just go with him to whatever meeting he has. Or at least be able to hold his hand or kiss him when we all gather together. It's hard, pretending we aren't spending every extra moment we can together. It's taking a toll on me. Sometimes I feel like his dirty little secret. It's a tarnish on how happy he makes me.

"We could stop sneaking around," I mumble, afraid to broach the subject. Every time we've discussed it before, he's already come up with some excuse as to why we shouldn't tell people we've been spending time together. We also haven't had the conversation where we've defined what we are. I'm too nervous he'll say something to break my heart, like we're just friends or something soul-crushing like that.

He stiffens in my grasp, his head rearing backward. "I didn't realize that's something you'd want."

I let out an angry sigh, pushing away from him so I can see his face. He's got to be kidding. "You didn't realize that'd be something I want?" I ask in disbelief.

"No, I didn't. I thought you were happy."

"I didn't say I wasn't happy with whatever we're doing here, but it'd be nice to not feel like a secret."

"You aren't a secret."

My eyebrows raise. "I'm not? Because it sure feels that way when you say things like, '*If I'm able to sneak away with an excuse.*'"

He runs a hand over his mouth, playing with his stubble. "I didn't mean it like that."

It's hard to be mad at him because I know he isn't trying to be cruel with his words, but it doesn't make it hurt any less. "Then how did you mean it, Poe?" I ask, resignation laced in my voice. I hadn't envisioned this being where our morning would go when he woke me up, but now that we're started, I can't let it go.

It seems I've finally become fed up with being his little secret. I'm tired of having to hide something that makes me so happy. If he's happy, why does he feel the need to hide it?

He reaches up to massage the back of his neck, his eyes darting around the room. It's obvious he doesn't know what to say. Sadness settles low in my stomach, spreading through the rest of the body with each second he stays silent.

"No matter how I answer your question, I feel like I can't win," he says tightly.

"What do you mean?" My voice is angry. I'm angry. I don't like the person he's turned me into.

"Because I'm on this fucking pedestal from you, and you've got to take me off it. For fuck's sake, Lennon," his voice is resigned, his eyes are sadder than usual, "I've been telling you that I'm flawed from the very beginning. I need to be taken off this god damn pedestal or I'm only bound to disappoint you more. Why can't you get that in your head?"

"I know this, Poe. What do you think drew me to you? It wasn't perfection. It was the raw hurt I could feel seeping from you in the first few moments I met you. My first thought when I saw you was me wondering what had made you so damaged. Hurt people know other hurt people, and I was dying to know more. I've never asked for perfection. All I'm asking now is for clarity on what we are and to maybe not feel like your dirty little secret."

He sucks an angry breath in, yanking at his hair. He looks just as heartbroken as I do. It doesn't stop me from my next words. "I've asked this once, and I'm going to ask it again because a lot has changed since then," I begin, keeping my voice steady even though I want to break down in tears. I hate that after all this time, he still can't explain to me why we have to hide this. "But what are we doing here, Poe? What are we?"

"You know what we are."

I shove myself off the bed, unable to sit another minute. So many emotions rip through me, I don't know which one to focus on first. "Don't tell me what I do and don't know. If I knew, I wouldn't be asking. If I knew, I wouldn't have been so fucking scared of asking until now."

His dark eyebrows pull in. God, I hate that even when I'm mad at him, I just want to close the distance between us and remove the frown from his face. Every time before this, I've been able to let it go. I've been able to take the scraps from him and tell myself I'm happy from it.

Now, I need *more*. I don't need a lot, but I know I need *something* more from him.

He looks sad, and for a moment I almost drop it. Only for a minute. His sadness can't stop me now because deep down, he's been making *me* sad. His failure to define what we are, to give me anything, has beaten down on me. Add in the fact that no one can even know we've been intimate for weeks now, I'm starting to no longer even feel like a secret—but it's beginning to feel like a dirty one, and I hate it. "Why have you been scared?"

He tries to take a step toward me, but I back up. Space. I need space from him. For once, I need to pull myself together around and him and stand my ground.

"Because I don't want to lose you," I answer honestly. My voice breaks at the end, and I can't hide the single tear that runs down my cheek. "I'm terrified that if I ask what we are, if I ask for more, that you'll run and we won't even be whatever we are now."

"Who said you'd lose me?"

Taking a deep breath, I run my hands down my face in frustration. "Could you stop answering my questions with another freaking question?"

"I'm not…" he begins, his jaw snapping shut when he realizes that's exactly what he's doing. He sighs loudly, his shoulders rising and falling dramatically. His cheeks puff out with the movement. "I don't know what to call us, Lennon. I wish I did. What I can tell you is that I feel something for you I haven't felt for anyone else, and it scares the hell out of me."

"Why?"

His lip twitches. "Now who's asking the questions?"

I roll my eyes, annoyed he can make me laugh at a moment like this. "Answer it," I demand. My arms cross over my chest as I wait for him to choose his words.

"Because once again in my life, I have something I can lose.

It's fucking terrifying because I don't know if I can lose someone else and survive it." His voice gets rougher. "I don't know if I could survive losing you, butterfly. And I'm so fucking scared at that realization."

He knows exactly how to erase the anger from my heart. As fast as I can, I'm closing the distance between us, throwing my body against him. I cling to him like I'm going to lose him. Maybe I will lose him, maybe we won't ever be able to come to an agreement between us. No matter what, for the moment, my heart is his, no matter how much he frustrates me. No matter how much he's fighting making his heart mine.

Poe's hands cradle my face. It's something he does all the time. I love the possessiveness of it. The scratch of his fingertips against the soft skin of my cheek has become something I've grown way too used to.

I look up at him, hoping he doesn't notice the water pooling in my eyes. "You're not going to lose me."

His thumb swipes underneath my eyelid, catching the tear that betrayed me and fell. "You don't know that, Lennon. Look at me, I'm already fucking things up."

He isn't wrong. It's partially my fault. I'd told him once I'd take him in any capacity I could have him. At the time, I thought that'd be enough. But now that I've had him in some capacity, now that my feelings have flown right past puppy love and ended at real love, I can't just accept scraps anymore. I want all of him. Even the ugly, jagged parts, the parts he thinks that are unlovable. I want it all and nothing less.

I lean into his touch, sad at the knowledge my heart will never beat like this for anyone else. Deep down, I wish I could accept whatever he's willing to give. Then we wouldn't be in a situation like this. Me needing more and him fighting tooth and nail to give me more.

"I just don't want to feel like I'm your secret," I whisper. More tears fall down my cheeks until they're a string. I'm embarrassed by them, but I do nothing to wipe them away. Maybe it's good he sees them. He needs to know how real this is for me, how the constant fear of the unknown is driving me mad.

"Then we'll tell whoever you want to tell." His voice sounds so sure.

The words take me by surprise. "Tell them what?"

His arms tighten on my face. "That we're dating? Fuck, I don't know, butterfly. Whatever you want to tell them. Whatever the kids are saying these days." He winks at me. I fight the urge to roll my eyes at him. He makes it seem like he's twenty years older, maybe even more, which isn't the case.

"You'd do that?" There's no mistaking the hope in my voice.

He attempts to wipe the smile from my face by kissing me. It doesn't work for long. The moment he pulls away, I'm smiling ear to ear. I hadn't expected him to say anything like this and there's no I'll try to even hide the elation from it.

"I told you, I don't want to lose you. If this is what you need, that's what we'll do. I'm just trying to think of the right time to do it. I don't want to make tonight about me…"

I nod my head immediately. "No, I get that. We don't have to tell anyone, or even tomorrow. I just want to know that soon I won't be something you're keeping tucked away, ashamed to tell anyone else."

Tonight we're all going to a big dinner to celebrate Nash officially taking ownership of all his music. He's signed his next few albums over to his old label, except they're under new ownership. This time, he'll own all rights to his music, the way it should be. I don't know a ton about this business, but I know that from what Nora says, this deal is huge and sets the precedent for many other artists of the future. It's a monumental day for Nash. I wouldn't dream of taking the spotlight from him tonight. Right now, I'm fully content knowing that we'll only hide this from those we care about for a little longer.

"I've never been ashamed of you, Lennon. It's never really even been about you. It's been because I'm fucked up that I haven't wanted to tell people. And quite frankly, I'm just a private guy. But I get why you don't want to hide this, and I want that, too. Can we just wait a little longer? Once all the excitement from Nash dies down?"

I rise to my toes, kissing him as my answer. I'd stay in this position forever, kissing him until my lips were raw, but eventually he pulls away. His hands find my hips, holding onto them tightly. "We've got to go or I won't end up leaving this hotel room."

I bite my lip. "That doesn't sound so bad."

He backs away, heading toward the hotel room door. It's just occurred to me he's already ready for the day. I'm impressed with how quiet he was because I'd slept through all of it.

I follow him to the door, the two of us stopping in front of it.

"I'll see you later," he presses a quick peck to my lips.

"Bye," I say, opening the door for him. He looks down both sides of the hallway before exiting. When I close the door behind him, I'm riding on cloud nine.

Soon, everyone will know about us.

CHAPTER
45

OUR MEETING ENDED AN HOUR AGO, and Landon is still giving me shit about being absent recently. Luckily, I had a bit of a reprieve from it while we worked on a new song with Nash. We'd booked a studio here in Glasgow, managing to lay down a few beats for the song before ending the session. If we didn't have the nice dinner ahead of us tonight, we would've stayed for much longer.

Nash almost canceled the dinner, trying to be modest about his accomplishments, but we wouldn't let him. The song will be there tomorrow or whenever. So many people have flown in to help him celebrate. That's exactly what we're going to do.

Everyone else has already gone inside to start getting ready for the evening. Landon wanted to smoke a cigarette, something he does occasionally, so I'd stayed out here to talk with him.

Now would be the perfect opportunity for me to tell him where I've been, or more who I've been with lately, but I hold my tongue. I don't want to tell him before Lennon gets the opportunity to tell her sister, or I get to tell Nash. Landon's my best friend, but I'm going to keep it from him just a little longer.

"Hey, I've been meaning to ask you something," Landon says, his cheeks drawing in to take a long pull from the cigarette. I hate that he smokes, knowing it's something that's bound to kill him one day. I'm not the best person to get on him for it, however, considering the things from my past I've put in my body.

"What's that?" I ask.

"I was going to ask Aiden since they're besties and all, but he's been so busy chasing after Monica that I haven't bothered, so I'd figured you'd be a good person to ask."

My interest is piqued. I'm curious to know where this conversation is going. "Ask Aiden what?"

Smoke billows from Landon's mouth. "Do you think Lennon would let me take her on a date?"

I choke on my spit. My hand swats at the air, trying to play it off like it's the smoke that he exhaled, even though that's the furthest from the truth. His words take me by surprise, planting a pit in my stomach at the mental picture.

"Why would you ask me that?" I snap, maybe a bit too defensive. I don't know if the reason he's asking me is because he's onto us, but if that were the case, I know he wouldn't be asking me in the first place. Landon thinks with his dick most of the time, but he's a loyal friend. If he knew what Lennon and I'd been up to, he would never ask this of me.

He shrugs, taking another pull. "The two of you seem to be friends. I know she used to be into you and shit, but I figured what the hell, if she was into you, she sure as fuck could be into me."

I never thought this would happen, but I want to punch my best friend square in the face at the words coming from his mouth. It's not like I can really blame him, he has no idea Lennon and I are anything. It doesn't stop my hands from balling into fists.

Pulling air into my lungs, I take a deep breath. I don't know how to approach this with him and I just need a fucking minute to think.

He must take my silence as an invitation to do it, or at least as an invitation to keep the conversation going. Too bad Landon and Lennon going on any sort of date will only happen over my dead body.

"What are my chances?" My best friend continues.

Fucking *zero* chance, that's what.

"I don't know, man," I say, fumbling to come up with an answer for him. One thing's for sure, I absolutely don't want him taking her on a date. At this point, I don't even want him looking at her if it means he's interested in her. "What would Nash think of that?"

Landon scrapes the cherry of his cigarette on the concrete next to him. Standing up, he throws it away in a nearby trash can. "I don't think Nash will care," he says, coming to stand in front of me again.

"Really?"

He nods his head, his typical shit eating grin on his face. "As long as I promise to take care of her, I don't think he'd mind. Plus, I'm not saying I'm going to marry her. She seems chill. I'd love to take her on a date and get to know her."

She's very chill. The dates I've had with her have been the best of my life, but that doesn't mean he gets to fucking do it.

"She doesn't seem your type," I throw out, grasping at straws here to get him off her scent.

This makes Landon laugh. It's obnoxiously loud. I don't know if he's ever found me this funny. "Poe, if anyone knows, it'd be you I don't have a type."

He's right. The man gives me whiplash on the women he's dated. Or attempted to date, it's never amounted to much with him. He grows bored easily, moving from woman to the next in the blink of an eye.

"Well..." I don't know what else to say.

"Well what?" His tone is annoyed. He can join the fucking club.

"Well, I just don't know if you should do it."

The excuse is pathetic. I could do better if I had more time to think on it. Or I could tell the fucking truth, but I can't get myself to do it. I don't want to tell him about Lennon like this. I told Lennon I was ready to tell people, and I thought I was, but now I can't. I tell myself it's because we haven't told Nash or Nora, but I don't think that's really the reason.

I hate myself for it.

"Is there something I don't know?" Landon presses. He watches me carefully. If my best friend wasn't a terrible liar, I'd wonder if he knows more than he's letting on. I know he can't possibly know what's happened between Lennon and me. If he did, he wouldn't be able to keep it a secret.

I shake my head at him. "No, there isn't. Go for it."

He claps his hands together in excitement. "Perfect. Then it's settled. I'm going to ask Lennon on a date. Tonight. After the dinner, or hell, maybe even during it."

No no no.

He can't. Not tonight. It's too soon. I can't watch him do that.

I'd easily be able to rectify this situation if I just came out and told him how I felt about the girl. He'd back away immediately if he knew I loved her. He wouldn't think twice about setting his sights on her ever again.

It should be easy.

It isn't.

My mouth stays closed. As my best friend walks toward the hotel room lobby doors, me following behind him, I don't say a fucking word.

He opens the door for me, his body holding it open so I can step inside. "I'm hyped man," he says. "She seems like the type of girl you'd settle down for."

Trust me, I fucking know.

"Happy for you," I bite out because I don't know what else

to say. It falls from my lips before I can think about the ramifications of it.

All I know is, I want to immediately find Lennon and tell her about this. I want to tell her to not give Landon the time of day, to shoot him down before he can even open his mouth.

It's a shame that Nash catches us in the lobby, not giving me any alone time with Lennon before the dinner.

CHAPTER
46

POE PULLS the chair next to him at the table out, gesturing for me to take a seat there. I don't even look at him as I walk right past it, angling around the table to find a different seat.

I find one right next to Landon. *Perfect.*

Landon looks shocked to find me standing at the chair next to his. Leaping out of his seat, he pulls the chair out next to him. "Take a seat," he says, rushed.

I give him my sweetest smile. "Thank you, Landon."

He smiles back, sitting down next to me once again.

Sneaking a glance across the table, I find Poe staring at us, dumbfounded. Monica sits next to him, not looking happy. I guess she never looks fully happy, but by the looks she keeps throwing at Aiden, my guess is the dirty look has something to do with him. Tyson sits on the other side of Poe, too busy on his phone to even hold a conversation.

I don't think it'd matter to Poe either way. He's too focused, staring at me with surprise.

He doesn't know I heard his entire conversation with Landon earlier.

Good.

It was an honest mistake. I hadn't meant to overhear their

conversation. It wasn't like I was snooping. I'd been out on a walk to clear my head. I'd been so excited after he'd left my room that morning, that I hadn't been able to get much done. Eventually, the excitement got the best of me and I needed a change of scenery. I'd been so used to going on daily walks with Pepper, and even though she's still in the states with a dog sitter, I found myself needing to move my legs.

I was coming back from my walk, pulling my headphones from my ears, when I'd walked up on Landon and Poe having a conversation. The look on Poe's face is what had stopped me in the first place. I'd never seen him look at his friend so angrily.

They were locked in the conversation, neither one of them noticing me standing there. It'd given me the opportunity to overhear the entire thing.

Landon had asked to take me on a date, which was hilarious because Poe must not know that Landon was already on to us.

"Pretend like you're laughing at what I'm saying," Landon says through a clenched smile.

I look at him, giving him a weird look. "What?"

He sighs, annoyed. "Poe is absolutely losing his fucking mind right now, seeing me talk to you. If you want to make him pull his head out of his ass, laugh. Right now."

I do as he says, still trying to figure out exactly what's going. Even though I want to, I don't look in Poe's direction. I heard it loud and clear, him telling Landon that Landon could take me on a date. 'Happy for you' he'd said. Well, then he can be happy about this.

It's pretty easy to smile at Landon. He's got an infectious personality. It's hard *not* to smile when he's already smiling at you. He reminds me of Aiden.

Turns out, I don't have to look at him. Landon's ready to give me the play-by-play. "Oh, he's so fucking pissed." He laughs, the sound coming deep within his chest.

"What's going on here?" I whisper, leaning in close to him.

It might look affectionate to lingering eyes. I wouldn't mind if it did. Poe took a dagger to my heart earlier today, it doesn't hurt if he feels a little bit of pain, too. It'd be worse if he didn't feel pain. Maybe he lied to me this morning, saying whatever he could to get me to shut up. I try not to think too deeply if he really doesn't care if Landon were to take me on a date.

Landon plays into the scheme. He leans in close, grabbing a strand of my hair and twirling it around his finger. Oddly, I catch Aiden's eyes in the brief moment I look away from Landon. He looks confused, which I understand. He's been on my case for weeks asking what's going on between Poe and I, and now he's seeing me with Landon. I can't keep up either.

"I told you this, book girl," he says the nickname without a hint of malice. I don't mind the nickname. I've definitely been called worse. "It's time Poe pulls his head out of his ass and realizes what he's got in front of him. You saw me try to coax him to say it when we were outside earlier, but he's even more hardheaded than I thought."

My jaw drops. "You saw me?"

He smirks, leaning back in his chair. "Sure did. I'd been planning on asking him before you showed up, but once you were there, I figured I should keep pushing it. To be fair, I didn't think he'd stick to his guns like that. The man's hands fisted the moment I brought up asking you out. I didn't know he'd let me get as far as I did."

The words *go for it* ring through my mind. I hadn't expected Poe to let it go that far either.

Yet, he did.

I rub my lips together, risking a glance in Poe's direction. He leans over the table in a defensive stance. Monica looks at him wearily, but for now she doesn't seem to be speaking to him. I don't know if I'd want to talk to him either with his current body language.

My eyes roll. He made his bed. Not my fault he now has to lie in it. "Yeah," I mutter. "I didn't either."

Landon bumps his shoulder against mine. He gives me a reassuring smile, but it does nothing to make me feel better. If anything, him bringing up his conversation with Poe earlier only makes me feel worse. "He didn't mean what he said," he offers, reminiscing on their earlier conversation.

I'd at first been excited to see him standing outside, having a conversation with his best friend. He looked upset. All I'd wanted to do was make him feel better. I was seconds away from making my presence known when I'd overheard Landon.

And then Poe broke my heart without even knowing it.

I'd been riding such a high after our conversation that morning. Sure, it'd started as an argument, but we'd worked through it. He'd made a promise not to keep it a secret anymore. We'd had an agreement.

Maybe it's my fault, for allowing myself to feel such a high after him. Eventually, you come down from the high, mine just happened to be crashing down.

"It hurt like he did," I say sadly.

He reaches to my lap, squeezing my thigh softly. It isn't intimate at all. It's something two friends would do. "He'll come to it."

Shaking my head, I take the champagne glass our server hands me. Nash stands at the end of the table preparing to give a toast. I don't look at Landon as I respond. "I don't want him to come to it, Landon." I keep my voice hushed, not wanting anyone to overhear our conversation.

"What do you want, then?"

"What I want is for him to not let his best friend ask me out on a date. If someone were to ask me if they should go out with him, I'd lose my mind. I want him to do the same. Or at least care enough to say no."

"He just didn't know what to say," Landon argues.

I quickly aim a dirty look at him. The server is finishing up passing out the champagne flutes. Soon our conversation will have to be over, at least for the time being, but I need to get this out. "His willingness to let you do it, even adding the 'I'm happy for you' definitely isn't the way to do it."

Nash speaks, bringing our conversation to a halt. He thanks everyone for being here tonight to help him celebrate the new deal. Once it's over, he looks down at Nora so lovingly; I feel a twinge of jealousy. Not because it's him, but because she has a man that isn't afraid to love her out in the open. I don't think Nash has ever been that way. He treats Nora like his prized possession, gushing about her to anyone who will listen.

I'm about to excuse myself, needing a minute alone, when Aiden pushes his chair out from the other side of me. Standing up, he taps his knife against his champagne flute. Everyone goes silent, all eyes on him.

He looks at me nervously. I give him nothing, having no idea what he's about to do. His eyes leave mine as quickly as they first landed here. His focus goes solely to Monica. She looks like she either wants to murder him or shrink into her chair and disappear completely.

"Monica," he says, his tone serious.

Her eyes widen, all focus going to her. I fight tears as my best friend gives the best speech I've ever heard. By the end, it looks like Monica may cry, too. Aiden just confessed his love to her. Something so touching I want to cry at the sentiment. It stings, knowing he's so willing to lay his heart on the line in front of all these people and I can't even get the man that I'm in love with to tell his friend not to ask me out.

My eyes connect with Poe. He watches me so intently I squirm in my seat. I don't know what he's thinking, but whatever it is, has his features molded into a face I can't read. He looks pained, but I don't know why.

A loud screeching sound fills the silence as Monica runs out of our private room. Aiden follows hot on her heels, leaving all of us in silence.

Nash clears his throat, holding up his water glass. "Well, I guess we'll cheers to that, too."

Everyone laughs, lifting their glasses and taking another sip. I don't do it. I'm too lost, wanting to run out of here just like Monica did. I shouldn't be this upset but seeing both Nash and Aiden so openly discuss their feelings has me feeling even worse about what Poe said earlier. I'm exhausted by having to keep things a secret. It's tiring, always wondering where you stand with someone. That's exactly the position Poe has put me in again. Everything was supposed to be fixed when he left my room this morning. We were *good*. It didn't even last a day before he wreaked havoc on my heart all over again.

Taking a deep breath, I plaster on a fake smile, taking a sip of my drink just to keep my lip from trembling. I shouldn't be feeling like this, and I definitely shouldn't be on the verge of falling apart at this dinner, but I can't help it.

I'm just tired of holding onto something that is bound to fail. I've desperately been trying to hold onto Poe, planting my feet in the ground to keep ahold of a possibility of an us. But my arms are tired. I'm over holding onto something, feeling like I'm the only one holding on for dear life.

It feels like I'm asking for the bare minimum from him, and I'm getting *nothing*. Nash writes songs about the woman he loves, never hiding how he felt for her, even after she broke his heart. Here Aiden, of all people, is confessing his undying love for Monica in front of a room full of people, not worrying if she accepts his love or not.

And here I am, feeling like I'm constantly rejected by the guy I've fallen for. Nothing screams rejection more than the man you love telling his best friend to ask you out.

Go for it.

I'm happy for you.

Everyone carries on with their own conversations while the room around me goes blurry. Standing up, I beeline out of the room.

"Lennon!" Landon shouts behind me. I don't respond to him.

Nora catches my arm as I pass her. Her face is concerned. "You okay?"

I nod, faking a smile. "I'm good, just feeling a little hot. I'm going to get some air."

She looks like she wants to argue, but she doesn't. "Need some company?"

"I'm good on my own. I like it that way."

She gives my arm a squeeze before letting go. The moment she no longer holds on to me, I'm rushing out. I'm having a moment of weakness, a pity party for one, and the last thing I want is to be around others.

As soon as I'm out of the private room, I look around to find the nearest exit. We'd really had to weave in and out of people to get to the back of the restaurant, and I really don't want to have to do that now.

My eyes land on a back door. It might be for employees, but at the moment, I don't care. I push it open, relief washing over me as I step into a near empty alley. There's a server talking on the phone a few feet away, but she barely spares me a second glance.

Walking past her, I make my way away from the restaurant, happy to be on my own.

I need to be alone with my thoughts.

Scotland was never somewhere I'd been before this tour. I'd traveled to various places around the world, but never made it here. I haven't explored Glasgow as much as I'd prefer, so that's exactly what I'm going to do now.

My feet decide my path through the busy street, my thoughts getting lost in my mind. I've never wanted to be this girl, the one so broken up over a guy. It was never my plan to beg someone to love me, but that's exactly what I feel like I'm doing with Poe.

It was easier when I barely knew him. My crush wasn't soul-shattering. It was silly, something for me to focus on. This is different. My heart got involved, and he really had me believing that his did, too. Now, I'm not sure.

One minute he's hot, telling me he could never lose me. The next, he's cold, giving his best friend the green light to ask me on a date.

This isn't what love should feel like. In a book, this would be the third act breakup. It'd hurt, but you knew the hero would do some sort of groveling or some epic grand gesture to get his girl back.

I feel none of those things. I don't even feel hope that he'll do or say anything.

And that's the worst part of it all. He's played so many games with my mind and heart, I don't know what to believe. What to hope for. What to think. So now I'm left with this uneasy feeling in an unfamiliar city, not knowing if the man I love will ever proudly love me back.

In fact, I'm not sure he'll ever love me *at all*. And that's no longer something I can accept.

CHAPTER
47

LENNON NEVER RETURNS to the restaurant. I know because my eyes never stop watching the exit. I hear Nora tell Nash that Lennon had sent her a text saying she was going to explore a bit. They both seemed disappointed by it but moved on quickly.

Eventually, Aiden and Monica also join the table, holding hands at that. Never did I imagine Monica doing any kind of PDA, but she and Aiden spend the remainder of the dinner sickeningly happy.

It hurts to watch. It sucks knowing that's what Lennon wants, but it's what I've failed to give her.

We're all on our way out to the waiting cars for us when Landon pulls me aside. He looks angry, at what I don't know. I honestly don't care. I'm too busy kicking myself for not following after Lennon. She didn't hide that she was upset very well. I should've chased after her and tried to figure out what was wrong. I should've been the one to fix it.

Instead, I stayed in my chair, too scared to chase after her because then it'd be obvious to everyone around something was up between us.

Now with her somewhere in the city, all alone, I don't really give a damn if people know about us or not. It doesn't matter to me. It never should've mattered.

Grabbing my arm, Landon pulls me into a secluded area. Our group decides they want to walk across the street to an ice cream parlor, giving us a moment alone. Except, I don't want to be with Landon. I'm still mad at myself for giving him the go ahead to ask Lennon out earlier and having to watch the two of them flirt; it still makes my blood boil.

"We need to talk," Landon demands.

I rip my arm from his grasp, unreasonably angry with him. "I don't want to talk."

"I don't fucking care what you want to do. There's something I need to tell you, and you need to listen."

My jaw clenches, but my feet stay planted. I'm ready to get whatever he has to say done with. "Get on with it then."

"I don't want Lennon," he deadpans.

Doesn't matter if you do or not. You can't have her.

"And you're telling me this because?"

"Because you need to know that she heard our conversation from earlier."

Oh fuck.

No.

We were alone. No one else was there.

Fuck fuck fuck.

When I don't answer, too busy internally panicking at what he's divulged, he keeps talking. "Yeah. I'd started the conversation because I wanted to see if you'd tell me the truth about you and her. I've known something was up for a while."

"You did?"

Reaching into his pocket, he grabs a box of cigarettes. He pulls one out, sticking it between his lips before pulling out his lighter. "It was fucking obvious you were into her. It went from she used to only watch you to you always watching her."

I think over his words. I'd thought I'd done pretty well at hiding it when we were all together, but apparently I hadn't.

"It was clear you were spending time with someone else when you kept making excuses to why we couldn't hang out. In the past, we've always been together. This international leg, we've barely spent time together."

"Maybe I didn't want to be around people," I throw out. I don't know what I'm trying to hide. It's clear he knows. I might as well be honest with him.

He laughs. "One day I bumped into Lennon in the elevator. She looked so blissfully happy, this weird bag wrapped in her arms like it was a prized possession. Right then, I knew she had to have been with you."

I don't think he means it, but him recalling the memory feels like a punch to the gut. I hate knowing she was so happy, knowing now how much I've hurt her with my ignorance since then.

"I'd tried to get her to tell me she was with you, but she wouldn't budge," he explains. He shakes his head, blowing out smoke. "She didn't have to. Knowing how obsessed she was with you, there was no way anyone was making her smile like that but *you*. Add in the part where you were MIA that day, and I just knew."

"Do you want a trophy for it?" I bite. Being a dick to him is unnecessary. I'm just in a shit mood and he's the only person I can take out my anger on right now.

He smirks around the cigarette. "No. I want you to get your shit together and treat that girl the way she deserves."

His words take me by surprise. I don't know if it's because they're from him, the guy who has never treated a girl the way she deserves to be treated, or if it's the words in general. It's one thing to think in your head that you're doing things wrong, acting in ways you shouldn't. It's a totally different thing when someone calls you out for it.

"If you knew we were involved, why in the hell did you ask me if you could take her out?"

"Isn't it obvious? I wanted you to come to your senses and realize how fucking gone you are for her."

I clench my teeth together, trying not to be angry with him. It wasn't his fault Lennon overheard our conversation, but I wish he hadn't said anything if he never meant it. Either way, it was my fault for saying what I did to him. For not shooting down his question the moment he asked for it.

And now I pay the price, knowing it no doubt hurt her.

Taking a step back, I lean against the building, trying to gather my thoughts. "Well, your plan backfired," I spit.

Landon throws his arms up in surrender. "Don't fucking blame me for this."

Sighing, I grab at my hair. He's right, all of this is my fault. I'm just angry at the world—mostly myself, for being such an asshole.

"She heard everything?" I ask, nervous to hear the answer.

He frowns, nodding his head. "Pretty much. It wouldn't have been terrible until you said go for it…"

"If only she knew how fucking terrible the sentence tasted coming from my lips."

"Is she the one?"

"The one what?"

He sighs at me, putting his cigarette out. "The one who finally gets you to love again?"

After Landon and I became friends, I'd told him about how Connor died and then how my parents died, and the guilt I carried from it. The conversation led into me telling him how my long-term relationship died out shortly after my parents. I became a shell of a person after my mom and stepdad died in the car accident. Guilt overtook me. I'd convinced myself if I'd made time to see them more, visited them sporadically, that they wouldn't have been hit by a drunk driver that night. It wasn't reasonable. My girlfriend at the time tried telling me that, but I didn't listen. One night, she told me I was too broken to love her. I was too focused on loving those who were already dead that I wasn't capable of loving those who were alive. She was angry at how much I turned to music instead of her.

It should've upset me, but I knew she was right. It's hard to move on when so many things are left unsaid when someone dies. Connor died thinking I was angry with him. My parents died when I hadn't seen them in months. I'd thought I loved that girlfriend, but I didn't love her enough to let go of my demons. I was in a really dark place after all of it, depending on music and drugs to keep me going. Landon had assured me one day there'd be a woman who could take the pain away. One who would convince me to forgive myself for my past and move on. I never dreamed of him being right.

But now, with his reminder of the past conversation, I know he was right.

It's her.

Swallowing the lump in my throat, I look to him, coming to terms with how much I've fucked things up. "Yeah, man. She is."

He throws his cigarette away, nodding his head to one of our cars parked on the curb. "It's about fucking time you realized it. Let's go fix your mistake."

CHAPTER
48

THE DOORMAN of our hotel yawns as I walk past him. I don't blame him. I've stayed out way longer than I originally intended. My night alone was exactly what I needed. Being lost in an unfamiliar city healing my broken spirit.

But now that I'm back at the hotel, no longer amongst the high energy of the nightlife, I'm exhausted.

I accidentally press the wrong floor on the elevator, creating one more stop on my trip to my room.

In a tired fog, the late hour getting to me, I trip over something in front of me. Looking down, I discover it isn't *something*, it's *someone*.

It's Poe.

He startles awake, ungracefully jumping to his feet. He has to steady himself by grabbing on to the wall.

"Lennon," he mumbles, rubbing at his eyes. "Hi."

I look at the floor he was just fast asleep on. He'd balled up a hoodie, using it as a pillow nestled against my door. "What are you doing here?"

He allows me to step past him to unlock my door. I leave it open, walking into my room to finally take my shoes off. I've had them on for way too long, my feet aching, blisters forming all over them. These blisters are nothing compared to the ones I used to get in ballet, but it doesn't mean they don't hurt like a bitch right now.

Looking over my shoulder, I find him still standing in the doorway.

"Are you going to answer my question?" I ask, not bothering to hide the defeat in my voice. I'm tired. The last thing I want to do tonight is have him tell me he's changed his mind about us. It was something I would've rather done tomorrow, but now that he's here, we might as well get it over with.

He scratches his chin. Looking around uncomfortably, he takes a hesitant step into the room. When I don't stop him, he fully steps in, shutting the door behind him. "I'm here because we need to talk."

"Do we? You seemed to say enough to Landon earlier."

My words don't surprise him, meaning Landon has already told him what I know. *Fine by me.* It saves me the embarrassment of replaying hearing him toss me to the side so easily.

"It's what I didn't say to Landon that haunts me."

"Truly, Poe. It's fine, okay? I'm tired and don't want to argue with you. I got the hint. You aren't interested, not really. We'll leave it at that."

"Like hell we will," he growls. It's only now I notice that he's got the worry stone I bought him in his hand. It almost falls out as he throws his hands around angrily.

"You were very clear that you don't give a damn about me when you told Landon to ask me out."

"It wasn't like that."

"Then what was it like?"

He looks down at his feet, his fingers running over the worry stone. I want to rip it from his hands, feeling he doesn't deserve the gift I got him. He can have the blanket back while he's at it. I don't want the reminders of what could've been if only he'd felt the same.

"I froze," he says. He lifts his head. The look in his eyes makes me want to believe him. His hair looks like a mess, probably from sleeping on the floor outside my door. "I fucking froze when internally I was losing my god damn mind at the thought of another man taking you on a date."

"You sure didn't make it seem that way."

"I'm sorry, Lennon." He swallows, taking one step closer to me. We're still a good distance apart, which is a good thing because I need the space. "I fucked up. Big time. But I didn't mean it."

Looking toward the ceiling, I take a calming breath. I'm tired of crying. I'd cried earlier alone on a crowded street. I thought I was done with the tears, at least for the night. But here I am, fighting tears from spilling down my cheeks. "It doesn't matter, Poe. I don't think I can do this anymore."

He looks hurt. "Do what?"

"This. Us. I've reached my breaking point. I'm not okay with caring more for someone than they care about me."

"I care about you," he argues.

"It isn't enough."

His nostrils flare. He dares another step closer to me. And then another and another until he stands a foot away from me. I want to back away, but I'm not strong enough. His scent that has become too familiar to me surrounds me, comforting me when the man who bears it is the one doing the damage in the first place. "I'll make sure it's enough."

"You can't. The damage has been done. You've been telling me from the start that I'd always be the one who loved more, and I thought I could accept it. I thought that we could heal the broken parts of each other and that'd be enough. I thought having some part of you—the *scraps* of you—would suffice. But it doesn't. I want you to be crazy about me. I want to feel like you can't live without me, because the idea of living without you guts me. I've cried all night at the idea, but the idea of loving someone who doesn't love me back hurts even more."

He reaches for my hand, but I pull it away. I can't touch him. "What do I need to do to prove to you that you're all I think about? Fuck, butterfly, everything in my life now revolves around you. You're the first thought I have in the morning and the last thought before bed. I used to eat, breathe, and sleep music. Now all I eat, breathe and sleep is *you*. You're my everything. You'll always be my everything. I'm just shit at showing it."

I suck in a breath, my vision going blurry from the tears. These are words I've dreamed of him saying, except now I don't believe him. "You're just saying that."

Lowering his voice, he looks at me sadly. "No, I'm not. I mean every word."

Lip trembling, I shake my head. "I wish I believed them."

This time, when he steps closer to me, I don't move away. When his hands reach up to cup my face, I don't stop him. He's my weakness. I can't say no, even when I know I should. I let him brush his thumb across my cheek, knowing that prolonging the inevitable will only make things worse for me.

He clutches me so tightly, like he's afraid I'll slip right through his fingers. His fingers firmly aim my chin up, making sure I look at him. "Tell me what you need from me, Lennon, and I'll do it."

What I need is for him to tell me he loves me. I want to hear it from his lips. That's the only thing that'll make me believe that I'm not the only one with the intense need for him. Him needing me, thinking about me, isn't enough. I want him to be earth-shatteringly in love with me. I don't want to ask him for it, though. It won't be the same.

Closing my eyes, I swallow my emotions. Being this close to him, makes me overthink everything. Like always, I'm rethinking what exactly I need from him. I love him so much,

I'm tempted to accept what he's given me, calling it his own version of love.

I don't want the watered-down version of love. The one where it's implied, but not said. I want the big, bold kind of love. One that's obvious.

And I'm scared Poe won't ever be that way. He has too much in his past holding him down.

His hands shake against my face. Maybe he is scared of losing me. I'm terrified of losing him, but I'd rather lose him than always wonder how he felt about me. "Lennon, I need you to tell me what you need so I can do it."

The first time I saw him, I knew he was broken. I didn't care. In fact, his brokenness drew me in. It rivaled my own. At night, I'd imagine the two of us fixing the broken pieces of each other, both of us ending up whole with the pieces of each other. Now as time has gone on, I realize I've willingly handed pieces of myself over to him to fix him, and it still wasn't enough. He took them, but they didn't fit him the way they should.

He's still broken and I'm missing so many of my pieces, never getting any in return from him. It isn't what love is supposed to be. It isn't supposed to be one-sided. It's supposed to mend, not break. And right now, all I feel is broken.

The morning after I told Poe about my past, I'd felt like an entirely new person. I'd finally got the weight off my chest. It felt like the weight I'd been carrying in my heart from the memory was suddenly gone. It created even more room in my heart for the man in front of me. The words he'd told me that night, the way he'd made sure to take care of me, god it felt like love. I was so happy, so naive, thinking we could live in that bliss forever.

But reality kicked in. She's a bitch like that. We went back to hiding things, and I pretended it didn't matter to me. When we'd agreed to tell people about us, I thought that'd be it. We'd be happy. It turns out, I still had on a pair of rose-colored-glasses. We still aren't over the biggest hurdle of all.

Him.

His eyes scan over my face, searching for something. Whatever he's looking for, I don't think I can give him. "I needed to not be hidden. I needed to not listen to the man I love tell his best friend to take me on a date. Now, what I need is to be left alone. I need someone who will prove to me that I'm their everything. That they love me. I don't need empty words that don't match up with actions."

"You're killing me, butterfly," he rasps. Both our bodies shake. If I'm not mistaken, I think one small tear rolls down his cheek.

Love isn't supposed to hurt like this.

Maybe we're both too broken to love.

Maybe I need love from a man that's whole. One who can give me what I need.

Maybe he needs to love a woman who's whole. One who doesn't take pieces of herself to fix him, burning herself out in the process.

"We'll still be friends?" I ask, the words tasting like acid in my throat. The last thing I want to be is his friend. It sounds like torture, to be around him, knowing what it feels like to be in his arms, to have him smile at me. But I can't be his secret either. I can't be the one that gives and gives.

So friends will be.

"Lennon, *no*." He emphasizes the last word even though his voice breaks. "I can't be your friend."

I can't be yours either.

"I can't be this. You were right, Poe. You said you'd only end up hurting me, and that's exactly what you did. Now I need you to stop hurting me and let me go before I'm weak enough to accept something less than what I deserve."

His hands freeze on my face. He freezes. The look on his face undoes me. He looks so hurt, so devastated. Maybe using his own words against him was low, but I needed to say something to get the point across. Overall, I just needed him out of my room before I did something stupid.

Slowly, the warmth disappears. He takes a few steps back, like I'd hit him. He's so taken aback by my words that he almost trips over my bag on the floor.

Closing his eyes, he scrubs at his face. My heart hurts, wondering if it's his way of hiding the tears. I'm not capable of hiding mine. They roll down my cheeks freely. I'm too exhausted to try and hide them.

He takes a deep breath in, holding it in his lungs for a moment before letting it back out. On the exhale, all hurt washes from his face. What comes of his features is something I don't quite understand, but it seems like determination. It seems misplaced for a moment like this, but I don't say anything.

I'm already resigned from the conversation, wanting to crawl into bed and go to sleep.

"You're right, butterfly. You deserve the world."

Turning toward the door, he rushes to it. For a moment, his steps falter and he looks over his shoulder.

I'm dumb enough for one small, fleeting moment to have hope. Maybe he'll tell me he loves me. Maybe he's coming to his senses.

He does neither. He just looks at me with regret before leaving my room completely.

As the door shuts, a sob rakes through me. It took all of me to keep it in until now. I can't see a thing, the tears keeping my eyes full. My knees hit the floor of the carpet, my body not strong enough to make it to the bed.

I don't know how long I lie on the floor, curled up in the fetal position, crying over a man who didn't love himself enough to love me back. I cry and cry until my tears dry up. And then I somehow cry some more.

Eventually, I stand up, promising to not let myself cry over him anymore. At least for tonight.

I'm not strong enough to fully wipe him from my memory. I slide his shirt over my body, inhaling his familiar scent. He won't be holding me tonight, he won't be holding me any other nights. But I'm not quite ready for his scent to disappear completely.

Climbing into bed, I doze off, wondering how I woke up so blissfully happy in his arms, now asleep alone with only the memories and the scent of him to kill the hurt.

CHAPTER 49

PUTTING a needle to my skin has always been a form of therapy for me. This time is no different.

Leaving Lennon standing in her room crying was the hardest thing I've ever done. With everything in me, I wanted to kick, scream, chain myself to her to convince her I was unbelievably in love with her. It took everything in me to not tell her that everything I'd said in the past was bullshit. It didn't apply to her. The rules never applied to her.

It took everything to leave our room. My mind had been flooded from a different argument, a different time, where the things that were left unsaid never had the chance to be said. I think back to Connor. I should've stayed and talked to him that morning. We should've worked it out.

I wanted the same thing with Lennon.

I was ready to fall to my knees, to tell her there's no way I could leave that room until she realized how she was everything to me. Walking away from her was brutal. If something were to happen to her before I could tell her how I feel, I wouldn't be able to live with myself.

But the look in her eyes said everything. Staying there would only hurt her, so I left, even though everything in me wanted to stay there and fight. She needs time, and I'll give her that. I'll do anything for her, and it's time I admit that to myself. I swore I'd never feel anything for her, but now I feel *everything* for her.

I'd convinced myself that doing her little bucket list, with a few half-hazard rules set in, would totally work. I was so fucking wrong. We hadn't even completed a single thing off her list before I was already gone for her, I was just too dense to realize it.

Now, that's all I realize. I hadn't been lying to her, she's all I think about. There's not a moment that passes by that she isn't on my mind. But she was right, she deserves someone who realizes what they have with her when they have it. Not after the fact. She needs to be appreciated, catered to, for someone to shout their love to her from the rooftops.

"What do you think?" the man next to me says, his accent thick and heavy. Looking down, I see the outline of a new tattoo on my chest. Only the outline is done, but it looks perfect, exactly what I was envisioning. He takes a rag, wiping the blood from my chest.

"I love it," I confirm, meaning every word. I couldn't think of a better tattoo or a better placement for what he's inking on my skin.

My phone vibrates. Looking down, I see a text from Nash. It's show day, our sound check happening in a few hours. I was exhausted after not getting any sleep last night. I'd managed a small amount when I'd fallen asleep against Lennon's door, but not much. After our conversation in her room, the one that completely fucking broke me, I barely slept a wink last night.

At one point, Landon had yelled at me, telling me to stop tossing and turning so he could get some sleep himself. I couldn't help it. My mind turned, replaying every single word said between us in Lennon's room. I'd replayed every moment we had together, wondering how something that felt so right could end up so wrong.

First thing this morning, I'd gone to speak to Nash. There were some things he needed to know.

I'd confided everything to him. Some things I couldn't keep from him any longer. If anyone knew how to fight for love, it was him.

I'd need his help to fight for mine.

I also made a call to Veronica, needing to talk about Connor with her. We both cried during the call, but it was what I needed. Finally, I've been able to release the guilt I have for the state of our friendship when Connor died. It'll always be a regret of mine, allowing us to argue over something so stupid, but I can't hold on to the pain of it anymore. I've forgiven myself, and that was healing enough.

Now I'm here because I needed to feel the sting of a needle against my skin. Desperate to put something important to me on my body permanently.

CHAPTER
50

MY SISTER OPENS the door to her suite immediately. She'd probably been waiting there from the moment I first texted her, asking if she was free.

I knew from the schedule Monica sent us that the guys were at sound check. There was a good chance she'd be alone, and I wanted to take advantage of that.

There are a few things we need to talk about. A few things I finally need to be honest with her about.

"Lenny, hi," she says, smiling at me. She invites me in with a nod of her head.

I follow her lead, marveling at how nice their room is. It's much bigger than mine, having its own living room and kitchen. There's even a dining table in the corner, large enough to seat at least ten people. There are papers scattered about the table, like Nora and Nash been busy planning something before he had to leave.

If I wasn't so nervous, a pit forming in my stomach, I'd ask her what they've been up to. Instead, I'm quiet as she leads me to a nice, large, plush sofa. She takes a seat next to me, two waters already sitting on the coffee table in front of us.

Nora watches me carefully. "What's on your mind?" she questions.

I take a deep breath, hoping this isn't a mistake. Part of me would rather die with this secret, knowing it's one that'll upset her. But a bigger part knows for us to get back to the way we used to be, or at least a version of it that's better, that I need to tell her the truth.

She needs to know what happened to me. She needs to know why I pulled away, why I left. I need her to know it wasn't her fault, but his, and I just didn't know how to handle what'd happened to me.

So that's exactly what I do. Reaching across the cushion to grab her hand, I wrap mine around hers. The large diamond from the ring Nash put on her finger digs into my skin, but I don't pay it any attention. All I focus is on her, on making sure I finally come clean.

At the end of it, we're both crying, snot all over our faces from letting our emotions out.

Nora pulls me into her tightly, the two of us falling backwards into the cushions. "Lennon, you shouldn't have kept that bottled up." The words come out clipped since she's still speaking through tears.

I cry into the crook of her neck, relieved to finally have it all out in the open with her. My hope is now she'll know that it was never that I was angry with her, I just had a lot I had to process on my own.

"It was my way of dealing with things," I say.

She clings to me. "I'm the worst sister, assuming it didn't go all the way when it did..." This sends her into an even deeper sob.

Pulling away, I look at her, trying to throw everything I can to convince her otherwise. "You're not the worst sister. I was in shock. I didn't know how to verbalize that it was more. In the moment, I'd wanted to pretend that it hadn't gone all the way.

That he hadn't *raped* me. It took numerous therapy sessions for me to admit to myself that it'd been rape, and that I had to confront that trauma to ever move on from it."

Sniffling loudly, she wipes at her face. "I know this is a terrible question, because how do you really get over something like that, but have you moved on?" She watches me carefully through her red-rimmed eyes.

I nod. "You're right, it's something I'll always live with. But I've put a lot of work on moving forward from it, on not dwelling on the hurt. He doesn't get to take the rest of my life."

She sits up straight, running her fingertips underneath her eyelids. "I think if I ever saw him again, I'd kill him."

A sad laugh bursts out of me. "Poe said the same thing."

This catches Nora's attention. Cocking her head, she gives me a look. "Poe?"

Shoot.

I guess now is as good a time as ever to tell my sister that for a short period, it felt like Poe was mine.

"There's something else I should probably tell you," I begin.

"Your crush on Poe?" she interjects. "I knew you had one. I just never wanted to say anything because I didn't want to embarrass you. I figured if you wanted to talk about it, you would."

My fingers run through my hair. I don't want to throw Poe under the bus and divulge things I shouldn't, but this is also my sister. I'm not going to tell her every detail of the two of us, or our time together, but I need someone to talk about it with. If not, the hurt will just stay pent up inside me forever and I can't live with that.

"It started out as a crush, but then it turned into more."

"What do you mean, more?"

"I mean, we became friends, and then we became friends who kind of hooked up, and then I didn't want to be his just his friend anymore. I fell in love with him."

Air whistles through her teeth as she sucks in a breath. "You and Poe?" she asks in disbelief.

I nod, chewing on my lip anxiously. "Me and Poe," I repeat, not loving the sound of it. It's a reminder of all the times I asked what we were and his only response was, "We're just us. Lennon and Poe."

"So you fell for him?"

"Yep," I clip. "I fell freaking hard."

Nora takes a moment to think about my words. Knowing her, she's choosing her response carefully. "What about him?"

Rubbing my lips together, I smile at her sadly. "He doesn't feel the same."

Once again, she reaches across the cushion to pull me into her. This one feels more normal. This is a topic an older sister should be comforting her younger sister about. Our earlier conversation was one neither of us should've had to endure.

Nora runs her hand through my hair. "I'm sorry, Len. For the years that I've known Poe, I haven't seen him serious about anyone. I think it's just who he is."

Her words are meant to be comforting, but they aren't. They're like pushing against a bruise, making the pain more intense. It doesn't help knowing Poe has always been like this and most likely will always be like this. It's depressing, knowing he'll never allow himself to love deeply again. It's a sad existence for someone to swear off love for good.

Nora's hand pauses in my hair. "I wonder if that's why he was here this morning," she says all of a sudden.

I lean away from her, giving her a look. "Who was here this morning?"

Nora sighs. "Poe. He stopped by first thing this morning like he was on a mission. He looked rough, Lennon. Maybe he's more upset about hurting you than you think."

My eyebrows pinch together. There's a small seed of hope glimmering in my chest. I don't let it become anything more. I can't let it become anything more for my own sake. "I doubt it. But it's fine, Nora. Really. It's not like he ever hid the fact that he'd never be interested."

Shrugging, Nora reaches for her glass of water. She takes a big sip of it, keeping it in her hand. "Then his loss, Lenny. Fuck him."

This makes me laugh. Nora doesn't cuss often, but when she does, she *really* means it.

"Yeah," I say with a chuckle. "Fuck him."

She reaches out to throw her arm over my shoulder, pulling me into her side. "Let's watch a cheesy rom-com and order a mountain of room service before the show tonight."

"That sounds perfect," I agree, pulling my feet underneath me.

"And then we're going to get ready and your outfit will show Poe exactly what he's missing."

If only that were true. I'm afraid it'll go back to how things used to be. He probably won't even notice me.

"Hey, Lenny?" Nora asks after we've settled in on the couch.

My eyes stay trained on the opening credits of the movie we'd picked out. "Yeah?"

"Want some good news?"

"I'd love that."

Nora pulls her baggy T-shirt up, rubbing a hand over her stomach. "I'm pregnant."

I'm up off the couch immediately. Standing in front of her, I shriek, "What?!"

She laughs, sitting up straighter and pulling her shirt back down. "It turns out that not everything that happens on the honeymoon *stays* on the honeymoon."

My eyes well up with moisture, but this time it's with happy tears.

I'm going to be an aunt.

"Oh my god," I whisper, still shocked and elated. "I'm so happy for you!"

She smiles, pulling out her phone to show me a picture. "Well, be *double* happy because they're twins, and I'm going to be needing all the help I can get."

Ripping the phone from her hand, I look at the picture on her phone. There's an ultrasound of two tiny little peanuts, one labeled A and one labeled B. I zoom in, unable to make out anything on them, but already madly in love with them anyway.

Happy tears overflow from my eyes. "You're going to be a mom of *twins*."

Nora nods. "Identical ones at that. Nash always said he wants a big family, apparently we're hitting the ground running on that."

I wrap my sister up in a hug, almost pulling her off the couch with the embrace. "I'm so freaking happy for you, Nora. For you and Nash. Oh my god, I just can't wait to love on the little nuggets."

Nora and I only half pay attention to the movie. For the entire time I'm with her, I forget all about the drama with Poe.

My sister is going to be a mom. I'm going to be an aunt. Nothing can steal my happiness at this moment. Not even the brooding bassist who stole my heart.

CHAPTER
51

THE CROWD GOES ABSOLUTELY wild in anticipation of Nash taking the stage. The dressing room walls shake with their excitement. Pulling my phone out of my pocket, I stress about the time for the millionth time.

She's a minute late.

When I'd planned out how this evening was going to go tonight, I'd needed some help. I'd recruited Nash, hoping he'd be able to convince Nora to pull some strings without making things too obvious. Maybe we should've told her more, ensuring she brought Lennon here on time.

We're only minutes away from having to take the stage, and there's something I need to do.

Someone I need to talk to.

Things I need to say.

But first, I need Lennon to show up so I can say everything on my mind.

I'm moments away from leaving the venue and tracking Lennon down myself when the dressing room door opens. Technically, it's Nash's room, since I don't think Lennon would've willingly walked into a room with my name on it.

Her eyes land on me immediately. I hate myself for the hurt that's in them.

Lennon looks over her shoulder at her sister. "What is this?" she asks accusingly, looking around the room. It took hours to transform this room after soundcheck into what I'd envisioned. Luckily, I had help from Nash and the band. Eventually, Monica and Aiden showed up to chip in as well. The room no longer looks like a dressing room, which was what I was going for.

Nora looks just as surprised as Lennon does. From over her sister's shoulder, I can see the look of shock on her face. "I have no idea," she answers, her eyes bouncing around the room.

Nash swoops in behind his wife, whispering something in her ear that makes her pause. Whatever she says back to him is hushed. I can't hear it from a few feet away.

I stop paying attention to them. I pin all of my focus on the woman standing in front of me, the woman that I love more than I've ever loved anything.

"Can I talk to you?" My heart thumps against my chest erratically. I'm so nervous that she'll turn around and leave, leaving all my plans for nothing. It'd be what I deserved for how I've treated her, how I've made her feel.

Looking over her shoulder, she says something to Nora that has Nora moving out of view. Nash gives me a thumbs up, closing the dressing room door to give Lennon and I some privacy.

I wait for Lennon to come near me, but her feet stay planted only a foot away from the door. The way she looks tonight steals all the air from my lungs. She wears a pair of black jeans that are tight around her waist but loosen as they go down her legs. A pair of boots are on her feet, reminding me of the pair she wore the time I walked her back to the buses from the show.

Her toned abs are on full display due to the top she's wearing being cropped. My mind flashes to the times I've kissed the soft skin of her stomach as I made my way down her body.

The crop top is tight, a knot between her breasts holding the two sides of the shirt together.

The long strands of her hair fall down her shoulders in perfect curls. She's got half of her thick hair worn down, the other half pulled back with a ribbon. If it were up to me, I'd pull on the ribbon and let all of her hair down. I love it when it has a mind of its own.

"What is this?" Lennon asks, her voice composed. She looks around the room, to the pages I'd ripped from books and hung all over.

Taking a deep breath, I try to smile through the nerves. With Lennon, I know I've only got one shot to prove to her how madly in love with her I am. I can't blow it.

"This is me telling you all the things I should've said from the beginning."

She's quiet, stopping at one of the pages taped to the dressing room mirror. Walking up behind her, I point to the highlighted spot on the page. "Here in this book, he tells her that he loves her by showing up to her dorm room in the middle of night and yelling it at her window until she'll listen."

"I know," she whispers. "I've read it."

Her eyes go from that page to the next one taped a few feet away, this one from a different book with a different highlighted page. "In this book"—I begin, reading over her shoulder—"he tells her loves her after his football team won the state championship."

Lennon follows me around as I point to all of the pages taped around the room, going over how each one of these characters tells his love interest that he's in love with her. I can tell she has questions, but she keeps them to herself. She allows me to take the lead, telling her scenes from books she's probably already read, but it doesn't matter.

By the end of it, we're back in the middle of the dressing room. This time, she isn't standing a few feet away from me, she's standing right in front of me and it takes everything not to pull her against me. I don't. I wait, hoping that my next words will hit home with her and it'll only be a little longer until I can hold her in my arms again.

"So now it's my turn," I say, my fingers reaching up to work at unbuttoning the buttons of my shirt.

"Your turn for what?" she asks.

"My turn to tell you what I should've said a while ago, when I first started to feel it."

Her eyes widen, but she doesn't say anything. That's okay. As long as she stays here, willing to listen to what I have to say next, I'll take it.

Once my shirt is all the way unbuttoned, I open it up until the fresh ink on my chest is revealed.

Lennon gasps, closing the distance between us so she can see the tattoo on my chest.

I witness her eyes get misty as she looks at what I've permanently etched on my skin forever.

Her.

Right over the spot where my heart threatens to beat out of my chest rests a giant butterfly. A bright blue one to be exact. One identical to the one at the butterfly garden.

"Poe," she says breathlessly, reaching out to run a finger over the outline. "You didn't."

I grab hold of her wrist. "Now it's my turn to tell you how much I love you, butterfly."

She looks up from the tattoo, a look of disbelief in her eyes. I grab either side of her face, making sure she looks at me while I speak. I need her to know I mean every damn word.

"Lennon Mason, I meant it when I told you that you're my everything. I can't picture the rest of my life without knowing that I'll spend it loving you. You once told me that butterflies were good luck, that they meant a fresh start, something new.

I'd meant it when I'd said *you're* my butterfly. You've taught me more about myself than anyone else ever has."

When a tear falls from her eyes, I lean down and kiss it, hoping she'll let me kiss her tears away for the rest of our lives. "What I'd failed to do in the moment, was not only tell you that you're my everything, but you're my whole heart, too. I'm madly in love with you. I feel everything you feel, maybe more. Definitely more," I add, kissing the top of her nose.

"Not possible." She giggles.

"I'll make it my mission to prove to you that you aren't the only one who feels this way. I've been terrible at voicing it, and I'll be better at it, but right here, right now, I need you to know that I love you. I love you so much that the idea that I could've messed things up so bad by just not telling you how I felt eats me alive inside."

Her eyes leave mine for a moment, traveling over all the pages taped around the room. "So what did mauling poor helpless books have to do with it?" she jokes.

I smirk, wrapping a hand around her waist and pulling her into me. "I wanted to point out all the ways your so-called book boyfriends told the woman they loved that they loved them."

"Because?"

"Because I will do every single one of those things just like they did if that's what it takes to prove to you that I'm yours. My heart is yours, if you'll have it."

She looks down at the tattoo on my chest. "And this?" she questions. I try not to shiver at the feel of her hand outlining the tattoo.

"This is me showing you that you, my butterfly, have permanently marked yourself on my heart. There's no me without you. My love for you is strong. It's permanent."

The crowd is almost deafening outside the four walls of the dressing room. Any moment now, we're supposed to be taking the stage, but I won't leave this room until I have the woman I love back. Until she's confident in how I feel for her.

"I'll do whatever it takes for you to know that I love you," I say. "If it means doing what those damn book boyfriends of yours do, so be it. If it means tattooing your name all over my body, I'll do it. Fuck, if it means walking out on that stage out there and telling twenty-thousand people that I love you, then I'll do it. I'll do whatever it takes. I can't lose you, Lennon. I've got so much more love to give you."

She isn't gentle when she pulls me to her level by my neck. I grasp onto her to steady both our bodies. Her kiss is the only answer I need. She kisses me with such enthusiasm, such promise, that I know I still have my girl.

The walls shake around us as we kiss until there's no way I don't have her pink lipstick all over my face. Finally, when we pull away, I reach into my pocket and give her the last surprise up my sleeve for the night.

It's a folded piece of paper, ripped from one of the books we'd last minute had an assistant get us. Handing it over to her, I wait for her to unfold it.

When she does, she smiles at the big bold letters I'd sprawled across the page.

Lennon Mason, will you be my girlfriend?

Smiling up at me, tears in her eyes, she nods. "I've been waiting forever for you to ask me that."

And then we kiss again. It's long and full of promise.

We kiss so long I make the entire band five minutes late to our set stage time.

By the smile on my face, and Lennon's from side stage, they don't seem to care.

I've got my girl back. And there's no way in hell I'll ever risk losing her again.

CHAPTER
52

It doesn't feel real, watching him from the side of the stage, knowing he's my boyfriend.

At one point, he looks at me from his spot, and taps the spot on his chest where the butterfly tattoo is inked permanently on him forever. When he mouths the words, "I love you," I just about run out to the stage and kiss him in front of all the screaming fans, not caring who sees.

Nora spends the entire night gushing about all the double dates we'll be able to go on. I only half listen to my sister. I'm riding the high of knowing that the man I pined over for months is finally actually *mine*.

He feels the same way about me. We're in love, and there's no better feeling in the world.

I'm still riding that high hours later, as we're riding the elevator back up to my room, finally alone once again.

Poe sticks his hands in the back pockets of my jeans, molding my front to his front.

"Have I told you I love you?" he asks, his mouth pressed to my hair.

"Not enough," I say with wonder. "I'll never be able to hear it enough."

"I love you," he answers.

"Not as much as I love you."

His hands cup my bottom through my jean pockets. Squeezing, he says, "I'll never tire of hearing you say that."

"Let's promise to never stop saying it then, okay?" I look up at him, wondering how any of this is real. This man is mine. His hair is a mess from the show, falling all over his forehead in a messy kind of way that drives my heart wild.

Poe pulls one of his hands from my pocket, holding it between us with his pinky waving in the air. He smirks. "Pinky promise?"

I can't help but laugh, remembering months ago when I'd made him make a pinky promise when our bucket list journey began.

Holding up my pinky, I wrap it around his, kissing my thumb for good measure.

He narrows his eyebrows. "What's that for?"

Smiling, I shrug. "I once heard that kissing your thumb during a pinky promise means it can never break."

"In that case," he bends down and dramatically kisses his thumb over and over again until the elevator beeps, alerting us that we've made it to our floor.

"So I've got one more thing on my bucket list," I tell him, my face going serious.

The doors are wide open, waiting for us to step out. For a moment, neither of us move. "What's that butterfly?" he asks.

"I want my boyfriend to make love to me, whichever way *he* wants."

His eyes light up with desire. Before I can say anything else, he's lifting me into his arms and speeding out of the elevator. Somehow, he manages to open up my hotel room door while still keeping a firm hold on me.

The moment the door swings shut, his lips are crashing against mine.

It's something I've been desperate for since the moment he finally told me he loved me. I've been waiting for us to be truly alone, and now, I want to take full advantage of that.

He still holds me in his arms as he guides us to the bed. Before we even make it there, I'm pulling at the knot between my breasts, freeing myself from my shirt.

Poe smiles when he realizes the shirt had a built-in bra and that fabric was the only thing keeping my hardened nipples from the outside world.

"I have so many things I want to do with you," he rasps, throwing me onto the bed.

I crawl across the mattress, smiling with glee at all the possibilities. "Where should we start?"

Rolling over to face him again, I stop in the middle of the mattress. I find him at the foot of the bed, his shirt stripped off, the freshly inked tattoo on full display. The skin around it is red and irritated from the freshness of it. It doesn't stop me from staring, from feeling amazed that he's permanently etched me onto his body forever.

Poe runs his thumb over his bottom lip. My breasts feel heavy just by the way he's looking at me. Keeping eye contact with him, I unbutton my jeans. I lift my hips, shimmying out of the jeans and tossing them to the side. My satin, pink panties do nothing to hide how ready I am for him.

"I don't even know where to start," he growls, taking a step closer.

I'll never tire of the hungry look in his eyes. He has a way of making me feel like the most powerful, sexiest woman in the world just by the way he looks at me. Wetness pools from me. I know he sees it.

Reaching out, he pulls me by my ankles until my bottom is hanging off the corner of the bed. He gets on his knees, lining me up perfectly with his mouth.

"The first thing I want is for you to come on my face, butter-fly." He coats his finger in me, taking a small taste.

"What about you?"

"Don't worry about me. The taste of you is all I need right now." He leans in, worshiping me with his tongue in ways that make my toes curl.

He sucks my clit, sending shivers down my spine. "This right here," he says, licking me up and down. "You. It's the best taste in the world. You taste like mine."

His words, that dirty mouth of his, sends me over the edge. I'm screaming his name, riding the waves of my orgasm as his tongue doesn't let up.

His mouth, his tongue, doesn't leave me until I'm certain he's lapped up all the evidence of my arousal. I'm about to slide off the bed and tell him it's my turn to do him when he's grabbing me by the hips and flipping me over.

My stomach hits the mattress.

"Now I want to fuck my girlfriend," Poe declares before I can even ask him. "But I want you to watch us in the mirror. Watch how perfect we are together."

Looking over my shoulder, I find him stripping out of his pants. Once they're off, he climbs onto the bed, wrapping an arm around my middle. He lifts, pressing my boobs into the mattress while my butt is in the air in front of him.

"Put your arms out in front of you, butterfly. Use the mattress to keep you propped. You need to be able to see in the mirror"—he points to the mirror next to the bed—"when I fuck you."

Moaning, I bury my face in the comforter, wet and ready to feel him. This time will be different from all the other times we've had sex. This time, I know that he's mine, and there's no way I'll ever let him go.

His tip glosses over my entrance. I moan again at the sensation, ready to feel him inside me. I've heard him say the three words I've been desperate to hear from him today, now I need to feel that desperate want and need from him.

He must need to feel it too, because he doesn't waste any time sheathing himself inside me.

Air hisses through his teeth. "God, you feel so good," he groans. "This position, you wrap around me like you were made for me."

He isn't wrong. Something about the position makes everything feel so much tighter. It almost feels like I won't be able to take all of him, but only almost. He's stretching me, molding me so I fit perfectly around him and only him.

"You need to look at us, Lennon," he says. Following his direction, I look up, incredibly turned on by what I see in the mirror.

"Do you see it?" he asks, pumping in out of me. I feel so full, on the verge of another orgasm and we've barely even started. "God, butterfly, look how good you take me."

I push back, feeling him deeper inside me than I've ever felt him before. "Good girl," he praises. "Look at you greedily taking every inch of me."

He rocks slowly in and out of me before he picks up pace. Eventually, the sound of our slapping skin fills the room. His words mixed with feeling him everywhere has me combusting, my chest falling to the mattress as my orgasm overtakes me.

Poe follows suit, the evidence of his orgasm hitting my back as he moans my name over and over. We both stay there, gaining our breath for a moment.

Suddenly, I'm getting lifted from the bed once again. My muscles feel tired, loose from what we just did. I go slack in his arms, already knowing exactly where he's taking us.

It's become our thing. Sex, a shower where he'll wash my body, sometimes making sure *every* part of me is clean, before we climb back into bed and cuddle, sometimes getting dirty all over again.

As the water beats down on me, Poe carefully scrubbing my hair for me, I realize I've gotten everything I could ever want and more from this man.

"Poe?" I ask, staring at the marble of the shower wall.

His fingers pause for a moment in my hair. "Yes, butterfly?"

"I don't think I ever want to stop checking off bucket list items with you. Can we keep doing it forever?"

He wraps his arms around me from behind, leaning down to kiss behind my ear. "Anything you want."

I laugh, snuggling in deeper into his arms. I can't wait to keep checking things off the bucket list with this man for the rest of my life. "I like it and don't ever want to stop."

He nips at my earlobe. "Then we'll never stop. We'll forever be getting ideas from those dirty books of yours."

"I love you," I respond, changing the subject because I feel such an overwhelming amount of love for this man.

It's crazy, that only earlier today I was afraid that there was no way two broken people could effectively love each other. I was wrong. Poe and I had been slowly fixing each other with the broken pieces of us. We took pieces of ourselves, handing it over to the other person. I was wrong to think it left us both incomplete, void of some of our pieces. Instead, we mixed all of ours up and filled in the holes together. Mine are filled with some from him, his filled with some of mine, the two of us now complete.

The way we began was as unconventional as love can get. I'd pined for him desperately, where he barely knew who I was. When he finally did notice me, it was almost transactional. We'd be friends with benefits, him helping me check things off my bucket list from the kindness of his heart. Time and time again, I'd told him about my feelings for him. Time and time again, he'd rejected them. I kept coming back for more, feeling solid in the way that I felt about him.

Eventually, it paid off. Now I have him, he's mine, and I'm his forever. I'd never dreamed of actually getting the man I pined over, but I'm so happy I did. Poe and I are proof that it might take a little bit of hurt, but in the end, the best love stories can be founded on rejection.

EPILOGUE
2 YEARS LATER

"WHERE ARE WE?" Lennon asks from the passenger seat.

"Why don't we step out of the car and find out?"

She gives me a look, turning her head to stare out the windshield. She squints, probably trying to see into the dark building in front of us.

"You know, instead of suddenly trying to get X-ray vision, we could get out of the car and you could get a glimpse of what's inside up close."

Even in the darkness of the setting sun, I can see the blush creep up her cheeks. The way she reddens so easily will always be one of my favorite things about her.

I don't give her the time to argue. I'm opening the door, rounding the back of the car until I'm on her side. Opening the door for her, I take her hand and help her step out. She wears a pair of nice heels, something she'd groaned about wearing when I'd first told her we were going out for a fancy anniversary dinner.

It's been two years since the concert in Glasgow. Two years since I knew I'd do anything to keep her in my life forever. I'd had this night planned out for ages, wanting it to be absolutely perfect for her.

As we walk up to the building, I replay all the things I want to say to her in my head. I've been waiting for this moment for years and I want to make sure it's everything she ever imagined —and then some.

When we reach the door, I halt, turning to face her. "I've been keeping a bit of a secret from you," I admit.

Her lips purse. "What do you mean?"

Smirking, I pull out a set of keys from the pocket of my suit pants. "I mean, I may have bought this building."

She looks at me in disbelief. "You *bought* a building? Why?"

"I did." Only answering part of her question on purpose, I stick the building key in the lock and unlock the door. I pull it open, gesturing for her to walk in ahead of me.

Lennon takes a hesitant step in, stopping immediately when her eyes land on what's inside.

"Oh my god," she says.

I step in with her, letting the door close behind us.

"Congratulations, butterfly. You're now the proud owner of a bookstore."

I watch her as she takes in every detail of the project I've been working on for over a year. When I'd first driven by this spot, seeing a for sale sign in the window, something about it had caught my eye. Maybe it was because of the small patch of grass next to the building, something almost unheard of in LA, or maybe it was because of the old brick of the building, a contrast to the typical modern, sleek look you find in the city these days.

Whatever it was that made me stop almost felt like fate. I'd turned my car around, needing to check the place out immediately. It had been an old thrift store, the couple wanting to sell and retire somewhere up North.

I knew from the moment I walked in that I wanted it to be Lennon's bookstore. I could already envision the patch of grass on the outside becoming her own butterfly garden. I could imagine the walls being filled with the plants she'd talked about, shelves lining the walls filled to the brim with books. There was even a perfect little nook where they'd hosted dressing rooms for a coffee corner. I envisioned us dancing through the bookshelves late at night. I even imagined a damn cat perched in the window.

It was all perfect, so I bought the place.

Buying it wasn't the only thing I needed to do though, I needed to get the bones of a bookstore going before I gave her the gift.

Her eyes take in the foundation of a bookstore I've laid. She beams, her excitement evident in every facet of her face.

"This is mine?" she asks, taking a step toward a shelf in front of us.

I follow behind her. "Yes, it is. Obviously it's not finished, I didn't want to take away from your dream. I want you to be able to make this into whatever you want, whatever you've always dreamed of. All I wanted to do was kickstart it a little. We'll have to go to the shelter and get a cat or two for the place, but I wasn't going to be the one to do that. You know how I feel about cats."

The last comment makes her laugh, her back still to me.

When she turns around to face me, there's black smudges underneath her eyelids from her makeup. She's crying, but they don't look like sad tears, they look like happy tears.

"Poe," she breathes out, "I don't even know what to say."

Grabbing on to her hips, I guide her toward a shelf at the front of the store. It's the only shelf here that actually has books on it. She's the book expert here, not me. I wanted her to be in charge of stocking whatever books she wanted in the place. "You don't have to say anything. Not yet."

The books in front of us are just something special. Something I'd been working on almost as long as I'd been working on this bookstore.

Lennon pulls one of them off the shelf, admiring the cover. "This is one of my favorites."

I smirk. "I know. All of them are."

Her eyes light up. She runs her finger across the spines, mouthing the titles for all of the books.

"Why don't you open one of them?" I ask, taking a step back.

She gives me a timid look over her shoulder. "Which one?"

My hands find my pockets as I shrug. "Any of them."

Turning around, she does as she's told, pulling one of the books off the shelves and cradling it in her hands. Her back is to me, but I can still tell the moment she finds what's written on the inside.

She spins on her heels, tears free flowing from her eyes when she finds me down on one knee. The book falls to the ground between us, open to the tip in page with the words 'Will you marry, Poe?' written by the author before being autographed.

Sliding the ring box from my pocket, I swallow, suddenly overwhelmed by the love I feel for the woman in front of me. "Lennon," I begin, my mind all of a sudden void of the speech I'd not only practiced in the mirror a thousand times, but in front of Landon and Nash as well. "If you were to open every single one of those books on that shelf, you'd find notes from all of your favorite authors asking you to marry me. It's something I've been working on for a while now."

She chokes on a sob in front of me.

I keep going, knowing if I wait too long, all the words I want to say to make this moment perfect for her will disappear. I don't want to forget them, knowing she deserves the best proposal in the world.

"When you popped up in my life, I had no idea how much you would change it. I've told you a thousand times that you saved me. I hadn't realized how dark of a place I'd been in, how bleak my outlook on life was until you showed me it didn't have to be that. You fell in love with me when I didn't even love myself. I can't imagine doing anything but spending the rest of my life with you."

My fingers shake as I open the ring box. She gasps when she takes in the ring, one I'd taken a leap of faith on and completely designed on my own. The emerald cut diamond sits on a gold band. The simplicity of the band lets the diamond take center stage. I'd looked at countless cuts and settings for rings, trying to come up with something I thought she'd love. Hopefully, the final ring is everything she's ever imagined wearing on her finger the rest of her life.

"Lennon Mason, my heart is yours forever. I want to spend the rest of my life reading your annotated books, dancing in the kitchen with you, running this bookshop with you, hell, even watching our own future kids running around this place. I want to continue to explore the world with you and watch awful, cheesy rom-coms with you. I'll do anything if it means it's with you. You're my butterfly, my home. Will you marry me?"

Lennon falls to her knees, catapulting her body into mine until we almost both fall over. She kisses me with such passion I know her answer before she says it. Finally, she pulls away. She swipes at the tears in my eyes, the proof of how much I love this woman.

She runs her nose against mine, a wide smile on her face. "Like I'd ever say anything, but yes."

Delicately, I pull the ring from the box. Both our hands shake like leaves, making it incredibly hard to slide the ring on her finger. Eventually, we get it done. She holds her hand to the ceiling, admiring the proof of our love on her ring finger.

"It's stunning," she says in awe, tilting her hand from one side to the other.

I kiss her temple. "I'm glad you like it."

Lennon looks down to my own ring finger, running the tip of

her finger over the bare spot. "I can't wait to put one on your finger," she notes.

I laugh. "Tell me when and where and I'm there, butterfly."

We're both on the ground. Grabbing my hand she pulls on my pinky, looping hers around it. "Pinky promise to forever," she says, her makeup smudged from all the tears.

Leaning down, I kiss my thumb. "Pinky promise to forever."

She does the same motion, kissing the spot on her knuckle where the smallest of tattoos is. It's the outline of an open book, a butterfly flying in between the open pages. It was her gift to me on our first anniversary. She'd told me if I got to wear her forever that it was only fair she'd wear her proof of love for me on her forever, too.

"I still can't believe you did all this without me knowing," Lennon says, laying her head on my shoulder.

"Do you like it?"

"There's not a word I can think of to describe how much I love it. You're just full of surprises."

I laugh, pulling my phone out of my pocket to the over hundred missed texts I have. "About that," I say, firing off a text. "There's one more surprise for you."

I've barely got the sentence out when the door to the bookstore is thrown open. Standing in the opening is a very pregnant Nora, a beaming smile on her face.

Nash races up behind her, holding a chubby cheeked boy in each arm. He smiles apologetically. "She's been staring at her phone since the moment you guys walked in here," Nash says.

Nora beelines across the store, engulfing her sister in a hug. "Oh my god, Lenny, you have no idea how hard it was to keep this secret from you."

Lennon is busy showing Nora the ring when the door opens once again, this time more of our friends and family pouring in. They'd all been waiting in the parking lot across the street, needing the green light from me before they came here.

Nash and Nora with their two kids and their third, a little girl, set to arrive any day now. We're on a bit of a touring break, allowing Nash time with his family. Nash has kept busy during the break, effectively keeping Nora pregnant for what seems like years. Next to come in are Sebastian and Riley, their two kids in tow. Lennon's parents follow after them, immersed in a deep conversation with Nash's bodyguard, Matt.

We all gather around the store, everyone congratulating Lennon and me on our engagement. Eventually, Monica and Aiden show up, the two of them a little disheveled, as if they'd found a fun way to bide their time, waiting for me to pop the question to Lennon.

Landon shows up shortly after, a couple of bottles of champagne in hand. Veronica and Maverick show up as well. Every time we talk, Veronica goes on and on about how she's excited to have a little bit of time away from her kids. She also spends half her evening convincing Nash to do a benefit show for the nonprofit she runs, Connor's Ocean. He keeps telling her maybe, but by the way he smiles at me, knowing how important the charity is to me, I know he'll do it.

There's not a lot of seating in the bookstore, but we make do. For the next few hours, I'm overwhelmed with gratitude for the people surrounding me. I'd gone so much of my life avoiding making attachments. After losing people I loved most, I didn't have it in me to risk ever losing anyone else again.

Until Lennon.

She showed me it was possible to love myself, to love others again. That I didn't have to be afraid of the what-ifs. Now, I've made my own little family, all thanks to her. I couldn't imagine a better group of people to celebrate getting to marry the love of my life with.

I pull her into me, floored that I now get to spend the rest of my life with this woman. Laying a kiss to her cheek, I'm shocked when she turns to face me, a sly smile on her face.

"I think I've got an item to add to our list," she says.

"What's that?"

She stands on her tiptoes, wrapping her arms around my neck. "Getting married as soon as possible."

"You tell me when and where, butterfly, and I'm there."

Continue reading for a glimpse into *The Consequence of Loving Me,* the first novel in Kat Singleton's Aftershock Series.

CHAPTER ONE: VERONICA

You don't drown by falling in the water; you drown by staying there.
– Edwin Louis Cole

Unless you actually drown.

The college campus bustles around me as I stare at the quote in front of me. I have no idea who this Edwin guy is, but I decide in this moment that I hate him. He probably has no true experience with drowning. And using it as some sort of inspirational metaphor, when it *actually* takes lives, is just shitty.

No one *willingly* drowns. They aren't like, "Hey, I fell in this water. I think I'll just stay a moment." No. They get lost in the vicious movement. They get pulled under, sucked in, until they see nothing else—ever again.

I continue to glare at the sorry mistake of a self-help poster that's stapled smack dab in the middle of the bulletin board. My eyes narrow on it one last time before I notice someone standing next to me.

"You're looking at that bulletin board like it just told you Zac Efron is gay," he says.

I slowly pull my gaze from the offensive quote and instead focus it on the guy behind the voice. First, I glimpse at his shoes —a pair of white Adidas. One point for him; every other male on the campus wears boat shoes that their stay-at-home mother probably bought them last time she came to visit. I continue my trek up his body. Black joggers. White T-shirt. Chambray shirt casually strung over his shoulders, slightly wrinkled.

Finally, I make it to his face. He stares back at me, a lazy grin pulling at the corners of his mouth—a taunt.

He raises his eyebrows, nodding toward the paper. "It must say he's gay. Oh god, let me see." He steps closer to the board, consequently stepping closer to me, and reads the words in front of us.

I accuse him with my eyes as his sweep over the poster, patiently waiting for him to become uncomfortable, but it doesn't seem to faze him. "Every ex-Disney star or current Marvel heart-throb could come out as gay and I still wouldn't care. Hollywood is overrated."

He smiles as his hand runs over his mouth. "Said no girl ever."

My lips part in frustration. "Says this girl now," I counter.

He takes a small step out of my space. A disruption catches his attention across the quad, causing his gaze to flick in that direction for a small moment before he looks back at me. "So, since we came to the conclusion it actually wasn't because Zac Efron came out as gay, what did that poster ever do to you?"

Then, he reaches up and plucks the paper from the board. A small ripping sound mixes with the noise of a college campus at three p.m. on a Wednesday.

He reads the quote out loud, his thick eyebrows bunching together. "What's wrong with it? Cheesy, *maybe*, but inspiring."

I roll my eyes, letting out a sigh that's half-growl. "It's beyond cheesy. He's using something tragic like drowning to motivate college students. I don't know why he thought *anyone* would eat that shit up." The strap of my oversized purse starts to slide off my shoulder, so I shift my weight and pull it back into place.

He laughs, managing to annoy me more than he already has. "You are on a campus filled with a bunch of sappy young adults. *Everyone* eats this shit up. Everyone but you, apparently." He neatly folds the piece of paper and tucks it into the back pocket of his joggers.

I glare at him before I turn back to the board, my lips pursing as I think about my plan of action. Finally, I swing my bag to the front of me and begin to rifle through it. My purse bumps against his arm, but to my dismay, he doesn't move. I finally find what I need—a flyer of my own, and the stapler I brought. I use one hand to hold the flyer up while my other staples it to the board.

Part of me was hoping Efron boy would have left me alone by now, but instead he uses this moment to step behind me and peer over my shoulder. My body tenses with his nearness.

"Looking for apartment or house available for rent. Not opposed to roommates. Call the number below if interested. Serious inquiries only. Veronica," he observes, his breath hitting my neck as he reads my words aloud.

He lingers on the last part—my name—dragging it out.

The heel of my combat boot makes a scratching noise against the floor as I hastily move back from the board and admire my handiwork. When I look down, I notice the paint splatters on my sleeve. If I cared what he thought of me, I'd be embarrassed.

He reaches in front of me and I watch in horror as he plucks the flyer from the board I *just* stapled it to. My mouth drops. "What the hell? I need that on there."

The guy chuckles, as he holds the flyer in his other hand. "Chill, *Veronica*," he says, dragging my name out again—and I hate it. "I'm just taking this off before a bunch of weirdos call you offering to be a bedmate, not a roommate."

I stifle the urge to hit him. There's just something about his smugness that infuriates me. And I consider if kicking his ass would be worth getting kicked out of school.

"Plus," he adds, "my roommates and I are looking for a new addition. It's your lucky day, Veronica! You can move in with us." His infuriatingly crystal blue eyes gaze at something behind my head before they once again focus on me.

"How do I know *you* aren't the weirdo trying to make me a bedmate and not a roommate?" I ask him. Disgust is clear in my tone and I don't try to hide it. My phone vibrates in the back pocket of my jeans, but instead of pulling it out to check it, I keep my stare aimed on him.

His eyes roam from the top of my head, down to my shoes, and back up again, unabashedly inspecting me. "Trust me, I don't want you in my bed. I do, however, want someone to help us cover the rent. Our last roommate fell in love with her professor and left without telling any of us."

To buy myself some time, I look around the quad, taking in the scene around me as I try to figure out the most polite way to tell him to fuck off. A tiny blonde cheerleader is thrown into the air by a man who looks like The Incredible Hulk from the corner of my eye. After watching her land safely in his hands, my eyes come back to the guy standing in front of me.

We both stare at each other, getting jostled by people passing by, until he moves. His fingers curl around my bicep. I have no choice but to move with him as he pulls me into the mass of people walking through our college quad.

His voice is way too close to my ear as he instructs, "Follow me. I need a coffee. But I want to figure out when you can move in."

"I never said I was interested in moving in with you." I yank my arm out of his grasp at the same time I plant my heels into the old concrete. People bump into me from all directions, but I stand my ground.

He turns around, raising his dark eyebrows at me. I wait for him to say something, but he doesn't. His shoulders rise and fall in a sigh as he also stops in the middle of the traveling bodies around us. We continue to stare at each other, and it's evident to me he has an iron will that rivals my own.

It's impressive, but not impressive enough to get me to move in with a complete stranger—an intolerable one at that.

I'm the first to break the silence. "I'm not following you. I don't even know your name. Plus, all you've managed to do in the few minutes I've known you is annoy me. We aren't off to the best start here." I scowl at another person who bumps into me while they rush down the sidewalk.

The stranger laughs at my reaction. It aggravates me. I let out a sigh and turn around, walking back to the campus board. I try to think if I have anything in my bag that I can use to replace the flyer this guy decided to rip down. Just as I round one of the corners, I bump into a firm chest.

"Veronica?" a familiar voice says.

I look up to see the guy I hooked up with last weekend.

I think his name is Chad?

I can't remember, but I *do* remember that Texas accent that drawls out of his mouth. If the accent alone didn't speak of his hometown, the cowboy hat that sits on top of his head would give him away.

"Oh, hi," I respond, looking over my shoulder to find demanding roommate guy standing directly behind me.

Why won't he just take a hint already?

"I tried texting you a few times since we saw each other last," maybe-Chad says.

Or is it Brad?

It doesn't matter. I just really need to focus on not rolling my eyes.

Don't guys know it isn't cute when they're clingy?

And now, there are *two* clingers surrounding me—one I don't even know!

"Yeah, I got them," I answer Chad-or-Brad, lazily twirling a piece of my long blonde hair around my finger.

His eyes widen a bit. He obviously isn't used to being ignored.

Luckily, his phone rings from inside his pocket. He gives me one last inquisitive look before pulling his phone out of his pocket, then shakes his head and walks away.

I look back to clinger number two to find that taunt of a smirk still on his face.

"That happen a lot?" he asks, with humor in his voice.

I shrug. It does, but I'm not one to tell that to a *stranger*.

He holds out his hand while I stare at it questioningly.

His long, tan fingers wiggle in waiting. "My name is Maverick, by the way."

"Maverick," I repeat, not moving.

He takes a deep breath. "This is where you shake my hand and *not* make it weird."

For some odd reason—maybe manners, or the fact that he looks so desperate—I decide to take his hand. His large hand engulfs mine in a firm handshake, and I want to snatch mine back.

Instead, Maverick takes his back and proceeds to run it through the length of his dark brown hair. The items in his backpack move around as he shifts his weight. "So, back to our earlier conversation. Based on the awkward run-in you just had with our star pitcher Chad, and judging from almost every male's eyes in this quad, I see you *are* used to guys wanting to be your *bedmate*, but believe me when I say, I'm not one of them."

I finally roll my eyes, unable to hold it back any longer.

When I don't say anything, he adds, "Look, you seem cool—"

"You don't know me," I snap. At the same time, I feel my phone vibrate in my back pocket.

He's *still* annoying me, so I pull my phone out of my pocket to see who keeps calling me. My mother's name pops up on the touch screen. I swipe to ignore the call and toss my phone into my oversized bag.

He sighs as his fingers nervously tap against his thigh. The look on his face when his eyes rest back on me looks like *he's* the annoyed one now. "Look, I'm not going to battle a stranger to move in with us. We need a roommate to help take over rent, that's all. You're looking for a place. So, it seemed like a good fit. If you want to say no, that's fine. Or you can think on it. Maybe I'll see you around if you change your mind. In the meantime, I really need a coffee."

He begins to walk away, and just before he's engulfed into the crowd, I remind myself I *desperately* need a place to live, and then I yell his name.

He turns around, obviously waiting for me to make the next move.

"Oh hell," I mumble under my breath, just before I make my way to him. I wait to speak until I'm standing right in front of him. My head has to tilt up in order to look him directly in the eyes. "You have the time it takes me to drink *one* coffee to convince me that toying with the idea of moving in with you isn't a complete waste of my time."

His face is puzzled, like he isn't sure if I'm messing with him or not. A few beats go by where he doesn't say anything, but finally he gives one curt nod and politely says, "Follow me, Veronica."

This time, I don't have the same urge to strangle him when he says my name.

Want to Continue Reading?
www.books2read.com/TCOLM

WANT MORE MIXTAPE?

Haven't had your fill of The Mixtape Series?!
Go to: https://BookHip.com/HDNDCCZ
to get the exclusive extended epilogue!

You can also read a free short story from Kat here:
https://BookHip.com/RHRVPKT

ACKNOWLEDGMENTS

Wow. I don't even know how to begin the acknowledgments for Founded on Rejection. It's hard writing this, and there's tears in my eyes right now knowing that The Mixtape Series is finally complete. I've been dying to tell Lennon's story from the moment we met her in Founded on Goodbye, but she just needed a little time before getting her happily ever after.

This book, *this series*, was only possible because I'm fortunate to have so many people in my life cheering me on.

First, I want to thank you, the reader. Whether you've just found my books or if you've been here from the very beginning, thank you from the bottom of my heart for choosing my world to spend your time in. This series started off as a passion project of mine and was supposed to begin and end with Nash and Nora's love story. It transpired into something so much more than I could've ever imagined since I first released Founded on Goodbye. Over the course of the four books, I hope you've fallen in love over and over again, and that these characters have found a place in your heart forever like they've found a place in mine.

To my husband. He's behind the scenes on so many things that have to do with my books and I wouldn't be able to do this without him. Babe, thank you for always being my #1 fan and for helping me chase my dreams. I love you forever.

Ashlee, you're the person behind the entire aesthetic of this series. Mixtape wouldn't be what it is if it wasn't for you. You're forever my best friend—my soul mate—and I love you so much. I can't wait to see what we'll come up with next.

To my #PantyThiefSquad. I literally couldn't have written this book without your constant support. The early morning and late night sprint sessions pushed me to write this book during the times where I didn't feel like I could do it. I love you all. Now let's get back to writing.

Tori, working with you has been a dream. Thank you for coming into this series and helping me make it everything it is. You've taught me so much and helped me become a better writer. I'll forever be grateful for you.

Cady, thank you for making sure my books are clean as possible. Your feedback makes these stories so much better. I appreciate you so much!

Nicki, I wouldn't be able to function without you. Thank you so much for holding everything down so I can focus on writing! You're the best and I really don't know what I'd do without you. Please stay with me forever.

Erica, thank you for being the first person to ever read Lennon and Poe's story. Founded on Rejection is what it is because of you. I value your feedback so much and like we always say, you're stuck with me forever. I love you.

To my betas. You've stuck with me through multiple books now and your feedback is everything to me. Your attention to detail is unmatched and I adore reading through all of your comments that make me giggle. Thank you for always giving me your real, honest opinions and helping me make my stories better. I love you and stay with me forever, okay?

To the authors I've gotten to know along the way in my author career. I'm in awe of your talent and the fact that I get to call you friends. So many of you cheered me on while writing these books and I'm eternally grateful for that.

To the bloggers, bookstagrammers, booktokers, and people in the community that share my books. I'm so eternally grateful for you. I've connected with so many amazing people since I started this author adventure. I'm appreciative of the fact that you take the time to talk about my stories on your platform. I notice every single one of your posts, videos, pictures, etc. It means the world to me that you share about my characters and stories. You're the lifeblood of this community. Thank you for everything you do.

To all the ladies at Give Me Books. Thank you for supporting me through the release of Founded on Rejection!

I have the privilege of having a growing group of people I can run to on Facebook for anything—Kat Singleton's Sweethearts. The members there are always there for me and I'm so fortunate to have them in my corner. I owe all of them so much gratitude for being there on the hard days and on the good days. Sweethearts, y'all are my people.

ABOUT THE AUTHOR

Kat Singleton is an author who developed a passion for reading and writing at a young age. When writing stories, she strives to write an authentically raw love story for her characters. She feels that no book is complete without some angst and emotional turmoil before the characters can live out their happily ever after. She lives in Kansas with her husband, her baby boy and her two doodles. In her spare time, you can find her surviving off iced coffee and sneaking in a few pages of her current read. If you're a fan of angsty, emotional, contemporary romances then you'll love a Kat Singleton book.

ALSO BY KAT SINGLETON

THE AFTERSHOCK SERIES

Volume 1: The Consequence of Loving Me

www.books2read.com/TCOLM

Volume 2: The Road to Finding Us

www.books2read.com/TRTFU

THE MIXTAPE SERIES

(Now a Completed Series!)

Track 1: *Founded on Goodbye:*

www.books2read.com/FOG

Track 2: Founded on Temptation

www.books2read.com/FOT

Track 3: *Founded on Deception:*

www.books2read.com/FODC

LINKS

Founded on Rejection **Pinterest:**

https://bit.ly/FORpinterest

Founded on Rejection **Playlist:**

https://spoti.fi/3KZ7EGT

CONTACT

Email:

authorkatsingleton@gmail.com

Facebook:

www.facebook.com/authorkatsingleton

Facebook Reader Group:

bit.ly/katsingletonSWEETHEARTS

Free Download of *The Waves of Wanting You*:

dl.bookfunnel.com/7buobclx4i

Goodreads:

www.goodreads.com/author/show/19920088.Kat_Singleton

Instagram:

www.instagram.com/authorkatsingleton

TikTok:

@authorkatsingleton

Website:

www.authorkatsingleton.com

Printed in Great Britain
by Amazon

44985734R00219